LOVE
and Other
SINS

EMILIA ARES

Love and Other Sins

Published by

SERA
PRESS

Hardcover: 978-1-7368140-2-4

Paperback: 978-1-7368140-0-0

eISBN: 978-1-7368140-1-7

Cover Design: David Drummond

Interior Design: GKS Creative

Copyediting: Elizabeth Cody Kimmel

Proofreading: Kimberly A. Bookless

Project Management: The Cadence Group

For Slava, Mila, and Sofia

Finally ... Always

And I think that's how the best relationships start—you're not looking for anything and suddenly, you have something.

PROLOGUE

Never let your guard down, *I scolded myself. How could I have let my guard down?*

I jerked my arms away violently but failed to slip out of his iron grasp, unaware as I gasped for air that I was only further perpetuating my own hyperventilation.

I parted my trembling lips, paralyzed with fear, trying to scream for help but not managing even a whisper. Heat circulated from my stomach to my chest and back down again. Clutching my shoulders, he propped me against the alley wall. My breathing became rapid and wild. This can't be happening to me. How could I be so stupid?

My instincts finally kicked in. I made the only move I could.

CHAPTER 1

MINA

Heathcliff had knelt on one knee to embrace her—

H ey, I noticed you always sit here. You got dibs on this spot?" said a
muffled male voice.

I put my Emily Brontë audiobook on pause, sliding my headphones
partially off my ears, and glanced up to find a guy looking down at me. It
didn't get more surfer dude than him: Vans, shaggy sideswept hair, and
the twitch he made at five-second intervals to propel said hair out of his
face. Dibs? I was sitting on the ground, leaning against a wall at the rear
of the school. I went there because it was peaceful and quiet. So yes, technically speaking, I guess I had dibs on the spot.

"Nope," I replied, nudging my headphones back into place. I rewound
and resumed.

Heathcliff had knelt on one knee to embrace her; he attempted to rise, but—

"Sweet. I dig the view from here, actually. You're Mina, right? I'm Tyler.
You always have headphones on, so I never get a chance to say wassup.
Hey, did you go to Paul Revere Middle School?"

I felt a ripple of irritation rising in my throat. I took a breath and slid
the headphones off again.

*Just answer the question, I told myself. It's not a big deal. Think likeable
thoughts. Try to smile.* "Nice to meet you, Tyler. No, actually, I didn't go

to Revere." I lingered to see if he was looking for more of a conversation, but he was suddenly preoccupied, typing on his phone in haste. I returned to *Wuthering Heights*.

Heathcliff had knelt on one knee to embrace her; he attempted to rise, but she seized his hair, and—

"Hey, can you believe she's making the AP Calc final cumulative?"

Pause. I looked up at him through lowered lashes, not because I was trying to flirt, but because I thought it might hide the aggravation I felt. "The actual AP test was yesterday, and that was cumulative, so it shouldn't matter if the final is cumulative."

"Yeah, but her exams are harder than the AP exam," he said.

"You think?"

He rolled his eyes. "Show-off."

I chuckled. "I'm sorry, but if I'm being honest, I don't actually recognize you from class."

"Hold on," he said, then began to pull a Clark Kent—literally. He slid a pair of reading glasses from his pocket and put them on. Then he swept his hair back into a ponytail with one hand, transforming himself into someone more familiar.

"Wow, that's funny; I recognize you now. So what's with the alternate look, then? Trying to fit in with the surf team, or practicing for the witness protection program?"

He released his hair and snapped his head back and forth as if to assuage it.

"This isn't a look; it's how I always dress. I just change my vibe for certain classes. Yeah, I am on the surf team, and teachers judge us. I'm automatically a space cadet and a stoner to them—an instant C average. But add some fake reading glasses, an ugly-ass sweater, and a little hair product, and suddenly they see someone focused, hardworking, and deserving of a good grade."

"Come on, that's not a thing!" I said, shaking my head. "You're kidding, right? You think that works?"

Like a magician mid-performance, he pulled a knit sweater vest from his backpack and shrugged into it, then tucked loose strands of hair behind his ears and cocked his head, staring earnestly at me through his glasses.

"Mr. Booth? Will there be an extra credit assignment for this unit?" he asked flatly.

I couldn't help but laugh as I realized he was as serious as a briefcase— the only item missing from his getup. He laughed too, and I began to wonder about him. *Maybe not so irritating after all,* I mused. He was funny and cute—why had I never talked to him before?

Well, because I didn't talk to anyone at school unless I had to. So why was he suddenly talking to me?

The sweet moment of laughter passed all too soon, followed by a whole lot of silence. I shifted my legs, suddenly self-conscious. My finger itched to resume the audiobook, desperate to discover what happened after Cathy seized Heathcliff's hair. But back in the real world, Tyler investigated further. "So where are you from?"

"I take the bus from Hollywood."

"No, I mean, where are you really from, like, originally? I remember your last name is something foreign."

So much for the woke youth of modern America honoring the culturally heterogenous scope of their fellow citizens. Anything approaching exotic facial features or an unfamiliar name still garnered you the age-old question, "So what are you?"

"Um, you mean, like, my parents?" I made sure the distinction was clear. "Well, my parents are from Russia."

"That's what I thought! No wonder you're always so serious and stiff." I stifled a sigh. "That's not a thing."

"Hell yeah it is," he intoned, yanking off his placebo glasses and flipping his hair. "I would know. Russians are always serious and never smile—well, the dudes, at least. The chicks are hot but bitchy, open-minded, and always packin' vodka—in which case, can I have some?"

Is he joking? I wasn't sure whether to laugh or be offended. *Keep it light, Mina. Smile.* "You sure love your overgeneralizations, don't you? A word of advice: don't drink the Kool-Aid."

"No, it's true!" he pressed. "Look, I can prove it. Don't your parents drive a Benz or a Beemer? Maybe one of each? Your dad's a big, scary dude who runs a bunch of other big, scary dudes. I mean, tuition here is pricey, am I right?"

This was why I don't talk to people. They tend to get real disappointing real fast. I'd officially lost interest in the conversation. "You should stop now."

"No, I got this—he's in insurance—an accident lawyer?" he snickered at his own joke, and there was an undertone of unpleasantness to it that brought my guard firmly up.

I made a monosyllabic sound of disgust and flipped him off.

"Oh, come on, lighten up, comrade! I'm just messing with you. It's called a joke. Joke-avitch! Like from Humorstan! But seriously, do you have a shit-ton of guns at home? Can you hook me up with a Kalashnikov?"

No meant no, dude. "A for effort, okay?" I snapped. "You're, like, practically a Rhodes scholar. Congratulations on getting through *Stereotypes for Dummies* in one sitting."

I yanked off my headphones and shoved them into my book bag, tucking my physics book under one arm as I pushed myself to my feet.

"Hey, don't go," Tyler protested, holding up one hand. "I'm not trying to be shady. I was just trying to work up the nerve to ask you something. Would you ever want to maybe . . ."

He glanced around then leaned closer and dropped his voice to a whisper. "Hook me up with a mail-order bae?"

I shoved him as he began cackling with laughter. "Is it true Ukrainian chicks will do anything to move to America? See, I know there's a difference between Russians and Ukrainians."

"Yeah, you're woke as hell. My bad." I went to walk around him, but he stepped into my path.

"Aw, don't get all salty! We can still hook up when I'm married to Katerina. She'll just take care of the guaranteed blowies, like an—"

I smacked his arm with my very heavy physics book, called him a waste of space, and started to walk away. A group of his eavesdropping buddies came out of hiding from around the corner, roaring with laughter as I marched past.

"Damn! She got you, waste of space! You owe me five bucks, Tyler! You thought she'd get through five minutes of negging? That chick?" one of them taunted, not bothering to keep his voice down.

Blood rushed to my face as I walked away, acting as if I couldn't hear. Things started spilling out of my still-unzipped backpack, and I stopped and bent to pick them up, swearing under my breath.

"Dude, she lasted, like, less than a minute, plus smacked him, plus cursed him out! This must be a new record! It's official: Russian chicks are un-neggable, the reigning neg champions!" said Surf Team Clone #2.

I shot him a poisonous look.

Like the rest of his buddies, he was still sporting the bottom half of his wetsuit from the early morning team meet. Did they really think keeping those suits on all day was going to help them get laid?

"Brah, that was most definitely longer than a minute!" Tyler argued.

I stuffed my things back into my pack and stood up.

"Nah, don't even try. I got the whole thing on video! I'm gonna Boomerang a slo-mo of her smacking you to that one song . . . 'Be Careful'—shit's gonna go viral!"

Livid, I spun around to find Surf Team Clone #2 waving his phone around like a demented man-baby. Weren't surfers supposed to be Zen and into recycling and saving the planet? Was I confusing surfers with Silverlake hipsters? I considered smacking the moron's phone right out of his overprivileged hand, but it was pointless; he likely had a cloud backup.

I turned on my heel and stalked off. Why did I blow up on him like that in the first place? I think the final straw was when he unintentionally named his imaginary Ukrainian sex slave after my *babushka*. The moral of the story? I could be violent and short-tempered, and left unchecked, I might at times perpetuate the angry Russian stereotype; but my intentions were good.

• • •

On the bus ride home from school, I scolded myself for losing my temper. Why had I let that over-tanned tapeworm rattle me? *You don't know how to handle drama because you've gotten so good at avoiding it,* I told myself, *keeping to yourself and living vicariously through the characters of your favorite books.* It sounded boring, I knew, but as far as solutions went, it had been a solid option for me—as efficient and predictable as my bus commute.

Public transportation wasn't the worst thing in the world, except for the countless stops, the rigid seats, and the prevailing stench—eau de marinated urine and stale air. On the upside, the public transportation experience was an unwavering source of motivation to work tirelessly and excel, and hence graduate to some form of private transportation, never to return to mass transit again.

Transportation notwithstanding, this was the last week of my junior year of high school—the last week I would ever attend a private school in Pacific Palisades. I was going to be making a big change for my senior year. I needed to transfer somewhere with some socioeconomic and ethnic diversity—somewhere grittier, more down-to-earth, more...real, where the neoprene-clad Cro-Magnon boys of the world were just one sweater-vest and pair of glasses away from the honor roll. Pacific Palisades had been a pretty bubble and looked great on a college application, but I couldn't spend another minute stuck in traffic on the I-10 at five in the morning. *Even the coast road gets old when you've been stuck on it for an hour every day three years running,* I told myself. Then I laughed ruefully and shook my head. Who was I kidding? The Pacific coast never got old, and I wasn't especially jonesing for more grit. The reality was my mother had lost one of her jobs and couldn't afford the tuition anymore. I was trying to focus on the positives.

Luckily, I hadn't put any effort into building lasting relationships that would complicate my transfer to a public school in Hollywood. How's that for a positive? Instead of a social life, I opted for a competitive GPA and a nearly perfect SAT score. Did I want to join Rafael Midoci's "study group" cult at the local village coffee shop every Thursday? Sure, why not? Did I want to go to Bianca Ramirez's "Kick Off the Summer" pool party last week? Of course I did! Did I want to go sailing on Troy Demur's family yacht? Who wouldn't? Was I invited to any of those things? Well, no. I was not. But surely if I'd put as much energy into smiling at people as I did into my grades, the invites would have started rolling in, right? Time was an investment, and I had chosen to bury all my capital in academics. Which meant if I wasn't accepted to one of my top-choice universities, I'd have committed social suicide for nothing, and the injustice of the world would shift our globe off its axis, hurtling us all into space to our inevitable deaths.

Back to Tyler—it was a shame, really. Sometimes, there would be a finely wrapped package covered in exquisite lace and rococo paper, but inside was a steaming heap of shit. You'd be looking around wondering, what's that smell? And sometimes it turned out to be nothing but a big old box of Tyler, tied in a shiny bow.

The scenery outside the window changed from shrubs to ocean as the bus turned left onto the Pacific Coast Highway. This short stretch of the coast was my favorite part of the ride home. I stared entranced as sunlight danced on the water, illuminating a path of silver all the way to the horizon. I'd have been happy doing nothing but looking at that view all day, except for the fact that I wouldn't have. Every second of the three years I spent slaving over my homework had been to give myself options in the future—to pave the way for me to choose what I wanted out of life, and not the other way around.

Beyond the whole paving metaphor, things were considerably murkier. I knew much more about what I didn't want in life than about what I did. I knew I didn't want to become some lonely professional with nothing but a collection of exotic cats and dry-cleaned, color-coded business suits waiting for me at home. How exactly did one safeguard against that? I guess I'd just have to casually stumble upon a sexually explosive yet emotionally stable relationship with a good *bad boy*. Maybe by then there would be an app for that.

I said goodbye to my final glimpse of the coast as the view abruptly went black. As we drove eastbound through a long tunnel that turned into the I-10, I held my breath but made no wish. An image came to me: a man standing just inside our front door, dressed in a navy wool coat with a cashmere scarf draped around his neck and passport in hand. Next to him sat a large, ungainly Saran-wrapped piece of luggage. It was clear from the size of his bag and the heft of his coat that he wasn't just leaving us; he was leaving the country, flying somewhere cold. His sad eyes were apologetic, but the ridge of his mouth was set in a hard, angry line. I didn't know it then, but that would be the last time I ever saw my father. The memory was like an aching tooth. I shut out the pain and hoped it went away on its own, but what if the tooth had gone rotten inside? I pulled my backpack in tightly against my abdomen, like this would plug the void and hold me together.

The bus screeched to a halt. We had entered the ironically named "freeway" where cars were bumper to bumper. As if on cue, a couple near the back of the bus began to bicker loudly.

The image of my father flickered into my mind's eye again. Traffic always gave my parents reason to fight. *Babushka* claimed they argued about almost everything, even from the beginning of their relationship, back when "the flames of young love had yet to burn out." I was told they even had a fight over what they would name me. My father wanted to name me Wilhelmina in honor of his late mother, while Mama wanted something more modern, something elegant but less serious. Mina was a compromise—Mina Nikolaevna Arkova.

My parents emigrated from the USSR to start a family in "paradise," a land free from oppression and a haven for dreamers. I'm not so sure about the oppression-free part, but America is the only home I've ever known. I was born and raised here, so I should have felt as welcome as anyone, right? For some reason, though, I always felt partly alien. Kids never seemed to recognize me as one of their own species. But I guess I was a pretty easy target back in middle school, equipped with unfortunately cut bangs tucked behind purple daisy clips, a large blue rolling backpack to prevent scoliosis, a never-back-down attitude, and naturally, no friends. Then there were my homecooked lunches that didn't smell like anyone else's lunch.

Mama always went all out when she'd pack my lunch: hardboiled eggs, *pelmeni* (small balls of pastry dough stuffed with minced meat), fresh cucumbers, *salat olivie*, *blini*, and lots of sour cream. Mama knew middle school was a hard transition; I think she wanted me to carry a reminder of home to make me feel less alone.

Much had changed since those middle school daymares—my confidence, for one. I'd become more accepting of myself and tried not to dwell on anything trivial. Back then, I was ashamed of the ways in which I stood out. To avoid being teased about the contents of my lunchbox, I ate alone in the bathroom for the first month of sixth grade, which was, in hindsight, not a great choice. Eventually, after rumors spread about me being a bathroom troll, I became a nomad, with nowhere to eat lunch in peace. Wherever I went, kids would point and pinch their noses. I was an insecure mess.

I studied myself in the bus window now. A pair of enigmatic hazel eyes outlined by thick, dark lashes gazed back at me. Remembering the profound devastation I experienced when those kids would call me "Bathroom Troll," I started to chuckle. Now I found it utterly hilarious. Why couldn't I see the absurdity of it all back then? But of course, I had no way of knowing that I was going to find a friend. I remembered spending weeks wandering the middle school halls and feeling so *other*—until the day I passed by my homeroom at lunch and saw that there were kids there just hanging out, eating and reading. I had no idea we were even allowed to be in a classroom during lunch. It sure beat hall aerobics, so I went in.

That was where I met my best friend, Nyah Wright. We had a lot in common. We were both ballet dancers and into the same type of books—dystopian fiction. She was close to her older cousin the way I was with Mama. And she never made me feel weird or different. To Nyah, I was just a normal kid—cool, even. Because of her, middle school became a happier place for me, relatively speaking. People still picked on me, but I knew I had a friend, so I focused on her. As long as she was there, I was okay. So when Nyah's parents decided to move to a ritzier neighborhood, we were both devastated.

Nyah and I put up a hell of a fight, I have to say. We boycotted the move and threatened to run away together. It was all very dramatic. Finally, our parents agreed to a compromise. Nyah still had to move away, but we got to go to summer camp and dance studio together. And now that her parents had promised to gift her the Honda when their new Tesla arrived at the end of the month, the two of us would be inseparable that summer.

Smiling to myself, I took a snap of the freeway and typed: *Ughh! FML! Miss you, counting down the days till summer.* But before I could press send, I received a message from her first.

OMGWTF Mina!!! u slugged some guy? R u ok? It's all over insta!

Perfect.

CHAPTER 2

OLIVER

What if something's gone wrong?

A hand touched my shoulder—*shit!* I almost fell out of my chair whipping my head around, only to find it was Remi. *Of course it's her—who else would it be?* I tried to relax, for her sake; it wasn't her fault I was jumpy. I gave her a reassuring smile, then checked the time: 8:25 p.m. Old Town Newhall Library in Santa Clarita had been closed for twenty-five minutes. Remi was the head librarian. She was also my only friend. No one should ever be fooled by her frail figure and her gray hair; the woman had the heart of a warrior. Deep wrinkles ringed her friendly eyes, hidden behind a pair of thick glasses that sat perfectly on the bump of her nose like she was born wearing them.

"You're going to have to forgive me, young man, but I've been calling your name from across the room for the past two minutes. You're on another wavelength tonight, aren't you?" Remi asked. She usually only called me "young man" when I was in trouble.

She fidgeted with the leather cord strapped to her reading glasses and dusted off the lenses with her turquoise blouse. Before I could gauge exactly what it was I felt about moving away from Santa Clarita, she offered another apology, "I really didn't mean to startle you; I'm sorry for . . . are you listening to me? Where's your mind wandering off to again? You worried? Nervous about the big move?"

She was right; my head was somewhere else completely. I was supposed to be out of here already—the library, not the city—but my client was an hour late. Which was weird. He usually let me know if something was up.

"It's not too late, you know. You can change your mind and stay; is that what you want?" Remi asked. I shook my head no. She gave me a scrutinizing look, then lifted her chin and sighed. "I have to lock up now, sweetheart. I wish I could stay a bit longer, especially tonight, but I promised Henry I'd pick up his prescription refills, and the pharmacy closes in half an hour."

"Yeah . . . no, I get it."

I checked my phone again for texts; still nothing. I pulled on my backpack and finally stood to face Remi. "Okay, guess I'm on my way, then." My casual words and tone belied the seriousness of the moment. I knew the two of us would never lay eyes on one another again.

She stood head high, with perfect posture, framed between the rows of the books she so proudly kept in order. I wanted to remember Remi that way, just as she had been the day I met her three years back—the best person I'd ever known. It may not have been saying much since I'd mostly only met dickheads my entire life, but I still doubted there was anyone like Remi out there. She was the first person who'd ever really given a shit about me, the only person who cared enough to talk straight to me when I needed it—like the mother I never had. I was seventeen years old. Do the math and you'll get a pretty good picture of my life.

She approached me slowly, reaching for my hands. I stiffened automatically, tensing at the prospect of physical contact. Despite my panic, I let her touch me. She gave my hands an encouraging squeeze, a gesture that told me she was proud of me. I was proud of myself, too. I barely flinched.

"Take care of yourself out there. I know it's what you said you want: to start fresh somewhere new, finish high school, be a normal kid, give yourself the life you should've had—the life you've always deserved. But that's not . . . last night you said something that's been bothering me. You said you didn't care about the money those jurors awarded you and that you won't touch most of it. I know that seems like a noble thing, but I think it's bordering on the quixotic. Don't let some arcane principle—"

"I will use it," I told her. "I'm using the check they sent me to get settled in New York. I don't think you got what I meant . . . "

"I understood you perfectly, Oliver. I always do. I'm not talking about a couple thousand dollars; I'm talking about the rest of it. It's expensive to live in a city like New York; I understand that you want to make a new name for yourself, start over again free and clear of this whole mess that you're leaving behind. And that's admirable, it is, but . . . I don't want you to put that kind of pressure on yourself."

"I'm not," I told her. "I won't."

"It's not too late to change your mind." I shook my head; she knew where I stood on this. What I wouldn't tell her, and couldn't tell her, was that the whole New York story was a ruse. My actual destination was Los Angeles. I didn't like lying to her, but I couldn't leave a paper trail. No one could know about my new life, not even Remi. Not if I was really going to have a fresh start.

She walked over and rested her hand near mine on the table, fingers thin and long. Remi's eyes filled with worry and she pursed her lips tightly. I smiled at her as she opened her mouth preparing to speak again. "Promise me one thing: Promise me you won't isolate yourself. Reach out to others, or at least join a support group out there as soon as you can. And don't give me that look—you know group therapy has helped you before. You may well need the support again if the anxiety resurfaces or you lose your grip on the anger." Her eyes welled up. I nodded and placed my hand over hers, letting her know it was okay, that she should say what she needed to say. "Someone who is willing to pick up and move to New York is someone who is playing for keeps, no matter what it takes, no matter who is standing in the way. And those are the people you have to watch out for— the wrong sort—the kind that unleash their demons on you. But, at the same time, you can't let those people isolate you. I feel like I'm making a mess of this . . . "

She buried her face in her palms, frustrated. Remi thought she was scaring me into staying, but she didn't have it in her. I'd seen some messed-up shit—a rare kind of horror. I'd endured unbearable pain. There just wasn't that much left out there that could still scare me. On the contrary, the thought of the new adventure actively thrilled me. I stood up from my computer chair, walked over to her, and pulled her hands off her face— her eyes were wet with tears, but she wore a wistful smile.

"Remster, you're a mess," I joked. She cracked up and her whole body shook with laughter.

She wiped her eyes with the backs of her hands, then dried her hands against her dark denim jeans. "You are right about that, young man. Just know that I'm here, okay? And you can always come back, or you can change your mind and go somewhere—anywhere—else. You're free now, but that doesn't mean you have to be alone." She smiled, knowing the weight of those final words, as another tear ran down her cheek. I felt a sharp stab in my heart. This must be what love felt like—the unconditional, family kind of love. The vulnerability of it was terrifying. I shut it out, shifting my focus to a splotch of dirt on the computer keyboard space bar, which I began to scratch off.

I didn't tell her I'd die before ever coming back to this place. Anyway, she already knew that, and I didn't want to hurt her even more by saying it out loud.

"Thank you for—" My tongue tripped on the words and suddenly, it felt as though a swollen dry lump was blocking my throat. I closed my mouth, giving up on the sentence. I shut my eyes, ashamed of my inability to deliver a simple thank you—one she'd earned fifty times over. Flashes of memories flooded the blackness of my closed eyes: her gaze always on me as she sat behind her desk; the frustration I felt when I didn't understand what this strange, intense old lady wanted from me; how I went from refusing to answer a single one of Remi's questions to letting her become my rock throughout the brutal court proceedings. Through it all, we built an understanding, one that really meant something to me. And now, I couldn't even thank her for it. *Pathetic.*

Maybe it's more than that? All this time, I'd been so focused on my plan to move away and erase my messed-up past that it was only now that it truly hit me: I was gonna have to erase Remi, too. My eyes grew hot and moist, and I shook my head to turn back the tears. I rubbed my forehead for a moment. When I took my hand away, Remi was watching me. I raised one hand, palm up, as if I was about to say something, and for a moment her pale blue eyes blazed with emotion. Then she closed them, and the faintest of smiles tugged at the corners of her lips. She nodded, almost imperceptibly, and relief flooded through my chest. That was her benediction, her blessing, and her goodbye. I turned and walked out of the musty dim room, pushing the heavy front door open and squinting at the glare of the setting sun. A warm gust of air hit my face as I headed toward the parking lot. At first, it felt good, like bedsheets on a cold night, especially after sitting under the AC for a couple of hours. It was still too hot for eight o'clock at night. The summer was fading, but not fast enough.

I was surprised to see the client I'd been waiting for in front of the library, standing under a lamp post by the dumpsters on the far end of the lot. Fifty was one of my oldest clients, but I knew next to nothing about him, not even his real name. We kept those out of it. He just called me

"Kid" and had me call him "Fifty." I asked him why that number once, and he said, "Got that name cause I always make sure everybody I do business with gets theirs. If I make money, you make money, fifty-fifty." *What the hell is he up to?* I wondered as I walked toward him. I was used to him running late, but he always texted me when he was, and he always came through, which was rare in my business. So the whole time I was sweating in the library, he was sitting out here in the parking lot?

"Took you long enough, Kid," Fifty said when I was within earshot.

"I was about to say the same thing to you. How long you been here?"

"Like ten minutes already, shit."

"We were supposed to meet an hour ago—"

"I sent you a damn text, didn't I?" he cut me off.

Did he? I went through my last burner phone a couple of days before.

"Well, I didn't get it," I said, holding my phone up. "Maybe you accidentally sent it to the other number. I tossed that one—"

"Man, you gotta get yourself a damn smartphone, not those weak-ass burners you always be using. Does it look like we're slanging dope? Makin' me change your damn number in my phone like you my side bitch or some shit. What network's that thing on, anyway? Give that shit here—"

I tossed him my phone. "Buzzy Wireless? For real? Sounds like a boot-legged vibrator company."

Be that as it may, I liked the privacy and anonymity a burner phone provided, so that was what I planned to keep using, at least until I got to L.A. When I filed for emancipation earlier in the year, I also petitioned the judge for a legal name change—for a clean slate. When I got to L.A., I'd buy a permanent phone under my new name, Oliver Mondell, and get a bank account—the whole nine yards. I wouldn't have to hide cash in the floorboards anymore. But I didn't explain any of this to Fifty. He pulled out a wad of cash; I took five smartphones out of my bag. We swapped. That was how I flipped: buy a broken phone, swap out the defective parts, shrink-wrap the box, and sell it as new to Fifty. Fifty sold to his exporter, and that guy shipped it out of the country. Everyone got theirs.

"Don't worry—you won't have to deal with me much longer. I'm heading to New York tomorrow," I told him.

This surprised him. "Serious? What business you got in New York?"

I hesitated. Screw it; it didn't matter anymore. "Nothing. Not yet, anyway. I just finally have my freedom, is all."

"Freedom? Whatchu know about living without freedom, kid?" Fifty asked, cocking his head to one side.

"No, I mean I got my emancipation papers."

"Emancipation . . . from your folks? They that bad?"

I zipped my bag shut again and said, "They're not my folks. Foster care."

Fifty cocked his head and arched his eyebrows. "Hold up—How old are you?"

"Eighteen in March," I said.

He lifted his chin and gave me an appraising look.

"Jesus, you're just a kid, Kid . . . it all makes sense now: the burners, the library, the motorcycle. Damn, and you already makin' moves? You know what? That's tight. Starting young, that's smart, man, you're smart. Shit, if I had my shit straight at your age, I'd probably be running New York by now. Back then, all I thought about was titties, new kicks, and my rep." He laughed, shaking his head.

"So, not much has changed?"

"Man, shut your mouth." He laughed. "No way—you got jokes now? How long we know each other . . . and you wait until your last day in town to make a joke? Been dealing with your boring ass all these years—I mean, what else don't I know about you?"

I laughed and hoisted my backpack over one shoulder, "All right, Fifty.

It's been good, take care—"

"Wait, hold up." He reached into his pocket and pulled out a couple of extra Benjamins. "For good luck, Kid. It's been good."

I stopped short, surprised at his gesture.

"No, you don't have to do that."

He took a step closer and shook the money at me.

"Don't disrespect—just take it. It's for good luck. My bad that I never asked nothing about you. Business is business—you know how it is. Most the time, the less you know, the better. If I'd have known, I'd have looked out—know what I mean? You do your thing out there. Find your grip, and maybe I'll come out one day. You can take me to a fancy-ass dinner on the Upper East Side or some shit, all right? Keep your nose clean, you hear me?" A hard lump sat in my throat from all the lies I'd told that day. I swallowed it down hoping Fifty didn't go looking for me in New York one day. But who knows? Maybe I'd end up there after all. I flinched as Fifty grabbed my hand, but he was just pressing the cash against my palm and closing my fingers into a fist over it. He nodded and headed back to his car.

Trying to find my voice, I called out, "All right, Fifty! See you!"

It always made me uncomfortable when strangers tried to help me out or take care of me, but then again, who wasn't a stranger to me? After what my mother did, anything anyone did for me was automatically an act of kindness. That is, until a man named Jack Burns came into my life. Jack ran one of the foster homes I ended up in, though it was a pretty big stretch to call it a home. The foster system was broken beyond repair: too many kids, too few supervisors, not enough places to go. I was stuck in a children's facility at ten, supposedly a temporary arrangement. I stayed there until I turned fourteen, when I was finally moved back into a foster home—Jack's foster home.

I had been so stoked when I first heard I was moving back into a real home. Like a naïve idiot, I thought that anything would be better than the prison I'd been in for the last four years. But if the facility had felt like a prison, Jack's foster home was worse than prison. It was hell. If I'd learned anything since then, it was that if something sounded too good to be true, it was. I pushed the crisp two hundred dollars into the pocket of my jeans as I watched Fifty's car disappear around the corner.

I hopped on my bike, a black 2006 KYMCO Venox 250. It was no Harley, but it did the job. I'd bought it with money I saved up, a token of my hard work and the freedom I'd always craved. As I rode up the street, the library building got smaller and smaller in my rearview mirror. I paused at the stop sign at the end of the road for a minute and said a silent goodbye to it, that building that had brought me solace—that building where I had met the woman who became my savior.

The blast of a car horn jolted me back to the present. The car behind me wanted me to turn already. I raised my hand, "My bad." That sound would have jolted me off the motorcycle a year ago. Maybe Remi was right; maybe therapy really did help. Time healed some wounds. I remembered the first time Remi had reached for my hand and I'd jumped back so hard I'd hit the wall. Seeing her reaction to my fear made me realize how messed up I'd become. It was in that moment that, for the first time, I started to feel some clarity that the things that had gone on in Jack's house were not only not okay, but that they might've messed me up for good. The realization hit me like a ton of bricks, and I'd just slid onto the floor right in front of Remi, drowning in grief over my own life. Remi ended up being the real deal, not just another stranger trying to take advantage. So, eventually I told her everything about Jack Burns, the piece of shit who had been beating and raping the kids in his care. I was fourteen at the time, but most of the kids he preyed on were younger than me—some much younger. Just the thought of it turned my stomach even then. I was the oldest, so it was up to me to save us. It was what I should have done the minute I knew what was going on.

I rode across the intersection, past closed furniture stores and empty shopping plazas. In hindsight, I couldn't believe how much I'd told her that day about the complaints we'd filed, and the multiple people we'd told of the abuse, including school counselors, social workers, police officers, and representatives working for the child abuse emergency hotline—professionals who'd been not just morally but legally obliged to initiate an investigation. And yet most of the complaints were simply ignored. The one time someone opened an investigation, all they did was send a few caseworkers to check on the conditions of the home. Jack naturally lied his ass off. We were interviewed too but he was present, so most of the kids were too scared to tell the truth. Jack's steely, dead-eyed glances made it all too clear there would be punishment once the caseworkers left. Faced with a lying adult and a room of terrified kids, the caseworkers did the worst possible thing: They filed it as a false complaint in the system. We were labeled as the kids who cried wolf. No one was going to believe anything we said after that.

"Have you ever considered hiring a lawyer?" Remi had asked gently, once I'd gotten most of the details out.

"No, we don't have any money." The thought never even crossed my mind as a realistic option. It seemed killing him would be easier.

"You don't necessarily need any money—cases like this are usually represented by public defenders, or by family lawyers doing pro bono work. We just need to find someone good—someone who's won a case like this before and is passionate about the work. We need to find you a firm of sharks who will fight for you until they've exhausted every option."

"Where do I look for someone like that?" I asked her.

"Well, we'll start with the American Bar Association directory." She pulled a fat book from a shelf, placed it on the table, and patted the seat next to her. I'd sat down and watched her thumb through the pages, sticking Post-It notes on various listings. Then she got on the phone and made a few calls, and before I knew it, I had a lawyer—and the rest, as they say, was history.

As I approached the Santa Clara River, I eased out on the clutch and turned my bike onto the bridge that ran across it. I had spent a lot of time there planning, thinking, pacing. When the river ran dry, teens hung out and smoked pot under that bridge, but so did a lot of creeps and tweakers. A girl from my last foster home had to fight off some crazy guy down there who had tried to rape her. For all Remi's warnings about New York, I was laboring under no misconceptions about L.A., or anywhere I might go in the future. This city was small and still I'd seen plenty of evil. Evil was everywhere.

I rode past another vacant shopping plaza. Everything out there was oversized: the buildings, the roads, the malls, the mega-stores, the parking structures. It was like someone had built it all in anticipation, like it was just a matter of time before the masses would descend. If you built it, they would come, or whatever. It could happen eventually, I guessed. But for now, there was just a lot of room for doing nothing and not a lot of room for business growth. There weren't enough buyers or exporters to move volume and so the seller market was becoming oversaturated. That was one of the reasons why I was moving out west.

The day that jury in my trial against the state had stood up and ruled in my favor, granting me two million dollars, was the day Los Angeles went from a faraway fantasy to an achievable goal. That win gave me a sliver of hope during a very messed-up time. It made me think that maybe a broken system could be fixed—and that possibly, though less likely, even I could be fixed. It was the first time I ever had something to live for and look forward to. That was one year ago.

That was also the day my application for emancipation had been officially approved. That, like everything else, was thanks to Remi. I had no idea there were programs set up to help kids in the system. Turns out help had been out there all along. I just didn't know how to look for it.

Remi and I found a website for in-state foster kids, fosteryouthhelp. ca.gov, which had a page listing the rights of all foster kids. Reading them made me sick, because almost all my rights had been violated at one point or another. The Independent Living Program provided money for vocational training, transportation, college, and 30 percent of housing. They also helped you get a computer, find a job, and access scholarship opportunities. But first, I had to write an emancipation preparation plan with my social worker and update it every six months.

It felt like pointless bullshit to me, just more obstacles blocking my way forward. But Remi explained to me that my rights were integral to the US democratic system. So if I wanted to turn my situation around, I had to know my rights and learn how to leverage them using the process inherent in that same system. So that is exactly what I did. And once I knew what federal law said I was entitled to, I stopped being an easy target. Every damn application I filled out got me closer and closer to my rights—my independence.

Enough with the life review, I told myself, as I pulled my bike onto the grass. Everything in this town reminded me of the most miserable years of my miserable life. I needed to let go of it all now that I was finally free of him. I needed to wipe him from my memory and never look back.

I had finally reached my destination: the Lily of the Valley Mobile Home Community. It wasn't much, but no one had been raped or beaten on the grounds so far as I knew, and that was as good as a five-star rating around there. I pulled off my helmet and walked up a short driveway to the small gray double-wide. Foster homes were "like a box of chocolates—you never know what you're going to get": a mansion (in your dreams, Orphan Annie) or a middle-of-nowhere shithole with no indoor plumbing (more likely). This time, I had lucked out, if you can call it that. It was probably not a matter of chance; the state didn't want bad press from shoving me back into a group home or a government facility while I filed for my freedom papers. Apparently, they had a list of "normal homes" behind glass that says, "break in case of emergency."

The door was unlocked; I walked inside and—*crack*. I stepped on something crunchy. Crap, I broke someone's something.

"Dinner," Breanne called out from the kitchen.

Braiden ran down out of his room, "Hey, what the hell? You broke my volcano project, Assface." Braiden was nursing a paper cut as though it was a massive wound. He cringed dramatically as he covered the cut on his elbow with an oversized bandage. I rolled my eyes.

"Summer school's over. Didn't you turn this shit in already?"

"Yeah, so?" He fired back, bugging the crap out of me. "I'm keeping it as a souvenir."

"Don't leave it by the door next time, Assface."

"Dinner!" Breanne yelled. She didn't like to repeat herself. The house sounded like a school cafeteria and smelled like burnt toast. She was probably trying to make homemade pizza again. My newest foster mom was as straightedge as they come. She was a forty-something ex-Marine with an American flag in her front yard. She recycled, paid taxes, followed the speed limit and made complete stops at every stop sign. She voted in every primary—even the June primary—because, and this was a house mantra: "Every vote counts." As if two kids of her own weren't enough, she'd taken in four foster kids, me included. She went back to working full-time as a family counselor as soon as her youngest foster kid, Julie, turned five last year, but somehow still didn't miss a beat at home. Breakfast and dinner were usually borderline inedible but always on time, and school lunches were packed the night before. Breanne was as decent a foster mom as they came, but she had her moods. On a bad day, she could be as cold as a snake. She liked rules—setting them and enforcing them: no grades below a B; extracurriculars were mandatory; chores were nonnegotiable; the cleaning chart was sacred; every week we washed the toilets, the stoves, the car, the floors, and the windows; we volunteered at shelter; no TV in the house; no smartphones; and we answered to her with "Yes ma'am" or "No ma'am." It was the kind of consistent structure I didn't necessarily like but could respect. I always knew where I stood with Breanne, because it all came down to her rules, and whether I'd followed them or not. That gave me a kind of strange control over my daily life that I'd never had before.

Her own kids were a different story. From what I could tell, Breanne got along better with her foster kids than her own, but that made sense on some level. Foster kids knew how bad it could get out there, even the ones who hadn't gone through hell themselves—the rumors got around. We knew enough to be grateful when we landed in a home that felt that safe, even if all the damn rules were choking the life out of you. Breanne tried to make me get rid of my motorcycle but that was one thing I wouldn't budge on. "I appreciate everything you've done, taking me in this year— my history and all. And I respect you, but no," I told her. "It's the only thing I have that's mine." And I guess my logic wasn't lost on her, because she didn't bring it up again.

Her husband, Jorge, worked in insurance—risk assessment or some kind of pointy-head thing, I think. He wasn't around much. Most days, if I stayed in my room, I didn't run into him at all, which is how I liked it. It was nothing serious; just that his shifty eye contact really bugged me, especially while he was explaining something super boring and random.

"Aren't you hungry?" Breanne stopped me as I headed for my room.

"No, ma'am, I ate already—but thank you very much just the same," I lied. I walked into my room quickly, shutting the door behind me. I sat on the edge of my bed, taking in the room. I shared it with Breanne's biological son, Franklin, who was thirteen. Noel, twelve, and Braiden, nine, were across the hall. I chose bottom bunk and liked to hang a blanket up for privacy. The room felt stuffy, so I got up to open a window, but almost tore my groin slipping on a dusty old video game poster in the middle of the floor. *How is this still here?* I kicked it out of the way, then kicked at it again out of anger. I missed and knocked my toes into the desk so hard that the reading lamp fell in a loud *clank*.

"Everything okay?" Breanne called out from the kitchen.

I took a breath. "Yes, Ma'am, I'm just working out . . . sorry. Everything's fine!" Breanne forbade pins, nails, or screws in her walls, so Franklin's entire video game poster collection had been stuck up by regular Scotch Tape. Most of the tape had lost its strength, and some posters were dangling by just one corner, while a couple had been collecting dust on the floor for months, but Franklin didn't touch them. I usually didn't pick them up either, out of principle. I'd been working with a court-appointed therapist on keeping my anger in check, but I had nasty slipups—more secrets to keep.

A nice foster home usually meant unbroken foster kids, so I was the only one in there with a history of abuse. Still, Noel Jopeecho—nicknamed Piss Miss because he couldn't aim for shit—always showed me respect. He looked up to me, tried to act like me, and once, I caught him trying on my jacket—but I put a stop to that shit real quick. It was cute and all, but the endless interrogation got irritating, especially when he made it personal.

"So, what's your story? Is it true that you beat up a guard in juvie?"

"No," I'd answer.

"Yeah, I didn't think so. You don't seem that crazy. Like, that's not what I meant—I'm not saying you're crazy but not that crazy. So . . . have you ever seen boobs in real life?" I had to push him out of the room and barricade the door to get him to shut up.

Then there was the youngest one—Julie, six—who followed me around the house like a duckling. I think I reminded her of her older brother. She showed me his picture once and said, "Just like you." They were separated by the system. She was brave and outgoing despite the burn marks that covered the right side of her face from a freak accident back when she was a baby. She used to cuddle up next to me on the couch at night while I made up stories about some princess and her unicorns or some shit. She would usually fall asleep before I ran out of ideas. But I had stopped the whole thing a few months ago. Julie was ignoring me lately, but whatever. Me? I just shut my emotions off and shifted my focus. It was for the best. I knew from day one it was only a matter of time before I moved out. I figured it would hurt her less if she didn't depend on me so much. I'd been trying to avoid the house in general that month.

Mona had been ignoring me for a while anyway, so nothing new there. She was the oldest, Breanne's nineteen-year-old daughter. I was low-key hooking up with her the previous year. She pulled me into the bathroom one night when everyone was asleep. I was surprised but . . . shit, I was down. She knew exactly what she wanted and wasn't shy about showing me. She used to say our hookups were just for practice. And it was fun for a while, until she started talking about us getting a place together when she transferred to NYU.

"That's not gonna happen."

She looked mad. "Why? It would be stupid to stay in separate places and pay double rent."

"I'm not interested. I'm sorry."

"Not interested in sharing a place, or in me?" I didn't answer. "Wow. Okay, got it. Screw you." And that was that.

But that was all in the past now. It wasn't like we'd ever had an actual connection. First thing tomorrow, I was going to the court clerk's office to pick up a certified copy of my emancipation order. It was the only thing still standing between me and leaving. That document was my ticket to freedom. Maybe I should have paid for ten copies right off the bat just to make sure I never had to go back.

I was already packed. I was always packed, out of habit. I didn't have much to take, anyway—just the clothes on my back, some files, and a gift from Remi—a book, *The Stranger,* by Albert Camus. There was something messed up about her choice, I had to say. *An absurdist, existential novel seems like an odd thing to give as a present, no matter what the occasion.* I think she was trying to say: *You think you're messed up? Read a book about this completely apathetic piece of shit—this total stain of a human—* and *you'll feel better about yourself.* I should have just left it behind, maybe passed it on to Piss Miss just to mess with him. But I couldn't let it go yet. Everything else I'd buy brand new in L.A.—brand-new things for my brand-new life.

CHAPTER 3

MINA

You could imagine my surprise when the most highly anticipated summer of my life came and went in the single beat of a humming-bird wing. I didn't think I'd ever step back onto an actual school bus again, not in this lifetime. But here I was: new school, first day, final year. It'd been fifty-two dance classes, thirty-six hikes, forty-one ice creams, thirty-six summer movies, seventeen rollercoaster rides, four-teen pool days, twelve sleepovers, eight bonfires, and three short months since that shitshow with Tyler had gone viral. I had since deactivated all my social media accounts, a transcendent experience. I'd have to thank Tyler one day.

But even coming off the busy social calendar of my summer didn't make it any easier to get onto a crowded school bus filled with rows of unfriendly and unfamiliar faces. Some glanced over momentarily, then quickly looked away. Strange faces, but familiar system: up front would be the people with motion sickness, control freaks, and the quiet ones who kept to themselves. That was where I would usually sit, but they were all taken. Apart from the two making out in the last row, the rowdiest bunch had reserved the seats in the rear. It was a party back there. A hefty boy with pants hanging far below his boxer shorts slapped his scraggly, self-bleached-hair buddy with a rolled-up bandana, cackling with every crackle of his homemade whip. A group of scantily clad girls chewed gum and applied eyeliner in a compact mirror while blasting the latest hits on speakerphone. They sneered as the two boys roughhoused up and down the center aisle. I turned to clock the bus driver's reaction to the scene, but he was too busy fidgeting with his keychain.

I took a seat by the window of an empty row in the middle section and strategically filled the empty seat beside me with my backpack, like I was reserving it for someone. On the surface, I was the perfect picture of the three C's: calm, capable, and cagey.

After the next few stops, the school bus was almost full, but no one getting on asked to sit beside me—the backpack worked. I stared out my window, past the sad eyes of my own reflection, as the school bus meandered through the City of Angels. What no one tells you is that ANGELS is an acronym for Angry, Narcissistic Gremlins and Egotistical, Lonely Sycophants. Or maybe I was just being too hard on the city. Whatever—I wasn't exactly a morning person.

Numbness tingled through my frozen fingers. *Russians don't feel the cold.* Nope, that wasn't a thing either. I warmed my hands by squishing them under my thighs, wishing the manufacturer had opted for a thicker fabric for my leggings. I guessed that was what you got for $15.80 these days at a back-to-school sale, but how in the world could I complain when ten thousand miles away, an Indonesian mother of seven was hunched over in a factory, sweaty, starving, sleep-deprived, and compensated a measly fifty cents an hour to make said shitty leggings? Suddenly, they weren't so shitty anymore—they were brilliantly put together, given the circumstances. Unfortunately, I was realizing more and more that to understand my own privilege was to know the misfortune of others.

In other news, my gut feeling about my new school situation was unsettling. Transferring to a public high school in the middle of Hollywood may have seemed relatively glamorous, but I knew better. The celebrity glitz the rest of the world associated with Hollywood was largely fictional, at least these days. I had already had the enchanting experience of attending an inner-city public middle school once before. The bullying had been so intense that Mama decided to dish out our life savings on a private school for me in the Palisades. To think I'd almost made it out of high school unscathed! Transferring for senior year—whose stupid idea was that, anyway? I did get to sleep in an extra hour because it was so much closer to home, but the looming sensation of the unknown was more nauseating than ever—or maybe it was the bus driver's sporadically spastic braking, like a child playing Whack-a-Mole with the pedals. If not for my music I'd have schized out.

I thanked the music gods for giving us Death Cab for Cutie and imagined dancing the choreography from the previous week's contemporary dance routine to "Underneath the Sycamore" in my head. Tension gradually left my body, but a chill made its way up my spine. I tried to ignore it, but then a gust of wind whipped my hair into my face. Someone must have opened a window, but it was barely sixty degrees outside—who would open their window when it's that cold? I felt for the zipper of my jacket and found it was stuck, so I yanked at it harder, then the pull tab broke off. Wonderful! I looked down to see the zipper eating up my shirt.

I tried to rescue my shirt from the jaws of the zipper but instead created an incredibly visible tear right in the center. *No!* Though I knew it was my own doing, I looked around menacingly for someone to blame, and what did I find? There, in the last three rows of the bus, was that same rowdy group of jacketless, immune-to-the-cold, window-opening assholes.

"Ugh! Look at this ugly-ass bitch," said the scraggly kid in the back of the bus, pointing at a woman on the street.

His friend, the hefty bandana whipper, stood up and hung out of the bus window, shouting, "Aw, shit, you're gross, lady! Don't eat that out of the garbage! Here, I got something for you to nibble on." He proceeded to hump the window.

"Ew, Kelvin, you're nasty! You'd hump that?" said a girl who could have been conventionally attractive but opted for the whole "I'll kill you in your sleep, then eat your baby for breakfast" vibe: Halloween makeup, excessive piercings, and forearms covered in marker scribbles.

Kelvin answered, "Yeah, after I put a trash bag over her face! Why not? I bet she's tighter than you."

"Shut up, stupid-ass!" the girl shouted.

I couldn't help but stare in disgust as he continued humping the window. He must not have been right in the head. Not to be outdone, the scraggly one threw a crumpled milk carton at the poor homeless woman picking through a trash can on the street corner. It was like they were competing over who was a bigger idiot.

"Damn, that's messed up," the girl remarked, chortling between each word. She didn't do anything to stop him—then again, neither did I.

Not a single person besides me seemed even remotely concerned about the insanity happening in the rear of the bus; they all just continued looking out their respective windows with total apathy. Shame on us. I so badly wanted to say something, but I didn't want to invoke violence or end up in another stupid viral video, and somehow, I knew that was how things would end if I got involved.

Screw it.

"That's not funny. Leave her alone," I intoned to the back of the bus.

"The hell?" The same girl chortled with laughter again. "Damn, Kelvin, that nosey bitch is schooling you fools."

"Bitch, mind your own business—turn around," said Kelvin.

Keep to yourself. Keep your slate clean, dictated a quiet but stern voice in my head, Mama's voice. I turned away and closed my eyes. Tuning out the unnerving cackles coming from the Neanderthals behind me, I pretended with everyone else that I never noticed a thing. When my mind was finally still, I sifted through my memory for some means of escape.

Then I was lying in the sand on a beach—one of my earliest memories. The cool breeze washed over me in contrast to the warmth of the sun heating the sand. When I dug my fingers and toes into those warm patches, a seagull flew by and squawked loudly, the tip of its wing brushing my skin. Startled, I sat up, gasping. My parents lay on either side of me with their fingers intertwined across my belly. Father opened his eyes and said, "Don't be afraid, Mina. The birds can't hurt you." Without a warning, he took me in his arms, hugged me tight, and then lifted me so I hovered above him like Superman. I loosened my grip on him and slowly let go, spreading my arms to mimic the birds.

Father read my mind. "See, there's nothing to be afraid of. Now you are one of them!"

"Careful not to be pooping from excitement on your father's head, little bird!" Mama teased. Father gently placed me back on the sand and rolled over to attack her with tickles; her laughter filled the air. I dug for a warm place to hide my feet in the sand but ended up stubbing my toe against the base of the school bus seat in front of me. I loved that memory but thinking about my father put knots in my stomach. I shouldn't have wrung my own nerves like that; it was masochistic.

"Wake up, princess! Let's just jack her shit." I opened my eyes to find the main building of my new high school outside the window. We'd come to our final stop quicker than I anticipated. I shifted my focus, tightened my grip on what was mine, and got up slowly without dropping my gaze from the girl glaring at me. She tensed and backed away instinctually as her friends' mouths formed Os of excitement for what was to come. Most of the students in the front rows had already cleared out but several stayed behind to see if the tension might escalate into something entertaining. I pressed past the girl and moved toward the exit with my jaw clenched so as not to utter a word. I reined in my temper and hoped she read the warning in my eyes as patience, not fear. But her next words told me she didn't.

Her voice was filled with exhilaration. "That's right, little bitch, run. I'll give you a head start—"

This would continue to escalate unless I put a stop to it right then. Fury filled me and spilled over too quickly to think my next steps through. I turned back, marching up to her face so fast that she didn't have time to finish her thought. She pushed me back out of fear before I had a chance to speak, so I grabbed hold of her wrists, twisted them inward to keep her still, and delivered my next words as quietly and calmly as my shaking voice could allow.

"Why don't you save your strength, and just focus—" She resisted against the strain I placed on her wrists, but I was stronger. "Focus on getting through the academic year, or one day you'll be the one picking through garbage while some kid chucks trash off a school bus at your head. Been skipping out on arm day, huh?" I got closer to her so she could feel my breath on her ear. "If you ever touch me or my shit"—she rotated her face away, but I followed—"I'll clip your hands off and use them to wipe my ass." I know, I know. That bit at the end was too much, but I needed to leave a lasting impression. Maybe she'd leave me alone for the rest of the year. That, or she'd stab me—it was risky business.

"All right, what's the holdup? Everyone off the bus. Come on, move it." Looked like the bus driver finally woke up from his coma.

"Let's go. It's not worth it. This bitch is crazy," her friend advised. Mission accomplished. I could go.

That must have been the school's welcoming committee, an enchanting first encounter. As I walked toward the building, I took it all in. Truly, it oozed with the charm of a penitentiary: walls and chain-link fences cocooned the fortress. It was a stark contrast to that private high school in the Palisades, where the campus was open and inviting, the buildings were more like a collection of single-story houses, pigeons were seagulls, and the smell of car pollution was a fresh gust of wind off the Pacific. That extra hour of sleep wasn't looking so sweet anymore. *Look on the bright side, Mina* . . . I wasn't going to hold my breath while I figured out the bright side.

After passing through security, a metal detector, and a random backpack check, I followed the rest of the herd to the school gym, where masses of students were told to pile into alphabetical order for class schedule distribution. Chaos, confusion, and profanity filled the overcrowded room.

I took a place in the A—G last names line behind over a hundred people, pressed play on my music app, and drowned the noise. Once I had my schedule in hand, I found the academic bright side: this year should be a breeze, grade-wise. I knocked out AP Calculus and AP Physics ahead of schedule last year, so all that was left was AP Statistics, AP Government, and AP Literature. The other three were a cakewalk and were all at the end of the day: Cooking, Computers, and Independent Study.

I treaded to my first-period class—AP Stats. Somehow, every seat was already taken. I rechecked my schedule to make sure I was in the right room. I walked back out to the hallway and double-checked the number on the door. *Yep . . . this is it.* I just couldn't believe how many students were crammed into this one classroom.

Our teacher requested four additional desks from the main office only to hear that they'd already given out all the extra desks. Apparently, they'd have to try bringing in a table from the library to seat the four of us who didn't have desks. The other students and I stood through most of the lecture, taking notes on our laps or against the wall, leaning on a shelf in the back of the room. I zoned out after our teacher had to explain the difference between mean, median, and mode three times because clearly the most vocal students in our class were also the least gifted in the art of retention. At this rate, it'd take all semester to get through the first chapter of the textbook, so merely getting a 3 on the AP exam would be highly improbable, no pun intended. I added a note to my to-do list on my phone: *Review Chapters 1 & 2 in Stats textbook. Solve practice problems (odd).*

"Excuse me, miss! Young lady in the back . . . hello? Put away your cell phone!" I ignored her; maybe she'd leave me alone. "Miss, put it away; no phones in class! Okay, you know what? Hand it over."

I looked up. "Ms., um, sorry . . . I can barely see the board from back here—" I looked for her name on the whiteboard. "Does that say Palloro?"

"Pallera."

"Ms. Pallera, I'm just using my phone for academic purposes, actually. I—"

"Right, and I'm Freida Pinto. Bring it to me now or spend your first week of school in detention. I don't care if you're sitting, standing, or squatting . . . I have a very strict 'no cell phone' policy. If I see it out, I take it," she declared in a nasal soprano. Great, I was her guinea pig. I had three instinctual reactions: argue, yell *Why me?* as I fell on my knees, and Google Freida . . . Panto? Or Pento? Instead, I strode up to her desk, trying to ignore all the eyes on me, with my knuckles white from tension, clutching my phone in frustration. I held Ms. Pallera's gaze without blinking, taking my sweet time to set the phone down gently and soundlessly on her desk. *Why couldn't you just hear me out, you unreasonable bitch?* Mama's voice chimed in like a voice of reason. *Be kind, Mina. Think some nice thoughts. Try to smile.* Ms. Pallera looked creeped out by my unexpected grin. I dropped it, turned away, and trudged to the back of the room. Great going, a superb first impression. That was the start of what was sure to be a delightful senior year.

Russians are sarcastic. Yeah, that was probably a thing. Or if it hadn't been, it was now.

My next class was AP Gov. It might easily be another overcrowded classroom, so I hustled over as quickly as I could. There was no way that I was standing through another hour of lecture. Luckily, the room was nearby, and I was one of the first students to arrive. Once inside, I suddenly felt detached and on autopilot, still upset about my phone getting taken away. *I'm just going to sit in the back corner and stare out of the window in silence, avoiding attention of any kind.* I picked a seat closest to the wall near the window, longing for a glimpse of life beyond the halls. *Why can't I just be an adult already?* As students continued piling in, I peered through the glass brick window. It allowed muddled light into the room, but nothing else of the world outside apart from a blurred tree silhouette. It must have been satisfying: to be grown, drive wherever you wanted, do whatever you wanted whenever you wanted. *Soon, Mina, soon.* The classroom was bright, filled with pastel hues, and equipped with fresh whiteboards and desks. I heard they finished building this place just the summer before. Someone, however, had already managed to vandalize my desk with graffiti, but at least it was a declaration of deep love: *Sasha + Joseph 4ever.* I was sure it was only a matter of time before fortunes shifted and cuffing season was over, and the desk revised to read something like *Sasha is ratchet AF.*

If I sounded cynical, it's because I was. Why shouldn't I have been? In my final year of middle school, out of principle, I refused to give up my place in the line for yearbook photos to an unreasonable bully of a girl, Charisa. Subsequently, she shoved me in the halls whenever she had an opportunity. Several painful days later, Charisa followed me onto my school bus, sat behind me, and violently kicked my spine through the seat-back for the entire duration of the ride. I felt helpless and on the verge of a complete breakdown, but my survival instincts kept me composed and alert. Still unsatisfied, she followed me off the bus and pressed her disgusting turquoise chewing gum against the back of my head with her thumb. Even then, I didn't break—not one tear. I just stood there, taking it. I hid my pain behind a nearly impenetrable fortress masterfully crafted after my "Bathroom Troll" days. I vented pain only in a self-designated safe space: at home or the dance studio.

The worst part was that those kids weren't really to blame—they didn't know any better. It was a messed-up system of circumstance, negligence, poverty, and perpetuated violence. I retained two lessons to survive unscathed: keep to yourself, and if you must express your opinion, express it silently. Clearly, though, I was terrible at doing both of those things, so I just opted for lesson three—the lesson I had learned from Charisa: when in doubt, bluff—convince them you're much more deranged than they are.

Tired of staring out a blurry window, I doodled in my notebook for the rest of class while trying my best to listen. Occasionally, I jotted down historical events that I wanted to investigate further. I'd have looked them up right then, but based on the reaction of my first period teacher, I'd been technologically castrated. Mid-class, the door swung open, and I looked over, eager for a distraction. It was a late arrival. He walked into class with a smooth strut like he was cat-walking across the surface of the moon, this new guy. My eye was immediately drawn to his hair, which sat in unruly waves with subtle streaks of gold atop an otherwise clean cut. It was like all the air had been sucked out of the room. Suddenly, I became conscious of the fact that I'd stopped blinking and breathing properly; I'd just been staring at this complete stranger, mouth agape. I quickly redirected my gaze to my desk, oddly embarrassed. But then I peeked back over—I couldn't help it. Striking, somewhat gray eyes illuminated his tan face, balanced by dark untamed brows and a neatly lined five-o'clock shadow. Most guys in our grade didn't have enough facial hair to trim into much of anything. I couldn't speak to his exact heritage, but he looked like a mix of many cultures: Middle Eastern or maybe Hispanic, but he could also have been Irish even, who knew? All I knew for sure is that his eyes were warm and inviting, even from afar.

But the longer I observed, the more I noticed hints of coldness in his demeanor. Maybe it was tension—awareness of us watching as he walked over to the teacher's desk? If it was nerves, he hid them well behind a steady, surefooted stride. Only his jumpy index finger betrayed him, tapping wildly against the edge of a paper he clutched like a broken metronome. He told so many stories without uttering a single word, and I was left asking myself, *Who is this guy?*

CHAPTER 4

OLIVER

'd never really been in control before, not for real. Life had dealt me more than my fair share of shitty cards, that's a fact. But I had to play the game regardless. As I wove through the I-5 traffic on my bike, it felt like the turn card had just been dealt and my luck had changed. It just might be time to bet big. With freedom paperwork in tow, empowerment filled me until I was almost a whole person. Each mile I biked now was a mile closer to my new life.

I exited off Hyperion Avenue—not far to go, then—and stopped at the bank to make a withdrawal. The judgement granted access to a very small portion of the total sum from the case. The rest was to be held in a trust until I was older. So, I filed an appeal and explained that I needed the money to relocate. Only after I pled my case in detail as to why the move was necessary for my well-being did the judge reluctantly grant me access to $15,000—and he tried to convince me that a nice, quiet life in Lake Tahoe would do me better than a big city filled with crime and sin. It was like I said: Evil was everywhere. And sin? Well, throw a rock and you'd hit a sinner.

If I'd budgeted correctly, the money should have covered my deposit for first and last month's rent, provided a little capital for my business, and still left some spare cash for everyday stuff for at least a month. The bank teller didn't really look at me until after she examined the check I wanted to cash. Then she scrutinized me like I was a tricky math problem and she had left her calculator at home. She asked me to take a seat while she got a manager.

The manager, Amid Mossaid, greeted me. He was young and had a generically ambitious look about him. He wore a cheesy smile as he took me to his office. He was wearing a sharp-fitted light gray suit and had taken the time to match his socks with his tie that morning—it wasn't exactly my style, but I could appreciate that kind of attention to detail. He sat me down at a mostly empty desk filled only by a computer, a nameplate, and a USC coffee cup. His diploma was displayed on the wall as well, and I wondered if it was meant to assure me that he was competent or to be more of a conversation starter. Maybe he was just a proud Trojan.

Amid tapped on his computer a few times then squinted into the monitor.

"Here's my ID. I need to cash this check, please. Here's the number of the Santa Clarita court clerk in case your supervisor needs to verify with them, and also, I'd like to open a business checking account and a savings account. I guess maybe we can just deposit some of this money into the new accounts."

Tap. Tap. Tap.

"Do you own your home?"

What the hell difference did that make? I wasn't trying to borrow the money.

"No."

"If so, what's your current mortgage rate?"

"Uh . . . not applicable." He didn't laugh with me.

"Did you know rates are at a historic low? By the way, do you have any outside investments?" He was reading this directly off his screen.

"No, just wanna open an account, that's all."

He ignored me. "Are you also interested in a credit card or a home equity line of credit?"

Had I not just established that I didn't own a home?

"No, I'm good. I just want to cash the check and open those accounts."

"Okay, let's get you those business checking and savings accounts so you can take advantage of those benefits right away."

It sounded simple enough when he said it. But two hours and thousands of keyboard taps later, I was still sitting in the chair and Amid was still squinting at his screen.

"Can I use the phone to call someone to let them know I'm running late?" I asked.

"Certainly."

I punched in the number I jotted down last night but got her voicemail. "Mrs. Goldberg, it's, um ... Oliver, the new renter. I'm very sorry, but I'm running late; the bank is taking a lot longer than I thought. I hope I'm not holding you up. I'm almost done here, and I should be there soon." I hung up and turned back to Amid. "Thanks."

"Not a problem at all. We're focused on the customer's experience, and I can only hope you will be satisfied with my service and give me a ten on the customer survey you will receive. I'm going to check in with my supervisor regarding the check status and I'll be right back. What denomination do you prefer?"

"So, five thousand dollars will stay in the business checking account as a minimum balance, right? Two hundred dollars in the savings account, for now, and the rest in hundreds, please."

"Sure thing. I'll provide you with temporary checks for your new accounts today, but I can order your business checks for you as well. Look through this booklet of sample checks and choose one that speaks to you."

The check ordering portion of the exchange took another half hour to complete. I began throwing pointed looks at the exit sign hanging over the front door.

"By the way, here, help yourself to some of my business cards. If you know anyone that I can provide the same great customer experience for, please refer them over to me."

"Will do. Thanks."

My new place was pretty much the perfect place to live. It was a small guest house in someone's backyard in Silverlake—"a quiet little neighborhood engulfed in trees, nestled in the nook of a hill" or some realtor shit. That's how it was described online, at least. As I pulled up to the house, I became self-conscious about how I looked. I parked my bike on the street and fidgeted with an unraveled thread that hung off the sleeve of my secondhand jacket. Mrs. Goldberg had seemed chill over email and on the phone but meeting new people in person was always stressful for me—it made me lose my grip on control. I needed control—I was a control fiend. I'd have to inoculate myself to the discomfort of meeting new people if I wanted to succeed in business, though.

The house was more impressive in person than in pictures. It was surrounded by a manicured lawn that bordered a garden of palm trees and weird-looking plants. That kind of upkeep took money, especially in drought-prone L.A. where a lawn like that was considered a luxury. Most of the neighbors had opted for succulents and gravel, probably to alleviate their water bill and mitigate the city-wide shortage, but not Mrs. Goldberg. The neighborhood really was as advertised: quiet and very, very clean. I rang the doorbell, hoping she'd gotten my voice mail and wasn't going to greet me with an explosion about tardiness. The door swung open and a blonde woman in her forties walked out wearing a white power suit and a matching smile. She looked like she'd just tumbled off the cover of *Malibu* magazine.

"Hello! You must be Oliver. I'm glad you actually made it!"

"Mrs. Goldberg, it's nice to meet you in person. Sorry I'm late. I got tied up at the bank. I tried to leave a voice mail."

She waved her hand through the air, "It's absolutely no problem, and please, call me Margret. Follow me, darling. Ah, is that a motorcycle helmet? I've always wanted to ride around on a chopper." I followed her through the garden toward the patio. "Can I get you anything? Water? Lemonade?"

"No, thank you, ma'am, I'm all right. Here is the check for first month's rent. Did the bank give you any trouble with the cashier's check that I mailed you?"

"No dear, it was absolutely fine," she said with another wave of the hand. "Aren't you darling? I'm just thrilled you're here. I've been very . . . selective. This is a very desirable neighborhood, obviously, and I can't let just anyone live on my property. God knows there's never a shortage of crazies in L.A. But after a minute on the phone with you the other week, I just knew you were the one! You sure know how to make a girl feel . . . safe, Oliver." She let out a glorious laugh, unleashing all of her pearly whites, but the rest of her face didn't move much—paralyzed as it was by all the Botox. Her long nails dug into my arm through my leather jacket, testing out my biceps, as she guided me through the rest of the garden. "Very, very charming. You're going to do just fine. How old are you, honey, if you don't mind me asking?"

"Eighteen," I lied, my heartbeat rising.

"A baby!" Margret's eyes lit up and her mouth twisted into a devious smile as she scanned me up and down. She fiddled with the pearls around her neck. "And getting a place of your own already? You're . . . oh, what do the kids call it? Oh, yes, you're *adulting!* Good for you. So, would you like the nickel tour?"

"Nah, I'm good. I saw the pics online and the video you sent was awesome. It's exactly what I'm looking for. I can just sign the lease now."

And the price is a steal, especially for this area. That was why I'd sent the cashier's check by mail, to secure the place before someone else snagged it up. It was still a bit over my budget, but nothing else came even close. I'd just have to work harder and affording the place would serve as good motivation.

"Just like that? When you know, you know, huh? Well, easy-peasy, then. I like a man who knows what he wants. Let me go get the paperwork and keys, and you'll be all set."

I looked around the garden as Margret walked away. Everything was blooming and bright. There were birds singing. There was even a lemon tree by a water fountain. I caught a glimpse of a hummingbird drinking nectar near a flowering vine and a pair of butterflies fluttered past the rose bushes then disappeared. *Is this a dream?* I felt my smile growing. Margret was a piece of work, but she was probably harmless. *Oh, what do the kids call it? Oh yes, you're adulting!*

Just then, the large entrance door of the house opened and a tiny head peeked out. It was a little boy, maybe seven years old—tiny but with knowing eyes. He ran outside, stopped a few feet away from me, and covered his eyes with his hands. "Hi," he whispered.

"Hello. I'm, um . . . Oliver."

He peeked through his fingers.

"Patrick?" called Margret from the house, and he turned and zoomed back inside. She came back with forms and a glass of lemonade and led me to the shaded patio. We took a seat on French bistro stools arranged around a small, marble-top table.

"Here. Did you meet Patrick?"

"Briefly," I replied.

"He's very shy." I just smiled and started filling out the renter's agreement, trying to think of a good cover story in case she asked for a copy of my ID. But she just handed me the keys as soon as I gave her the paperwork, no additional questions asked. We both stood up, and just as I'd had time to think, *That was easy*, she asked, "So, how are your parents dealing with you moving out so soon? Your mom must be a wreck. Do you have any siblings? If you don't mind me asking, that is."

Why did she have to go there? Everything was going so well. "They're fine with it," I answered automatically, but didn't elaborate, creating an uncomfortable silence on purpose.

"That's great—oh, the guest house is out back." My heartbeat steadied as she stood, gesturing toward the walkway that led to the back of the house. "Just take this path; it wraps around the house and will lead you straight there. I'm so sorry that I have to rush off on you, but I have an appointment on the other side of town. But call me if you have any questions or need anything at all." There was that famous Hollywood smile again.

I followed the paved path to the back of the house like she told me to. Across yet another perfectly mowed lawn and against the backdrop of some tall-ass hedge, sat a place—my place, my . . . home. On the outside, it was like a mini-me of the main property. Eager to get inside, I headed straight for the heavy mahogany door. I turned the key, and it opened to reveal a living room with surprisingly high ceilings that created an illusion of spaciousness. The wooden floors were scuffed, but the walls wore a fresh coat of beige paint. Bow windows flooded sunshine into the space. The cottage was divided into three areas: an open kitchen which was connected to the living room and a bedroom. The ad didn't explicitly mention that the furniture in the pictures was included with the place— the bed, the dresser, the TV, a super-expensive-looking couch—but it was all still there, minus a few decorations and random crap like pottery bowls and tiny gold tables that I didn't need anyway. That would save me a shit-ton of money. I didn't think the grin would be leaving my face anytime soon. I couldn't even recognize the idiot smiling at me in the mirror.

I sprawled out on the giant bed and soaked it all in. Could this really be *my* life? I'd never lain on a mattress that comfortable; it hugged all the curves of my back. Imagine sleeping on something like that your whole life. *Okay, break's over.* I sat up and looked around, making a mental list of everything else I needed. Then I jumped to my feet, hid my transcript and freedom papers under the mattress, and headed out.

First, I stopped by an electronics store in a Glendale mall. If I was buying a phone, I was going to buy the best phone on the market, with the largest storage capacity and the fastest service provider. No more second-rate shit, especially if I was trying to be someone in the industry. I needed reliable service and voice mail—no dropped calls. A successful image begat success—I actually read that in *Success.* Sounded lame, but it checked out. Research was how I taught myself most everything I knew. I'd seen the statistics—they all said the same thing: because of my past, my trauma, I was more likely to end up an alcoholic, a drug addict, locked up in a looney bin, or in prison, or even a sexual abuser of my own kids. But hell, no—screw that! I wasn't a statistic; I was a person, and I had a choice. No one else was gonna write my script for me, so I'd made up my own lessons—self-education, trying to eat right, staying drug-free, working out regularly, and reading articles—lots and lots of articles. Articles were like home school for life. All the little maxims and acronyms they provided helped me maintain an illusion that I was brought up by actual parents. At least, I thought they did—the hell did I know about being raised by real parents?

The sales rep took me to the counter and rang up the phone. He looked at me funny when I paid for it in cash, like there was something wrong with that. I could practically feel his thoughts take a turn. *What'd you do, rob a bank?* Whatever. It'd take more than that to mess with my good mood that day. I put my new phone in my pocket, threw the packaging in my backpack and walked out of the store feeling like a king.

I needed new clothes, shoes, and office supplies, so I roamed through the Galleria and walked into a department store packed with back-to-school shoppers. Little kids ran ecstatic circles around their parents while teenagers trudged past, hunched over, hiding from one another under shitty haircuts or anonymous hoodies as if being spotted with their family would mortify them. Idiots—they didn't know how good they had it—someone giving enough of a shit to take you shopping.

I refocused, holding up a pair of designer jeans and rubbing the tips of my fingers against the soft fabric. The button was carved with elaborate detail, the zipper moved like butter, and the stitching was seamless. I examined the tag, printed on thick, chic paper in an elegant, tiny font was a not-so-tiny price somewhere in the triple digits. I'd never bought new clothes from a store before, so I wasn't sure what was a fair price for a good pair of jeans. Everything I'd worn had been secondhand. I wanted to dress nice, but I knew I shouldn't blow all my money on something as trivial as clothes. I bought five pairs of the cheaper brand but splurged on a fine leather jacket that was on clearance. I also dished out for a very nice pair of brown leather boots to replace my pre-owned, worn-out crap. The boots and the jacket would serve me for years, so I figured I was being practical. I also grabbed a pack of socks and a dozen white and black cotton tees and made a quick stop by the underwear section. *All right, this and done.*

A salesgirl appeared out of nowhere. "Hi!" She flipped her hair and batted her glued-on eyelashes wildly. "Can I help you find anything?"

"I'm all right." I turned my attention back to the underwear packages, looking for my size.

"Here, I'll help you find your size—32-34?" She squeezed closer to me, placed her hand on my chest to move me over slightly, and bent over to flip through the packages on the bottom shelf, glancing back at me periodically to see if I was watching her.

I took a few steps back. She was being so obvious in her desire to be admired. I couldn't help it—I had always pushed girls like that away, but it had the opposite effect, like they could sense my reluctance and they found it appealing. Girls might call me a player, but in reality, I was hella selective with the type of girls I ended up actually sleeping with. Well, unless you included my first time.

I mean, after the trial finished, and as soon as I got placed in that temporary foster home, I felt like I had to have sex as soon as possible just to prove to myself I could do it on my own terms. I wanted to make sure Jack Burns hadn't messed me up that way, even though my therapist at the time was highly against it. She said we had a lot of work to do before I was ready for anything like that. So, obviously, I did the opposite. That first time I met up with this one girl who had started hanging around the library—let's just say, she wasn't the library type. Again, she was a bit older than me, and way more experienced. So, she texted me her address and told me to bring rubbers. I was nervous as hell. I went over, her parents weren't home, she dimmed the lights in her room, and set up some music—it was a vibe. I had a box of condoms in my backpack, athlete mentality—I was ready to go. The whole time we were doing it, I was checking in with her like, "You okay?—Oh, shit . . . You okay? You good?"

She was like, "Yeah, are you okay, though?" That's when I realized my eyes were shut the whole time, my fists clenched, and my body rigid—just fixated on suppressing messed-up memories instead of being fixated on the gorgeous, naked female below me. She rolled her eyes and went, "Is something wrong? Here . . . just let me get on top." I did. It was all downhill from there. Therapist was right—I wasn't ready. Like a poison, toxic shame had ruined sex for me.

With time, I learned that I was able to enjoy myself only when I was emotionally detached from my partner and things were purely physical. As I grew more experienced, I learned how to choose the kind of girls—or women—who enjoyed intense sex with no emotions. Those kinds of opportunities started to arise more often than I expected, even in my days at the library—especially there, you'd be surprised. It was always the quiet ones. They eventually wanted something more, though, and that's when I ghosted them. I didn't know, nor did I want to know, the first thing about being someone's boyfriend. I was still trying to figure out my own shit.

"Got it!" the salesgirl exclaimed, waving the underwear in my face and snapping me out of my flashback.

I grabbed the package and mumbled a quick thanks before heading to the register. After paying for everything, I made my way to the exit, hoping everything I bought would fit in the new backpack I got. Just as I neared the exit, the girl from earlier stopped me in my tracks.

"I'm Bree, by the way."

I looked at her, said, "Thanks for your help, Bree," and tried to make my way past her.

Bree's carefree façade wavered in light of a disturbing possibility. "So. . . what's your name? Are you, like . . . running away from me?" she asked loudly and made an uncomfortable giggling sound. A few customers overheard and stared at us in passing.

Don't be an ass. "Look . . . I'm sorry. I'm, um . . . Oliver." I tried to produce a genuine smile, and she turned on like a lightbulb.

"Oliver! Cool, I'm on break in half an hour, if you wanna grab a bite?" she asked enthusiastically. She had a habit of running her tongue over her lips after every sentence she uttered.

"I would love to, Bree, but I got a lot of stuff I gotta do today."

"Oh, too bad! Take down my number, though," she insisted. I hesitated, but finally pulled my phone out, unlocked it, and handed it to her.

"Nice! I love the new iPhone!" It took her under ten seconds to program the number in—impressive!—and then she was browsing through my contact list. I snatched the phone back. "Oh shit, that's crazy! Aw, I'm the first number in there! Text me, so I'll have yours."

Luckily, a coworker called her over. She waved goodbye before bouncing away. What a strange, sweet, sad girl. That was the kind of girl you hook up with and then regret it. The sex would be good, but you wouldn't call or text back, and before long you'd be getting fifty texts from her a day. Then she'd set your house on fire. I might have been wrong, but that's the vibe I was picking up.

The first thing I did as soon as I got back to my place was to browse the App Store on my phone. I couldn't wait to get online and see what the market was like. Now that I had a fixed address, I could finally set up some online accounts and order units to come straight there. I quickly realized the network required a Wi-Fi passcode, so I tried *goldberg*. Nope. I tried *margretgoldberg*. Nope. I tried *goldberg4567*. Nope. I tried *patrick4567*. Nope. Finally, I tried *patrick2013*. That did the trick. Lucky squirt.

After a few hours of research, I set up a meet with a guy whose number I'd dug up on Craigslist a while back. He was selling ten phones back then and I figured maybe he'd gotten his hands on more product already. This was going to be the biggest quantity of brand-new, high-end smartphones I'd ever purchased thus far—mostly because I'd never had enough cash before. I asked him to meet me at a nearby plaza. My stomach growled; the timing was perfect, as I had to make a grocery run anyway.

I waited for him in the parking lot for five minutes before he finally pulled up in a Nissan GT-R. An Asian guy got out of the car. I walked up to him, stuck my hand out, and said, "I'm, um . . . Omar. You're Tee? That's a nice car."

He looked at my hand but didn't shake it. "Yeah."

He didn't trust me; I didn't trust him either. First-time deals were normally stiff.

"Phones are brand-new and sealed?" I asked, taking my hand away.

"Yeah," he said.

"Do you have the receipt?"

"Yeah. Ten gold iPhones, brand-new, sixty-four gig, unlocked—like I said in the text. You got the cash? It comes out to sixty-two hundred dollars even."

"Can you do fifty-nine hundred?" I asked in a flat voice.

"No way in hell. What is this? Don't set a meet and then lowball me!"

I narrowed my eyes at him.

"The new one just came out. The price on these just took a major dip. It will drop again overnight and keep dropping—might as well sell to me at fifty-nine hundred tonight," I explained.

"Sixty-two hundred dollars is the best I can do. I'm not making shit on these, either."

I shook my head.

"Fifty-nine fifty. You won't even get fifty-eight hundred tomorrow. Come on. Think about it," I said firmly. I pulled my keys from my pocket and jangled them—a signal that I was ready to walk away from the deal with the cash still in my pocket.

He whipped out his phone, said "Hold on," and dialed a number. There was no answer, so he hung up quickly and tried again. Still no answer.

"Okay. Let's do it."

Perfect. After digging through the leading online forums for a few hours and calling around, I'd already found someone with an exporter connect looking to buy these older units. He was willing to go as high as $6,300—that's $35 a phone and $350 total profit for the night. I always made a good profit on the old models when the new one came out and the sellers got desperate to liquidate units. I took out the money. "Let me see the phones." He opened his trunk and handed me one; it came in a small box white box. The logos were in the right place; it looked authentic. The weight felt right. I checked the seals to make sure the phone really was brand new and not resealed. The receipt checked out as well—$599 a unit retail. Looked like they were purchased legit and tax-free in Oregon a couple weeks back. I counted out $5,950 quickly and handed him the wad. I stacked the phones into my backpack while Tee counted the cash and marked the bills, checking for fakes. He was satisfied, because I put my hand out again and this time he took it. "Let me know when you have more product," I told him.

"I always have more product; let me know when you have more money."

"I'll text you tomorrow." I headed over to Albertsons while doing some mental math. If I could keep it up, I could potentially gross over ten grand a month. *But don't get greedy,* I cautioned myself. The first thing I needed was a safe for my cash—I couldn't just keep depositing that kind of money and then withdrawing it the next day. That would raise a red flag with the IRS; I'd become a liability—and the bank would kick me out and shut down my account. I had to start brainstorming ways to get my business off the streets. I needed to legitimize myself—make it a real business—but all of that would be easier to do once I was eighteen. For the time being, no landlord would take me seriously enough to lease an office to me.

I needed to remember to order some bedsheets online. It was hard to do more than a few errands at a time when I had to get everything home on my bike, so most things were going to have to come by mail, and I was going to need to look for a used car on Craigslist. *Adulting.*

I zipped through the aisles of the grocery store, grabbing essentials: cucumbers, tomatoes, bread, cold cuts, eggs, bacon, chicken, a frying pan, and some toiletries. I headed toward the checkout, but then doubled back for the nonessentials: Red Bull, Pringles, Sour Patch Straws, Oreo cookies, and Belgian chocolate. At home, I stuffed my face with as many salami sandwiches as I could eat while I shopped online. I ordered silk bedsheets, fine goose down pillows and comforters—I was really livin'. I also added a safe to my cart, bought some kitchen essentials, and threw in a few vintage art pieces. One was an artsy piece with a nude mermaid or sea-creature girl caught in some ropes. The description detailed a painting of a figure onto which real rope had been affixed, giving the illusion that the figure is entwined in the rope. It was glass framed. *Fancy.* The other was a poster of a smiling dog playing the piano. I'd always had a thing for mermaids, which admittedly was kinda bizarre. As for the piano . . . well, I'd always wished I could play. So, if a dog could do it, there was still hope for me, right? A part of me wanted to just order an electric keyboard and have fun with it—maybe I could teach myself? I placed a rush delivery on the bedsheets and let everything else arrive through normal shipping. I smiled, picturing Margret's reaction when all those packages started arriving while I was in school.

I put away my phone and tried to fall asleep, but I just ended up staring at the ceiling for what felt like an hour. I tried streaming some music on my phone. It asked me for a genre, so I chose classical, and the Mozart "Requiem" started to play. I vibed to it, closed my eyes, and sort of swayed. I laughed at the thought of what I was doing—soothing myself with Mozart, feeling classy as hell. But after five minutes, I concluded that shit wasn't working. I dropped to the floor and got into a plank position and started doing push-ups. I kept going until my body gave out and I was lying sprawled out, face down on the floor, panting. What was that? That had to be like five—maybe even ten minutes of nonstop push-ups. I was still panting like an old man. Was I getting out of shape, or was that a good amount? *I gotta hit the gym or some shit and ask a trainer.* I stared at the ceiling, smiling at the idea of having a trainer, but my smile faded quickly.

Something was off here. I looked around the empty room. *What's throwing me off about this place? It's perfect, isn't it? Where's that stupid smile I couldn't wipe off my face earlier today, and why can't I fall asleep? Am I nervous about school tomorrow?* No answer—only the crickets. That was probably it—it was the silence. Not Franklin's snoring, not Braiden whining about something across the hall, not the sound of Breanne's and Jorge's hushed conversations or a radio station playing the oldies, not the neighbor's barking dog or the sound of a juvie guard beating up a loudmouth, or the sound of Jack Burns's TV set blaring upstairs, muffling our screams from the basement. Nope, none of that—only silence, only the crickets.

My phone alarm went off at 7:00 a.m. I stretched, showered, fried some eggs, and put on a pot of coffee, letting it brew as I got dressed. My smile was back. I threw on fresh clothes and my new jacket, dropped a notebook and pen in my backpack, and went out to the patio to finish my coffee. I texted the Glendale guy that I could meet him with the phones around 4:00 p.m. The birds were up and chirping away. *I feel you guys; I'm right there at your level.* I needed to leave soon, though, or I'd be late to my first day of school.

Los Angeles morning traffic was no joke, and it was no wonder—narrow streets with a hundred times more cars than they were built for. I'd never been more grateful to squeeze past so many frustrated sedans, or more scared to navigate through so many crazy people who drove like they had nothing to lose. I found a spot between two cars across the street from the main entrance and parked my bike. The school was pretty big, but it was about half the size of the one back in Santa Clarita. The hallways were packed with more than twice as many students, though. I'd read that there were over four thousand students enrolled there that year— the entire population of my old neighborhood. I walked into the main office and there was already a long line to speak to a counselor. When my turn was finally up, I gave her my name. The woman tapped away at the computer, then peered at me over her glasses.

"I'm sorry, Mr. Mondell, I can't seem to find you in our system."

"That's bullshit! My bad, I mean—you must be mistaken—please check again. They promised me the transcripts were sent over and everything was all set." I dropped the anger from my voice and reminded myself to stay calm.

"Take a seat, Mr. Mondell. We'll sort it out." So, I sat and they "sorted it out" while I missed all of first period. My records were eventually discovered in an envelope underneath a stack of papers on an unattended desk. At least this process was faster than opening a checking account.

It really irritated me how the school system was run, like the way everyone was supposed to fit into the same mold—a bullshit, cookie-cutter style of learning, based on memorization and pointless quizzes. I sucked at standardized testing. I hated memorizing random facts when I didn't get how they applied to real life—I couldn't learn like that. Trust me, I got the necessity of our educational system enough to respect its significance in shaping our minds and setting us up for adulthood and shit, theoretically. I guess that was why I was there, getting my diploma—no one was gonna take a high school dropout seriously.

I went to my second-period class. According to the map on the back of my planner, it was in the same building I was in, the main building, but on the second floor. I looked through the narrow window in the door before walking in—the teacher was sitting at his desk reading from the textbook and the few students I could see from there looked bored as hell. It was my first time taking an AP class. I was nervous I'd fail, but history had always been my favorite subject and I usually did well without even studying, if the teacher was any good at lecturing. I was still surprised they put me in AP; I guessed there wasn't much interest in an Advanced Placement government class. *Screw it, let's do this.* I finally pushed the door open. Dozens of eyes looked over at me as I stepped inside, eager for a distraction.

Whenever I felt like I was being watched, I usually started to perform. My posture morphed, my spine stiffened, but I felt strangely weightless as I started to move forward. *Are they all still staring?* I didn't check; I continued to look straight ahead. The teacher stopped reading and looked up at me as I approached him—visibly annoyed by the interruption. *This is painfully awkward*—the silence, the staring, the walking. I gave him my schedule to sign and quickly found an empty seat.

"The AP exam is comprised of two sections: multiple-choice, which is one hour and twenty minutes and worth fifty percent of your total score"—*I wouldn't be facing the limitations of flipping them on the street if I could figure out how to ship the units straight to the customer. I mean, there's no question there are towns out there without nearby electronics stores for miles. So, those folks would buy online even at a markup . . . not now—listen to the lecture. What's this dude's name? Mr. Gerald?*—"and worth the other fifty percent of your total score. Those four responses will ask you to apply political concepts in real-world scenarios, compare the decisions and implications of different Supreme Court cases, analyze quantitative data, and develop an argument using required foundational documents as evidence."

I tried to focus on what he was saying, but my mind kept moving back to thoughts of work: profit, price drops, product, maximizing on the dips—*What haven't I thought of yet? What am I missing?* The bell jolted me. *Shit—what'd I miss?* Everyone was getting up. I grabbed my backpack and got up too. I started to walk forward, but a girl leaned over to grab her stuff, blocking my way. I considered going around back, but decided to wait, and couldn't help noticing her clothes. She was dressed like a hitman, black and sleek from head to toe. There was something hot about it—maybe the fact that she was giving me a great view of her backside at that moment. She straightened suddenly, and before I could move, her elbow jabbed me hard in my stomach, almost knocking the wind out of me.

"Sorry!" She turned to see her victim and her face changed when she saw me. There was something about her—her eyes. Well, not so much her eyes, physically, but more like what they said about her: she had this look—a kind of restless intensity.

"It's okay," I finally said. I tried to look away, but I couldn't make myself break her gaze. Déjà vu hit me, sending my head spinning. I felt a powerful compulsion to reach out and touch her, as though her body was a familiar place—as though she's someone I'd known all my life, someone I was relieved to see again. I looked down at my arms; thank God they were still at my side. What the hell was going on with me? *This is embarrassing—get the hell out! Go!*

By the time the lunch bell rang, I regretted leaving like that, bolting without saying a word. Was it *weird*? Probably. I found myself scanning the halls, the stairs, the quad for her tightly bound ponytail or her fitted black jacket. The whole thing played in my head in a repeating loop— those eyes, burned into my memory—a stranger so familiar, that intense but fragile bearing. I distracted my mind by getting as far away from the crowd as I could. I walked over to the isolated classroom buildings in the back of campus. I sat down on a curb under a tree and pulled out *The Stranger*. I was really feeling the main character, Meursault. I envied his cool detachment from the world, his easy indifference. I had to get lost in that guy's head instead of my own. So, I did. Page after page, I was reading faster, totally lost in the plot, but just as Meursault was about to run into Marie Cardona—*thud*. I was pulled out. I looked up to find someone by the fence, but it wasn't just someone: it was a black jacket and a tightly bound ponytail. It was her. My heart started beating faster. Did she see me? What was she doing? Why'd she throw her backpack over the fence? Yeah, she was ditching—probably didn't think anyone was watching.

She took a few steps back and ran at the fence. It was a long way up. Nervous, I stood. But she climbed quickly, nimble and surefooted as a cat. When she reached the top, she perched there for a moment, like she was soaking in the view or something. Was this girl crazy? What was she thinking, climbing a tall-ass fence like she was in *Crouching Tiger, Hidden Dragon*? Was she stuck? Should I say something? Something told me she'd be fine on her own.

A few moments went by like that. Then she swung her second leg over, slid halfway down, and jumped the rest of the way. What a strange and impulsive creature. She moved like a cobra: not at all and then all at once. I felt a sense of relief as she landed on her feet, and I continued watching while she reached down to grab her backpack and something small that fell out of her pocket. It hit me, then: she was about to leave.

Say something.

CHAPTER 5

MINA

He's just some guy, Mina. Stop it—wipe the drool.

Yep, I was still staring. But he had the most unexpected manner of carrying himself. The way he walked was confident, not arrogant or self-conscious. I pictured him wearing one of those posture-perfecting contraptions they'd been selling online, then giggled the image out of my head. I straightened my back as his eyes glided through the room. As a dancer, I appreciated grace. I wished I could be invisible even for just a minute, so I could get a closer look. I wondered what cologne he wore. *Get a closer look? Eww . . . stop it, Mina! Who are you right now? How does he smell? This isn't Alien vs. Predator.*

I remembered what happened the last time a guy caught my interest. I met him at a party last summer—Stuart, or was it Steven? Anyway, let's call him Stan. Stan and I ended up alone in someone's room after he asked if I wanted to go "someplace quiet." I thought he wanted to go on a walk or something. I didn't get out much, so it didn't register that what he meant was he wanted to take me to a random bedroom in a stranger's house and immediately start making out with me like the world was ending.

At first, I just let him do his thing, because he looked so excited that this was actually happening, and I felt bad for him. But pretty soon it all became tragically sloppy and wet, and I remember thinking, *Okay, great, now we're making out. Oh, God, he's trying so hard that it's actually hurting my lips! Isn't this the part when I'm supposed to feel turned on? I don't really feel anything. Oh, man, his breath isn't the freshest, which isn't helping. I really wish he'd chewed gum before sticking his tongue in my mouth. Ow! Yep, our teeth just clanked. How much longer do we do this? Oh shit, I forgot to put the laundry in the dryer!*

I worried something was wrong with me for having such mundane thoughts in a situation that was meant to be intimate. Nyah offered her wisdom: "Maybe you're a lesbian?" Then she offered to make out with me to test it.

"I don't think that's how it works, babe." I laughed it off. But later that night, I lay awake wondering, *Maybe I am a lesbian.*

Today was different. For the first time, I felt completely entranced by a guy. All the while, he didn't even know I existed. *How could he have? He just walked into a crowded classroom a few moments ago! You, however, have spent way too much time drooling over him,* like a dehydrated nomad at the sight of a coconut. *Look away! It's only a matter of time before he catches you staring at him and labels you a psycho!* I tightened my grip on my pen, took a breath, and gathered the resolve to look back down at my notes.

Suddenly, he spoke. "My schedule, sir." *Sir?* Either he was raised right, or he's fresh out of boot camp. His timbre was appealing—soft but deep. I smiled to myself, eyes glued to my notebook.

"Have a seat, Mr. Mondell, and collect this from me after class," said Mr. Gerald.

I stole another glance toward the boy at the mention of his name. I wondered what his first name was. Mr. Gerald continued his lecture, and I doodled *Mondell* in my notebook. Repeatedly forcing my gaze down made class feel drawn-out and uncomfortable. What was worse, my stomach started turning with a strange, hollow discomfort.

Great, I was having some kind of physical reaction. *Is this an anxiety attack? This is ridiculous!* I found myself begging for the bell to ring, but just as it finally did, my heart sunk, knowing we would no longer be in the same room. *What is happening?*

I didn't even know the guy. He could be vain, rude, and a complete disappointment, especially considering the luck I'd had. It could be Tyler Syndrome all over again. I got up and tried to grab my backpack off the floor, but one of the straps was wedged beneath the table leg. When I finally got it loose, I decidedly turned to leave through the back door but accidentally elbowed someone in the stomach.

"Crap. Sorry!" I exclaimed.

I looked up with an apologetic smile, but as soon as my eyes found his, I realized I should look away before he guessed what I was thinking.

He was a bit shaken at first but brushed it off quickly. He chuckled and rubbed his stomach. "That's okay." There wasn't a trace of vanity or rudeness in his glowing, bottomless eyes. I was caught under his gaze as the light essence of bergamot and white ginger drifted to me. I couldn't turn away from him to save my life.

I was staring long enough to notice he wasn't in any hurry to find a distraction either but suddenly, the light in his eyes was gone—his gaze went cold and neutral—and he took a few steps back into a desk. I waited for him to say something—anything—but he turned and walked off silently. I must have creeped him out. *He saw it in your eyes, the desperation.* I walked out after him, but he was gone.

Ever wonder what you look like from the outside? I did—especially right then. All I could picture was me staring at him with Gollum eyes, like he was my precious. Shit, I hoped not. More than anything, I always endeavored to be composed, never revealing what thoughts lay beneath the surface—"endeavored" being the key word. My temper was an unpredictable wild animal. The goal was to keep a low profile in school, purposefully keeping my opinions to myself and wearing neutral or bland colors, based on the belief that those who flew under the radar survived longer. The old Soviet mentality to avoid government suspicion had stayed with many people. *"Ni brasaisya v glaza ni zdelayut zla,"* as Mama always said. It meant "Don't cry for attention, and you won't end up in tears." The only place I let myself be vulnerable was at the dance studio. Actually, besides home, that was the only place I had friends, spoke to people, or even smiled, really. I guessed that might not be normal behavior, but it worked for me. Until now.

At lunch, I went back to first period to pick up my phone only to see a text from Nyah:

Manny's here! He's taking Shondra's contemporary class @ 2. U better get ur ass down here right now! I'm losing my shit!

Shondra's contemp class? Why aren't you in school?

I ditched. He posted on Shondra's page this morning, and I couldn't resist but I don't wanna go alone. You have to come!

Typical Nyah, very dramatic. Manny, one of the most talented dancers from our studio, made it onto a big Hollywood dance show last year, but still came back for classes on occasion. We'd both known him since we were kids, but he was a few years older and had never given us the time of day—not that it stopped Nyah from swooning over him since before she could sit in center splits.

"I'm older, I'm wiser, and I've got boobs now! Sure, the memo may have gotten lost in the mail, but it's time he sees I'm not a child anymore," she explained to me one night.

Don't get me wrong—I wanted Nyah to find her happiness more than anything, but I was almost certain Manny didn't swing her way. I just didn't know how to break it to her that his *port de bras* was far too fabulous. Now, I realized, I was in no position to judge. I just practically drooled on a complete stranger who ran away from me like I was a rabid dog.

I desperately wanted to leave. I needed to go to the dance studio and work these emotions out of my system. It was still lunch and I had two classes left, but I could just say I felt sick and forgot to sign out through the nurse or something—Mama would understand. I headed to the front entrance, where I found guards on high alert for school shooters—ever since the shooting in the Valley, administrators everywhere had upped security. I turned back and made for the edge of campus, where a chain-link fence was designed to keep us in. I walked along the fence until I reached a quiet place at the back of the school hidden behind single-story classrooms. I made a mental note: *This is a good lunch spot.* The fence must have been a good fifteen feet tall—a lot higher than I'd climbed before, but it was now or never. I threw my backpack over, so I officially couldn't pussy out. I made impulsive moves like this sometimes and sometimes ended up regretting it. Hopefully this wasn't one of those times.

After taking a few steps back, I ran at the fence and willed myself to keep scrambling until I got to the top. I swung a leg hastily over the edge and stayed there a moment as the fence swayed. Once it felt stable, I worked out a strategy to get down and found a grip with both feet, but they slipped. My fingers were strained, and the soles of my shoes kept slipping against the metal. My knees were getting banged up and my arms shook as I struggled to hang on. I inched my way down slowly at first; then, halfway down, my fingers began to give out. I made it as far down as I could, then jumped the rest of the way and landed on my feet. Pain shot up through my legs as though a thousand needles hit my soles simultaneously. I was okay—nothing was broken—but I wouldn't be trying fence-hopping again anytime soon.

"For a moment there, I thought I might have to rescue you," declared a smooth, deep voice.

I stopped in my tracks and turned around guardedly, looking for the source. A figure leaned against one of the single-story classroom buildings on the other side of the fence. Mondell! I couldn't believe I was so preoccupied with the idea of getting over the fence that I didn't notice someone there. He was leaning against the wall, book in hand, with a cryptic smile on his lips. I held his gaze, wondering what book he was reading, until I finally worked out that I must've looked like a brainless turd just standing there in silence.

Girl, you better snap out of it! I shook my head, chuckled at my own uncharacteristic gawkishness, turned to walk away, and promised myself not to look back.

Too much nervous energy coursed through me to wait for the bus, so I ran to the dance studio instead. I'd always loved the feeling of being on the move and how it kept my mind from overtaking me with its monkey chatter. It was only a couple of miles anyway, and there was half an hour left before class. I got there with a few minutes to spare, entered through the back, and ran up the stairs to the fourth floor.

As I walked through the door, Nyah ran toward me. "You made it!" She pounced and wrapped her arms around me, clinging like a little monkey— she was a featherweight. I gave her cheek a big smooch and smacked her butt, signaling her to get off.

"Let me go sign in."

"I already signed in for you—just in case." She beamed.

"Thanks a lot. They charge for that, you know! What if I hadn't made it?" I snapped.

"Then I'd have crossed it out. You're kind of crabby today—PMSing already? Come on, she's starting warm-up. He's in there right now. Feel my heart."

She grabbed my hand and slammed it flat against the center of her chest. I chuckled while shaking my head. "Okay, crazy. Let me get changed— go in without me."

"No way! I can't go in by myself. I need you. I'll wait."

I held her face between my palms and looked her square in her big brown eyes. "Yes, you can. You walk right in there, and don't stop until you are in the center spot of the front row. Find his eyes in the mirror and hold them as you slowly slide on down into your gorgeous center splits like it's what you were born to do, because it is. I'll be right there."

Nyah looked up at me with her lost puppy eyes, shaking her head. I turned her around, gently nudged her forward, and then ran to the bathroom to change. I changed out of my school clothes, threw on my shorts and sports bra, splashed water on my face, and hurried into Studio G.

As I stretched, I looked over at Nyah, still sitting in her center split, happy as a clam. She was chatting away with Manny beside her, listening and laughing. She was such a superstar—I didn't know why she ever doubted herself. There was nothing more beautiful than the smile on Nyah's face in a moment of happiness.

Shondra walked into class with a sassy strut. "Beautiful people, let's get some legs in the air on this divine Monday afternoon." She turned to look at Nyah and me. "Hello! What are my baby chicks doing out of school this early?"

"It's a half day today," I answered quickly before Nyah had time to freak out.

"Exactly," Nyah added. I looked at her. *Don't push it.*

"Sure, it is." Shondra remarked, sarcastically. Thankfully, she let it go and connected her iPod to the sound system.

Normally, we warmed up first and then completed a series of short choreography from one side of the room to the other repeatedly. The goal was to disobey gravity. I wiped the sweat from my brow as soon as I got to the other end of the room, feeling lighter after letting go of some of the frustration from the day.

Sometimes there were strength training and endurance exercises in between to build discipline and technique. Our reward was the dance routine we learned at the end of class, where our blood, sweat, and tears were given a chance to pay off. We carved the choreography into our minds, and after we'd learned it and danced it over and over, the new goal became to look within ourselves to bring an element of depth to the movement.

So we dug and dug further, until we found the trouble—the pain—which we all carried deep within, and we brought it up to the surface to work through it and share with one another. In turn, we gained temporary access to the boundless, intangible energy that encompasses our universe—the energy that created and sustained our souls—and together we were supposed to heal. The problem was that for me, it'd always just been a temporary fix. The emptiness inside had deeply planted roots. Like a tenacious virus, it always came back.

I loved the physical strength that dance training gave me, but I could have done without the bruising—I could already feel one forming on my right kneecap as I hobbled home. Mama and I lived in a townhouse with tiny rooms but great closet space. She bought it a few years after the last housing market crash. We had refurbished it to look both modern and comfy. My favorite part, hands down, was the balcony, which was where we spent most of our time.

I heated up some food, tidied up, and chipped away at homework. By the time Mama pulled into the driveway, I was catching up on a few of our favorite shows. Without a doubt, she'd had another miserable day working under her delusional hag of a boss as an in-house accountant for a luxury real estate brokerage. I ran downstairs to greet her, and she plodded in, drained, but still managed a genuine smile. We melted into each other with a long hug, an asylum from the plague that is loneliness. Mama was a superhero, and the only person who could always see through the one-way mirror shield I carried. I took her bag off her hands and carried it upstairs for her.

"How's your back today?"

"Even don't asking me about it." She shook her head and clutched her lower back as she climbed the stairs. Hunching over a computer desk all day could really mess you up. I felt for her—when she hurt, I hurt. "Honestly Mina, I feel as I was most happy working as cleaning lady when we was fresh from the boat."

"Then quit."

"Be serious, Minachka." We cuddled up on the lounger in the corner of our tropically decorated balcony, equipped with a portable fire pit, a TV, and fairy lights overhead. We watched our favorite teen drama while eating dinner, followed by ice cream and green tea. These times were the good times. Guests always thought it was funny how we spent more time outside our place than in it; in the summer, when it was warm at night, we even used to sleep out there—until the plague of mosquitos descended upon the city. As we rested on the balcony and chatted over a *shisha*, I thought about how I could spend the rest of my life not moving from that very spot.

"I'm bad mother. I even shouldn't be smoking *shisha* next you, let alone with you. Your *babushka* would kill me if she was here. We talk this morning, you know? She read an article from the health magazine how smoking *shisha* like smoking one hundred cigarettes. Maybe she's psychic."

There we went again. "Mama, she isn't psychic; she probably saw the *shisha* in the background last time you were Skyping with her. Plus, you're the best mom. Do I really need to tell you that? Think about it like this: it's better that I smoke this nice, clean, beautiful, premium glass *shisha* with you than a crappy, cheap, rusty one that's been passed around to over fifty people at some party in the Valley. Besides, it isn't even slowing down my dancing . . . yet." I paused. "Let's just both agree to cut back."

"All right, okay. Defense, please rest your case. How was school? Did you teach your teachers anything?"

"Very funny. You know I like to keep a low profile. By the way, I need a doctor's note for tomorrow, please. I left early today to catch Shondra's afternoon class."

"Mina, today was your first day! Do not built habit from this, please."

"It's 'don't make a habit of it.' You know I won't make it a habit, but it's very cute when you try saying those typical cheeseball mom lines from TV shows to me." I grinned at her, and she rolled her eyes and tried to smack me with a pillow. I saw it coming and ducked. Upset that she missed, she fumed at me, or tried to at least. "Mama, you look kind of constipated," I laughed, which made her crack up. We both had the least attractive laughs on planet Earth—a low guttural sound. Let's call it hearty.

Something bright in the sky caught my attention. I'd been subconsciously suppressing thoughts of Mystery Mondell Man all that time, but there he was again—smack-dab in the middle of the moon. Apparently, that was where I tucked away my thoughts of him. Mama cupped my face in her hands contemplatively and furrowed her brow. I was amazed once again at how quickly she noticed something was wrong. I couldn't be that obvious, could I? It wasn't like I'd never stared at the moon before.

"Mama, I met this guy in my history class today. I think he's new like me, but I started freaking out around him for no reason. I accidentally elbowed him in the stomach when I was leaving class, though, and he literally—and I mean literally—ran from me." I waited for her reaction. It didn't come. Oh, great, she was speechless. "That's why I went to dance. I was so embarrassed." I mumbled.

"Mina!" she exclaimed. "Wow, Mina—I haven't seen you had a crush like this since elementary school. Remember Christopher, very cute dorky boy with crazy hair—math genius? You told me his hair was magic, like a dragon fire, and if you didn't marry him you can die?"

I suppressed the urge to grimace. "Of course, I could never forget my first love."

"Oh, Mina, you was a special kid. You cry and cry about him. But you getting over him quickly."

"Quickly? It broke my heart into a thousand pieces when his family moved away to . . . I don't even know where. That was seven years ago, and I've only just recently found and glued back that last piece of my heart—now it's a mosaic," I joked.

"Just in time for your new love. I hope he's fan of Gaudi." She had jokes too.

"I can't explain it. Everyone is so—unimpressive at school—they're all the same. And then out of nowhere, he just walks in. He misplaced everything in my head; I was concussed throughout the rest of the day. Why do I always do that, Mama? Either I don't care at all, or I fall hard and fast. Couldn't I get some kind of warning from the universe? Then I could prepare and become obsessed gradually and, hopefully, reciprocally."

"That's not how it work, Mina—you know this. The funny thing is that poor boy doesn't know what's coming." I looked at her; I didn't get it. Mama laughed. "Oh, come on, you know what I'm talkin' about. Let's just say you tending to get what you want in life, always. There is conditions, of course: first condition, you must want it very much, and, second, you must pursuing it actually. If it taking too long, though, for you to achieve then you beginning to lose interest. Ironically, it works out in time, but by this time, you don't want it anymore. So, it's too bad really for this poor boy."

I scrutinized her face to see if she was just making fun. "I don't do that! That's awful. What are you talking about?"

"I'm talking regarding Joel and this one foreign kid from your middle school—oh, and light-haired boy, Samming? Sammy? I'm talking regarding piano lessons. I'm talking in regarding to this video game you was obsessed with. You try and try and finally you getting somewhere, and as soon as you getting close, you lose interest and find something else."

Where was this coming from? "You are so wrong! It's different with him. Look, he didn't even notice me, anyway—well, not until I jabbed him with my elbow."

"How do you know he didn't notice you if you trying to ignoring him the whole time?"

I felt acutely uncomfortable, as if someone was shining a powerful spotlight on me. Just as she gathered the breath to say something else, I cut in with a change of subject. "How was work?"

"Work was eh—nothing new. This bitch breathing fire all day. I thought, maybe I implode—or worse, maybe I explode!"

I grinned at her. "That's not worse; it's better. Explode! Give her a piece of your mind. She has it coming."

"That's reminds me, can you please call to the insurance company tomorrow regarding our downstairs burst pipe? Here, I'll text you phone number and claim number. Maybe you can call when lunchtime at school tomorrow?"

"Weren't they supposed to call you today?"

"They call, but you know how they are with me—once time they hearing my accent and see my last name, they don't take claim seriously. I can see by this questions and attitude he think I burst pipe on purpose to collect insurance. So you should try to call; they listen to you for sure."

I smacked one hand onto my thigh in exasperation.

"I don't get it, Mama. The entire room got flooded, and the adjuster they sent already inspected it and signed off on everything. What possible fraud could there be? The pipes have to be replaced, and even if we find cheap labor, there still won't be much money left over. Plus, our rates will go up after this claim, so why would we lie?"

"Ah no! You just reminding me. Insurance will like crazy for sure going up when we renew the next year."

"Yeah, well, that's insurance. You pay for a service you hope you won't have to use, and if you dare use it, you will be punished. Don't worry—soon I'll graduate law school, pass the bar, intern for no money at a promising firm, work my way up the ladder, and after winning a few high-profile cases for them by doing all their bitch work, I'll become a junior partner. Then, all I'll have to do is bring in a few multimillion-dollar clients and leverage them to become a name partner—easy. We'll use the money to develop properties while we vacation in Mykonos, Ibiza, and Sochi for the rest of our lives—or whatever's left of our lives. I'll be forty-five by then."

Mama kissed my head, and we took a deep breath and sang, "Ah! Sochi," in unison as the fire danced before us.

"Your plan becoming more specific. I like it. Wait, but this means I will be in seventies! So—so old already at this time." She groaned. "Maybe new plan?"

...

The next morning, I was drowning in a pile of rejected clothing options. It was bizarre. I normally wore whatever to school without any thought, but I'd already changed five times—I even tried on a *skirt*. I must have really been losing it. Noticing the time, I thought, *Screw this*, and threw on the usual: a dark denim jacket over a plain gray T-shirt and black boots over dark jeans.

Mama looked like she was in a rush too as she handed me break-fast money and laid a big smooch on my cheek on her way out. For a moment, it felt like everything would be okay. We smiled at each other, then parted ways as she drove off and I walked in the opposite direc-tion toward the bus stop. I heard brakes screech loudly and whipped my head around. Was she okay? My heart pounded against my chest.

Her reverse lights came on and she backed up toward me, rolled her window down, and leaned out.

"Loving you, my baby."

"Are you crazy? You scared me—"

"You saying crazy to your mother? Mina, where's the your respect?" she asked sternly.

"You're right, I'm sorry, loving you."

"Mm-hm." She closed the window, shook her head, and raced off. That was my mom in a nutshell.

No one bothered me on the bus that morning. It was like I didn't even exist—just the way I liked it. I made it through first period, but it felt like the longest, most tedious class I had ever endured. *Because you wanting to see him again,* Mama's voice whispered in the back of my head. The bell finally rang and I all but sprinted to second period, qualifying for the Guinness Book of World Records fastest classroom commute time.

As a result, I was way too early. I put my earbuds in and sat against the wall outside of class. I watched as students passed me, guessing what might be going on in their lives that they didn't want others to see. I caught sight of Mondell as he glided down the hall and I quickly looked the other way. I jumped to my feet after he went inside, tightened my ponytail, counted to ten, and walked in after him. He'd already grabbed a seat near the window in the second row, the seat I'd been in yesterday; I moved toward an empty seat on the opposite side of the room and then stopped. *Screw it.*

I planted myself in the desk directly in front of his. I despised sitting in the front row, but I had made my bed and now I had to lie in it. I could almost smell him from there. I needed to stop thinking about how he smelled—I was sounding more and more like a fetishist, even to myself. *Quick, think about something else. I wonder if he snowboards or skis? What difference does it make? You're so random.*

Mr. Gerald started roll call, and I doodled. I'd just put the finishing touches on my snowboarding alien's antennae when something landed on my notebook, making me jump. A note. I was pretty sure it came from the seat behind mine. I froze, then took a slow, deep breath. Was it for me, or did I have to pass it? I looked around trying not to be obvious, but no one was looking back my way. I picked up the neatly folded paper slowly and opened it.

Inside, I found two words in a slanted scribble: *Hello Mina*. I swiveled around in my chair. Mondell was looking straight at me. When he saw me looking he nodded slightly.

My heart thudded so loudly that everyone probably heard it. How did he know my name? *Roll call, duh. Shit! I could've heard his first name if I'd just paid attention.* Should I respond? My hands, however, had a mind of their own; they scribbled something, folded the paper back up quickly, and tossed it over my shoulder.

"Ow."

Oh, God, tell me I didn't hit his eye. It sounded like he was opening it and scribbling something back, and my stomach turned. *Chill out and breathe. Who cares?*—Me.

I finally managed to slow my accelerated heartbeat by focusing only on the sound of my breath when suddenly, the note landed back on my desk and wild horses began racing around in my chest again. I opened it quickly and reread my own response: *Hello?* Was that all I said? Brilliant. I really couldn't have come up with anything more interesting?

I read his response: *I'm Oliver. What are you thinking about?* What the flying duck? What was I thinking about? That was a little intense. I was thinking about how he made me feel like I was somewhere between being on ecstasy and free-falling from a plane, and I'd never even *done* either of those things. Who did he think he was, asking me something so intrusive?

So far, he was entirely unpredictable. I liked it.

How I'd rather be snowboarding. Yeah, that was good—sounded cazh. Also, it normalized his super intrusive and uncomfortable question. I turned and placed the note on his desk that time; I should have made eye contact, but I chickened out and turned back before looking up.

When he passed it back to me, his fingers met my shoulder for a moment. I'd never been so fully aware of my shoulder before. I opened it and read: *Really? I thought you would rather be climbing fences.* I couldn't help smiling from ear to ear.

"Ahem."

I looked up to find Mr. Gerald standing a few feet away. I felt the eyes of the entire class on me. "I came over to find out what on earth could have made you so ecstatic, young lady. Unfortunately, it looks like our discussion of the eighteenth-century Act of Union wasn't it."

How long had he been standing there?

Crap! Mr. Gerald snatched the note out of my hands and read aloud, "Hello, Mina. Hello. I'm Oliver. What are you thinking about? How I'd rather be snowboarding. Really? I thought you would rather be climbing fences." He stopped. Some kids chuckled. "The beginning of a thrilling conversation, I'm sure. Let this be a lesson for the rest of you—I read notes out loud. This is not an appropriate time or place to socialize. Do it on your own time, not mine. Don't be so easily distracted, Mr. Mondell. And you, Miss . . ."—he flipped the textbook on my desk to the first page and read—"Arkova . . . not an ideal first impression." I just looked down— stay quiet—but he continued addressing only me. "Now, perhaps you already know about the Acts of Union and how they relate in this case, so I'm only boring you. I'm sure you can enlighten us about it."

Don't say a word, Mina, not a word.

"Silence. Yes, I really didn't think so. It would do you well, young lady, to focus on things of importance, things that can last. After all, unlike knowledge, looks are fleeting."

What the hell? What a chauvinistic prick! I didn't see him lecturing Oliver on how to prioritize his looks. The classroom filled with chuckles. How was it fair that he was giving me a harder time than Oliver when I didn't even start that stupid note? Humiliated, I blurted out my only defense. "It's, of course . . . debated, but having failed to— *ahem*—having failed to, um . . . to conquer Scotland, England used the economy and Parliament to ultimately add Scotland to its collection of territories. To England's surprise, Scotland ended up taking them at their own game, becoming more successful in industry, commerce, *and* education than anyone ever imagined. The Scottish Enlightenment was something England didn't see coming, and it elevated Scotland . . ."— silence—"You want me to go on? How it relates? How the British Parliament grew stronger, more powerful, and refocused on America? They wanted a stronger military presence in the colonies after war with the French, so they passed the Stamp Act to fund it, but we were all, 'Nay! We have our own colonial assemblies! We don't need a double tax.' Which is how we came up with 'No taxation without representation!' Speaking of which, I can teach the rest of class today but maybe you should do it yourself. So you can . . . you know, actually earn that undersized portion of our parents' tax dollars that funds your unique tie collection."

No . . . crap! The room exploded in *ooh*s and *damn*s.

Someone made a comment. "Actually, this makes sense now. She explained it well. Ha ha!"

Revenge! whispered a voice in my mind.

"That's enough. Quiet! I said." He walked back to his desk and slammed the textbook dramatically. "Enough! And that bit at the end, Miss . . . Arkova, was extra. While you're in detention, think about finding the line between feelings that are appropriate to convey in my classroom and those best kept in your head along with your regrettably twisted outlook on history." He turned and went to his desk to write my detention slip. Everyone was still looking at me, hungry for more. I hated being stared at—it was disconcerting. This teacher was so going to make it his mission to mess up my GPA. That made two out of six.

Could I be mistaken, or was that the sound of Oliver's chuckle? I looked over my shoulder at him with anger on my brow, but as soon as our eyes locked, my ire evaporated. He wasn't laughing at me. *Wow,* he mouthed. He was impressed. His gaze seemed to penetrate my carefully composed shell, reaching deeper and deeper through the layers.

"Come collect your detention slip, Miss Arkova," Mr. Gerald taunted, pronouncing my last name with a ghastly accent. "I'm not surprised—Peter tried to Westernize his federation, but he was still just a war-hungry tyrant ruling over a horde of barbarians," he muttered almost too quietly, but I had exceptional hearing.

And to think . . . I was about to apologize. Somehow, I couldn't keep my mouth shut that day. "Inappropriate much? What does that have to do with my detention slip? And for your information—"

"Young lady—"

"For your information, in Peter's time—as in over three hundred years ago—it was the Tsardom of Russia, not the Russian Federation. Last time I checked, it's the twenty-first century, and, despite my last name, I am an American." This guy had to be the primary specimen in experiments in Artificial Stupidity. I grabbed the slip out of his hand, walked to my seat, took my things, and walked out just as the school bell delivered liberty.

Detention was held in the gym at lunch, although I didn't really see how it was supposed to be punishment. I climbed to the top of the bleachers and queued up an audiobook file on my phone—I finally managed to track one down toward the end of summer after months of shit luck. For lunch, I opted for a cheeseburger and a Coke. I smiled, remembering the

Belgian chocolate bar in my bag. I'd thrown it in there the night before in preparation for a bad day—an emergency picker-upper.

Just as I was about to bite into my cheeseburger, I heard, "What are you smiling about? Detention is serious stuff." I looked up, mouth still half-open. It was Oliver. I closed my mouth so fast that I bit my tongue and yelped. I could taste blood.

"Are you okay?"

"Yah, aye yust bid my tongue," I laughed at myself. *It's okay, just accept that this is you.*

He laughed with me. "Sorry—and I'm sorry about getting you detention. I stayed and explained to him that it was my fault. Okay . . . my bet is he was rejected by a cute Eastern European girl who was way out of his scope either, like, last week or, like, way back in the day or something, so now he's just biased against like all things Soviet."

"I'm not Soviet," I snapped.

"I know that."

Soften up. "Wow, so he gave you detention for . . . umm, taking blame? You should've just let it go. But still, thank you." He smiled like the resurrection of chivalry was a major side project for him.

"No, he didn't give me detention. I figured I'd come and at least apologize. I thought I'd keep you company, but I'll let you enjoy your music."

"Oh, it isn't music," I said quickly before he left.

Oliver blinked. "Huh?"

"It isn't music playing in my headphones; it's a book."

"You're listening to a book? Why don't you just read it?"

I hesitated, but he didn't sound condescending, just curious. "I hate reading." That sounded stupid, so I added, "I mean, I don't hate it, but I guess I'm easily distracted. Love books, hate reading. Audiobooks keep me focused on the story . . . I guess I just prefer hearing it read to me like my mom would—it's not as enjoyable if I read it myself. Plus, I need both hands for this burger."

He laughed, "Now that sounds like the real reason. No, I get it. Everyone has their own way of doing things. What book are you listening to?"

"Right now, *The Buddha in the Attic*—it's stories of Japanese women who came to America in the early nineteen hundreds to marry men they'd never met. It was actually really difficult to track down the audio version of this one. I thought I'd end up having to read the thing myself," I explained.

"Sounds fascinating. I'll let you do your thing, then."

Well, that's twice now that I've scared the poor guy away. Don't leave, Oliver. I'll put my headphones away. He was already down the bleachers and out the door, though. I scowled. Screw the burger; I needed to proceed directly to dessert. Half the chocolate bar was stuffed in my mouth when it dawned on me: I was totally going to break out from crushing that hard.

After the final bell rang, I exited school through the main building, my iPod blaring the end of a Linkin Park oldie. Not in the mood to endure any potential conflict on the bus, I decided instead to walk home and calm my jitters. I crossed the street and turned a corner into a narrow alley.

Several yards away, a dark SUV with blacked-out windows crept down an alley perpendicular to the one I was on. A disquieting lump manifested deep in my gut, insisting something was wrong, but I was aware of my paranoid tendencies, so I continued ahead. The SUV screeched to a stop, blocking my path, and the lump in my gut mutated into a knot.

This time, I didn't hesitate; I immediately turned back to run when, with sickening force, I crashed into the chest of a huge man. I ricocheted, stumbling backward, and would've been on the ground had he not grabbed hold of me. A thank you would have been appropriate, but my gut still knew something wasn't sitting well. The dark-haired stranger towered over me with a menacing glare. A bowl haircut outlined his dark, deep-set eyes that sat under a bulging forehead. I jerked my arms away violently but failed to slip out of his iron grasp, unaware as I gasped for air that I was only further perpetuating my own hyperventilation.

I parted my trembling lips, paralyzed with fear, trying to scream for help but not managing even a whisper. Heat circulated from my stomach to my chest and back down again. Clutching my shoulders, he propped me against the alley wall with the full weight of his enormous mass. My breathing became rapid and wild.

My instincts finally kicked in. I made the only move I could: a sharp knee to the groin. But either the guy had balls of steel or he'd been castrated, because aside from a grunt, he barely flinched. Instead, he hit me in the stomach and I collapsed to the ground, stunned by pain. He lifted me back up against the wall and pressed the palm of his oversized hand firmly against my mouth to keep me from screaming as he pulled out a pocketknife and raised it to my throat. My knees turned to gelatin, numbness spread through my body, and a ringing throbbed between my ears.

I hate this damn song. I skip it every single time it comes on ... why can't I ever remember to delete it off my playlist? My earbuds were still in. The colossus seemed to notice this at the same time, and he yanked them roughly from my ears, instantly killing the whining voice playing in my head. He slid his other hand up to my throat, making breathing harder than it already was, and traced the curves of my face with his blade. *What did he want from me?* Every scenario to escape was reckless, and I was struggling to stay conscious.

He brought his mouth a few inches from my ear and slithered harshly, "*Tvoĭ* papa behind on payment. You tell him we are not some *Americanskiy* bank. Understand?"

My father?

He squeezed his left hand so hard that I started to choke. "Yes?"

I gasped for air but only found pain; sharp burns sent spasms across my chest as though my heart was being churned through a meat grinder. It took every ounce of strength and desperation left in me to nod through the intolerable agony. He relaxed his grip slightly and I inhaled greedily, but the oxygen burned my throat more than his chokehold did. I surrendered to a brutal coughing fit.

"*Horosho.* Here, a souvenir."

No, God, please! Not again . . . He covered my mouth again and pressed his blade into my skin, slicing my cheek. I let out a muffled cry as my tears flew into the open wound; it stung badly.

"No!" shouted a voice.

The colossus took his hands off me as we turned toward the source.

Oliver?

"Not your business," the figure growled, taking several steps forward, but Oliver didn't move. My eyes darted back and forth between them. Oliver barely blinked as he matched the giant's glare. Suddenly, I was faced with a different kind of fear.

"Kiril!" barked a husky voice through a rolled-down window of the dark SUV. So, the guy's name was Kiril. *"Hvatit."*

Enough, said the man in the car, but there was amusement in his tone. He was having a good time, watching. I tried to make out his face through the darkness, but the car was limo-tinted. Kiril chuckled and did as he was told. He sauntered back to the car and opened the door, but then stopped abruptly and turned to face us. He stretched his arm out, squinted one eye, aimed his blade at me, and bent his arm at the elbow, as though preparing to throw it.

This is it, I thought. Then I was knocked to the ground. The only other thing I could remember from that moment was pain, Kiril's sneer, and the sound of the SUV screeching away.

Balled up in the fetal position, I asked myself, *Where does it hurt?* Everywhere, but there was no sharp, stabbing pain in any one place.

Oliver rolled off of me and onto his back—panting and visibly shaken, as was I. I tilted my head up and opened my eyes, scanning his body for the knife, but there was nothing there—he was fine. He jumped to his feet like he just thought of something and ran after them but there was no use, they were probably blocks away by now. I looked at the ground around us, the corner, the wall—no blade anywhere. *It was a bluff—sick bastard.* The walls, sky, and ground all blended together into a single rotating sphere, and I lay back down, overwhelmed by shock.

Oliver walked back over and kneeled down next to me. "It's okay. You're gonna be okay." Whatever shock had been holding me together melted as tears streamed from my eyes to drip against the concrete. He carefully brushed the hair out of my face; the strands were wet with blood. I looked up at him and somehow found it in myself to be embarrassed. "What the hell was that? Do you know who those guys are?" he asked.

I finally produced the word "No."

He gave me a scrutinizing look, then nodded slightly.

"I'll go with you to the police station. You need to report this right away."

"No. I'm not reporting anything."

"Why?"

I let out a labored breath. "What would I tell them? 'These guys attacked me. I don't know who they are, but I don't think they're registered voters, and I don't have anything to go off besides the fact that one of them had an accent and spoke Russian. So . . . what do you say, Officer? You think the department can spare a patrol unit to follow me around for a while, just in case?' Come on, Oliver." I should've shut up. It was wrong of me to be anything but grateful to him.

Somehow, he forgave my outburst. "Why not? You think every person that walks into a police station has their attacker's Social Security number? That's not how a police report works. They can actually be really helpful in the right circumstances. Especially if you can describe your attacker with specifics . . . like that giant, ugly-ass mofo. Plus, we got his name, so either they're dumb as hell or cocky . . ."

"Look, I just don't think it's a smart move on my part—it could make things worse for me." I explained. What I didn't say was 'My father has obviously gotten involved with some very dangerous people.' Going to the police was only going to get someone killed.

After a moment, he let it go, and shrugged. "What can I do?"

"Nothing. I'm okay. You can go, don't worry."

He didn't look like he was going anywhere. I pushed myself up and he helped me stand. "I can't just walk away. You were just attacked."

I stared at him for a while, spaced out. "I'm gonna walk home. You can walk with me if you want."

"You're absolutely sure you don't want to report this? We could give them a description of the car, at least."

"A black SUV with California plates. That would narrow it down to a pool of about a million," I retorted, and put an end to the conversation.

After about five minutes of silently walking by my side, Oliver stopped in front of a gas station. "Hold on, just let me grab something in there." He ran in and I followed slowly. By the time I made it inside, he was already paying for some sort of mini first-aid kit. "Come on, let's go around back." I followed him back outside, around the building, and into one of the bathrooms. He was about to lock the door, but changed his mind and left it open—it smelled horrid. He turned the faucet on and gently moved me toward it. He looked at me with uncertainty at first, and then his hesitation disappeared. He brought his free hand to my chin and carefully angled my face as he dabbed at the cut with an antiseptic wipe. It stung intensely, and another wave of dizziness washed over me. I leaned forward onto the dirty sink to keep from falling.

"It still doesn't make any sense. If it was supposed to be a random attack, why didn't they even try to take anything? Why take the time to do the whole intimidate-with-knife routine?" he asked.

My gaze shifted from the wall I'd been staring at over to him. Only then did I realize how close together we were standing. It almost made me forget something terrible just happened. I stepped back, grabbed a Band-Aid from the kit, unwrapped it, and applied it to my cheek in the mirror—securing the gauze in place. I looked terrible, puffy eyes and disheveled hair. Nothing I could do about the eyes, but I redid my hair into a tight, high bun. When I turned back to him, he was still studying me, wanting an answer.

"They weren't there to steal. It was a warning . . . for my father. That Kiril guy said he owes them money, or took their money—I don't know. The only thing I'm sure of is that I don't know anything."

"A warning. For your father."

I simply nodded, not meeting his eye.

"Okay. Well, when you get home, you'll tell him what happened, and he'll know what he has to do," he reassured me, but he really wasn't sure.

"He doesn't live with us." I moved to exit the bathroom; he followed me out.

"When's the last time you saw or talked to him?" he asked carefully, our fingers sometimes brushing as we walked.

"Last year, on my birthday. It was a short conversation. He basically said, 'Happy Birthday, Mina. I love you. I miss you. Be a good girl.' That's it—nothing about where he is or what he's doing or anything. My mom doesn't talk about him anymore, and I don't ask." *What is it about Oliver that makes me want to spill everything?* Cracks were popping up across my normally impenetrable dam, and I was leaking information all over the place.

"How did those guys know about you, or where you go to school?"

"I don't know."

"I really think you need to get hold of him. This isn't okay, what he's put you in the middle of. He needs to settle his own shit—"

"No shit! Don't you think I know that?" I snapped, regretting it as soon as it left my mouth.

"I'm sorry. Look, I get it, okay? I know how you feel," he said quietly, so I could barely hear it.

Softer, Mina. "Don't be sorry. Who knows what would have happened if you hadn't walked into that alley when you did? Though sooner would have been better. What, did you have some other girl to save on the way to my alley?" He laughed and I added, "But don't worry about it. Really. I'll figure the rest out on my own."

"I don't think it's a good time to leave you alone. Let's get you to your house at least."

We walked through two more miles of silence, but surprisingly, it was the farthest thing from awkward. It was nice, actually, like I'd known him for a while. Well, enough that we didn't *need* to talk. When we got to my front door, we stopped and faced each other.

"I never thanked you, did I?"

"You implied it."

"But I never said the words. Thank you, Oliver. I'm not—I really don't know how it would've turned out if you hadn't stepped in."

"I have a feeling you can handle a lot more than you think. Either way, I'm glad my Sherlock senses were tingling when I saw that guy follow you into the alley. Something told me he wasn't boyfriend material."

"I'm glad your sense of humor is still intact," I teased.

"I'm glad you think I had one. Can I see your phone for a sec?"

"Yeah."

He took it and dialed a number, his pocket vibrated, and then he handed it back with a naughty smirk that would look stupid on anyone else. "Since I'm sure you were about to ask for my number anyway. Good night. Get inside."

When I got upstairs, I hurried to the balcony to watch him go, catching him just as he turned the corner at the end of my block. I wondered where he lived and where he was going next. After pulling out my phone, I sent a text to the number he dialed.

My mom'll be home soon, and she can drive you.

The house always felt empty when I was alone in it. I hated that feeling. I curled up under a blanket on the balcony, which usually made me feel better. My phone lay beside me, waiting for his response. Finally, it buzzed.

Thanks but my bike's back at school

I quickly typed back *She can put it in her trunk, it's no prob.* I barely had time to put my head back down when he replied immediately.

Not that kind of bike.

Of course.

. . .

"Baby." Mama's voice brought me back to reality. We'd come to a stop. I opened my eyes and felt her gentle touch on my re-sanitized and re-bandaged cheek—as if she would ever trust another person to do her job adequately. "Vso, we're here."

It was the first time Mama had said anything to me since we left home after packing us a bag in silent fury. She hadn't stopped checking the rear-view mirror the whole time she was driving, and her hands still shook as we pulled into the parking lot of some boutique hotel I didn't recognize. I wasn't ready for the explosion that came after I told her what happened to me. First she started yelling at me, demanding to know why I hadn't run or called for help. When I explained that there had been no safe way out and that I'd been entirely overpowered, she cradled me in her arms crying and apologizing, as though it was in some way her fault.

Rancho Mirage was where we always went whenever life became too much for either of us, and I guess this was no different. It was as though the desert had healing energy. I'd only just stepped out of the car and already the sweet, warm air told me everything would work itself out.

Mama met my gaze and offered a smile. She felt it too—the calm washing over us. She checked in and paid cash up front. They didn't want to do it at first—against hotel policy, they said—but Mama could talk a Mormon into a tequila shot. We settled into the room, stowed our legal documents and computer hard drives in the safe, hung a few things in the closet, and laid out toiletries in the bathroom. There wasn't much to unpack—we'd brought only the essentials.

I played music to fill the silence, but Mama said, "Turn this off, Mina. We need to hear everything what is happening outside that door at any time."

I did as I was told, and then asked, "Do you want me to email your work—let them know you can't come in?"

"No," she answered quickly, "I will handle this myself."

I lay on the bed and fiddled with my jacket zipper. My phone went off.

"Mina, I think I told you already! You must to turn this thing off—now!"

I picked it up to see a text from Oliver: *How did it go?*

I quickly typed back, *She flipped. We had to leave town . . . gtg.*

I also sent Nyah a quick message—I knew she'd freak if I went MIA for too long. *Mom took me on a surprise trip to the desert and just fyi reception sucks out here talk as soon as I can.* Then I shut it off.

"Mina!"

"It's powering off." I turned it toward her. "See?"

"Okay, good. Thank you. Jacuzzi?" she asked suddenly.

"Sure." I jumped up, grateful for a distraction. It felt like summer all over again when I slipped into my favorite bikini.

"Ah! Minachka . . . your knees."

I looked down at my knees, purple and blue. "No, it's okay, Mamachka—those are from dance, not today." *At least, I think they are.* I grabbed a pair of towels and gestured toward the door before she changed her mind and packed us up again to go someplace even farther from home. "Come on, Mama, let's go soak away our troubles."

No one was enjoying the hot tub at that hour—it might actually have been officially closed. I dipped a toe in, and the water was perfect. Mama tiptoed over the cold cement to start the bubbles, and I admired her figure. "Mama, you look like a model . . . you been hitting the gym low-key? Or is it just the stress?"

"Oh, come on, it's the dark. Tell me this in morning when my stretching marks says: *Hello!*"

"Sorry for the stretch marks."

"Never sorry for this. I am wearing it with pride. You must to understand I am—" She looked down at my hip abruptly; I looked down too. There was a patch of fresh cement rash. "You will telling to me this is from the dance too?" she asked. I walked deeper into the jacuzzi to hide it. Bad idea—man, it stung! She observed my movements in silence, detecting every ailment. She was too sharp to fool.

"*Ngh* . . . it's from the fall. When that degenerate aimed a knife at me and pretended to throw it, Oliver reacted by knocking me down to the ground to get me out of harm's way." I sat closer to her. "He surprised me. There's more to Oliver than I thought. Mama? Do you know what's going on with my father? Does he really owe those people money?" I searched her body language for answers, because she didn't respond and tried to hide her face. Her hands began to shake—soon her entire body trembled uncontrollably. *She doesn't know*, I realized. "No . . . please, Mamachka, don't cry. I'm sorry. Let's talk about it tomorrow."

"No—my baby, I am sorry. *Prosti menya*. If I took the care of you how I should have—if I picking you up from school by myself like does a decent parent do—this would never happen. I would being there, and this would not . . ." she mumbled through tears. I'd never seen her so help-less. Not sure what else to do—I held her.

"How could you have known, huh? Tell me. How are you supposed to work and take care of everything else at the same time? You can't do every-thing—it's not physically possible. You do too much already." I stroked her hair. "This is his mess—he needs to clean it up. This isn't on you."

"He won't picking up his damn phone! Maybe he change his number. I email him too, I mail him a letter—I even sending him a freaking SMS. I call Peter. He didn't heard from him in many months. Where is he? If he not fixing it—what can we do? And now they go after his child who is having noth-ing to do with it? How long we have to hide? I'm afraid to calling Babushka, Dedushka—bringing to them unnecessary danger." She wept, covering her face with her hands. I held her to my chest, trying to keep it together.

I'd never seen Mama that way, even when my father left. Although I knew that she was deeply depressed, shut down in so many ways, on the surface, she was the poster child of immense strength and stability. She normally had this insane command over her emotions—maybe it was to protect me. Seeing her so broken and afraid terrified me, and told me it was my turn to be the strong one.

We sat silently in the tub for a long time—maybe an hour. Mama got out first. She held out a towel to wrap me in, her way of letting me know that her inner storm had passed and that she was back and taking care of me now. When we got to the room, I watched TV while she showered. She came out of the bathroom wearing fresh clothes and headed to the door.

"I will be back soon, Minachka. I will going to the lobby; I want to sending some emails to your school and my work. I will use cover for IP address, okay? I know—I see what you already gathering breath to tell-ing me. Relax, okay? I say to them we feeling sick . . . blah blah blah. I can get Marina to write some doctor's notice later." She doubled back to kiss my forehead. "Try falling to sleep. Loving you."

"Loving you." As soon as the door shut, I grabbed my phone, stepped out onto the balcony, sprawled on the lounge chair, and took in the view. What a sight—the brilliant stars of the desert sky glistened against the black night. You could trace the velvet ridgeline of the mountains on the horizon.

I played with my phone, flipping it over and over in my fingers. *Screw it.* Finally, I just turned it on and stared at the screen as it awoke from slumber. I waited, unblinking, as the bars appeared at the top. No messages. I sulked and put my phone down on the glass table beside me.

Bzzzz. Bzzzz. Bzzzz. Bzzzz. Bzzzz. Bzzzz. Bzzzz. Bzzzz. The delayed texts finally rolled in. Yes! I grabbed my phone so fast that I almost dropped it. They were all from him, and my smile stretched from ear to ear as I opened them.

> *damn! for good or just for a bit?*
> *out of town where?*
> *you think you ever comin back?*
> *?*
> *no actually don't write back*
> *especially DON'T talk about your location, just to be safe*
> *That's crazy that you had to leave like that, I guess it's serious, huh? But I hope this isn't goodbye.*

Then, according to the time stamp, a few minutes later he added:

> *if it is goodbye . . . take care of yourself, glad we got to meet*

Chills ran up my arms. I hoped this wasn't goodbye, either. Life was so ironic and complicated. This had been one of the worst things that'd happened to our family since Mama—*don't go there.* Anyway, it was just strange because, yeah—it was awful and frightening, but it had also brought Oliver and me together. We had something now that we had both lived through together. Now I just had to figure out a way to reach my father and hope he could figure something out.

I must have been going mental, because the thought of not seeing Oliver again scared me more than the thought of running into those men again. I really had to sort out my priorities. In hindsight, I had a hard time believing they were serious about killing me; they would've been way more low-key and taken me somewhere private. They wouldn't have left a witness, and they wouldn't have used someone as memorable and identifiable as Kiril to threaten me in the first place. Their objective was clear: to scare me into getting my father to get them what they wanted—to send him a message. Once they had it, they'd leave me alone, I thought. I walked back inside and jumped into bed. Sleep came quickly, but it didn't come alone.

I was somewhere strange—a place I was sure I'd never been but that felt oddly familiar. I climbed a seemingly endless wall of boulders piled on top of each other. Finally, I reached the wall of a dam, so there must've been water on the other side. The scorching sun heated the boulders so much that my hands burned as I gripped them, but I kept climbing. One misstep and I would fall to certain death.

What was I doing there? My arms were very weak, so I knew I'd never agree to anything like that voluntarily. Was I running from something? I looked down to find nothing but the steepest slope I'd ever seen. My limbs went numb from fear only for a split second, but it was enough time to make me lose my orientation. Before I could react, my left foot slipped, throwing me off balance entirely. My fingers clutched the rocks; I gave up and practically let go of my steady grip—something I would never do. *Maybe it won't be so bad? Maybe I won't feel any pain?*

Instead of the sensation of free-falling, a firm grip clasped onto my forearm, suddenly inspiring me to fight for my life. As I scrambled to hold on, I looked up to find Oliver struggling to pull me. Suddenly, as though the earth had shifted on its axis, the diagonal drop was now a vertical one.

"I've got you!"

He seemed certain, and it comforted me, but I began slipping out of his grasp and was hanging on by only a few fingers. His fingers quaked as he fought to hold on. Inexplicably, his expression changed—the emotion drained from his face until all that was left was utter apathy.

"It's too hard," he said, and he let go.

The sound of my own gasping breath and the jolt of my body jerked me awake. My heart rate slowed as soon as my eyes flew open. It was the middle of the night, and I was still in the hotel room in Rancho Mirage. Oliver's final words echoed through the darkness. Mama mumbled something in her sleep, untwined her legs from mine, and rolled over to the other side of the bed.

What a bizarre dream. I'd never dreamt about anything so vividly, as though it were really happening. My dreams were usually symbolic, fuzzy, and incoherent; also, I normally forgot the specifics as soon as I opened my eyes. This felt like real danger, like I was really going to die, and even though I was awake, I still remembered every detail. Uneasy, I cuddled up to Mama and tried to put it out of my mind.

The next time I opened my eyes, the sun greeted me, shining in through the translucent white curtains. I looked over to Mama's side of the bed: it was empty. I stretched my arms overhead, put some space between each vertebra, and wiggled my toes awake. I reached for my phone out of habit but then remembered there was no point.

By the time I finished my morning routine and stepped out of the bathroom, Mama was back with coffee and in a suspiciously good mood. "*Dobroe utro*, baby. I save us the great spots at the pool. Yoga class starting in thirty minutes, but first, let's adding some love to our love handles. *Da?*" She handed me a chocolate croissant.

"This is heaven. I should get attacked in alleys more often," I blurted before thinking. I instantly regretted it when I saw pain flit across her face.

"Don't say such stupid things like that, Mina."

"It was just a joke," I mumbled.

"It's not funny joke."

"I can't help that it's not funny, Mama; humor is hereditary." She laughed—a good sign. We finished breakfast on the balcony when I finally mustered the courage to ask "Mama . . . did you hear back from him?"

Her smile wavered, then disappeared altogether. After several moments of silence went by, she exhaled and simply said, "Yes, I did. He sent email. He writing he will calling me back later today."

"What? That's great, I think it's a good sign. What time?"

"We will see . . ."

"What do you mean? Oh, by the way, can I turn my phone back on?"

"Mina! How many times should I repeat this? It is not safe."

"Mama, you emailed and called him, and they're probably tracking his phone and his computer. Even if you're very careful, I think they will find us if they need to. What's the point?"

"The point is to be smart and safe, okay? Just in case, okay? Can you not live for one single second without this thing?" I bit my tongue. It wasn't that big of a deal, not if it meant bringing Mama a little peace.

"You're right. I'm sorry, just forget I said anything." I really didn't want to upset her over something stupid when she was finally feeling better. "Come on." I pulled her up. "Let's go perfect our crow poses. I feel it. Today's the day we finally keep our asses in the air for more than three seconds."

After yoga, Mama and I laid by the pool, biceps burning from the instructor's fascination with *chaturanga*. When she wasn't looking, I reached for her margarita, but it was so far away and my body was so exhausted that I lost balance and almost fell out of my lounger.

"Mina, tell me you not trying to drinking my margarita."

It was honestly creepy sometimes, the things Mama knew.

"I'm not trying to drinking your margarita."

"Don't making fun of my English. Go do some handstands in the pool."

"Mama, I'm not ten anymore."

"Yes, unfortunately." She laughed.

"Come on, let me have a sip," I whined.

"Okay. If you can holding your breath longer than me in the water, you can finishing the whole margarita. Okay?"

"That's bullshit."

"Why bullshit? I give you chance. You young, good shape—it should be so easy for you."

"Maybe if you didn't have the lungs of a superhuman." Mama had held her breath for over two minutes before—I timed her myself. I was good, but not *that* good. I remembered practicing in school to beat her record. I used the clock on the wall to keep track of time as I held my breath during class, but some assholes started making constipation jokes, so that was the end of that. Tyler Syndrome strikes again.

"How about a game of backgammon?" I was already reaching into our beach bag for the miniature backgammon set.

"Okay. See, I don't chicken out, even against your super-brain."

"That's because as soon as your luck kicks in, my brain is just super useless."

"That's not a luck, baby, that's a skill." She rolled the dice and then said to someone behind me, "Oh, excuse to me? I don't know if you saw this, but your baby just putting something in her mouth, some dirty plastic stuff."

I turned to see who Mama was talking to: a woman working on her tan on a nearby lounge chair. Her baby girl, who couldn't have been older than a year, or maybe a year and a half, was crawling on the concrete beneath her lounge chair, chewing on a filthy plastic wrapper of some sort and staring at the pool in awe.

"Hmm?" the woman asked irritably.

Mama repeated herself. "Is this your baby? She chewing on some trash plastic from on the ground, so I telling to you because I was thinking you want to know this."

"I can't understand a damn thing you're saying! Where are you from?" She laughed.

"She said your baby's chewing on some plastic trash so you should probably get it out of her mouth," I overenunciated before Mama repeated herself a third time.

"*Ni nervnichiy, davai egrai.*" Mama told me to let it go and roll the die.

The woman scowled. "Are you kidding me right now? I don't need to be told what to do with my goddamn kid, got that? She's just fine, a little bit of germs never killed no one. Where are you people from? Hmm? What language are you talking in? This is America. Speak English! Okay? Don't come into my country and tell me how the hell to behave and then yap with each other in some gibberish. Just go back to wherever you came from!"

Believe it or not, this wasn't a first—my mama being told to go back to her country. It was a favorite go-to for the small-minded.

"First, don't raising your voice," Mama told her. "Second, this not only your country—you are the immigrant, too, just as we are. You should learning the history before you just screaming at people. And I'm feel sorry for this baby who will growing up with a influence by somebody who thinking about this world like you."

"Mama, *astav.*" Now I was telling *her* to let it go.

"Bitch, you need to shut the hell up!" the woman snapped, jumping up out of her lounge chair.

Is this lady crazy?

Mama shook her head. "No—just sit down. I'm sorry I ever was trying to help you."

"Whatever, nosey immigrant bitch. Can't even relax in peace anymore in this goddamn country! Come here, Elsbeth—get that crap out your mouth!" She jerked the plastic wrapper away violently and threw it in the pool. The baby cried.

Mama and I played backgammon in silence.

"What time did my father say he'd call?" I asked in a low voice.

There was that look. She was deliberating what to say again.

"What's wrong?"

"Okay, baby, I'm sorry. I don't know why I lie before. I just don't want it you to thinking that, just because . . . Look, I already talk to your father."

"What? When?"

"Last night, when I went down to lobby. He did send me his new number. We talk."

"So? What did he say?" I leaned forward in anticipation.

"He say do not worry and that he would handling everything today. I ask him how much he owe. He wouldn't answer and just say the interest was hard to pay, so he falling behind on these payments to this financial branch with a ties to Russian mafia. Over there, everything tied together to mafia. He kept repeat saying he is really feeling sorry and that he would taking care of everything."

We looked at each other, quiet for a few moments. I didn't really know what to say.

"He say he loving you and want to call to you and talk to you soon."

"Bullshit. My phone number's no secret. He could've called anytime. You don't really buy that, do you? Whatever. I'm not talking to him. I don't care what you say—"

"Stop," she snapped. Then, hearing her own harsh tone, she softened her voice. "Minachka, the *last* thing I will do is forcing you to talking to him, especially now. Okay?"

"Well, great. I'm glad he's taking care of his own problems for once; it means we can go home. Let's stay today. We can head back tomorrow— less traffic, but I still won't miss any school."

"We will not going back. After what they did? Are you out in your mind?"

"Why not? Are you seriously considering running away somewhere? Where? There's no point. He said he's taking care of it today. Anyway, do you really think it was hard for them to find me in L.A.? They'll look me up at any school, anywhere we go, and there is no way I'm going to stop going to school. I'm not just going to give up my life."

"Please calming down. I'm not say that. I just need time to think, this is all. Don't pretending this isn't about Oliver. We're not put our life in danger for some boy you meet yesterday."

I sighed and shook my head.

"I'm not pretending anything. You can't deny that I gave up the past three years of my *youth* for school." She started laughing, which made my blood boil. "Second, he isn't 'some boy'. He put his life at risk for someone he didn't even know. You should be grateful to him." I grabbed her drink and chugged it down.

"Really, Mina?"

Before she could scold me again, I dove into the pool and sank to the bottom. I stayed under for as long as I could to cool down. When I couldn't stand it any longer, I came up gasping for air and my eyes found Mama. "How long was I under? Did I beat your record?"

Her shades were on. She shook her head. With a heavy exhalation, she leaned back in her lounge chair feigning indifference. She knew I couldn't stand it when she ignored me. I climbed out of the pool, walked over to her chair, and got into plank position directly over her, dripping with cold pool water. She continued the charade. I collapsed onto her and forced her to hug me.

"Don't be mad."

"You have cut on your face. You thinking it's smart to jumping in this dirty pool and getting some infections?"

"Yeah, I know . . . I realized that after I got in the water but it was too late. Order a shot of vodka to sanitize it?" She rolled her eyes behind the shades. "Mama . . . loving you." No response from her. "You loving me? You should, while you can. If I die tomorrow, you'll be sorry you ignored me and wasted the precious time we had."

"I said to you a couple of times already not to saying stupid things like this, Mina," she scolded, but hugged me back.

Sweet victory. I lay in her arms like I used to when I was little; she stroked my wet hair and ordered a shot of vodka from the cocktail waitress. We looked out across the picturesque desert scenery emerging from beyond the gates of our hotel—like something from an old postcard Frank Sinatra sent to Marilyn Monroe. Out of the corner of my eye, I noticed a middle-aged couple across the pool gawking at Mama and me with curiosity and disapproval. I think they thought we were a couple, and as their facial expressions grew bolder, they really started to get under my skin. Like, who cared? Why couldn't people just mind their own business? Okay, so she wasn't really my sugar mama, but even if she were . . . what gave people the notion that they could judge others for who they loved?

Mama interrupted my staring contest with the couple across the pool. "Okay, how does this plan sounding to you: if your father convincing me that he can handling his business with this men, and he has the real plan for debt repayment, like new loan from someone . . . then maybe it will be safe for us to going back to Los—"

"Deal, yes . . . makes total sense to me." I interrupted before she could finish.

"Not so easy, Mina. Nikolai has big debt to the bank here in America, he paying only interest rate so each month thousands of dollars he just throwing away and it is not even bringing principal loan down, simply he is like running in the sinking sand. He struggling for very long time, and our home was in the jeopardy of bank seizure a few times—"

"Why didn't you ever tell me? I could have gotten a job. I could've helped out."

"No way for you to help this type of loan, babychka. Just listen . . . suddenly, one day last year he starting to wiring me some new amount, a big amount and telling me this pay for the interest on the second mortgage and the remaining amount can help to pay down principle loan, finally. I was happy, but honestly, I feel still very nervous. I knew this was seeming too easy, but much more easy for me to closing my eyes to this than asking some questions and starting some fight with him. I told to myself maybe he must be having made the successful new business. I keep taking this money he sending me each months and paying the second mortgage down, no questions because I was just too tired for this questions."

"It's not your fault."

"Mina, he was, he is my—we will always being partners in this world . . . no matter what. He is my family, and we are team. Does not matter what he did or what he does, you understand this . . . yes?"

"I don't know, Mama. All I feel when I think about him is anger. He left, period. What kind of team is that?"

"Only team we have. This is what I was trying to telling you before. If he shows to me it is safe for us to going back home, then we will, but things are going to be changed, Mina. Do you understand? I will taking you myself to wherever you need to go. I will driving you—"

"It's drive you, not driving you."

"Huh? Oh, okay. I will drive you. What I saying before? I lose my thought . . ." She shook her head in frustration. This was why I didn't normally correct her English. Why did I do that just then of all times? "Yes, I remembering now. When you coming home after your school, you staying home. You need to going somewhere else? Okay. But you must tell to me each step you make—no more doing whatever you want and skipping school this day and that day for the dance class, okay?" She held my gaze without humor in her expression. She meant it.

I nodded, kissed her cheek, and went back to the backgammon set.

"Let's negotiate the terms of my loss of freedom over a game." She frowned, unamused. "Kidding—I'm kidding! You're the boss."

"You are such the little monkey. You driving me bananas one of this day."

I smiled big, revealing all my teeth and channeling my inner chimpanzee. We ate lunch at a chic little café in a nearby resort; we fed the ducks, made bad jokes, and laughed too loudly. Then we hit the town center, eating ice cream as we meandered through pop-up carts of handmade jewelry and past tiny boutiques displaying the latest in desert fashion in their windows. We kept our conversation light, talking about old times, like when I was little and my sandal strap ripped in this exact same plaza. Mama was going through a DIY phase, so she tied a rubber band around my foot to hold the shoe together. We laughed now at how I had to limp clumsily the whole way back to the hotel when she could have just bought a cheap pair of flipflops. Aside from being yelled at by that shit-show of a human earlier, this was turning out to be a perfect day in paradise.

"Look there . . . beautiful." Mama gestured behind me as we walked back to our hotel. I turned around to find the sun setting beyond the hills. The sky was stained in a gorgeous spectrum of pinks and blues.

One earth axis rotation later and we were on the road home, listening to Keane's *Under the Iron Sea* and watching the same sun paint a new canvas. My father must have come up with the money and thoroughly assured Mama of our safety, because by the time I woke up the following morning, all our belongings were packed. "I call to him last night for information. An old military friend of Nikolai's has a brother in fur business; your father saying he is a good man. Nikolai flew to him, they meet, sign some document and this man has wire him the sum necessary— that's it, very few words. You can imagine asking your father some more information is pulling the teeth of a shark. I think maybe he must doing this man some favor now, but he did not saying to me any more detail. He say to me 'It's safe, go home.' He is very sorry, loving you very much, and everything okay. I don't know what I should do, Mina. Are we really supposed to going home? I pack for us, but I am . . . what if—?"

"Mama?" I hugged her. "I believe him. He wouldn't . . . I think we can go home."

Leaving limbo was bittersweet. A no-worries nirvana certainly had its appeal, but if you stayed more than a day or two it became monotonous. I wanted to get back to my life—things were finally getting interesting. Oliver, of course, didn't know I was coming back. I daydreamed about our first reunion, running through a series of ridiculous and improbable scenarios like getting assigned to each other as partners in AP Gov class and having to go watch a political film in a dark theater for extra credit. Finally, we reached downtown L.A. The city lights welcomed us home. Suddenly, it felt like anything was possible again.

CHAPTER 6

OLIVER

And that's when it finally hit me—damn, she's really gone. I never even got to know her, so this feels crazy, but I'm all messed up over it. Like, I'm sad about what could've happened between me and her . . . which is crazy—right? I mean, I don't really know her. Right?" No one answered. That wasn't really how it worked anyway. Questions were automatically rendered rhetorical. No one was allowed to offer any advice to each other; all we could do was listen and share about "our road to recovery." The guy in the beanie hadn't stopped staring at me throughout the entire support group meeting. He sat across from me in our little circle of victims. He cleared his throat and nodded his head in support of whatever the hell I had just said—which I honestly didn't even remember anymore. Where was I again? Oh, yeah. "So this girl, Mina, she leaves town. And now I'm in a support group . . . ! Like, what the hell? And I was doing well too, like . . . no offense, but it kills me—being here, listening to you all."

The woman sitting beside me, wrapped in a colorful wool blanket, started wiggling her foot nervously. She avoided eye contact with me and instead stared off into a distant corner. I scratched my neck, regretting the direction I was heading with the share. "I know, I'm not supposed to say things like that and I'm sorry, okay? But it's just true.

I thought this would help me to not feel so alone. But I look around this circle and I'm—all it's doing is messing me up more. I mean . . . have you seen the websites for these support groups? Have you guys seen how many of these meetings there are all over this city? Think about it—how many people are there like us? How many never even make it to a meeting and jump off a bridge or slit their throats? How many of these degenerate pervs are still out there doing this to people, hurting kids, messing them up for good?"

The support group facilitator stopped me before I led the entire group off the rails. "Oliver—"

"Yeah, I know. Sorry, I'll stop. That's not where I was trying to go with my share, anyway. I just—I don't know what the hell happened. You guys might be thinking something in that alley must've triggered me. But I'm telling you, no! I was completely cool afterwards. I was just grateful she was okay and glad I was there to help. But then she wrote to me saying she had to leave town, and that's what really messed me up, I think. Like, I know it's a good thing. Right? I mean that she's safe, not that she's gone. I was starting to worry about myself with her anyway. She's nice, you know? And, holy shit, is she smart—"

Now the co-facilitator chimed in. "Oliver, I don't mean to interrupt, but I just want to make sure we stick to the script and that everyone gets a chance to speak about the specific step they're on in their personal recovery timeline. Since you're new here, just remember that the objective is to share your own experience and feelings related to your recovery, and with no comments on another person's share within the five minutes allotted for each person—"

"I've finished this entire friggin' program! These damn steps you keep throwing in my face—? I did them . . . every single damned one. Don't you get that? I've completed every last step, and now some girl leaves town, and just like that I'm back to barely surviving? Last night, I wanted to drive my bike off a friggin' cliff. I'm just trying to figure out how I got here, okay? I've regressed—just let me get this out. So . . . now, I'll get to it. Last night, the nightmare came back. It's been a year since I dreamed the worst one, it's the one with the . . . the nail-covered bat. I was back in the basement, naked, on my knees, chained to the floor, bent over the wood plank . . . he was—he was there, behind me like always. I couldn't turn to see his face, but I knew it was him, and he was punishing me for the trial. Everything was burning, scorching. I couldn't get out of it, the nightmare. I was screaming at myself to wake up . . . but the nightmare, it shifted when I heard this sound, like a whisper. It was Mina . . . she was just standing there, watching me through the window. I yelled at her to open the door, to help me, but she just watched. He was loving it, the sick bastard . . . he was laughing as he punished me. I looked back over to her, but now the window was empty . . . she was gone. I finally woke up. And I couldn't just fall back asleep. So, I got on my motorcycle and rode the streets, and then the canyons, to clear my head. It helped for a bit until I realized how easy it would be to just let go and ride off the side . . . I caught myself in time. I started thinking, what if I miss out? What if the rest of it—my . . . life—would have been completely epic? And I gave up because . . . why? A bad dream? That would be pathetic. And just like that, that tiny bit of hope got me to the bottom of the canyons and back home in one piece. That's the power of thought, of outlook, of mental health. Understanding that, even when pain is everywhere, all around you—"

"Remember, try to use 'I' and 'me' instead of 'you'," the co-facilitator chimed back in.

I inhaled, exhaled, and tried again. "Even when the pain is everywhere, all around me—in my blood and the air I breathe—even then, the pain is temporary and one day . . . it'll pass. When it finally does, I'll be glad I held on. And I'll be glad I knew what I had to do. It saved me once, so, yeah"—I exhale, feeling lighter like at the end of a climax— "this helps, this feels good once you finally, I mean . . . once—I—finally get it out of my mouth. Ugh! The whole 'I' thing is hard to get used to, though."

"Yes, it's easier to separate yourself from your feelings by assigning them to the Platonic you and far more difficult to claim them as your own. Thank you for sharing, Oliver. . ." One of the facilitators, a bearded man in his late forties who was trying his best to look like a psychologist or a professor, opened the circle up for comments while almost everyone averted eye contact. "Any comments on Oliver's share? Anyone? Okay . . . Edward."

"I feel your anger, and I have it too. I just think it's dope how you were able to get yourself down that cliff and to a meeting." Of course, it was the gawker in the beanie.

"All right, Edward, thank you. You want to share today?"

Edward nodded. "It's been a hard few months for me. Mother finally died." *The Stranger* kinda started like that, if I was remembering it right. "She was my trigger. I almost used again. This last week I've been thinking of using almost every moment of every day. It's really hard 'cause I've got all these beautiful memories of her, and then there are the ones I . . . uh, the bad ones. But . . . anyway, she was . . . she was my abuser."

I went into group autopilot, maintaining eye contact and nodding every once in a while but totally tuning out the Edward's story. I'm not going to stand in the way of anyone's catharsis, but there came a point where I just wasn't willing to keep listening to other abuse stories.

After the meeting, I helped put the chairs away and held the door open for the people who walked out behind me. That guy, Edward, patted my back and put his arm around my neck like we were old buddies. "My man! That was so crazy, right? So, you wanna get coffee?"

"Um . . . yeah, okay." Why not? What else did I have going on? *Nothing.*

Edward paid for coffee—he insisted. While we waited for our order, he went to the bathroom. When he came back, he walked up really close to me and said "Forget her. You have to." I shook my head at him. I didn't follow. "That girl you were talking about."

"What are you talking about?"

"You need to forget about her," Edward stated, staring at me with his hands on his hips like some kind of Little League coach. "You know exactly what I'm talking about. She's dangerous for you. Because of her, you're back in group. You care too much about her and you don't even know her. You need something simple for now. Someone that doesn't affect you so much." He said it like it was the most obvious thing in the world.

"How? How do I forget someone like that?"

"Easy. Screw someone else. If it doesn't work, do it again and again and again until it does."

He sounded so wound up. "Edward, are you okay?" He didn't look good. Then I noticed a faint residue of powder around his nostril. "Tell me you didn't snort some shit while you were in the bathroom. Come on man!"

"Yeah, it was so powerful, man. It felt real in there. I just gotta do the same thing next week and I'm solid, man. We should hang after, for sure."

"What do you mean . . . do the same thing next week? Another meeting? Edward, you used . . . do you have a sponsor you can call? You're not still on probation, are you?"

"Naw, man. I'm not an addict. I'm an actor. I'm doing this film about addiction and shit. We go into principal photography next week. *Whoo!* It's so hard doing what I do. I just want it to be authentic, you know what I mean? Like, genuine, so I can represent you guys well. I don't want people like you to watch it and say, like, 'That guy's bullshit.' That would really suck ass. Like, I hate when I'm watching a show and shit doesn't feel real."

My blood boiled and my hands trembled in anger. I felt a strong impulse to strangle him on the spot. Our coffees were ready. I ground my teeth, considering my next move. Moving slowly, I picked up my cup. He walked to a table and sat down. I followed him, still trying to process what he had just revealed to me.

"So your share . . . about your mom—"

"Yeah, that's my character, pretty much. Super screwed up, right? I think it's partially based on a true story. I want the pain to be as real as possible when I do this scene, you know what I mean? I just want it to be real. So, listen, I want to ask you some questions about your dream, man—"

"You want the pain to be real?

"Yeah, exactly man."

"You sure?"

"Of course!" He nodded his head eagerly.

"Well, I think I might be able to help you with that." I walked around the table, removed the lid from my coffee, and poured it over his crotch. "Channel this"—he screamed—"those meetings are sacred, for victims only. Don't ever come back."

CHAPTER 7

MINA

The alarm blared through my dream world. It was the last thing I wanted to hear at 6:35 a.m. after a weekend of lazy afternoons under the Rancho Mirage sun. As I clambered out of bed, my feet connected with a glacial bedroom floor. Picking an outfit that inspired thoughts like, *Wow, I've missed you, but also, is it hot in here?* was turning out to be a real challenge. So far, the closest I'd come was a short sundress that said, *Cute, but trying way too hard and also completely inappropriate for a prison-like mid-city high school.*

I threw my fifth attempt at an outfit across the room in frustration and eventually settled for some jean shorts to showcase my fresh tan, a white tee, sneakers, and a letterman jacket that I hadn't worn in a long time. When I looked in the mirror, the girl I saw looked like she'd somehow become trapped in the nineties. I needed to go shopping one of those days.

I checked the time and swore under my breath. Only a few minutes left until I had to leave the house. I ran into the bathroom, brushed my teeth, tied my hair, and grabbed my bag.

Mama was sitting at the kitchen table, drinking coffee. "Morning!" I ran past her, kissing her cheek on the way to the bread box. I opened it up, grabbed a bagel from the bag, and almost bit into it when I spotted a stain of green mold. "Ew!" I exclaimed, dropping it into the trash.

"We will go to the grocery shopping after your school today, okay, baby?"

"Yeah, sounds good." I headed for the door.

"Do you want to taking some tea or anything?" Mama asked.

"No, I'm super late. Gotta go, loving you!"

"Go? Where you have to go?" she asked, following me to the door. "We talking about this already. I must to driving you."

I stopped in my tracks and turned slowly. Wow. She was serious about making changes. "Aren't you going to be late for work?"

Mama shook her head. "Half hour is no a big deal. I will talk to them and explaining. End of day, it's just a job—this is your safety and my peace in mind."

"Peace *of* mind." I walked back into the kitchen and poured myself some coffee. If I wasn't taking the bus, I had plenty of time. Mama always taught me to be independent: basic self-defense, public transport, common sense, and street smarts. I'd gotten myself to dance class and the school bus stop on my own since I started middle school. Truthfully, though, getting a ride from her was so much better than having independence.

She pulled up right in front of the main entrance. We both looked around nervously, just in case. No dark SUVs, no scary men. Mama reached over and stroked my cheek. She smiled weakly, as though as to encourage me not to worry. All the while, her own sleep-deprived eyes were filled with fear. She sensed me reading her and looked away, hiding behind her uncharacteristically unkempt hairdo, her loose curls reaching out in every direction. I loved it when her hair was natural and wild like that, but she hardly ever let it happen. I brushed a few strands away and leaned over to kiss her goodbye.

"Everything's fine, Mamachka—try not to worry."

"Promise you be careful, my baby—stay sharp, keeping eyes open. You must to call me as often you can. Texting me too when you can do it, letting me know you okay. I'll picking you up after your school."

"How are you going to do that? What about work?"

"I will handling that. Look, Minachka, you should not having to be worried about my work. This my responsibility. If they not understanding, that's okay. I will finding another office who understanding. Of this one I am tired anyway. Okay, go ahead, baby."

"Okay. Good luck. Loving you." I hugged her, gave her another kiss, and headed toward the main entrance, but I turned back before walking in. She was still there; I waved. This would take some getting used to.

First period dragged on. Ms. Pallera spent an hour describing the difference between discrete and continuous data. It wasn't really her fault—people keep asking the same dumb questions over and over. I worked on the homework assignment for the night to help make the time pass until I could see Oliver. When I had gotten home the night before, I'd thought about texting him to let him know I was back, but surprising him was more my style.

As we headed over to my second period class, I stopped by the bathroom for a quick touch-up. I added a dash of powder to my shiny forehead, a bit of lip balm to my chapped lips, and a splash of perfume that I took from Mama's bathroom. I popped a mint into my mouth, just in case, and hurried out. My heart was beating like I was competing at the World's Fastest Drummer competition. I checked the time: two minutes until the bell rang. I walked into the room with purpose, eyes searching for his, then suddenly found them. *There.*

I saw disbelief wash over him. As I walked over, I panicked, because I realized I hadn't prepared anything to say. *Just breathe,* I told myself as I stood before him. He didn't say anything either—just looked at me.

"Hi," I finally produced.

"Hi," he said dryly, suddenly avoiding my eyes. He looked down at his phone instead, ignoring me completely. I couldn't believe it. I gave him a moment to address me, but he just continued to stare at his phone.

"Is everything—"

"Sorry, I'm just busy right now," he interrupted me before I could ask what was wrong.

I knew our first interaction wouldn't be anything like my daydreams—not even close—but this was something I hadn't even considered. Standing there, being ignored like that, was just humiliating. I turned on my heel and walked away, taking a seat as far away from him as possible.

Maybe he told his parents what had happened and they convinced him how dangerous it was to associate with me.

"Miss Arkova, are you with us?" snapped Mr. Gerald. "Pass the assignment back."

Shit! Stacked on my desk was a pile of assorted papers. I checked to see if Oliver was looking—he wasn't. Mr. Gerald had handed out some sort of rubric and a permission slip. Our first paper was due next Friday, and there was a field trip the next week. I tried my best to pay attention for the rest of class, but it was hard to concentrate on anything besides feeling disappointed at the way seeing Oliver had gone.

After mulling it over a hundred times, I decided I should just talk to him when class was over. As soon as the bell rang, I stood up and walked over to his desk, but he was already on his feet and headed toward the door. "Hey, can we talk a second?" I called after him.

He slowed down but barely looked at me. "I can't right now," he said, without stopping. Then he walked out the door.

WTF? Crushed, I made a silent vow that I would not approach him first again and walked through the rest of the school day in an autopilot deadpan sad-song-in-headphones haze. The next time I even cracked a semi-smile was when I saw Mama's car.

After we dropped off groceries—mostly chocolate—at home, I convinced Mama to watch my class at the dance studio. Nothing got my ass into gear like having an audience. The last time she watched an entire class start to finish, I was twelve. Over the past few days, it was like I'd become her baby again, and I loved it. I worked twice as hard, pushed further, and leapt higher than I ever had before.

When the class was over, Mama grabbed me in one of her fierce hugs, old-country style. In the car on the way home, she went on and on about me.

"Mina, your dancing is another level now. Wow, I am very impressive by you! This was beautiful to watching! God gracing you with such a gift"—Mama was spiritual, but she didn't usually talk about God—"you must never letting it go. I am so proud that you still very dedicating and balance your time with a school and this and homework and everything," she told me. "So, Minachka, I am thinking how about we driving over in Burbank and register to purchasing some guns?"

"First you mention God, and now guns? What's next, Mama, you becoming Republican?" She shot me the same look she would give the TV when the newscaster reported something inconsequential.

"Just Beretta—something that just reliable and simple. Why not? We should make protection for ourself. To do nothing is very stupid."

"But guns are dangerous! Especially if we don't know what we're doing. I mean, you don't even know how to hold one, right? So, what's the point?"

"Excuse to me, Mina, I can holding a gun very well and much more. I never having the reason to share this information with you, but this doesn't mean I am some *oftza*," she said, spitting the Russian word that meant a domesticated sheep.

"You can hold a gun and *much more*? What does that even mean? You can't just say that to me out of nowhere. You can't keep things like that from me my entire life and then one day just mention them casually! I don't know anything about you, do I?" Mama rolled her eyes at me like I was being extra, which riled me up more. "Here I am, sharing everything with you—"

"Stop to being such a melodrama, Mina. I am telling this to you now. Not big deal. In old country, your *dedushka* teaching me how to hold, shoot, assembling, disassembling, clean, loading, and unloading firearms starting from somewhere like nine or ten year old. Plus, not just regular gun like we have now, but old-school handgun, different style, rifle, the shotgun. Crossbow and ax is put under the bed and table in each room all around house—it was norm of times. I never wanting that for you, though—never thinking you would needing this here. That reason why we coming to this country in a first place: for a freedom and opportunity, but also for a protection from this horrible people who can walk in your house any time they wanting to and taking everything whatever they want. The men who are like a gangsters. There was so many of these groups, too many, and my homeland becoming broken because everything they touching turning into *gavno*."

I stayed silent, eager to hear more. Mama almost never talked about the old country, and I certainly had never heard her call it "my homeland." I forgot she spent most of her life in another country, and that there was a time when her tiny hometown in southern Russia was all she knew. She and my father had left everything and everyone they loved behind to search for a better life, on practically another planet—and started over from scratch. I couldn't imagine ever possessing the courage it took to become an immigrant.

"How everything went with the Oliver?" She changed the subject as we pulled into the garage.

I turned away, fixing my gaze out the window at the garage wall. "Fine," I answered flatly. I heard her shift her position and lean forward, and knew without looking that she had fixed me with one of her intense stares.

"What's happened? Look on me." I turned and met her eye, and she wrinkled her forehead.

"He's avoiding me for whatever reason. I don't know," I explained.

"I sensing something is a different in your energy this moment you walking outside of school and sit in the car. You having posture, very defeating, very slouchy. I was thinking maybe after you going to dance class maybe you feeling different—and it is—but now I see slouchy coming back. Looking at your shoulders like they trying to touching each other under your chin. The boobs are giving a high-five to your thighs. Babychka, *nyet*, you do not let a man affecting you like this—chin up, shoulders back, smile."

My posture? Well, actually, she might have been right about that. My spine cracked as I straightened it. "I'm fine, Mama, I promise. I don't even care. It isn't him; I'm just tired. I'm gonna go start on homework." I headed inside and went straight to my room.

I tried everything as a distraction: music, drawing, cyber-billiards. But Oliver was like a black hole—harder to resist the closer you got. In fact, attraction had much in common with the phenomenon of black holes, in my experience. Time slowed down and space became infinitely distorted.

I finished my homework for stats, gov, and lit, but it was more busywork than homework. This school assigned twice as much as my old school, but the problems were so straightforward that I finished them all in under an hour. It sounded great, but it really just meant we were on our own in terms of doing well on the AP exams.

I lay on my back, stared at the ceiling, and tried to forget his name, his face, his existence. I wasn't just bummed and confused about Oliver, but everything else on top of it. I was angry at my father who borrowed money from loan sharks who stalk people's kids. I was irritated with my new school and how much everything sucked there, especially the teachers. I breathed deeply, noticing the air filling my lungs, and tried to fill them all the way. I held the air and let it rest inside me like they told you to do in yoga class. Then I slowly released it, wondering where it would go. *How far will my exhaled air travel? Will it ever reach Ireland? Australia?*

Probably not. Will it reach Oliver? What if he inhales the air I just exhaled? I pictured my air entering his perfect mouth. *What is* wrong *with me?*

It was stupid that I was even pining over him after he basically blew me off. I should have made posters and put them up all over the neighborhood: "Lost: Pride. BIG REWARD. Last seen on September 7th. Warning: may inspire strong feelings of self-worth."

I spent the next week of my life quiet on the outside and frustrated within, finding it difficult to match Oliver's indifference. I kept my word to myself and didn't approach Oliver again. I waited for him to come to me, but it never happened. He just went about his days pretending like we were complete strangers. The hardest part was putting on a smile for Mama the whole time, knowing how unforgiving she could be toward people who hurt me. If I showed her my true pain, let her know how Oliver ghosted me, I was afraid she'd hate him. Which was funny, because why should I have cared if she did? I supposed it meant that a part of me was still hoping for things to resolve between us. *This will get easier.* It had to. How much longer could I possibly feel that way, noticing everything he did—every noise, cough, and gesture? Most of the time he stared out the blurry window in class. I wished I could hear his thoughts, and I craved to be under his gaze again, but he gave me nothing.

The only thing that kept me going was dance, where I didn't have to hide and could let it all go. I released my frustration. The freedom was so intoxicating that I didn't bother to look out for the other dancers at all, and I barely felt it when I kicked Nyah during the pirouette arabesque. I didn't even slow down.

Nyah yanked my arm to stop me from finishing the routine. "What the hell, Mina! You just clocked me!" I stared at her in confusion. "Is anyone home in there?" She knocked on my skull, and I slapped her hand away. She glared at me incredulously.

"I'm sorry," I mumbled as it became clear: *I'm really losing it.* I ran out of the room, grabbing my bag from the cubby, and rushed through the exit door. Out of breath outside, I slumped against the brick wall of the building and let it all go. The pain, tension, and frustration poured from my eyes. I heard the door burst open but didn't look up.

"Mina, what's happening?"

I really didn't want anyone seeing me like that, but I supposed if it had to be someone, I was glad it was Nyah. I looked up at her; she was a blur through my damp eyes. Her hair was gathered in a ponytail, and a curly strand hung down by her heart-shaped face as drops of sweat collected on her worried brow.

"Get inside," I whispered hoarsely. "It's windy; you'll catch a cold."

She shook her head and slumped down by me. "The longer you take to start talking, the longer I'm out here, and the more likely I'll catch that cold. 'Kay?"

"You're impossible."

"I know—I learned from a pro," she said and shivered a bit. I took my oversized hoodie off and draped it over both our shoulders.

"Look, Nyah, I'm sorry I got you in there. I just lost control and didn't even see you. I . . . I've just been so out of it—"

"Stop apologizing. You think I don't know you're going through something? Of course I've noticed—I'm not an idiot. I've just been waiting, hoping you'd come to me yourself. Obviously, that's not gonna happen. So just tell me, because you know I'll get it out of you somehow."

"It's stupid. It's so pathetic that even in my head it sounds weak, but saying it out loud to someone? No."

"Well, I'm not just *someone*, am I?"

Wow, a guilt trip? It was low, but effective. "Fine! This guy at my new school just crashed into my life, and he's screwing with my head. From the moment I first saw him, I couldn't stop thinking about him, and then he helped me out of a tough situation—"

"What tough situation?"

"Nothing, just something stupid at school. You wanna hear this or not?" Nyah folded her arms around her knees and hugged them to her chest. Listening mode.

"Okay. So, after he helped me, we shared a connection that's hard to put into words. I could swear it was both of us, not just me, you know? I'm not demented. He really seemed . . . I don't know, interested? And then I come back after the weekend away, and nothing. He doesn't even want to look at me. He keeps saying he's busy or that he can't talk right now."

She took a few moments to process what I just told her, and then, out of nowhere, she started cracking up.

"What? You're such an ass! This is not funny!" I yelled.

"Yes, it is! Are you kidding me? I thought someone *died*. Jesus. This is all over some guy not giving you enough attention? You would so laugh at me if the tables were turned."

"It's not just this I'm having problems with; it's other stuff too! I'm not explaining it right—"

"In fact, you did laugh at me when I was in this exact situation, but then you gave me the best advice anyone has ever given me, and you know what? Manny and I went out last night."

"What? Where? Why didn't you tell me?"

"Good morning! I called you like a thousand times and nothing—not even a text back."

"Shit, sorry, Ny. I was about to call back, but then—"

She reached out and brushed a lock of hair from my forehead, then pulled out her lip gloss and handed it to me. I applied a coat.

"Please, it's fine," Nyah said, giving my freshly glossed lips an appraising look. "My point is, you're the one with the best advice when it comes to guys. You said he told you he's busy? Well, did you ever consider that maybe he is, and it's nothing more than that?"

"It's more than that; there's this look in his eyes like he couldn't care less. Detachment. But it makes zero sense based on his last text to me."

"Okay, then; take your own advice. Stop zoning out and zone in. Do you have any classes together?"

"Yeah—gov."

"Good. It's time to take your power back. You should walk right up to him in class tomorrow, look him in the eye, and reel him in the way I know only you can. And just as it dawns on him that you're what's been missing his whole life, put the wall up, take a seat and go about your day. All it takes is one powerful moment and the ball's back in your court."

"I tried doing something like that . . . sort of."

"Try harder."

"Oh, lord, what have I done to you? Is that seriously what I sound like when I give advice?"

"Yes. It's brilliant."

"It is completely nutty! Wait, so what happened with Manny? How did it go?"

"Really well; he's such a sweetheart. He's got too much on his plate right now—he opened up to me about his hectic schedule."

"Did anything happen? Did you kiss?" I asked cautiously, unable to control my disbelief.

"No." She hid her face behind her knees. "You'll never believe this, but Manny's gay."

"No! Really?" I feigned surprise as best as I could. "Oh, Ny! I'm so sorry. Are you okay? Is he okay?"

"I know, right? I was really embarrassed at first, and mostly surprised, but thank God I managed to play it off! Yeah, so, as soon as he told me, I just shifted gears and played it cool. Okay, I mean . . . I, you know, I did say something slightly awkward at first. I was like, 'Oh wow! You're gay? That's . . . that's really awesome! My cousin's gay!' and he said, 'Cool. I'm seeing someone, though.' It was painfully awkward. Like, I sounded like some idiot trying to hook up the two only gay people I knew. But then he just took the reins of the conversation. He told me about how hard it's been for him and his boyfriend. Apparently, the producers of that awful dance show he was on, all they cared about were ratings. He told me about how they forced him into a fake relationship with his dance partner for ratings. He had to hide who he really was from his fans or they threatened to eliminate him from the show."

"It sounds like a total nightmare." I rubbed her back as she started shivering again.

"Anyway, now it makes sense, you know, why he was never interested in anyone at the studio. We don't have any cute guys there at all. Oh my God, and listen to this: He told me he just had to get drinks with this fierce diva from class who took front and center like it was her destiny. I totally love him. We pretty much became best friends overnight, so at least there's that."

I raised my eyebrows and gave her shoulder an affectionate shove.

"Best friends? I'm off my game for two seconds, and you replaced me already? That's cold." We chuckled, but I couldn't help feeling sensitive to her joke. I didn't think I could handle Nyah ghosting me too, and getting a new best friend on top of everything else that'd happened these past few weeks. I'd have to step up my friendship game and be there for her more. "You're taking this really well, though, Nyah. It makes me look pathetic. You're stronger than you look, munchkin." I pinched her cheeks. Her face was freezing cold. She slapped my hand away. "Nyah, holy shit! Your cheeks are frozen solid. Get your butt inside. My mom's about to pick me up."

"'Kay, but you *have* to tell me how it goes."

"Every detail," I lied, even though I held back almost all the details a few moments ago and had no intention of saying much more than that in the future. I wanted to hoard every detail about Oliver in my own head and heart, keeping him for myself like a selfish little gremlin—telling no one a thing, not even my best friend who had always shared everything with me. I didn't know why—I just did. I could still be there for her; I just didn't feel ready to talk about him to anyone. I was afraid if I did, then the magic of him would start to fade away. Mama pulled up before my face could betray me. Grateful for the timing, I hugged Nyah goodbye and ran to the car.

•••

"Heylo! A somebody is looking a very beautiful in this morning!" Mama exclaimed as I came down the stairs. "Is it a picture yearbooks day today?"

I disguised the pleasure I felt at her compliment by placing my hands on my hips and feigning irritation.

"Seriously? Am I normally ugly?"

"No, you know you're always a beautiful. No matter the what. But is just a usually you looking like you don't a really caring how you looking, like pajama style, and today you looking like, yes, you caring finally and putting in some efforts."

Way to damn me with faint praise. "Awesome, thanks."

As I exited the car in front of school, people were already looking at me before I walked into the main building. People continued to stare as I walked through the halls to class. My heart was beating against my chest, and I dug my fingernails into my palms as I caught my reflection in a window. Everyone was gawking at me like I was an alien—okay, I may have overdone the makeup a bit. Feeling flushed, I ran into the nearest bathroom to splash water on my face the way I always did when I was feeling that anxious. But as I stood at the sink, I caught sight of my reflection. *You can't splash your face today—the makeup will run.* Instead, I held my red palms under the cold water to soothe the nerves. I patted the back of my neck with a wet paper towel. Today I was wearing my hair down. It was smooth, dark, and straight, and hung around my shoulders like velvet drapes, slightly covering the right side of my face. It felt strange, not having it tied back in a tight ponytail the way it usually was—I felt less in control this way.

I stared at my winged eyeliner in the mirror. Nyah sent me a text this morning: **Winged liner! A must! HUGE confidence booster 4 u cuz I swear u get so fierce when ur wearing it on performance days.** Beneath my lucky leather jacket peeked out a delicate silk blouse. I ran my wet palms over my plum wax-coated jeans, the ones that always made me feel like I was in a punk rock band or something.

As I hurried to first period, I was surprised to spot Oliver standing by a wall near the main entrance near a familiar group of students. Well, here was my opportunity. *I should do it now*, I thought. It was a better place to do it than a crowded classroom. I'd have the element of surprise if I did it right then. I was gonna do it. *Come on, just do it. You are fearless. You are in control. You are fearless. You are in control,* I told myself as I walked over.

We locked eyes almost instantly. I made myself concentrate on just putting one foot in front of the other until I was standing close enough to brush my fingers against his—not that I did. I took in his sculpted biceps, the delicate line of his carotid artery in his neck, his sharp jawline, and his soft parted lips, only stopping once I reached his eyes. My own eyes softened. His brow was furrowed as if he was trying to parse what was happening—what was different about me. As I held his gaze, his eyes sparked with heated desire. My knees trembled and my entire body was flushed with heat. I took that warmth and transferred it back to him through my eyes as if to say, *See what you do to me?*

But just when I thought I had a rein on the situation, an unexpected connection manifested. This inexplicable, pure, all-consuming emotion filled my eyes with tears. What the hell was going on? I felt thoroughly exposed, and suddenly felt the need to pull back, to step behind the iron curtain again. How was I going to do that now? I had to break eye contact. I looked at the floor.

He played you hot and cold. You are nothing to him, so now he is nothing to you. You're numb. You. Feel. Nothing. I felt my eyes go cold, emotionless. Dead eyes. I looked back up at him. Oliver's expression changed to confusion, then concern, and I instantly regretted the way I was toying with him. Why was I getting revenge? Why was I sending mixed signals? So what if he hurt me? At least he was being subtle about it. I turned away quickly to hide my regret. I let my hair fall over my face—my shame concealer.

I turned to bolt and ran smack into a crowd of students, all of them from my second period AP Gov class. What was happening? Why were they gathered there so early?

"All right, everyone, follow me outside. The bus is here," Mr. Gerald announced. They all started moving toward the main doors and I looked around, lost. "Miss Arkova? I don't have your signed permission slip."

"Permission slip?"

"From your parents and the rest of your teachers? Based on the look on your face, I'm assuming you don't have it. Either that, or you enjoy wasting everyone's time." I shook my head. "You can't just stand here all day. Go to your first period class, Miss Arkova. Later, Mrs. Garver will supervise you in the library during second period. She has the makeup assignment; you will find all the answers you need in the source material that I have set aside. Stay there until the Nutrition bell rings," he instructed. *How could I have forgotten about the field trip?* That was how distracted I'd been. I was losing my grip on life. I stole a glance back to

Oliver. He was still studying me, confusion in his eyes. Embarrassed, I quickly turned away and left.

After a miserable first period, I miserably trudged over to the library, where I sat marinating in melancholia. I was bleak and monochromatic, like something Picasso would have painted in his Blue Period. I considered leaving altogether but decided to stay in school and do what had been asked of me for once. No more running; I had to face things head-on, starting that day. After checking in with the librarian, I took an empty chair in the back, happy to be engulfed by rows of books. I folded my arms on the table, desperate for an academic distraction.

Halfway through Mr. Gerald's assignment, my mind was still stuck on the earlier events. Regret had dissolved into abject humiliation. I was engulfed by gloom as I relived the moment in the hallway over and over again. Defeated, I dropped my head into folded arms. *Such an idiot. Who did I think I was approaching him like that?* I squeezed my arms tighter around my head, trying to block any light from coming in, and the tip of my nose pressed against the table. I disregarded the germs, the smell, and the fact that someone might have smeared their boogers on that exact spot. I couldn't begin to care about things that had once repulsed me now. Instead, I channeled my energy into holding back tears. I wanted this day to end.

"It's just a field trip—don't cry."

His voice hit me like a stroke of lightning. I lifted my forehead off my folded arms slowly, sucking back the tears on my way up. He was standing right in front of me, hands on his hips, regarding me with a smug smile. Damn him and his smirk. I couldn't help but smile back, realizing what a pathetic sight I must be. He took a step closer and my heart picked up the pace. "Come on, let's get out of here."

I was taken aback by the suggestion. "I . . . I mean, I should probably stay here," I said.

"Yeah, you *probably* should." He cocked his head to one side, grinning.

Great. Now what? The good news was, he wasn't leaving. He leaned forward and planted his hands on my desk, leaning so close I could smell his cologne. His fingertips brushed my arm, and I felt an electric pulse where he'd touched me. He took my hand and gave it a playful tug, signaling we should go. What should I do? My response would bear consequences. I'd have felt the weight of that if I hadn't been floating on a cloud. I stood and led him toward the exit.

"Mrs. Garber? Excuse me, but I'm not feeling well. Oliver's offered to escort me to the nurse's office in case I get dizzy on the way there. Can you please write us a hall pass?" I asked the librarian, with an Academy Award–level tremor in my voice.

She looked bored and distant, like she was on a different planet in her own mind. She deliberated for a moment and then answered, "Feel better." I reluctantly let go of Oliver's hand to grab the hall pass.

As soon as the library door shut behind us, we shared an exaggerated, diabolical grin. I was getting the sense that Oliver shared my aversion to authority. He led us toward the back of campus.

The last thing I ever thought I'd be doing was climbing that fence again, but there I was. I scanned the area for a guard, but I didn't spot anyone. Oliver reached the top first and offered his hand to me. I let him pull me up, then straddled the fence as he jumped down. I hated this part. Oliver made me more nervous, because as much as I loved an audience, I didn't want to look like an idiot and break my ankle. *Screw it.* I didn't have much of an option at that point, so I used the same technique as before—holding on as long as I could tolerate as I worked my way down, then jumping the rest of the way. He kept me steady after I landed, but all I could think about was his hands on my hips.

"Hey!" someone shouted, cutting into our moment.

A security guard was running toward us from campus, shouting for us to stop. *Shit.* Where'd this guy come from? I looked back at Oliver, and his eyes lit up as he realized we'd been caught.

"Come on!" He grabbed my hand and together we sprinted like crazy. "We just . . . gotta get to my bike . . ." he panted.

I didn't think the security guard was dedicated enough to chase us over a fence, but I didn't plan on standing there to find out, either. Running side by side, Oliver and I shared a moment of exhilaration.

When we finally reached his bike, he grabbed his helmet and turned to put it on my head. As he secured the strap, I asked, "What about you? No brain-bucket?"

"Better me than you," he joked, and got on, looking over to me expectantly. "Hop on," he coaxed with a wink. "I'll be fine."

I hesitated. The memory of a knife at my throat and the taste of fear on my tongue flashed through my mind. Our lives were so short; to live every day with fear of dying was not living. So, in a decisive moment, I climbed up and wrapped my arms around Oliver. We roared away without looking back.

At first, I felt tense and uncomfortable—the thought of literally hanging on for life was terrifying—but I tried to let the tension go, relax the pressure out of my shoulders. I closed my eyes and envisioned blank space. Soon, all the anxiety I'd bottled up was blown away by the cleansing wind.

It's a mystery how quickly life changes as the minute hand ticks forward on a clock somewhere. In the end, the best moments—the ones you keep going back to—are the ones that aren't governed by a clock at all. They are the ones in which time is of very little importance. I already knew this was the kind of transcending moment that I would revisit for the rest of my life—riding on the back of this motorcycle with Oliver, not knowing what would happen next but smiling at the thought of how close I came to divinity.

We passed the Griffith Park sign and pulled over across from the Greek Theater. I realized it was time for me to get off, but I didn't know how to go about it. Trying to maintain a cool and stress-free facade, even though every nerve in my body was on edge, I loosened my grasp on his torso and attempted to dismount the motorcycle with some semblance of grace. I pulled the helmet off and shook my hair out. It cascaded over my shoulders as I contained my enthusiasm under a simple smile and handed his helmet back.

"So, what next?" I asked.

He cleared his throat. "I . . . uh, live close by, moved here not too long ago, couple blocks down. Figured it's about time I explored the neighborhood. Wanna go for a walk?"

"A walk?"

He nodded. I looked down at my boots—they were platform, but they should have been fine.

"Yeah, okay."

I followed him along a wide road to a narrow, semi-steep hiking trail. "Just a walk, huh?"

He responded with a crooked smile. "You'll be fine."

I couldn't keep it in any longer. "That was incredible, by the way, riding over here on your bike."

"Yeah, it was fun. I was living it through you. It felt like my first time all over again." I wondered if he was teasing me. We made our way up the hill along a winding dirt trail.

I tried not to sound as winded as I felt. "How did you convince your parents to let you get a bike? You have to share your secret strategy. My mom would quicker encourage me to enlist in the army than let me set my butt on a motorcycle."

"Remind me not to mention this little adventure around her."

"Yeah, never. Please." I laughed. "She's freaked out enough by everything that went down in the alley. Actually, the other day, she just casually mentioned to me that she's thinking of getting a gun. Can you imagine?"

He turned and looked at me in surprise.

"Really? Yeah, well, I don't know much about her, but it's probably a good idea. I'd do the same if I was her and then some."

"What do you mean?"

"I would never have come back here—for one, I'd have split and kept on moving."

"This is our home. Where exactly are we supposed to go? Stay in Rancho Mirage until we shrivel up like prunes? She talked to my father, and now we're back, so that means whatever was going on is over now. He took care of it."

"No, yeah, I'm sure he did. Sorry, I know it's not my business," he said.

I waited for him to say something else, but he didn't. I had so many questions for him, but I wanted them to come out naturally and not like an interrogation. Instead, I took in my surroundings, noticing the way the sun shone between the trees and how birdsong filled the air. Life was an unpredictable beast. To think I was on the verge of a serious depression less than an hour before—now I was on top of the world.

The observatory peeked out at us around the corner as we made our way up the winding trail. "I haven't been here since third grade," I said, mostly to myself. My inner child was elated to be back and I picked up the pace, skipping like a jubilant elf the rest of the way. Oliver chuckled and shook his head.

Tourists swarmed the observatory with fancy cameras dangling from their necks. Herds of eager school children took a break from their field trip and ate lunch on the freshly planted green lawn. I wove through the madness toward the tall front doors and looked back for Oliver, who quickly caught up with me. I reached for the door, but he beat me to it and held it open for me.

Somehow, on top of charm and the whole cool factor he'd got going, he possessed something even more rare: manners. I suddenly felt challenged to step up my own game like never before.

Once inside the observatory, our attention was drawn straight to the enormous Foucault pendulum in the middle of the hall. I ran up to it and looked over the edge, observing the large bronze ball swinging back and forth over the pendulum pit until it knocked over one of the pegs that measured its rotational progress.

"I remember being too small to see over this barricade," I recalled. "I was convinced the whole thing was a cauldron and thought the pendulum was an oversized, enchanted stirring spoon. Now I realize this pendulum is yet another reminder me of how small we are in the scheme of things. Isn't it funny how the earth rotates beneath our feet all day, every second of the day, and we hardly notice a thing?"

"At least there was a time when you believed in magic. Not everyone can say that."

"What? You never believed? Not in Santa, or the Tooth Fairy, or anything?"

He smirked at that but went quiet again.

"*The pendulum is essentially disconnected from the turning of the Earth, and once started in motion, it continues to swing in the same direction, regardless of what the Earth does,*" he read off a tablet. "Oh! Everything you were saying finally makes sense. I was like, what is this girl going on and on about? We're small, and the world keeps turning. Now I get it."

"Ha ha! You're absolutely hilarious," I responded with mock laughter.

"I'm just glad you aren't having an existential crisis . . . or are you?" he teased, nudging me playfully. I nudged him back, but he continued. "I have an idea. Next time, when you're randomly freaking out about, you know, the world rotating and stuff, what we do is we come here, and we climb on this pendulum thing. And problem solved . . . we'll be the only two people on the planet who are standing still while everyone else is turning. I mean, yeah, technically, I guess we'll be swinging back and forth, not standing still, but you get the gist. Deal?"

I shook my head firmly. "No can do, sorry. No more climbing for me, thanks very much, but that was a very clever idea—very funny." My eyes followed the pendulum to the vaulted ceiling, where they rediscovered the beauty of Hugo Ballin's murals of figures from celestial mythology.

"Now that's extraordinary." I gestured to the ceiling. "When I was a child, these murals were the most majestic part of the observatory for me. I would study every inch of that ceiling, from Atlas to the Four Winds. And I'd make up stories that went along with them until my neck was sore from looking up. But I just this minute realized that they actually portray constellations and the planets as some form of deities—science and religion together. That's interesting . . ." I brought my eyes back down from the ceiling to find Oliver watching me quietly. He didn't say a word, and his silence made my stomach flutter. He was so mysterious, while I was more like an unfiltered rambling buffoon.

I led him to the white stone balconies that looked out over the city, but instead of facing forward and looking out as I did, he turned his back to the view and sat on the ledge, facing me. Again he watched me in silence as I looked out over the city. I tried to act natural under his gaze, but it was hard to act natural and feel that nervous at the same time.

"So, religion or science?" he asked unexpectedly.

I smiled. Looked like he was listening back there inside. "Well, of course, without science, there is no progress."

"And? Go on."

"And without faith, there is no soul," I concluded and look over to meet his gaze. "So, I guess I believe in the marriage of both."

"They are too different to coexist," he said.

"They might be two separate branches reaching in opposing directions, but they come from the same tree. In the end, they are the two components that comprise all living things, don't you think? Genetic makeup and molecules and atoms all sum up to a human being, but he does not breathe without that spark we like to call the soul." I hoped he understood what I meant. "That must have come out of my mouth a total mess, but it made sense in my head," I admitted.

"Naw, don't worry, it came out crystal clear." He shook his head. "You have strong opinions, and I like that. They're contagious." I wondered if that was a compliment. "You talk like you've had a lot of time to consider it and you choose your words carefully—which is crazy, because I put you on the spot, sort of—and it's like you had an answer ready." I beamed like a foolish little girl who gave the correct answer to a thorny question in grade school. "Have you thought about it before?"

"Thought about what?" I asked.

"Religion versus science."

"Oh . . . yeah. A lot, actually." But my mind was neither still nor at ease. I had questions of my own. I bit the bullet and just asked him, "So, listen, what was wrong the other day?" He just stared at me with a blank expression. I could see him scrambling for a veil to hide behind—his poker face. *Oh no you don't!* "I came over to say hello to you in class, and it was like you didn't even know me."

He didn't answer right away, but he turned and looked into the distance. Finally, he said "It was a just a really bad day—a bad mood—and, you know . . . I'm not proud of it. I took it out on the first person who approached me. I'm, you know . . . I'm sorry. It was tactless." It wasn't what I wanted to hear; it sounded pat and generic. But I'd have to accept it—what else could I do? Interrogate him further? Not worth it.

"I want some *shisha*." The thought spewed through my malfunctioning verbal filtration system.

"What?" he asked.

"Just thinking out loud. *Shisha*'s like fruit-flavored tobacco, and you smoke it through a water pipe," I explained.

"Sounds weird, but I'm up for trying something new."

"Have you really never heard of *shisha* before? Hookah? Qalyan? Narguile ... no—?" He looked at me with a blank expression. "You been living in a cave or something?"

"Close. Santa Clarita," he answered, but immediately got tense, making me feel uneasy, like I wasn't supposed to hear that. I seized the gem and tucked it away in my treasure chest of information next to fiery gaze, unpredictable, and impossible to read. I changed the name of the virtual treasure chest from Asshole back to Oliver.

"All right, let's go," I said.

"Where to?"

"Over the hill and across the way."

"Huh?"

"The place I usually go is in the Valley. We can take the 101 to Sherman Oaks and it's right there on Ventura."

"Okay, sounds like a plan."

As soon as we walked back down to the bottom of the hill where we parked his bike, it hit me.

"Wait, shit! We can't go to the Valley. I'm not letting you get on the 101 without a helmet—there's no way."

"Okay. I'll take Mulholland," he offered.

"Oh, and that's so much better? It's a winding cliff, probably even more dangerous. Let's just take the Metro like normal people."

"The Metro?" He rolled his eyes, put the helmet on my head, and snapped the strap under my chin.

"What?" I protested. "Could be fun—" The breath went out of me as he grabbed hold of my waist with both hands, almost giving me a heart attack. Then, with a theatrically overexaggerated groan, he lifted me off the ground and set me on his bike.

"What are you doing?"

He then took a step back, as if to examine my level of volatility. "I just suddenly had this impulse to do that. All right, fine. You win, let's go."

"Metro?"

"Helmet." He hopped on in front of me and he reached back, searching for my arms. As soon as he got hold of them, he pulled them around his body. That was him being playful, I guessed. I laughed and held on tight as his bike came to life and we flew down Vermont Avenue.

I wondered, if I had wings and tied a rope between the motorcycle and my waist, could I have flown? I pictured it: sailing up into the sky towed by Oliver, and uncontrollable laughter took over at the thought of my own absurdity. I may have been losing it; being on the back of his bike took me to some subconscious place where I forgot where and who I was. I only realized we pulled up to a motorsports shop after he tapped my leg to signal that he needed the kickstand down.

"Be right back," he said and jogged into the store.

I stretched my hands over my head, putting some space between each vertebra—bad idea. The bike started tilting over to the side opposite the kickstand. I made a quick move up to the front and gripped the handles to steady her out. Sitting up front, I wondered how quickly I could learn to ride. She seemed hard to control, but I loved a challenge. I undid the helmet strap so I could pull it off and shake my hair out.

Another motorcyclist pulled up next to me, looked over, and nodded. I nodded back, unsure if it was some sort of fellow biker greeting. He wore a black beanie under his helmet, which accentuated his defined jaw. He was a good-looking guy in his midtwenties, confidence oozing from every pore. I looked away, refusing to feed his palpable self-satisfaction, but I could sense his approach with my peripheral vision.

"Nice ride." His pearly whites blinded me like they'd been soaked in bleach.

"Thanks," I responded, a reflex. I didn't mean to make it sound like it was mine.

Before I could elaborate, he reached out to touch the bike. "KYMCO Venox—nothing on my Ducati, but you never forget your first." Ugh, what a douchelord. This was the kind of guy who undoubtedly relished the sight of his own reflection in shiny objects. "How old is she?" he asked as he glided a finger over the body. As soon as he got within a foot of my leg, I scooted away. Then I decided to follow through with the movement and get off the bike entirely. Carefully, I swung my leg over, crossed my arms, and took a firm, wide stance a few feet away from him, the bike now between us.

"Not sure. It's not mine," I finally responded. He walked around the bike toward me, taking his time like it was a game to him. He pushed me to say it: "My boyfriend's inside. He'd know." And there it was.

"Yeah?"

"Yeah."

I gestured vaguely toward the store, not expecting to find Oliver walking out. Perfect timing. Worry lines appeared between his brows; he assessed the situation as he walked over. I turned back to the guy, hoping he wouldn't quote me on the "my boyfriend" thing, but the guy was already on his way toward the store. As they passed each other, there was a silent intensity in the air between them. The Ducati guy was quite brawny, I realized, once I saw them side by side. Oliver was leaner but taller, and the look he was giving the other guy was absolutely feral. I would never have wanted to be on the receiving end of that glare. Something must've happened inside the store to put Oliver in such a bad mood. The moment between them passed, and so did the gravity of Oliver's expression. By the time he reached me, the glare had vanished into thin air. He looked as if nothing were ever the matter at all, which made me question whether or not I imagined the glare in the first place. But as he handed the brand-new helmet he'd bought over to me, I noticed something strange. His hand was injured, covered in blood.

"You all right?" he asked.

"Me? Yeah, what about you? Your hand—ouch! Are you okay? What happened?"

"Oh, uh, yeah . . . it was stupid. I wasn't looking where I was going, tripped over a folded stepladder an employee left in the middle of the aisle. I caught myself but scraped my knuckles against the screws when I landed."

"Wow. That looks bad! You should talk to the manager—" I said.

"It's no big deal—"

He was hiding something. It scared me a little, because if he was lying, he was a good liar and I should be careful. My eyes kept darting back to the store, as if someone was going to run out after him. He wouldn't have hurt someone in there, would he have? *No.* "Well, hold on. Let's clean it up, at least."

"Nah, I'm okay."

"Come on, Oliver, we have to disinfect—"

"I told them and I'm telling you, I'm good. Trust me." he declared in a tone that indicated the subject was permanently closed.

"So . . . you really got me a helmet?" I asked him, emphasizing the personal touch of his gesture.

"Well, after you started talkin' about the Metro—I should have a spare, anyway." Before I could make a joke about him starting a motorcycle ride sharing app, he asked, "What did he want?"

"Who? Oh, that guy? He was just asking about your bike, actually— probably isn't used to seeing a girl on a bike and figured . . . well, you know how guys can be." He didn't say anything, but his playful nature had disappeared yet again. I tried on the smaller helmet; it fit my head much more comfortably than the first one. "Does this thing come with a parachute?" He smiled, then got on the bike and looked away so I couldn't read his face.

"I do know 'how guys can be,'" he acknowledged. "I can give his Ducati a nice, hard kick if he crossed any lines." Both grateful and alarmed by his offer, I gripped his torso tightly as his engine purred to life.

"No, it's cool," I managed, the dinosaur in my stomach giving one giant flap of its wings.

He took Mulholland. The City of Angels glistened in a golden glow of smog and sunlight, but it was a lovely sight as we cruised through the Hollywood Hills at 60 mph. Once again, the sensation of being on the motorcycle with him lulled me into near delirium. Seriously, how did I get there? It felt entirely like a hallucination, or one of my crazy daydreams.

We pulled up to an outdoor shopping plaza. The *shisha* place was inside on the second floor. I pointed to the parking entrance, indicating that he should take the ramp down to the underground garage. We parked and hopped off the bike near a huddled group of teenagers. Oliver noticed the kids passing around IDs and studying them.

"What are they doing?" he asked as he headed toward the main entrance. I grabbed his hand and pulled him toward the opposite direction.

"No, let's go this way." I guided him to the back entrance and explained, "Those guys are getting their ID situation in order."

"I don't have an ID on me. You didn't say anything about needing one."

"It's all good—that's why we're going in through the back. You shouldn't be driving without an ID, by the way."

"There are a lot of things I shouldn't be doing," he teased.

I laughed and finally let go of his hand, wondering how much longer I could have gotten away with holding it before it got awkward. We passed through the kitchen as I nodded to some familiar faces.

"The bathroom's right here. You can clean yourself up." I pointed to the door on the right and he looked at me, confused. "Your hand, remember? Disinfectant."

"Oh, yeah. I forgot already. It's no big deal, but yeah, let me go wash it with some soap. I'll meet you inside," he said.

"When you're done, just follow this hallway out that door to the patio and make a right," I specified.

The Arabic music came in louder and louder the deeper I walked down the hallway. I caught sight of the manager, Jo, as soon as I reached the outdoor patio. As he made his way over to me, I looked around for Mama to make sure she hadn't made an unexpected visit.

"Minaaaaaa," Jo pronounced in a warning tone. Jo was your average guy in his early twenties with very poor taste in fashion. He was of average height, above average intellect, and a very charming smile. He was too skinny in the eyes of his Persian mother and grandmother, too liberal in the eyes of his Arabic father, and too smart to be the manager of a *shisha* place. His dark circles and tired lines gave away just how overworked the man under the fatigue-denying smile was.

"Jooooooooo." I mimicked the way he called out my name.

He chuckled. "Cute, but the answer is no."

"Jooooo! Jooooooey, *joon . . . aziz . . . habib!* We came all the way from Hollywood. *Lotfan?*" I pleaded with him in Farsi. "Please" was the only Farsi word I knew besides *joon, aziz,* and *habib,* which basically all meant "darling."

"Who's we? Who did you bring here? I know it's not your mom this time of day."

"I'm with a friend. *Lotfan!*" He pressed his lips together and folded his arms across his chest.

"Don't *lotfan* me. Why aren't you in school?"

"Short day. Come on, please don't embarrass me in front of my friend."

"Short day, my ass. Mina, you can't go around telling people they can come here if they're underage. Cops do random ID checks, and you can only be here with a parent or guardian. My job is on the line—you know that."

"It's the afternoon; we both know they usually come at night. Besides, they only check around once every two years, and they've already been here this summer. Your words, not mine. Come on, please don't be an ass, *lotfan*."

His eyebrows shot up.

"Listen to me, *jigar*, I'd rather be a living ass than a dead pushover. If your mom found out I let you stay, she'd murder me."

"That's why she won't find out." I offered a charming smile and tried a sultry voice. "Just this once? It won't be a regular thing, I promise. Come on, Jo *joon*." He sighed and shook his head in defeat. I'd worn him down.

"Okay, but you owe me." It worked. "Are you the friend?"

I turned around to find Oliver had joined us. He extended his hand to Jo, who shook it. "Oliver," he said his name in an even deeper tone than he normally spoke.

Jo led us to my favorite table—well, it was less of a table and more of an ornamental rug laid over a raised wooden platform accompanied by an uncoordinated variety of decorative pillows you would only find at a garage sale. "Oliver, I'm assuming you're the same age as Mina here," Jo muttered. "As in underage?"

Oliver didn't respond right away. Instead, he offered me a hand to help me climb onto the platform, took a seat, and said, "Well, I'm emancipated, so I'm legally an adult."

"Congratulations. So legally you can do anything except vote, purchase alcohol, pornography, lottery tickets, and firearms . . . oh, and be here."

"Enough, he gets it!" I exclaimed. "Jo's a law student and thinks he's gonna rule the world. I guess you can keep the throne warm for me until

I pass the bar exam and wipe the floor with you in litigation like a true Queen of Dragons."

"Don't push it, Mina. I know you think your charm is limitless, and maybe it is, but leave a man some dignity. Also, it's Mother of Dragons—don't get it twisted," Jo advised.

"Loud and clear. Meanwhile, how about a *shisha*—the usual flavor—and a green tea with mint for me? Oliver? Sorry, I know you haven't had any time with the menu."

Oliver scanned the menu quickly. "Uh, no, that's okay. Can I just get one of the sandwiches?"

"Which one?"

"Turkey . . . the way it comes is fine; and . . . *ah*, a Red Boost slushy—of course, only if you think I'm old enough for one." Oliver spoke sarcasm! Yay!

"You're old enough to know that crap's terrible for you," Jo commented wryly.

"Sounds delicious," Oliver responded.

"You sure know how to pick your friends, Mina. This one's almost a bigger pain than you are." Jo walked away. Oliver and I smiled at one another politely, both unsure what to discuss next.

"What was that all about?" Oliver asked.

"He was just giving me a hard time about coming in with an under-aged friend," I explained. "It's nothing personal, it's just Jo's way. He likes breaking rules, but he's in denial; he's conflicted. Just ignore it—I do."

"Have you two known each other a while?" he asked.

"My mom and I used to come here all the time back when my . . . uh," I stopped myself. *What am I doing? Don't tell him random, sad, personal crap.*

"When what?"

Too late, now you have to explain. "After my father moved away. My mom was under a lot of stress and I was trying to figure out a way to prevent her from smoking again. She had the hardest time quitting cigarettes; patches and gum didn't really work for her and the only other thing I could think of was *shisha*—it's something like less than one percent nicotine. Plus, it's not something you can just pull out of your pocket and smoke—it's a bit high maintenance and expensive. The key is not to smoke it for like an hour. Anyway, we'd talk for hours, I'd study, she'd catch up on work . . . it was nice. I miss it."

"You're lucky. Your mom sounds chill."

"Chill? Yeah, I guess. Not so much anymore, but she used to be. I don't know what I would've done if it wasn't for her—it would've been really lonely." Like a bad habit, I immediately sank into the dark, spider-infested corner of my mind where the big, hairy monster called What If resided. I snapped out of it just before I was sucked in for good.

"Anyway, what about you? Are you closer with your dad or your mom? Wait, actually, you mentioned that whole emancipation thing. Were you joking, or was that true?"

He deliberated a response and opened his mouth to speak, but a server arrived with our *shisha*. The man was somewhere in his late thirties, avoided eye contact, sported a close shave, and judging from the look of his hands, he'd most likely labored as a mechanic before prepping charcoals and *shishas*. He looked disinterested—probably overqualified. He moved smoothly, with confidence, and all the while, handling the flaming charcoals with ease.

"Coconut flavor?" the server asked, and I nodded in confirmation. "No one ever orders just coconut flavor by itself," he added as he places the *shisha* down before us. I'd never seen him during the night shift, that was probably why my order wasn't familiar to him.

"Try it. You can start mine if you want. I bet it'll be your new favorite." I handed him the hose.

"All right," he answered.

Oliver fidgeted with his silverware, his expression grave, as though all the earth's sadness was his alone to bear. I gave him a "What's up?" nod, and he shook his head. I offered a crooked reassuring smile, kept questioning him with my eyebrows, and then danced them up and down. He started to laugh—and I mean really laugh. It was a beautiful sight, especially in comparison to how incredibly stupid I must have looked right then, but I couldn't have cared less. My goal was a smile, and I got a laugh—bonus points.

"Very good . . . smooth flavor," the *shisha* server decided.

"Yeah, it's a good one, glad you liked it. Thank you . . . Gabriel," I read his name tag.

"Thank you, miss," he said as he turned to leave.

I turned to Oliver, who leaned back to make himself comfortable. He sprawled out on the Arabic rug, resting his head on the tufted pillows. Just as I started to lean in, my phone went off loudly, making me jump. I guess I'd forgotten to turn it to silent at school. It was Nyah. I'd call her back. I set the phone to vibrate and threw it back in my bag.

"So, Mina, what else do you do for fun besides hiding from thugs and smoking *shishi . . . shishu*?"

"Oh, well. Interesting question," I began.

My phone vibrated nonstop in my bag. I couldn't keep ignoring it. Nyah's wide-smile selfie lit up on my display. I shot her a text: **hey what's up?**

I finally answered Oliver. "Umm, a lot of things."

"So . . . not much else?" He smirked. Was he flirting? I thought there was definite flirting going on there!

I got a text, another, then a third, fifth, and sixth.

"Oh my god, Nyah," I murmured under my breath as Oliver had a laugh. I opened my phone and read:

OMG!!!

Dude pick up your phone!!!
You're gonna die!!!
Ok not die, but scream
You'll 4 sure scream
Ahhhhhhhhhhhhhhshfkhflakh

The phone rang again.

"I'm so sorry," I said. "It's my best friend. She's very persistent."

"It's cool, just pick up," Oliver suggested.

"She's having a conniption. Nothing new, she does this from time to time. But yeah, I probably gotta take this."

"Of course, go ahead," he said, and took his own phone out. Ugh. I couldn't believe a second ago we were almost flirting, and now we were just two people on their phones doing separate things.

I picked up. "Nyah? Everything okay?"

"Oh. My. God. Where are you right now?" I hesitated. "Mina? Hellooooo? Are you hearing me? I have to talk to you right now!"

"Okay, talk."

"Wait, where you at?" she demanded.

"I'm having *shisha* on Ventura at my usual spot," I explained reluctantly. All I needed was for her to rush over here.

"For real? That's perfect! I'm right by there . . . see you in five." *Click.* Crap.

"Brace yourself, she's super amped about something," I warned Oliver, who looked up from his phone. I tried to hide my anxiety at the thought of the two of them meeting by taking a puff of *shisha*. It would probably be okay, but you never knew what'd come out of Nyah's mouth if she was feeling talkative, which she usually was.

"So . . . back to my question: What else do you do for fun?" he asked.

"Let me see: reading—fiction and non, old films, foreign films—especially old Italian cinema—De Sica, Bertolucci. I love a good law show or a funny political podcast. Sometimes I'll go see an exhibit at LACMA, any kind of art, really, music, of course. And hobby-wise, some light sketching—very light—I'm not good at all. I love singing, but only if no one can hear me, because I sound like a wounded dog. As far as actual skill goes, I'm a dancer—it's my only real talent."

"Oh? What kind of dancer?"

"Pole, mostly," I joked.

"Professionally?"

"Very," I went with it.

"Like actual stripping?" He was unsure if I was messing with him. I didn't answer. Instead, I nodded vaguely as I took another drag of the *shisha*. "You can't do that professionally unless you're eighteen," he argued.

"You can't do this unless you're twenty-one." I exhaled a large cloud of smoke through a smirk, head slightly tilted up.

"Fascinating. I've never known a stripper with so many interests."

CHAPTER 8

OLIVER

A stripper with interests? That was idiotic.

After a deafening silence, Mina finally spoke. "So you think exotic dancers are simple-minded? Incapable of complexity, of curiosity, empathy, or exhibiting an interest in art?"

"Hell no, I just—" *Crap. Oliver, think!*

"You shouldn't assume an entire group of people are a certain way. What people do to make a living doesn't define them, especially when it comes to people who don't have the luxury of choice. Most exotic dancers work multiple jobs trying to save up for something important: providing for a child they have to raise without any support, or trying to afford the completely insane cost of higher education—education that's designed for the privileged while the rest of us have to figure out how to sell our organs just to pay for the textbooks let alone the tuition."

Perfect, she friggin' hates you now. "Look, I swear I didn't mean that the way it sounded. For real, like, when you said dancer . . . I thought you really meant like you do some salsa or, you know, friggin' ballet dancing or whatever, or . . . like, Zumba or some shit—"

You should listen more, talk less. Of course, once I started talking, it was hard to shut up. "Honestly Mina, I thought you were messing with me with the whole stripper thing. So . . . I was, you know, just trying to fire a joke back—a super lame joke—but, you know…look, I'm sorry. I respect you. I wasn't—it wasn't meant to be, like, an insult, or, like, me hating on women who strip or whatever, you know, like you said, exotic dancers. I mean, not just women. I know that men strip, too. That's not the point…shit…what's my point?" I chuckled weakly, begging for mercy. Mina failed to hide the smile creeping into the corners of her mouth, and it turned into a full-on laugh. There was no question about it, I was a complete moron.

"Were you messing with me? Yeah? Seriously? This whole time? Oh, man. Okay, you got me…stripper…okay…okay, I see how it is. Mina, you're … you're good. I'ma get you back though, don't you worry. I am so gonna get you back." I shook my head in disbelief.

"But I *was* serious about not judging people for what they do—" she justified.

"Yeah, yeah, no, I get it. Lesson learned."

She offered a very welcome change of subject. "I think it's about time you relax and try this *shisha*."

Manipulative and merciful—a strange combination. It reminded me of that prick she was talking to outside the bike shop earlier. I caught a glance of the two of them through the window of the store but couldn't look away; I was prematurely pissed off. So pissed off that I'd punched the wall by the cash register. This was one of the reasons a girl like Mina was dangerous to me—because she made me vulnerable. Vulnerable not just to pain, but to my own uncontrollable anger. I knew that jealousy and anger were closely related. What if I hadn't taken my anger out on the wall, but had blazed outside in a jealous rage? I didn't even want to think about what could have happened.

How was I supposed to feel, though? That manager guy, a grown-ass man, had been totally drooling over her. I could still see him in my peripheral, watching the two of us talking from the corner. How many friggin'

Jos was I gonna have to worry about? A girl like Mina? Probably a lot—an endless amount of Jos.

But that was life. I guessed when someone was worth getting to know, there was always a line. I didn't think Mina was aware that she even had a line, and I had no clue how to tell her I was standing in it. I mean, first of all, I had no business standing in the line—I was completely unqualified to have any kind of relationship . . . with anyone.

Then why are you here?

That was the messed-up part: Having spent the afternoon with her, I didn't think I could let her go. Whatever this was that we were doing, I wanted it. Not just today, but every day.

I took a puff of the *shisha*; the smoke filled my lungs. It was like inhaling a vaporized coconut. The flavor lingered in my mouth even as the thick cloud of smoke escaped. I gazed into her exotic upturned hazel eyes. Just because I wasn't ready for her didn't mean I couldn't admire her from afar. We could be friends.

You don't know how to be that either. I chuckled.

"What's funny?" she asked.

"Uh, I was just thinking about how crazy it is, being here. I mean, it's like . . . yesterday my life was a prison. Santa Clarita was like a prison—nothing to do, no room to grow. Look at me now—smoking *shisha* with a beautiful girl in Los Angeles."

"I'm sure there are *shisha* places in Santa Clarita."

I laughed. "You know what I mean, though. Life's insane, after everything somehow it's led me here, where I never thought I'd be." Well, that wasn't an outright lie, it just wasn't the whole truth.

Suddenly, she remembered something. "Someone once told me: 'Life's like having unprotected sex: you'll catch the STD even if you fake the orgasm.'"

I burst into laughter, mostly surprised. "What the hell does that even mean . . . and who the hell—I'm sorry. Who in the world said that to you?"

"No one, actually, maybe I read it somewhere—I guess it sounded wittier in my mind."

Just as we both cracked up, a petite, perky, curly-haired girl crept up behind Mina and pounced on top of her.

"Mina!"

"Jesus, Nyah! You scared the shit out of me. Wait, did Jo see you?"

"That grumpy dude over there? Yeah, I told him I'd be in and out of here in a flash. He wasn't happy about it." Nyah waved at Jo and mouthed "Five minutes."

"Careful, you're about to knock the *shisha* over," Mina warned her. This must be the infamous best friend, she of the incessant texts. That shit was crazy, how different they were. Their voices were night and day—Mina's had a deep and raspy quality, while Nyah's reminded me of the bell Salvation Army volunteers rang. Mina was taller than the average girl; she'd got curves most skinny girls didn't, and the vibe of a grown woman. Nyah was cute, like a doll. She had these big eyes, velvet skin, and round cheeks that gave her face the shape of a heart. She was covered in little freckles everywhere, especially around her nose. Also, she had a shit-ton of energy exploding outward even when she was just standing there.

Nyah turned to me. "Hi, sorry to interrupt this . . . whatever this is." She got shy when our eyes met and looked back to Mina. Suddenly, it was like I wasn't even there anymore, and her energy went back to a thousand percent. "I'll make it quick. You're gonna die in T-minus-five seconds!" Nyah squealed energetically. "Guess what?"

"What?" Mina indulged her with caution.

"Guess!"

"Okay, it starts with a hot guy and you're in love but then something, something, something. Am I close?" Mina asked.

"Ha-ha, funny!" Nyah rolled her eyes, but then admitted, "Okay, fine! There's this guy at my school, Jake, who I never had a chance to talk to before, but now he hangs out by our benches because Hammid and Sarah know him from lit class. The fact that he's cute isn't my point right now, though, so listen! He was talking to a bunch of us the other day when he casually mentions that he's going to that rave downtown, and then, all of a sudden, he turns to me and says, and I quote, 'Maybe I'll catch you there?' Can you believe it? Oh my God, Mina, I melted—I mean, there was, like, a heat between us"—Mina cleared her throat loudly, but Nyah continued—"He really is so cute, though. Like, the way he styles his hair, so meticulous, and the way this little dimple forms in his cheek when he thinks of something funny to say. Also, this time, I'm almost one hundred percent sure that he's into girls. That's not the point, though. The point is, we *have* to go, or we'll both be totally missing out on life itself, like being a hippie in the eighties and missing Woodstock." Nyah talked like it was a race to the finish line. Is this actually how girls talk about guys? Or was this frenetic babbling something exclusive to Nyah?

Mina asked, "Wait, back up. What's a rave?"

I stepped in. "It's like this giant dance party like a massive electric music carnival—multiple stages, DJs playin' sets till the sun comes up. EDM, neon lights—like, glowsticks and shit—drugs—sweaty, almost naked people—any of this ringing a bell?" Mina smirked. "How do you know all about *shisha* but not what a rave is?" She shrugged.

Nyah suddenly jumped in, "She knows what a rave is. She's just being annoying." I glared at Mina, frustrated with my own gullibility.

"Oops, sorry. I never introduced myself. I'm Nyah, by the way."

"That's actually my bad," Mina explained. "I should've done the introducing, and I'm sure I would've, had you not jumped on me and thrown me completely off my manners earlie—"

"You must be Oliver." I caught Mina pinching Nyah. I raised my eyebrows in surprise. *How much does this girl already know about me?* My curiosity spiked. "I mean, I haven't heard, I'm just assuming you're— *Yeow!* Anyway, so, yeah, just our luck!" She ignored me again and turned completely back in Mina's direction. "They made it eighteen and over this year because some girl ruined it for everyone last year. She just had to be super extra and overdose on E and die."

"Nyah!"

"What? Do I look like a monster? Like, RIP, and no offense, of course!"

"I don't know. You just don't sound like yourself right now. But, okay, so how do you plan on going to this thing, then? A fake?" Mina asked.

"We. How do we plan on going?" Nyah corrected her. "I'm glad you asked. Remember Kierra?"

"No," Mina answered with zero enthusiasm.

"Knows every lyric to every rap song Kierra?"

"No."

"Eats jalapeños like candy Kierra?"

"No. What about her?"

Nyah wasn't a quitter. "Pushed that guy who didn't get 'no means no' into the bonfire this summer Kierra?"

"Okay, yeah. What about her?"

It was like I wasn't there at the table the way they were talking to each other—like I'd been discreetly beamed up to my starship. But I didn't mind. It gave me a chance to observe Mina—to get a sense of what she was really like with someone who knew her really well.

"Kierra's cousin's friend's boyfriend lives next to the lady who hires the dancers and contortionists for the company that throws the raves. Kierra said she can hook us up with audition slots, easy. Isn't that sick? That means if they hire us—which they will 'cause we rock—we get all-access tickets to the rave and get to be on stage with the biggest DJs in the world! I know, right? Doesn't it sound incredible?"

"It sounds incredible. I can already picture having that convo with my mom. 'A rave, Minachka? Yes, great idea. You totally going, here are pasties and please, don't forgetting to having the fun!'" Mina exaggerated a thick Eastern European accent.

"I mean . . . yeah, well, minus the pasties, that's probably what she'll say, isn't it? What? You were being sarcastic? No way! Since when? Lily's the best! Now, my parents—there's a hopeless case. I was actually planning on telling them I'm staying over with you," said Nyah.

So Mina's mom's name was Lily. The name automatically triggered memories of my last foster home back in Lily of the Valley. Julie's little face resurfaced first; I took a big gulp of the ice water in an attempt to swallow the images away, yet they still rushed in with impressive force. Breanne's rare smile, Miss Piss laughing at all my lame jokes and making me feel like I was worth a damn even though I wasn't, and Franky just being the other body in my room, giving me mysterious anti-loneliness protection. I push back against the memories, afraid to drown in them, but it was too late. Remi's face surfaced—a vivid ghost. Maybe I should've called her, to see how she was? *No, I'm nothing. She has real family. She can talk to them.*

I focused in on Mina's voice and it brought me back to the present. "Yeah, so . . . I don't know. She's just been hovering over me like that lately. She's been freaked out because of what she . . . um, saw on the news, and showing me all these clips nonstop, warning me about every little thing. I just doubt she'd let me go." Mina didn't say more, which I was guessing means she hadn't told her best friend about what happened to her that day in the alley.

"She'll let you go if you explain that it's a legit performance. They'll be paying us, so it's all totally professional. You can show her the money, and everything—just don't tell her it's a rave. Seriously, how will she ever find out? It'll be fine, I promise. Okay, so, auditions are next Saturday at eleven downtown. I'll text you the info. All right, I'm out. I'll leave you two to—*haha*, I mean, I should go 'cause grumpy dude's mad-dogging me from over there." She gave Mina a big smooch. "*Mwah.* Bye. Nice to meet you, Oliver."

"Same." The girl was a force of nature, that was for sure. I don't think she'd stopped to take a breath for the entire time she'd been at the table.

I stood. I read somewhere that a man should stand when a woman left or arrived at a table. But I regretted it as soon as I did, because it felt like a weird thing to do, and also, I didn't want Mina to think anything of it. Plus, I bet that those two would have gotten annoyed by some old-school move from the patriarchal past.

"Oh, are you going to the bathroom? You can walk me out . . ."

"No, I—" Before I could sit back down, though, Nyah suddenly hugged me goodbye.

"Oh! You just wanted a hug," she said. I turned to Mina, who looked amused but conflicted. "It's like I already know you." Nyah stepped back and her face grew serious. "Mina's special, Oliver. You want to be her friend? Treat her nicely and keep her out of trouble," Nyah warned.

"I can do that," I assured her.

"Okay! Love ya, bye," Mina insisted. Nyah bounced away.

"It's like she's connected to a Red Boost slushy IV," I remarked. "So, really? She knew who I was already? How much did you tell her about me?"

"Mostly the bad stuff. You know, kind of an asshole with major mood swings, treats me like shit when he's having a bad day. Yadda, yadda."

"Yeah, I figured."

A waitress came by with my sandwich. Mina asked her, "Excuse me? Can we also get a backgammon board, please?" The waitress nodded.

"Looking for some competitive tension, are you?" I teased.

"Scared?"

"Of a little backgammon? Nah. How hard can it be? But why backgammon?"

"When in Rome—" Mina responded.

"What's Rome got to do with it? That's where you learned to play?"

"No, it's like the expression: 'When in Rome, do as the Romans do.' But we're in a *shisha* bar, so like, 'When in a *shisha* bar, do as the OG *shisha* smokers do.' Get it?"

She lost me halfway. My mind went somewhere else when I noticed the glow of her skin along her cheekbone. I imagined tracing the curves of her face down the soft skin past her jawline and down to her neck with my fingers. Then I replaced my imaginary fingers with my lips traced the same path down her neck. I pictured grazing the skin of her shoulder with my teeth, a soft bite that almost tickled, then a harder one as I kept going down her arm and reached the skin on her wrist, then palm, and then the pads of her fingertips. *Chill out, Oli. Focus.* What were we talking about, again? *Backgammon.*

"Yeah, don't worry, I'm a quick learner. Plus, I've played a couple games online against the computer when I was like thirteen," I told her.

"Good, so you won't mind if we make it interesting?" She tilted her chin down but foxily kept her luminous eyes on me.

"How?" I asked as the waitress returned with a backgammon set.

Mina opened it and began setting up as she explained. "Each time either of us is hit during the game—that happens if I roll the dice and one of my pieces lands on yours, or if you roll the dice and one of your pieces lands on mine . . ." she explained.

"Okay, what do you want to happen every time you land on me or I land on you? I don't think Jo's gonna be okay with a game of strip backgammon, do you?"

She laughed. "No, not stripping. What is that, the theme of the day? If either of us gets hit during the game, the person that gets hit has to reveal something—something like a story or a fact about themselves. Something that we don't know about each other yet—kind of like a secret."

"Why?" I asked. The last thing I wanted to do was play emotional roulette.

"Because I can tell that talking about yourself is something that makes you uncomfortable." She smiled again. "And I'm all about getting people out of their comfort zones."

"All right, let's play. Which direction do my pieces move again?" She motioned counterclockwise. "Oh yeah, it's all coming back to me now."

Mina came out swinging with a roll of double threes and started building a defense by the gates of her home board. Her moves were smart but predictable. My turn—I rolled a five-three. Unlike her, I didn't play by the book. Instead of building my own defense, I did something crazy and moved my checkers out of her home board, leaving them open and completely vulnerable to get hit. I could tell she was an ace-point game kind of girl, so I knew my move would bother her.

"Wait, what are you doing?" she asked.

"Playing."

"That move is so suboptimal that I can't even let you make it. You want some advice?" she asked.

"No, that's okay. I know I could've built my defense. I like to take the road less traveled."

"The road less traveled, like the Frost poem?"

"The road less traveled, like the choices I'm going to make during this game. They aren't going to make any sense and it's gonna frustrate the hell out of you—just a warning."

It took me a couple of rolls to get the hang of the game and remember all the rules. As we continued to play, though, I could see Mina realizing that kicking my ass wasn't going to be the piece of cake she thought it was. My moves were unpredictable, irrational. Sometimes, I played by the book, and then randomly threw in a surprise move when I felt like it and offered up my pieces to be hit without protecting them using my other pieces. What was really driving her nuts was that while my pieces were completely exposed, I kept getting lucky and the dice wouldn't give her the numbers she needed to hit my open pieces.

"Beginner's luck is an understatement when it comes to you," she complained, frustrated.

I'd backed her into a corner. No matter what, she'd have to leave two of her checkers vulnerable and I would be able to hit them. It was like an electric current was running through my fingers as I picked up the dice. I needed to roll a six or a one.

God, or Lady Luck ... either one, or both—whoever's listening, really— give me a six or a one, please. Actually, if you really can hear me ... I don't ask for much, do I? Just a six, and a one.

"You've got a concentration unibrow," Mina commented. "Chill out. This isn't life or death, Oli, and I'm the one with my pieces on the chopping block—"

I released the dice before she could finish. They danced across the smooth wooden surface of the board and landed on a six and a one. My heart rate spiked. I threw my hands in the air, truly surprised. Oh shit, I could actually hit both of her pieces—that was two secrets! But if I did that, then I'd have to face the consequences—two of my own pieces would be exposed. I could just hit one of hers, pull a pick, and pass. That should have guaranteed safety for all my pieces and still counted as a win. But my hand moved on its own, serving my reckless, greedy nature and paying no mind to repercussions. I hit both of her checkers and put them on the bar in the center of the board where she'd have to start over from the beginning. I looked up at her and stated the obvious: "You owe me two secrets." Her eyes grew wide— she was still processing what had just happened. Catching her off guard felt good. I didn't think she was ready to reveal a single secret to me, let alone two. Had she really been that sure she could beat me at backgammon? Her lips were parted like she was unsure of what to say. I wanted to press my mouth against the curves of her plush lips. *Stop it. Just focus on her eyes.*

She laughed a constricted, nervous laugh. "You want two secrets so badly that you've left both of your pieces completely exposed?"

"I'm just playing the game; you made the rules. Don't stress, Mina. It's not life or death, remember? No rush—one secret at a time." I tugged lightly on the *shisha* hose. "Hand that *shisha* over to me. You won't be needing it while you're revealing your deepest and darkest." I grinned.

She smiled back, confidently, and started with the first secret, "Okay. Relish. I can't stand relish. Hate it, actually. Not sure why. Always have, always will."

I stared at her blankly. "Relish?"

"Relish." She smiled like she thought she was gonna get away with that lame-ass "secret."

"As in the hotdog condiment?"

"Yep."

"That's your secret?"

"Yep."

"You call that 'revealing yourself, getting out of your comfort zone'? All right, cool . . . easy. I can come up with a thousand facts like that about me," I said.

"Hold your horses. I was just joking, buying time to think. You'll have to excuse me; I didn't expect to be sharing first. I honestly thought I was gonna wipe the floor with you, but you're lucky as hell," she said.

"Skilled. Skilled as hell," I disputed.

"Yeah, yeah. Okay, let me see," she hesitated, opening and closing her mouth a few times, like she was unsure where to begin or how to say what she was about to say, but then she finally committed to something. "One of the main things I remember about when I was little is how much time my mom spent with me. We were together, just the two of us, almost every minute of the day. My father worked a lot, she didn't have any help because my grandparents still live in Sochi—that's a city in Russia. The thing about my mom—what made her different than most—is that despite the fact that I really was just a little kid, she always treated me with the respect you give an adult. She always behaved like I was her equal—her friend. So she'd ask for my opinion about a decision she had to make, or my advice in regard to an issue she was having. I didn't know at the time that what she was doing was something extraordinary. To me, she was just being my mom, you know? I really love that about her—anyway, so that's a little something to make up for the whole 'I hate relish' thing. So, that's the first one and the second one . . ." she made a labored exhale.

That explained a lot. It explained how she was so confident and steady. She'd been told that she mattered, that her opinions mattered, that her voice mattered, from the day she was born. Her long eyelashes fluttered when she was uneasy. Her eyes became glassy and fixed on a point inside her mind—her memories. She was looking for a secret. As soon as she found it, she looked at me with quiet horror in her expressive gaze.

"And, um, for the second one . . . well, she was pregnant once when I was little. I had no clue at first—I mean, not until I finally noticed how protectively she held her belly. She told me I came up to her—I think I was around five or something—and finally asked her, 'Mama, what are you hiding in your tummy?' She laughed; she thought it was funny, and she cupped my face, got really close, and whispered back, 'Your sister.' Somehow, I understood, even though I was just a child.

"Her belly started to show, and so did my excitement. I couldn't wait to have a sister and h-h-hold her in m-my—" Mina's eyes were brimming with tears as she stared off at the wall. It hurt me to see her in pain, like the time in the alley.

"I couldn't wait to play with her—teach her things. I couldn't wait to meet her. But my mom ended up having a miscarriage. The baby died. I never got to meet my sister. Anyway, I guess I still carry that. So that's my secret number two."

She wiped the tears off her cheeks, and her face went blank. She was shutting off her feelings; the tears stopped like she had cut off the water supply or something. Mina regretted it—telling me. I could read it off her face and in her body. I should've let her leave it at relish and kept it light. But she came up with the game herself, and she was the one who decided to get super personal. God, I was shit at being supportive or whatever. I had no clue what I was supposed to say or do.

We both heaved a big sigh at exactly the same time, which we both found funny, and thank God, because it lightened the mood. Without thinking, I reached out and tucked a loose strand of hair behind her ear, cupped her face, and stroked her cheek with my thumb. After I realized what I had just done, my mind filled with thoughts like: *Is this too much? Should I hug her? Should I pull my hand away?* My heart pounded hard. I leaned forward and left a kiss meant for her cheek. It landed somewhere else, though—not her mouth, but near enough that the corners of our lips were almost touching. I drew back. Our eyes locked and something clicked, like . . . *it's okay.* She didn't lean away or move away. She was there, closer than we'd ever been. The way she was looking at me—she was so steady. She seemed so sure of herself. I loved that about her—it was my favorite part. I needed to learn from it.

I wanted to be close to her all the time. I don't think I'd ever wanted anything else that much. It was a dangerous thing for me to know what I wanted. I wanted freedom, and, against all odds, won it. My body flooded with an unexpected feeling of warmth that made the hairs on my arms stand. My insides were melting. It was a strange sensation, the thawing of a frozen heart.

Just then, a grating, vibrating sound interrupted our silence. I tried to cling to the moment, but Mina had already broken our eye contact. As soon as the vibrating finally stopped, it started all over again. *The moment's over.* Mina looked in her bag, but I knew it was my phone that was ringing, not hers. I pulled it out of my pocket and checked the caller ID . . . it was Tee. *Crap—he better not be calling to cancel our meet.*

"What's up?"

"You're late," Tee complained, agitated.

"Late? It's two o'clock right now. We agreed on eight."

"Oh, yeah. All right," he said, and hung up.

What the hell, Tee? I murmured to myself. "Sorry about that—"

Mina began digging through her bag frantically and finally yanked out her phone. She turned it back on in a panic, shaking it, like that was going to make whatever she was afraid of go away. Her eyes went wide when she saw something pop up on the screen.

"Shit! Is it seriously two o'clock? How does time fly like that? It was just—ugh, never mind. Shit! We have to go right now! I mean, please? I'm sorry, I mean, please can we go?"

"What is it?"

"I completely forgot about my mom. She picks me up from school now, and I forgot, like a complete idiot. She's gonna be there in like ten minutes—"

"Just call her—"

"I can't! I don't know what to say yet, so I can't lie—she'll know I'm lying. She'll kill me for ditching, and if she sees me on your bike, she'll really lose it. She might freak out enough to make us leave town again, this time to who knows where."

"Mina, calm down. Let's just call her. I'll take the blame for everything and say it was my idea—"

"No way, that won't work. She'll think I'm being disrespectful if I let you talk to her instead of me—"

"You're the one who said your mom treats you like an adult and listens to your thoughts and opinions or whatever, so I thought maybe it wouldn't be such a big deal and she'd get it if you just explain—"

"I said she *used* to. And please don't do that. Don't throw my own words back in my face like that."

"I'm not, I'm sorry—"

"I'll tell her myself in my own way. It has to come from me, okay? Let's just head back quickly, I'll text her something vague in the meantime and I'll figure out what to tell her once I get back. Let's just go." She waved down a waitress. "Can we have the check, please?"

"No need. Here." I got up, handed the girl a hundred dollar bill, and gestured to Mina: *Let's go.* She didn't budge.

"What are you doing? The bill won't be more than fifty bucks, tip included."

"Well, I don't have smaller bills on me. It's not a big deal, let's just go—"

"No way. Look, it's my fault. I'm sorry. I overreacted. Here, I'm literally texting my mom right now and telling her I'm gonna be late." Mina typed something into her phone while addressing the waitress at the same time. "Can you please bring us the change? I'm sorry for the rush and for the confusion." She found her wallet in her bag and held out twenty-five dollars, offering it to me. I shook my head, refusing to take it. She folded it and shoved it in my back pocket anyway.

"Here you go." Jo came back with the change instead of the waitress. "Everything okay? What's the rush, you two?"

"Later, Jo—thanks for everything." Mina offered no explanation to Jo, who arched his brow as she rushed past him. He narrowed his eyes at me. I shrugged and told him thanks.

I ran out after Mina, disappointed in myself but unsure of why. I'd probably messed everything up. Seems like that's what I always did in the end.

CHAPTER 9

MINA

Have you ever felt two strong yet opposing emotions take over your conscience at once? That was what I was feeling right then on the back of Oliver's bike as he pulsed through traffic like the line on a heart monitor screen. I was lightheaded, and a sensation of weightlessness had overcome my body. He had kissed my cheek. Was he attracted to me? Or did he just feel sorry for me after the dead baby sister story?

Anxiety filled me as I imagined Mama's growing fear for me. Texting her was starting to feel like a huge mistake. She'd probably just pulled up to school. She could've been calling me right that moment; but it wasn't like I could pick up a phone while we flew down the freeway at seventy miles an hour. What would I say? Why hadn't I been answering? At first, I couldn't help but think she just wouldn't get it—she wouldn't understand why I ditched school with Oliver. But now that I'd had some time to consider what I was going to tell her, I realized he was right. I should've just called her, even if only to tell a lie—to say I had forgotten she was picking me up and started walking home from school. But I was afraid—afraid to get caught in a lie, afraid to tell the truth. She'd be pissed for sure, but maybe I could even have been able to finish hanging out with Oliver. Or maybe she might have driven over there and dragged me out of the *shisha* bar by my ear. That was the problem: She was unpredictable, that woman. As cool as she could be, she could also be extremely harsh. All I knew was that if I got caught in a lie, she'd punish me, and worse, she might never trust me again. I got a tighter grip on Oliver, praying we made it back in one piece. *She'd kill me if I die on this thing.*

"Thanks for getting us back so fast—thank God there was no traffic. Okay, I'm gonna run. Sorry about all this," I added quietly as I climbed off the back of his bike and we had pulled up around the side corner of the school, hidden from the main street by a wall. I wondered what was waiting for me around the corner. I dug through my bag for my phone.

"You don't have to apologize to me. I have some business to take care of in Hollywood anyway, so I should get going. Don't worry, though, and let me know how it goes." He smiled reassuringly.

I handed back the helmet. "I'm scared," I admitted through a suppressed chuckle.

"It'll be okay. Just picture the worst thing that can happen. Go ahead, really picture it."

I did. I pictured Mama dragging me into the car by my hair in front of Oliver and driving me far away so that I never got to see him again.

"So whatever it was, it's going to be better than that," he said. Strangely, I was comforted. Part of me wanted to stay there and talk to him forever. I wondered what sort of business he'd needed to handle in Hollywood. My fingers finally found my phone in the bottom corner of my bag. After I smiled goodbye, I walked away from Oliver as I pulled it out and took a look. *Oh, God.* Thirty-six missed calls and four voice mails. I was only nineteen minutes late! *Had she texted me back?* I opened the text message box between Mama and me. *Oh no. Oh, shit!* I stopped dead in my tracks as I processed the red exclamation mark next to my message and the red "Not Delivered" sign under it. *What the hell?* I threw the phone in my bag, and broke into a sprint, realizing Mama must have been losing her shit with worry.

I rounded the corner and kept running until I reached the main entrance of the school. A lump formed in my throat as soon as I saw Mama sitting on the curb, holding her head in her hands, clutching her phone against her forehead, surrounded by several administrators and school security. Words couldn't describe the utter fear on her face as she got up and started to argue with one of them about something. *Oh, Mina . . . what have you done?*

Some of the administrators saw me running toward them and pointed. Mama turned to look. As soon as her eyes found mine, there was this beautiful serenity that overcame her; she'd been relieved of an unbearable burden. It made me run faster, and I didn't stop until I was in her arms. She held me like a baby, rocking me back and forth, and gasped for breath as she pressed her wet cheek into mine.

"*Spasiba. Slava Bogu. Slava Bogu,*" she thanked God.

"Mamachka, *prasti.* I sent you a message, a text message."

"What kind of messaging? I was calling you for a hundreds of times, Mina!" I felt like a pile of garbage. It wasn't worth it—the date, any of it. I should've called. Why didn't I just call?

"I'm so, so sorry Mamachka, that I wasn't able to pick up your calls. I was—" But I just couldn't say it, especially not in front of all of those administrators. I'd tell her the truth later, when we were alone. "I walked home and forgot—so, the calls . . . my phone died while I was walking back here. That's why I couldn't pick up. I guess I must've—I didn't plug it into the charger properly last night. I completely forgot that you were gonna pick me up. I wanted to call but I saw that my phone had only one percent battery life left, and—" The moment was gone, and her face morphed from exhaustion, relief, and confusion to sheer anger.

"Jesus, Mina! Just a one phone call could saving your mother from the heart attack. You can borrowing a phone or going to a pay phone, anything!"

"I'm sorry! I just assumed my text went through—"

"*Ne vri.*" Mama warned me not to lie to her.

"*Ya skazhu tebe vso v mashine, abishayu,*" I promised to tell her everything in the car.

There was silence—it was broken by one of the administrators, a reed-thin woman in a pantsuit and gaudy oversized glasses. "Excuse me, young lady. You say you walked home after school, but all of your teachers say you were absent, and Mr. Chavez saw you jump a fence with another student during second period," said the no-nonsense kind of woman, who may have been our principal or vice principal. She gestured to the security guard, who I guessed must have been Mr. Chavez.

My heart thudded as I wove my next lie. I scanned the vicinity for security cameras. There were none. *He doesn't have proof that it was me; it could've been anyone.* I addressed the security guard. "Me? You say you saw me jumping a fence? What? That fence?" I pointed to the metallic perimeter bordering the campus—he nodded. "That thing is fifteen feet high! I don't know who you saw, but it wasn't me. It's not possible. I'm terrified of heights, and I don't know how to climb a fence. You're mixing me up with someone else, sir. I've been feeling very sick all day today, spent almost the whole day in the bathroom—"

"Why didn't you go to the nurse's office?" asked the woman.

"I was planning on it, but the bathroom was closer. I kept thinking that it'd get better in five minutes and if it didn't then I'll go—didn't want to make a big deal out of nothing. But you know how it is, once you get settled in a comfortable position, you don't want to move. No? No one?"

"That's ridiculous. You look absolutely fine to me."

"My stomach was hurting, then it finally stopped—it's my period. I felt better, so I walked home . . . like I already said," I explained, almost convincing myself of this new narrative.

"Come Mina, let's going to home," Mama said. Her tone was cold. I knew she was deeply disappointed.

"Excuse me, ma'am, we need to continue the dialogue about this incident. Firstly, we should have a discussion in my office about the men who you thought took her, as you said, 'under our nose,' and why these men would do that. Secondly, now that we've spoken to her and established that she is safe, we must address her absence. She absolutely cannot go unpunished for truancy."

Mama feigned confusion. "This men? No. I've been clearly mistaking. It's because we were having the scary incident recently with a some men who we were not recognizing, and they were following us one time a few days ago from the store after they just trying to stealing my purse, and I did not letting it go. So they following us while we driving to the whole way home. And we calling to cops but they leaving already. I have been afraid and kind of a paranoia from this time. But you heard it what my daughter has explaining. She having a stomach pain, she was waiting in a bathroom until this pain subsiding, and she walking home and coming back when she realizing I was been waiting for her here—that's all whole dialogue. Thank you please for your helping me. Goodbye." Mama grabbed my arm and led me to the car.

I broke the silence on the way home.

"*Mamachka, prosti.*" I asked for her forgiveness.

"*Prosti*? I was thinking that I can never see you again—that those men just taking you t-to . . . finished the job on you. You almost killed me today, Mina," her hands shook as she gripped the steering wheel.

"*Prosti menya.* I can't believe I forgot you were gonna pick me up."

"You forgetting everything today, like information that *tvoya* mama is no idiot. Mina, your *menstruatzia* has never causing you the stomachache in your life, the last thing on a planet you are fearing is a heights, plus you climbing any fence in the sleeping mode if necessary because you climbing even from your crib at a one years old to just getting some water. Maybe I can let you to lie to this people and your teachers. But this only for not to ruining the education you working all your life so hard. I will always putting your school reputation in front of everything else, but you don't ever think to lying with me like this way again, *slishish?* Now, open you ears to me very careful; I will only asking to you this one single time." Mama hadn't been this angry at me since . . . in a very long time. "One time, do you understanding me?" I nodded quickly, startled. "Where have you been?" she almost growled.

"Okay, the truth is that there was a field trip today. I forgot to get the permission slip signed, so I was sent to the library. Oliver stayed behind too, and we snuck out and went for a hike in the hills. I'm sorry for lying. I was scared you'd get mad. By the time I remembered you were going to pick me up, it was too late to get back on time, and I really did text you that I'd be late, but I guess there was a glitch and it didn't go through—"

"Enough," she said in a dry, sharp tone. I knew better than to argue.

We drove in silence. The only sounds were the muffled Los Angeles traffic through thick window glass and the hum of the air conditioner.

"This is a my fault," she said suddenly. "I creating this problem by myself because I always have been letting you do whatever you want—dressing whatever you want, making you own decisions, giving a weight for your opinion, closing both my eyes to when you talking back to me. Your *babushka* always warning me about it that I am too much a liberal with you. She was saying, 'It's seeming like harmless for now, but you will ending up in many tears one day.' I just always ignoring her because I was not wanting to be as a strict and very much unreasonable as she was to me . . . but it's turning into she was right." Mama's eyes sparked with anger, her tone turning dark. "Don't worrying, Mina. One thing I am knowing for sure is it is never late for teaching a some discipline."

That was a threat if I had ever heard one; if things didn't change, I'd be sorry. My heart began to race, but I kept my mouth shut.

"Ditching again the school, skip all classes for what? For the boy? This just a loser move—not a serious person move. A girls who's easy doing this kinds of stuff. This behavior not matching for you, Mina. Think carefully about it, because if you just saying bye-bye to every goals and dreams you had and all responsibilities and later, the boy is deciding, 'Hmmm . . . no, I don't like this girl with a zero future.' What will then be left for you, Mina? A nothing."

Geez Louise. I couldn't keep quiet any longer. "Okay, I think you're making more out of this than it is. True, I messed up, but it's just one day, and—"

"Enough from you. Now I will talking. You will just shutting your mouth and listening to me. From now, you will living your life to my rules. A rules that beginning and ending with my word. My word is a law not a question. You will be dressing what I want—with a no questions or arguing. You will be attending each single class each single day and being on time, always, no matter what happens. Not one single excuse note for the absence will be coming from me. All those privilege was for adult person, and it is becoming very much clear that this is a child in this car, so I will treating you as one. And your dancing? Never again during the school time and putting the limit to four times per week."

"Fine! Whatever you want," I rolled my eyes at her bylaws.

"Phone . . ." She held her hand out without looking at me as she continued to drive.

"What?" She couldn't be serious.

"Give to me your phone." She was serious. "Mina—"

I placed the phone in her open palm, crossed my arms, and turned away from her. We didn't say another word to each other the rest of the way. I was livid and humiliated. Yes, I should have called her—how frustrating was the clarity of hindsight? I also knew that she would've been pissed no matter what. And yes, she was doing the right thing—the mom thing. I deserved those regulations. I should have been grateful, really—but in the moment, I was just angry.

As soon as we got home, I ran upstairs and slammed the door to my room, locking myself away from the person I loved most. It was a childish move and something I never thought I'd have stooped to. Boy, had I regressed! I thudded down on my bed, competing with Mr. Gerald for Drama Queen of the Year, and stuffed my face into my pillow, screaming away the frustration and self-hate at the top of my lungs, all the while wondering if I were only doing it because of the movies. Still, it felt good... for about five seconds. *Great—now what?* I was stuck up there. I couldn't believe I was missing that night's Jazz Funk at the studio, led by guest choreographer Zeek, winner of Norway's Favorite Dancer last year. I had watched the whole season on StreamSite and used to follow him back when I still used social media. His routines were insanely creative. I'd been looking forward to taking his class since it was announced in the monthly news blast.

Sprawled on my back on the bed, I stared at the blank, beige walls of my room—no posters, no ballerina globes, no generic artwork reprints. I had never thought there was a point; with a schedule like mine, there was hardly ever time to stare at walls. Music would make the confinement more bearable—something loud and rebellious—but she'd take it away just to make a point. I sat up, threw some headphones on, and connected them to my laptop. It'd be a silent rebellion. I migrated from Black Sabbath to Procol Harum too quickly and both started and finished the big ten-page assignment for AP Gov, which wasn't due until finals week in December. I considered texting Oliver or Nyah through my cloud messenger, but I didn't really feel like talking right then. Besides, everything I did on my laptop would be mirrored on my phone, and she knew my passcodes. I couldn't risk pissing her off and getting my laptop confiscated too—it was the only thing keeping me from going insane. I drifted off to sleep ten minutes into an abysmal romantic comedy without having dinner and, technically, no lunch either.

At some point late at night, I woke up to the sound of a wailing ambulance siren and an ache in my rumbling stomach. My alarm clock said it was 3:00 a.m. It was pitch black outside my window. I tiptoed downstairs even though Mama was a heavy sleeper and it took a lot to wake her. I inhaled a salami sandwich and brought a second one back upstairs with me. I gave the rom-com a second chance, but those two had less sizzle than Ashley Greene and Jackson Rathbone. Twenty minutes in, I finally submitted to exhaustion and drifted off again.

My morning alarm tried to wake me, but I snoozed it and kept sleeping. My body felt too heavy to move. I eventually turned the alarm off altogether, and the next time I opened my eyes, it was one o'clock in the afternoon. I couldn't believe I'd slept through so much of the weekend. I wondered if Mama'd been in here to check on me. Was she still mad? Of course she was.

I stretched out my body, bringing life back into my fingers and toes. I finished my morning routine in the bathroom and tiptoed down the stairs. *Why am I tiptoeing again?*

Mama was in the kitchen. I came in offering an apologetic smile, but she stood with her back to me by the dishwasher and didn't turn as I walked over. She didn't look at me or say a word. I tried to hug her, but it was awkward and unreciprocated.

"Good morning, Mamachka . . . or afternoon, technically. How did you sleep?"

She didn't answer. The silence hurt my feelings even though I'd expected as much. I made breakfast in silence. She continued to load the dishwasher quietly. It was a cold and uncomfortable start to the day. After I ate, I went out onto the balcony where Mama was drinking coffee.

"Mamachka, it's nice outside, perfect for a hike—shall we go?"

She turned her face to me slowly and her eyes said it all. "No. This is not how it will be. You will asking me. 'May I go to the hiking with you, please?' Not telling me what you want and saying 'Let's go,' no. You will be asking always just for a permission."

This is getting ridiculous. But I did as she said. "Mamachka, may I go hiking with you?"

"No. Go to upstairs. Go into your room and stay there. You are a punished. You have a many things to do for the house: you have to washing a laundry, making floors of your bathroom a shiny, vacuuming the room. Just open your eyes and look around a house what needing to be done and then do it."

"Okay, I'll do all that, no problem, but maybe while the sun is still—"

"No. Stop a talking."

"But I—"

"Just shutting up, please. Open the ears to me and I will repeating for last time. Go to upstairs and wash everything that's need washing. Go."

That's messed up. I turned and went inside. I stormed up to my room and shut the door aggressively. Then I began to make my way through her entire list with dogged determination: the laundry, the bedsheets, the bathroom, and even the dust. I vacuumed and then I mopped. I made pasta for lunch and brought some to Mama. Again, she said nothing. But she did nod, which told me I'd made a small step in the right direction. After I finished washing the windows in my room, I went down and did the balcony doors. My back ached as I looked out across the cloudless sky; the sun was on its way to setting. It was probably around a quarter to six and it was starting to get chilly. I was in the middle of mopping the balcony floors when Mama walked out.

"This is inside mop, not outside mop. You just making this mop very dirty and unusable for house. Did you asking me permission to using this mop for outside? Did you asking me, 'Mama, is there exists a special mop you using for a balcony?' No. You just doing whatever you like, same as before. So, you just learning nothing from yesterday. Now, you will taking this mop you ruin and take a bucket . . . go to outside and washing it with a water from hose and soap from a laundry using also a very small amount of bleach," she commanded coldly. I shook my head.

"I'm sorry—"

"Sorry? What can I do with all this sorry you giving me? Nothing. For you, say sorry is like making a pee—too easy." She was absolutely unbelievable. "Go." *She has no idea what most daughters are like. The ones I know don't execute a single command their parents give, let alone do every single little freaking thing they are told, like I always have. Why is she being like this to me—after one mistake? It's not fair.*

"Did you hearing me? Maybe you brain not working so much anymore after the boy coming into your life?"

Enough.

"Screw this." I dropped the mop and moved to leave the balcony, but she grabbed my wrist and held me in place.

"What you saying to me?" she tightened her grip.

"Don't touch me." I yanked my arm free, got inside, and stormed back upstairs. I ran into Mama's room and grabbed my phone off her nightstand. Back in my room, I quickly changed into my dance clothes—threw on a grey hoodie, pulled the first pair of jeans I could find over my dance shorts, and slipped into my black combat boots, remembering it'd been a little chilly at night lately. I couldn't find my dance bag anywhere, so I ran downstairs and searched around the living room for it.

"You not leaving this house, Mina." I looked up to find Mama holding my dance bag. "Not to the dance class even."

"This is bullshit! I did everything you said . . . more, even . . . but all you do is go ballistic over a stupid mop and make me feel worthless. I've been trying so hard to make up for my mistake but apparently nothing's good enough for you, and no amount of effort on my part is going to change that. I can't breathe in this house . . . I'm suffocating. Give me my bag."

"You will not make a one single move without my permission. I do not letting you go to the dance class today—"

"Screw it. Screw dance, keep the bag. I can't stay here, I'm sorry." I bolted out the door and run across the wet lawn.

I didn't look back or slow down. For now, I wasn't thinking—I was reacting. Running. I made sporadic lefts and rights on small, random streets to take a route unfamiliar to Mama, in case she followed me.

I picked up the pace even more as I passed the halfway mark between my house and the dance studio, but a sharp pain spiked in the right side of my rib cage. I clutched it and stopped to catch my breath, looking around to see if I was being followed. There was no one there.

I walked the rest of the way, clutching my side. *Mother Nature, is this what I get for lying about having menstrual cramps?* Luckily, the pain was slowly subsiding. My phone buzzed and a text came in. It was from Oliver—his name shone in bright white letters across my phone screen. I traced it with my finger and then opened the message.

Mina, all good?

Well if that wasn't the $64,000 question. Then I noticed there were a couple more texts from him above this one. I guessed that they'd come in late the night before and then a few earlier that morning.

hey havnt heard frm you, everything go ok?

morning

. . . ?

startin to wonder if she rly did make u pack up&leave town

My heart rate accelerated; my stomach turned. I hated my body's natural reaction to him. I reread the most recent message: **Mina, all good?** **Yes**, I typed, but something stopped me from sending it. I wanted to see him—that night. I deleted the reply and instead said **Not exactly. Can you meet me later?**

He replied almost immediately. *sure where?*

I exhaled, basking in the elation of potentially seeing him.

I'm gonna be at my dance studio on Cristi Ln between Santa Cruz and N Palm st.

wat time? he asked.

pretty much now I'm almost there. See you after?

for sure.

K I'll text you.

I began to jog again, groaning when I realized how crappy I must look. I hadn't even gotten a chance to freshen up after cleaning all day. I slowed down, looked around for signs of Mama following me again, then texted Nyah. **Nybear, do you have emergency kit on you? You going to 6:30 jazz?** There were a bunch of unanswered, old texts from Nyah that must have come in last night as well. I'd explain everything in person.

hey is evrything ok? missed u last night . . . Yeah I do and duh I am!

Thanks, see you soon and I'll explain.

Okay, good. I made a right on Cristi Lane and jogged half a block, and my phone started buzzing again—Mama was calling.

I slowed down and picked up, looking around again. "Mama, I'm fine. I am safe but I just need some space."

"*Ya sechas tebe pakaju* 'space'! *Ty polnost'yu soshla s uma chtoli—*" I ended the call and winced. She was gonna kill me. *But I need to do this,* I kept telling myself—though I knew it wasn't completely true. I was a liar and a drama queen—I'd become my own pet peeves.

Regardless, I walked into the studio and headed to reception to sign in.

"There she is," my favorite soprano voice called out behind me. I turned to find Nyah's everlasting grin, but it faded into a cringe. "Did you break up with your hairbrush? Oh, Mina, you've seen better days. Actually, this makes me feel better about you not texting me back last night."

"That's messed up," I laughed, my eyes filling with the tears I'd been suppressing since Mama berated me over a mop.

"Aw, boo . . . come here—tell Nybear what happened."

"I'm okay."

"Come here," she walked toward me, opening her tiny arms.

"I messed up." I didn't know what it was about Nyah's hug, but it opened the floodgates to the worst kind of tears—tears of frustration and self-pity.

"Oh, okay, no. Shh . . . no, please don't cry out here. BB three, hello?" She dragged me to the bathroom.

(BB three: *noun* \'bē-(,)bē\: Badass Bitch. Rule N°3: No crying in public. Ever.)

Nyah and I made those rules when we were still in middle school. It sounded a lot more legit back then. I didn't know why she still insisted on quoting them. I collapsed to the floor by the far wall of the bathroom. Nyah sat by me, performing a clumsy combination of hair stroking and back patting.

"What happened, bae? I haven't seen you like this since your dad left. Did something happen with your dad?"

"No. It's me. I really screwed up, Nyah. I keep screwing up. My mom is so mad at me—"

"I know. She called me. I've never heard her like that, Mina—"

"She called you? What did you tell her?"

"I told her you weren't here and that I didn't know where you were, which was the truth. That was right before you texted me."

"After what I did today, leaving the house like that . . . I don't know how she's ever gonna—"

"Calm down. Just walk me through what happened."

"You know how I ditched with Oliver? Well, she found out. Right after you left, I remembered she was gonna be there at school waiting to pick me up. It completely slipped my mind because, you know, I usually get home on my own. By the time I got there, it was too late; she was with a bunch of administrators in a state of total panic. She thought I had been kidnapped or something—"

"Why didn't you just call her?"

I sighed.

"Yes, I know I should have called her. Anyway, later, in the car, she completely exploded on me after I told her the truth about where I was. Then she just went military with all these new rules and regulations. She took my phone, by the way, that's why I didn't pick up any of your calls or texts."

"Makes sense," Nyah said.

"I spent the whole day trying to make it up to her, cooking and cleaning. I did everything she said. But it was like she was dead set on making me feel like shit to teach me some massive lesson once and for all and she just completely tore me down. She wasn't even letting me come here; she confiscated my dance bag. Like, really? I couldn't stand it anymore. I just left. I told her 'Screw dance.' So, hopefully she bought it and thinks I'm not here. And . . . whatever, I'll be fine without my half soles—that's all I really needed from my bag, anyway. I'll just go barefoot."

"I have my old ones with me . . . they might—"

"They won't fit. It's okay—actually, I may have also needed my deodorant and body spray from that bag, because on top of everything, my dumb ass asked Oliver to meet me here after dance."

"Looking like you straight up walked out of a mosh pit and came here. You need more than some deodorant, girl. Come on, stand up. Up, up, up, off this dirty-ass floor." She pulled me to my feet. We both turned to the mirror instinctually as Nyah made theatrical air circles, gesturing to my smeared day-old mascara, chapped lips, dry skin under chunky foundation residue, and the bird's nest that'd formed on top of my head. "Ya see all this? BB five! You look like a hurricane survivor without the hurricane."

"Nyah, come on."

"What? I'll be right back—wash your face and your pits and all the other bits." She ran out of the bathroom in a flash.

(BB five: *noun* \'bē-(,)bē\: Badass Bitch. Rule N°5: Never let a crush catch you looking like a wreck. Ever.)

I'd just finished washing up when Nyah burst through the bathroom door with her pride and joy in tow—her customized makeup and hygiene emergency kit. "Glam kit to the rescue!" It was purple, sequin-covered, and fulfilled all needs, ranging from a simple day at the beach to an extravagant night at the Royal Palace Masquerade Ball on planet Zorfon. She set the hefty duffle bag down on the countertop, unzipped it, and began selecting.

"Okay, we don't have much time, so let me just give you the ShortNotes version. I don't know what's been going on between you and your mom lately, and I won't pretend I know the quick fix, because you know I suck at giving advice, especially when it comes to parents and crap. Don't stop . . . here, dry your face and take this." She soaked a cotton ball in eye makeup remover. "You didn't get all the smeared mascara off. Wipe gently . . . *gently*. I'm no expert in parental disciplinary drama, but I do know this: I've never in my life seen two people as tight as you and your mom. So, no matter what you did, it can't erase everything you've been through together, and she'll have to get over it, eventually. Be patient. So, for now? You know the drill."

"Dance it out."

"Just dance that shit out. Go home refreshed and calm and just apologize. Moms love apologies, especially when you mean them."

I laughed through my shitty mood. "I love you. I don't know how, but you make everything lighter, better. And you give good advice."

"I know. Try my new mascara; it's waterproof. Oh, and here—blush, lip gloss, perfume, deodorant, hair spray, mints—scrunchy? Yeah, definitely a scrunchy. At this point, only a deep conditioning mask and a long hot shower can save your hair. Just do half up, half down. I signed you in, by the way."

"You're my savior."

"I know. Now save that face." She left me alone to do my thing. Class started in five minutes. I finished up as quickly as I could, not bothering with much of the makeup because I'd sweat it off anyway. I undressed and packed everything away in the cupboards, then joined Nyah in the studio lobby.

"Okay, my turn." She put both hands on my shoulders and got very serious. "Never forget who you are—a gorgeous smartass with a badass leg extension." She turned me around and nudged me forward the way I always did to her.

"Ow! I don't do it that hard." But it was already happening—I felt unstoppable as the music roared to life in the main studio—class was starting.

"Left foot, Mina," warned Damari Fegan, contemporary ballet master. I was so caught up in perfecting the *développé*-turn-leap progression that I hardly noticed I'd been on the wrong foot. As I recalibrated, a figure standing in the viewing window caught my eye. It was Oliver—he was here. He made eye contact with me and we shared a smile. I was taken by surprise, my *port de bras* still in fifth.

I brought my attention back to class and became faster, stronger, and better than I ever thought I could have been. I knew he was watching, so the stakes felt high, and somehow, impossibly, I was in the zone like

I'd never been before. There was even this perfect moment in the final routine: a scissor leap. Normally I couldn't gather nearly enough momentum for a decent scissor leap, but something about the fact that he was right there gave me the ability to leap so high that I hit the cleanest midair split I'd ever produced. It was powerful.

Nyah kept throwing meaningful looks my way. Even the legendary Fegan commented, "You're on fire today, Arkova."

I tried to play it cool even though my heart fluttered like a wild songbird trapped in a cage. The class came to an end. Nyah wished me luck, I thanked Fegan for an amazing routine, and I finally walked out to meet Oliver, who was now on a phone call.

"Hey, I can't believe you made it." I smiled stupidly, soaked in sweat. He held up his finger and mouthed to me: *Sorry.*

"Yeah, same quantity as we agreed on—nothing's changed. Sealed," he promised whoever was on the other end of the call. *Please tell me he isn't a drug dealer. I doubt it. He wouldn't be having this conversation in front of me if he was one. Right?*

I stood around awkwardly—waiting at first and then deciding to go back into the now-empty dance room and do some cool-down stretches while he finished his conversation. Nyah followed me in and palmed in the air like, *What's happening?*

"I dunno," I whispered, and sat in my splits. "He's on a call, I guess."

"Okay." She enunciated the word out, slowly.

"No big deal."

"Yeah, duh." Nyah was unsure what to do with herself. "So, should I . . . ?"

"Go home? Yeah, totally. Don't worry."

"I'll call you later. Text me when you get home."

"I will," I promised. She squatted down to hug me, and just as she zoomed out of the studio, Oliver peeked in through the door.

"Sorry 'bout that. Wait, was that Nyah just now?"

"Yeah. She moves quickly. I can't believe you watched that whole class."

"You're pretty amazing . . . for a stripper," he smiled coolly.

I laughed. "Thanks. I had a lot of frustration to work out."

"Oh, no! So, what happened? How much trouble did I get you in?"

"I'm basically grounded for the rest of my life. My mom freaked out pretty badly. You can imagine, after everything that happened." I kept my voice low.

"You don't look grounded," he said.

"Yeah, well, I could only take so much penitence, old-world style. I ran out of there. I had to dance."

"That's not good. Hey, you wanna talk outside? It's kinda hot in this room." *He's right.* The room stank of sweat and dancer feet.

"Good idea." He followed me out to the lobby. "Let me just change really quick. I'll meet you outside." I grabbed my jeans, hoodie, and boots from the cupboard and ran to the bathroom. I peeled off my sweaty sports bra, dance shorts—and even my underwear—and put them in a plastic hygiene bag, hiding them in the maintenance cabinet under the sink behind the toilet paper rolls. I'd get them later. I washed up with wet paper towels in the bathroom stall and put on my hoodie, jeans, and boots. Yep, no undies and no bra felt dangerously uncomfortable, but better than the alternative. I wet my hair in the sink and tied it up in a high bun. *Ready.*

Oliver was by his bike right outside the studio. "Nice parking spot," I said, and he looked up.

"Perks. Listen, do you mind coming downtown with me? I have some business I gotta handle and maybe we can talk after. We could maybe go somewhere fun. Just no more *shisha* . . . throat's been killing me since yesterday." *Are you kidding?* How was I supposed to resist? That was just too tempting. I was too curious—*what* business downtown? Then I pictured being back on his bike with my arms wrapped around his waist as we raced through downtown L.A. I remembered the feeling of Oliver's body vibrating between my legs as we rode through the streets and the sweet smell of him filling my lungs. Just a few more hours—I was screwed anyway. I texted Mama: **I'm fine, please don't worry.**

"Let's go downtown."

CHAPTER 10

OLIVER

She pulled me in with her walk, the sway of those sexy hips, the subtle bounce in her step. It took all my focus not to picture her in my arms, caressing the curves under that grey hoodie, those legs wrapped around me—legs powered by rocket fuel, judging from the air she got in that dance class. Guess I wasn't that focused on being focused. Effortlessly sexy, that's what she was; wet hair like she'd only just showered, and none of those layers of makeup most girls coated on those days.

She was distracting, to say the least, especially when I'd had several meetings downtown that I couldn't cancel, especially with CJ involved. CJ was my biggest potential client at that moment, and most likely an exporter judging from his purchase pricing. So far, I'd been dealing with the middlemen—like Freddy, my client in Orange County. But the night before, I got a call from a 310 number, and right there on the other line was CJ. He told me that word had gone around about a new kid in the business, and he was curious. He wanted to do business direct, which was huge—guys like him didn't show up in person for meets anymore. They had people for that. Going direct would increase profit margins for both of us, but the move would also cut the middle guys out, potentially pissing them off.

I had to be on time and focused, and the units I bought from Tee had to be on point—brand new and legit. I couldn't afford to be distracted, but distraction was exactly what Mina needed to take her mind off things at home. It wasn't just that, though. She had opened part of her world to me—letting me watch her dance. I wanted her to see mine too—my world, the part that I was proud of. I wanted her to see me as a man the way I saw her as a woman.

So, there we were again, riding through the city of streetlights. Her arms were wrapped around me and the feeling helped me forget how lonely of a place the world was. I wove through the 110 South carefully—couldn't take any risks with my fragile cargo. The meet with Tee was up first. We pulled up to an empty parking lot under the bridge running over the L.A. River—Tee was already there. Mina seemed confused by the place and uncertain as to what we were there to do, exactly, but didn't ask questions, which was convenient. She waited silently as I checked the phones one by one—opened the seals, made sure they were authentic, brand-new, and unlocked.

Suddenly, she walked over, picked one up, and asked me quietly, "What should I look for?"

She trusted me. She didn't know what this was—if it was legal or something less legitimate. I'd never have brought her to anything shady—but she didn't even ask. I only showed her what to check for once and we went to work as a team. She was a fast learner—no surprise there. I handed Tee a fat wad of cash totaling $21,000. Mina's expression slackened in surprise when she noticed the quantity, but she recovered real quick. I loaded an empty duffel bag with the thirty iPhones and started securing the bag to the back of my bike with bungee cords.

"Sorry, it'll be a tight squeeze. I really need to buy a van," I told her.

"*I'm* sorry. I had no idea you had work stuff to do. You should've told me you were busy. What's stopping you from getting a car?"

Good question. "Well, I don't really wanna buy a used car, but I still haven't figured out all the emancipation specifics—like, if I can even lease one on my own credit yet—that kind of thing," I replied. "Anyway, hop on. We gotta go."

She did, holding on to me more comfortably than before. She closed the gap between our bodies this time and rested her chest against my back. Even her grip was more relaxed. Before, it felt like she was attempting the Heimlich maneuver. Now she was even leaning into the turns with me, making the bike a lot easier to control.

I was on edge before the meet with CJ. Money was money, and wherever cold hard cash was on the table, trouble could follow. CJ had insisted on meeting in front of the Chandler Pavilion, which was a strange and inconvenient place for a meet, but the fact that it was heavily populated helped put my nerves at ease—though not completely. Paranoia didn't die; it slumbered.

Mina and I parked in the underground lot and took the stairs. As soon as we reached the street level, I got a text: **Concrete bench to your right.** Those instructions led us to an unassuming man sitting quietly on a bench across from the central fountain of the square. He wore simple clothes—a black button-down dress shirt with rolled up sleeves, jeans, and sneakers. His watch stood out right away, though, as did the pendant hanging on a leather cord around his neck—depicting what looked like one of the Indian gods. He stood just as we walked up and extended his hand to me. I shook it and said, "Hello, you must be CJ." He nodded at me and acknowledged Mina with a smile but didn't offer her his hand.

"I am honored to meet you, Mr. Mondell."

He was being formal. "You can call me Oliver, Mr. CJ, let's—"

"Just CJ is okay for me. Oliver, have you had a chance to admire the exquisite statue before us, right there in the middle of this glorious fountain? Did you know this fountain was first built in 1969, but a new fountain—one that was far more technologically advanced—replaced it in 1989? The important thing is that the statue in the middle remained intact, which is significant. Why? Because it is a prayer for peace built by Jacques Lipchitz in response to the Vietnam War." He gazed at the fountain as he talked. I turned and looked at it too, trying to see where he was going with this—hopefully somewhere.

"You must be asking yourself why I'm sharing this with you. It is because I want you to understand the story this fountain tells: that technological innovation coexists with the pursuit of peace. I want our relationship to be prosperous, profitable, and more importantly, peaceful. It is a ritual of mine to begin all new business dealings in this pavilion. It does not matter to me whether you bring in twenty or two hundred units. What matters is that we do not allow greed to interfere with the pursuit of peace. Do we have an agreement, Oliver?"

"Yeah. Sounds good, CJ."

"Wonderful! Here you are, then: twenty-seven thousand dollars, as promised." He handed me a shopping bag, which contained three white business envelopes in a thick blue rubber band. "You can leave your duffel bag right where it is. Thank you for meeting me, Oliver. I hope to see you again soon—you seem like a capable young man."

Seriously? He expects me to just trust him and, what, not count the money? Is he not going to check the units either? What is this? I didn't move. There was an awkward silence. I looked over to Mina for the first time since we'd walked up here. There was a nervous look in her eyes, probably because she could tell this was unusual. I didn't get it—was he joking around? I slowly reached into the shopping bag and started unwrapping the rubber bands from the envelopes.

"Oliver, please stop. I thought we had an understanding. I explained, didn't I? The fountain, the significance of trust?"

"Don't you want to check the product? Those could be bricks in there."

"Are they?"

"No, but—"

"Then good. Young Oliver, a relationship built on trust is tested by falling blindly. Let's start there. Clear?"

"With all due respect, CJ, human error is still a factor."

"Errors, human or otherwise, are unacceptable. Let me be clear, Oliver: if you count that money before we go our separate ways, this will be our final transaction."

I hesitated. This was crazy. Everything I had was riding on this deal. If I lost the money, I might have ended up on the street. This guy could have been totally full of it. He had a reputation, sure, but this could've all been some batshit setup or a huge opportunity with a very weird dude that I was potentially throwing in the garbage. Unable to make the call, I looked to Mina again. I jerked my chin up, silently asking what she thought.

"Russians have a saying. *Doveryai, no proveryai*—trust, but verify."

I nodded. "I like it." She was right; it would be insane to trust this guy and walk away without verifying the funds. I didn't care who he was.

I reached into the shopping bag and ripped open each of the three white envelopes. Two of them contained about $10,000 each and the third had a bit less. I stacked the hundreds and counted out 270 bills. It was all there. "Looks good."

CJ smiled. "Smart girl—smart boy for asking a smart girl. Always a good idea to verify funds on the spot, Oliver." What the hell? Was this some kind of test? "I will contact you with the date of my next export deadline."

As Mina and I stood to leave, two men, presumably undercover security officers, approached the bench. One picked up the duffle while the other stood in silence beside CJ. *Falling blindly, my ass.* I couldn't believe I hadn't noticed them walking around; they were both gargantuan.

Mina smiled as we descend back down to the parking garage. "That was fun."

"Good call back there, Mina."

"Would you have actually considered it if I wasn't there?"

"I have no idea. But I have a feeling you were meant to be there today."
I wrapped the plastic of the shopping bag tightly around the cash and put it in my backpack, looking back to see if anyone was following us down. "Want to learn to protect yourself?"

"Isn't that what you're here for?" she asked, teasing me. "All right," she added, smiling again. I smiled back, and I felt it linger on my face all the way to the L.A. Gun Club on 6th.

Mina grinned up at the sign. "A shooting range? I thought you were going to take me to some super-secret underground martial arts gym and turn me into Gina Carano overnight."

"Damn, girl, you don't hold back on your expectations, do you? But seriously, you do get that no weaponless self-defense training can get you ready for suspicious alley thugs that quickly, right?"

She stood up straight and crossed her arms defensively. "True, but I'd kick their asses at backgammon."

I laughed. "Probably. My point is: Sometimes you gotta even out the playing field to have a chance. Only a weapon—a gun, a knife, a bat, a pencil, whatever is lying around—can help you do that. You don't ever want to be in a position where there's a gun on the floor next to you that can save your life, but that you don't know how to use. You gotta get familiar enough so you can just go for it, not freeze up."

"What ever happened to 'the pen is mightier than the sword'?"

"Like I said—a pencil, a pen . . . whatever you can get your hands on. But if there's a gun, don't go for the pencil."

Mina rolled her eyes. "If something bad is going to happen, it'll happen, period. It'll be sudden and unexpected, just like last time. What's the point of getting ready when it can happen at any moment? It could be in my sleep, on the way to school, or even now!"

I got that deep down she was scared, but that was no way to live. "No! I don't believe that bullshit for a second. You don't really mean what you just said. That look you've got in your eyes right now? That's fear. It's as unnatural to you as telling a lie or staying quiet when you have something to say, so just get rid of it. I know those guys who came after you shook you up. I understand the repercussions that come with being terrorized like that, believe me. But you have to push back against the fear, and the only way to do it is by arming yourself with knowledge and practice. Why? Because when it's all over, even if you die and are rotting in the ground, at least you'll know you didn't leave quietly."

"Wow. With a speech like that, Lyndon B. Johnson could've rallied twice as many troops . . . who all would've died in Vietnam."

I stood my ground, refusing to let her sarcasm derail my point. I needed for her to hear me.

"I'm talking about protecting yourself, not trying to prevent Communist aggression in South Vietnam. Yeah, that's right . . . I know some shit about history, too." She didn't answer, she just stood there smiling. Then she turned around and walked away from me. "Where are you going?" I called after her.

"Inside, to bust a cap in your ass with my itchy trigger finger. Where do you think I'm going?"

"You can't say shit like that around here." I followed her up and through the door. That's when I realized we had a problem: we needed someone over twenty-one to sign for us. "Mina, hold up. Let's go back out a sec."

"Why?"

"Just come on."

We exited back out to the parking lot. I looked around for any new arrivals—someone who would be laid back about it. Most of these guys looked like off-duty cops or military. It didn't feel right to approach any one of them.

"You looking for someone?" Mina asked.

"We need someone over twenty-one to sign up with us. I didn't think about that."

"Oh, shit. I figured you knew a guy, like I know Jo."

"It's cool, we'll just ask someone," I said.

We waited around for a couple of minutes until a new group of people drove up and got out of their Jeep. It was a group of three, somewhere in their midtwenties. They approached the staircase toward the entrance looking like members of a heavy metal band. *These guys would be perfect.*

"Hey, what's up?"—I talked to the guy closest to me in a low voice— "Listen, do me a solid, will ya? Let my friend and me sign in with you guys and I'll pay for your session today. You're over twenty-one, right?"

"Yeah." He turned to his buddies and laughed, starting up the stairs. "You gonna pay for all of us? You sure you got enough on you? You ever been shooting? It ain't cheap."

"Yeah, I got it. Don't worry."

"Well, okay, big man, let's do it. You guys don't care, do you?" he asked the other two.

The lady with full sleeve tattoos shrugged. "Nah, I don't give a shit."

"Free's my favorite number," said the other dude.

"See? Easy," I told Mina.

We followed them inside and filled out waivers. "You're not gonna do anything stupid in here, are you, kid?"

"Like what?" I asked.

Mina pointed to a wall displaying several large Soviet AK-47s. "Whoa!"

"Yeah." I eyed the guns. Their power was seductive—what I wouldn't have given to have that kind of power in my hands when I needed it! But then I would've been rotting in prison—not standing there thinking of excuses to get closer to Mina.

CHAPTER 11

MINA

Oliver took hold of the gun in my hand, demonstrating how to release a magazine and load bullets. As he did, his fingers grazed mine—and I felt a nervous inner buzz and familiar weightlessness. Loading bullets wasn't fun—it was hard on the delicate pads of my fingers and became more challenging with each bullet—not to mention that I could hardly stand still because he made me so nervous. Despite the allure of his muscular arms guiding mine into shooting position, I managed to retain some information. Tension overcame me as Oliver's body pressed up against mine—his arms around me, fingers guiding mine to the trigger to help me aim. But as soon as the bullet left the chamber, the power of the recoil, the sound, the casing grazing my cheek—everything about the shot—shook me deeply. Our sexual tension became a nonissue, overshadowed by visceral shock as I jumped back, startled. My hand darted up to my cheek, the skin by my cut burned. I was frozen, mouth agape, hands trembling, still gripping the gun but unable to lower it or move at all. I wasn't in the shooting range anymore; I was back in the alley. I could feel the bite of the blade against my cheek.

Oliver's voice was in my ear, steady, reassuring. "Breathe, Mina. Breathe slowly—" His voice brought me back to the shooting range. "It's all right; that wasn't bad at all. Did the casing get you in the face?" I nodded and took in three shallow breaths; it was all I could manage. "That's okay, that just means your wrists were soft. We'll fix that. Inhale slowly. Good...now hold it, hold the breath. Release it slowly. Focus on the target. When you're ready, take a step forward...one foot in front, one in back." He grasped my hips and centered them. Then he glided his fingers over my thumb. "Bring both thumbs over to the left, pointed at the target. Mash back against your right hand with your left and rotate your left hand forward. It should feel uncomfortable—that's how you know you have control of the gun. That way the muzzle doesn't rise, and you don't miss." I put so much tension on the gun my hands almost began to shake. This was definitely harder than I'd thought it'd be. "Good...yeah, exactly."—Instead of letting the fear swallow me up, I honed in on Oliver's voice, following each detail of his instruction as best I could—"Now line up the front and back sights height-wise and center it, slightly covering the target behind the alignment—does that make sense?" I nodded. "As you exhale, try to squeeze the trigger as you let go of the breath, but don't forget your grip ...keep tension here"—he tapped the fingers of my left hand—"always." I realigned the front and back bumps, but it was hard to keep them lined up without holding my breath. I inhaled again and started over. I held my breath at the top of my inhale, lined up the sights, gripped the gun hard, exhaled, and squeezed. *Bang*—a hole pierced the top corner of the target.

"Good! Keep going!"

Bang. Bang. Bang. Oliver let go of my arms and stepped away. *Bang. Bang. Bang.* I was on my own, on a roll, hitting just left of center. *Bang.* Now just right of center. *Bang.* I was out of bullets. I placed the gun down on the felt-covered shooting stand and turned to face Oliver, who walked toward me with a huge smile on his face. I smiled back at him, proud of myself. Just as I opened my mouth to thank him, shots fired from the neighboring station. Even through the earmuffs, the sound was so loud and jolting that I shut my eyes, tucked my chin to my chest, clenched my hands into fists around my head, and folded forward. My forehead hit Oliver's chest.

"High-caliber bullets," he said loudly, as if to reassure me with the validity of his statement.

The sound of the next-door round was so intense that I felt it in my bones. When it finally stopped, I looked up at him and took a few steps back. "Sorry"— I flinched from another round a few booths down—"It's just really loud, caught me by surprise!" I yelled. Another round of shots began from a booth on the far end of the range—when would it end? "It's like World War II in here!" I guessed I'd just have to get used to it.

Oliver yelled something back at me, but it was lost in the deafening noise.

"What?"

"Nothing! It's good! You're doing good!"

Time passed, and I did eventually stop jumping every time someone fired their rounds. Also, my aim was getting better; by the third round, each bullet that left my gun hit the man on the target paper, and a few even got him in the center of his chest. But my accuracy didn't last—with each passing round after, my aim grew less and less accurate until finally it was worse than it had been in the first place.

"You're probably getting tired. Your aim's getting sloppy, Arkova," Oliver declared.

I smacked him playfully. To my surprise, he flinched hard and tried to play it off by laughing at himself. By the time we got to his bike, Oliver was back to his old self.

"Yeah, well, maybe if you weren't flexing, holding your breath, and clutching the gun in a death grip the whole time, you wouldn't be so tired?"

"You're hilarious," I replied flatly.

"You hungry?" he asked.

"I could eat. Let's grab something quick, though—maybe take it to-go, eat up in the Hills—somewhere with a view? I know a place," I offered.

"I'm always up for a view."

The ride up Outpost Drive was a cold one, but on the bright side, the view ledge was surprisingly vacant of other people. Normally you couldn't get a decent spot on the ledge without being elbow-to-elbow with some-one on either side of you. I guessed it was late and tourist season was winding down. As I stood overlooking the city, a shiver ran through my body. Maybe it was more than just the weather. Being near him had a way of making my shoulders shake and my stomach throb—so strange. Not a star in the sky thanks to the light pollution, but it was still a beautiful night. The city sparkled below us with the dazzle of a Las Vegas showgirl.

His gaze rested on me.

"What?" I asked him.

"Nothing—you here or somewhere else?"

"I'm here," I answered, but the look on his face said it didn't satisfy him. Even though my stomach was still turning and my teeth were chattering up a storm, I went on. "It . . . it's a reality ch-check up here—"

"You okay?"

"Yeah, it's just getting a little chilly." He quickly took his jacket off and put it over my shoulders.

"No, don't give me your jacket! What about you?" I offered it back to him.

"I'm good." He wrapped it around me again, and the warmth of it smoth-ered any further protest of mine. "You were saying?"

I blinked. "I forgot already."

"Oh, come on! It was getting good, I can tell."

"I lost my train of thought. Something about . . . oh yeah, being up here—it's a reality check to see the tiny buildings and their little inhabi-tants down there, everyone living their little lives with their little problems.

At least from here, that's what it looks like. And then you realize you're one of them. We're all part of that herd down there."

Oliver nodded, and I continued. "But I'm also thinking, hey, it's me on this planet, in this body, in this country, at this moment in time— no one else. Things all coming together like that—what are the odds? I could be gone. I could've never existed in the first place. It makes me realize that when I die, I want to leave something behind—make something of myself."

I meant to stop there, but there was more. I turned my body to face him and took a step closer. The more I revealed, the more familiar with each other we got, and the brighter the fire inside me burned.

"What were the odds of you and I meeting—the odds of you coming to Los Angeles, walking into Gerald's class? What were the odds of you ending up in the alley with me that day? It's crazy when you really think about it. Every day, something incredible can happen that changes your whole life; every choice can be the choice that takes you in a completely different direction. It opens an infinite number of possibilities. Like, the simplest choice I make, whether to go left or right, could change my entire life. Our entire future is constantly being bet on the next roll of the dice. But we can't think like that, and we shouldn't—we'd lose our minds. Anyway, that's not my point. The point is: I don't want to just wait for things to happen to me. I want to be a woman who does what makes her happy instead of just dreaming about it. A woman who knows what she wants and makes it happen." The last few inches of empty space between Oliver and me were charged with electricity. "That's what I was thinking about," I whispered.

I stood, lips parted, awaiting what could have been the most highly anticipated event in my as-of-yet very bland love life. His eyes were dark and mysterious, but they were tinged with uncertainty—like he was fighting something. Just then, a dreadful sound pierced the air as a dark vehicle flew by us, emitting the screech of a banshee and jolting us both.

"Slow down, for God's sake! Who drives like that?" I yelled after the car. I looked back at Oliver, and he shrugged like he didn't know what to say. Neither did I. It had certainly spoiled the mood. "Should we go?" I turned away from Oliver, disappointment taking the place of my jittering nerves, and started back for the parking area where we left his bike.

He followed, but he stayed a few paces behind me. It was probably a good thing that we were interrupted—it saved me the embarrassment of standing there and talking about being "a woman of action" while mentally begging for a kiss that may never have come.

As I walked, I felt his hand wrap around my wrist. "What's—?" He spun me around to face him, ran his fingers through my hair, cupped my cheek with his palm, and pressed his lips to mine. A strange feeling washed through me—a feeling that this kiss had to happen no matter what—and a mere roll of the dice, or screech of a speeding car, or even Oliver's own ambiguity, could not stop it.

I ran my hands up the side of his neck into his untamed hair. He traced my spine with his finger. I grazed the soft skin of his hip under his shirt, and he trapped me between the parking pay station and his body. He was strong, but so was I. I caught my breath by resting my head against the side of the pay station when his fingers ran up the curves of my hip over my jacket to my breast, past my collarbone, and to my neck, where he replaced them with his lips. He kissed my neck as I trailed my fingernails up along his lower back. His kisses became less gentle. He sucked on the tender skin until my neck burned—that's when I felt his teeth—soft at first, then harder.

It didn't hurt—just took me by surprise—so I let out a gasp. I didn't stop him or pull away; he was the one who stopped. He backed away from me like I'd scared him, cleared his throat, ran his hands through his hair, and turned away. My heart continued to pound wildly. I moved toward him, took his hand in mine, and gently laced my fingers with his, but his body went rigid. *Be brave.* I got on my tiptoes to reach his lips with mine, but he didn't reciprocate. He just stood there, unyielding. I was mystified. *He doesn't want affection now?* I finally pushed him away in frustration. "What? So, you can bite me, but I can't hold your hand? Everything's gotta be about what you want? Well, you're dead wrong if you thought I'd be down for that." I turned away and stormed off.

"Wait—" He caught up quickly and took my hand into his. I pulled away and backed up. "I'm sorry, Mina. Listen, I'm not . . . I can't be what you need. You see? I'm already hurting you. There's a lot you don't know, and it's not . . . it's heavy stuff from my past that no one needs in their lives, least of all you. I just want to keep you from it, and keep this thing we have light and, you know, fun. You feel me?" I didn't respond. *Light and fun? He'd better be joking.* "Mina, look . . . honestly, you were right before. That day you came back, I was acting weird, and it was because I was trying to just do the right thing and stay away altogether, but eventually I couldn't. I knew I was being selfish, so I told myself, okay, cool, you wanna chill with her? Fine, but at least keep it light for her sake—it's for you, not for me."

For me? He was unbelievable. "That's a new one. You do realize you sound like every guy who's ever tried to hit it and quit it, like . . . ever, right?"

"That's messed up. I'm tryin' to be honest with you."

"Oh, okay, so, you're emotionally unavailable, but only as a personal favor to me. How sweet of you. I guess I should say thank you."

"I get what it probably sounds like, but it's hard to explain. It's just . . . when you let me in like you did back there, I couldn't think straight. You said all those things—how you didn't want to live life in your head— and sometimes, God . . . when you talk about how you're feeling, it's like you take my own thoughts that I've always had but never understood, and you find words for them. It's like you know me and I don't feel alone in my thoughts anymore, like we could be the same. But you don't know me, not really . . . if you really knew me—I promise—you wouldn't be standing here."

"Why?" I demanded. Silence. "You don't just say something like that and then stay quiet."

He didn't answer, and I hadn't a clue. I really didn't know anything about him. Nothing compared to what he knew about me. Suddenly, I felt cheated. I wanted to open up to him, but now I could see that he never gave me that same courtesy. I'd been so naïve. When I laughed this time, it came from some dark and cynical place.

"What's funny?" he asked.

"Oh, 'What's funny?' I'm sorry, you don't get to ask me any more questions. It's my own fault, really. I guess that's what you're used to: You ask, I answer. I open up and pour it all out in front of you, but I shouldn't dare to even think about asking you anything. That's what's funny. I'm laughing at how stupid I've been. I don't know a damn thing about you, and that means you don't really give a shit about building a relationship. You just wanna hit it, plain and simple. I know all about guys like you—making a little stand against Mommy and Daddy because life's just too whitebread to bear—then reenacting the hot/cold cycle with every girl you meet. You're good, Oli. I mean, you almost had me."

His stoic posture stiffened, and his jaw clenched.

He shook his head, but finally he spoke. "You wanna know about me? Okay. Foster homes, youth facilities—my whole life, a deranged psychopath, a friggin' cuckoo supposed to be caring after children instead routinely molested and abused us. Oh, and the bike? You wanted to know why I get to ride this motorcycle—motorcycles are dangerous, right? Well, Mina, here it is: I get to ride it 'cause I don't got any parents or relatives or anyone who gives a shit if I die. You wanna know about me? Cool, cool—let's see . . . my life's top-notch, I live alone—moved to L.A. so I can blend in—you know: big city, lots of messed-up people. Are we bonding yet?"

I was aghast. I'd unraveled him. I was such an idiot. *Say you're sorry.* But now I was the one who was frozen. He was laughing and breathing heavily, his eyes wild and unfocused—getting himself riled up. My eyes followed him as he paced. "No, for real, I actually feel better now, thanks. Hey, you know what? You're right, I shoulda done this earlier. I shoulda told you all this shit before, wrote it in that note in Gerald's class. Yeah that would've been *perfect*—he'd read it out loud to all those friggin' people in class, and you know, and th-then maybe we could've all held hands and sung friggin' 'Kumbaya.' How great would that've been, *huh*?" He was angry, out of breath.

His words cut like a blade. Such a beautiful person—such a horrific past. Of all the things, all the truths there could've been, this hadn't even been on my spectrum of possibilities. There was nothing I could say. Nothing.

I didn't look away. He probably wanted me to, but I wanted to show him I was there. So I said it with my eyes, I said it in my mind: *It's okay. I'm here. I'm sorry.* It must've gotten something through to him, because eventually I walked toward him and took his hand again. This time, he entwined his long fingers with mine, and we walked back silently to the ledge overlooking the city.

"So, you said you live alone now?" I asked after a while.

"Yeah. Wanna see?"

I didn't think about it. I just nodded.

We roared onto Bonvue Avenue, a quiet street in a very expensive part of town where the sound of a motorcycle's exhaust felt out of place. Oliver pulled over halfway down the street and cut the engine. We climbed off and I followed him toward the front gate of a massive house. *How does he afford a place like this?* We walked under an arch of red roses, through an elegant iron gate, and into a garden of blossoming cherry and lemon trees. Instead of walking straight to the front door, however, we veered right and headed along the side of the house to the backyard.

"I rent the guest room out back. I don't own this place." He smirked. "Not yet, anyway."

By "guest room," he must have meant "guest house," because his place was almost the size of our townhome. Once inside, he excused himself to go to the restroom. Meanwhile, I scoured the walls for posters, pictures— anything that could give me more insight. The kitchen was bare, but he did say he had just moved in. I noticed the door to his bedroom was open. I walked up and leaned against the doorway, peeking inside. Moonlight flooded his bedroom through a gorgeous picture window.

The bed was large and low to the floor, and the sheets were a simple white cotton. The décor was bare—minimalistic—so the keyboard sitting in the corner of the room caught my eye quickly. I walked up to it and glided my fingers over the keys. I heard the bathroom door open. The sound of Oliver's footsteps grew closer until he was beside me.

"Do you play?" I asked him.

"I don't"—he smiled his Oliver smile—"Yet."

"Goals?"

"Goals," he repeated in agreement.

"This Casio's not bad for someone who doesn't play."

Something glimmering under the moonlight on the nearby wall caught my attention. I left Oliver's side to get a closer look. It was a peculiar piece of art, a strange woman—creature-like, maybe a mermaid—was caught in something, a net or a wire. Her face was angelic, but a subtle darkness haunted her expression, and behind the damsel façade was a profound satisfaction in being caught. She was enjoying it, the pain—or was I imagining it?

"What did it for you—the mermaid or the ropes?" I asked, still admiring the piece.

Again, there was only the sound of his footsteps, and then I felt the heat of his body pressed up behind me. He didn't say a thing. I waited for his next move, heartbeat accelerating by the second; he swept my hair over my shoulder, slowly, and ran his lips up along the side of my neck. I'd never felt as vulnerable as this; the tungsten heart in my chest had suddenly become as malleable as putty as he grazed the small of my back with the tips of his fingers. His hand slipped up my jacket and glided to my breast. I didn't stop him. He moved his other hand to my hip, pulling me in harder, rubbing against me. My breath caught. He moved the hand that was on my hip lower until his thumb latched onto the top of my jeans. Like before, he trailed kisses along my neck, but this time, I was overthinking it—unsure what to do with my hands. I kept them at my sides, entranced by his movements. He slid his fingers down my jeans, gliding them lower and lower until I took a sharp breath and closed my eyes. He was everywhere, tongue against my neck, palm cupping my breast, warm fingers dancing on my core. Overwhelmed, I released a stifled moan. *But I want to make you feel good too. I just . . . don't know how—what's the right way to touch you?* I was afraid—afraid of doing something stupid or wrong, of making a fool of myself. I didn't want to just stand there like a mannequin either. I placed my hand over his jeans against his crotch and rubbed gently. He grabbed my wrist. *I barely touched him—did I do it wrong?* He turned me to face him and lifted me up, wrapping my legs around his waist. Before I could overthink and overanalyze everything that had just happened, in one swift motion he walked over, laid me on his bed, and kissed me. As he lowered the rest of his body over me, he put most of his weight between my thighs.

I kissed him back passionately—at least this I knew how to do. My body responded to his touches on its own. I wasn't wondering what I should be doing anymore—this was a dance. He pinned my hands down with his and reintroduced his lips to my neck. This time, the kisses weren't soft—his mouth was powerful, relentless—he was devouring me. My body shook. He constricted my movement so that every time I shifted, I rubbed against his weight. He brought my hands around, down, and beneath my back where he tucked them under. The tension built; he didn't stop until my neck was on fire and I could no longer suppress my moans, despite my best effort to remain silent in ecstasy.

He lifted himself off me but stayed on the bed. I searched for my breath, chest rapidly rising and falling, legs spread, arms still trapped beneath me. His eyes were hungry, and every move was calculated.

I was frozen as he pulled down on the zipper of my hoodie, so distracted by each newly exposed inch of skin that I could barely hear my phone ringing. Blood rushed to my face when I remembered that I had nothing on underneath my jacket—no bra, no panties, and already in bed with him—details that may have left the wrong impression of me. There was an instinct to cover my breasts as the zipper revealed more and more, but my hands were still trapped beneath me, and I couldn't bring myself to move them just yet. He didn't stare at my exposed breasts. Instead, as though to comfort me, he bent back over and kissed me again. His lips were soft and his fingertips light as they ran up and down my abdomen. But everything was getting more and more intense now. The hard friction of his hands was rubbing against my bare skin, one hand on my neck, the other on my backside. His teeth grazed the tender part of my neck, traveling lower and lower down until he reached the center of my chest. Maybe it was because I suddenly realized that he was sucking on my breasts, or maybe because I could feel him through his jeans against my thigh, I began to grasp the course of this trajectory. I grew uncomfortably nervous, and my anxiety deepened when my phone began to ring again. It had to be Mama. As soon as my mind went there, I knew it was too late, and I wouldn't be able to think of anything else. How could I forget? I needed to go home.

I pulled my hands out from under me, gently moved Oliver out of the way, and got off the bed, zipping up my jacket as fast as I could.

"Are you okay? Did I hurt you? I'm sorry, I should've asked before—"

"No, just—my phone," I explained, and ran to it without looking back at him. As I unlocked it, I saw that all the calls were from Mama. That wasn't all, though; there was a text from her too. Nausea hit me as I read, **You just breaking my heart. What I did to deserving this from you? How many times should I calling you? You thinking this a normal for behaving such a way? You must to coming home and staying in a your room until I say. Not just to going where ever you like! If you will not to coming home in a one hour then do not coming home tonight.**

"It's—I have to go, Oli, I'm sorry." I grabbed my things and ran out.

"Mina, hold on a sec!" he called after me. "Where you goin'? Is everything okay? Let me give you a ride."

"No, it's . . . it's better if I go by myself—I should go on my own. I'm sorry," I called out without slowing down or looking back.

This landed me on my own—like I wanted—sitting on a cold, hard public transport seat, rereading the text from Mama for the fifth time. The lump in my throat got bigger with every passing minute. I regretted running out of the house then more than ever—that damned hindsight again. As if jeopardizing one relationship wasn't good enough, I had damaged two. Running out on Oliver with no real explanation was cowardly. I didn't know why I'd done it. I could've just explained it to him, but after finding out about his past, I was too ashamed to show him how I'd treated Mama just to spend time with him. Maybe I was also a little scared of what would happen if I stayed to explain. *You weren't ready to go where it was heading. That's why you bailed.*

I was nervous to get home; my intestines felt knotted up in dread. I've been away too long to have just gone for a walk—she'd sense where I've been, I was sure of it. I went straight to the person she explicitly forbade me to see. Now I'd have to look her in the eye knowing I didn't just go see him; I rode downtown with him on the back of his motorcycle to an electronics hustle, paid off strangers to shoot guns, and a whole lot of other things I dared not get into. As the bus came to my stop, despite a strong urge to stay seated, I stood and got off.

There's nothing to be ashamed of. Just explain it to her from your perspective, and she'll get it. I continuously told myself that on the rest of my walk home. It was only a couple of blocks, but by the time I crossed the threshold and my eyes met the morose expression on Mama's face, all that confidence crumbled away. Her tired eyes and knitted brow made it clear she wasn't in the mood for my perspective and that nothing I could say would ever make this better.

"You should be a shame," Mama's voice was fierce, filled with anger. "Do you hearing me, Mina? You should be a shame to even looking at me in a eyes. Lower down the gaze onto the floor. You having no respect for me. You just completely losing your mind! I don't know who this garbage person you becoming?"

Her words were salt on an open wound, but I didn't lower my gaze—instead, I answered "I'm so sorry, I am, but—"

"Silence!"

"All my life—"

"Just closing your mouth!"

"For the first time, I did what I want to do, not what you wanted me to do. Welcome to the average daughter—"

Her hand slapped across my face like a burning whip. "Am I been the average mother?" she screamed, but then stopped herself abruptly.

I couldn't hide my shock; my eyes welled with tears. I pushed her—this was on me. But this was also my chance to stop the arguing; it was a way out. I ran upstairs and closed the door to my room. Overcome by a wave of emotion, I let my pillow absorb the tears until it was soaked in a veritable lake of self-pity. After a while, the door handle turned, and the door creaked open. I remained motionless, but when her hand touched my shoulder, my back muscles tensed.

"Look at me." I waited a few moments, but then I did. She was so drained—drowning in weariness—that I didn't dare hide my empathy. She reached her hand out to me and I took it. "I'm sorry, my baby. *Prosti menya*. You really just push me to a limits of my patience." Her eyes filled with tears. I was terrible. I was a horrible, horrible person. I felt like the scum of the earth, lying there and subconsciously contemplating strategies to minimize my punishment while my poor mama was in so much pain.

Finally, I responded through my tears. "Of course I forgive you. I can't even ask for your forgiveness. I don't deserve it. I'll try, though. I'll do everything I can to earn it. I'm sorry, I really am. What I did . . . running out like that, it was a terrible thing to do. I'll never do it again. I love you."

Too exhausted to respond, she laid beside me, filling in the empty space behind me like the perfect puzzle piece. I felt ashamed. *I don't deserve you.* The thought stung my eyes and put a lump in my throat.

"Don't crying, I crying enough for you and me today." She whispered weakly, wiping my cheeks. She murmured something to herself. I heard the word *Dedushka*—my grandfather. I exhaled heavily. We laid together in quiet stillness until I asked her something that'd been on my mind. "Mama, how are you coping? How are you okay living so far from your parents, from Babushka and Dedushka? Moving here by yourself?"

"It very hard. Not so okay like you think. I missing them each every day. I was not alone. First I was coming here with your father. We winning the green card lottery—a blessing. Not a thing you will saying to 'No, thank you.' People in our town would doing anything for such opportunity. Still, some time, I just wanna only stay in a bed and giving up on leaving house, on a work, but I'm thinking about you and finding a strength. Of course, I also still to having this hope, too, hope one day we are all to be together, the real full family."

"You should go out with your friends Erica, or Rachel. You never do that anymore. Why don't you call them?" I asked.

"How can I worrying about my going out when I just a worrying about you going out?"

I shook my head forcefully.

"I won't do that again. I'm sorry for what I did. I don't know why I behaved that way. It was impulsive."

We didn't speak for a bit. I almost drifted off, but the thought still nagged me: "I don't get it. What's going on with my grandparents' visa application? We filed years ago—"

"You knowing all facts—no new news for a now. It's more complication right now with a politics. It's off of our control," she explained.

"What was *Dedushka* supposed to do—let his family starve? Employment wasn't voluntary, and to get a job he had to join the Communist Party purely for survival, a formality—I explained it all in the supplementary letters we sent in. Can't they see that it's the truth?"

"I knowing that. You do and I do everything we can do and I have spending almost whole emergency fund of ours on the immigration lawyers and a translator who it is clear can't do so much like we think they will. If it is my choice, Babushka y Dedushka would being here long ago, legally or not. But it is not my choice, it's they choice, and you knowing just how they are—proud stubborn. They cannot do something not decent like come to a country without the formal invitation, especially your Dedushka, military man respecting all rules. So this the only way, just a waiting. Or ... just hurrying up receiving the law degree and then you can do better job than useless lawyers we hiring."

"Easy to say. Hard to do," I mocked her favorite expression, and we shared a laugh.

"You should knowing this, Mina, *Dedushka* very sick. I don't wanting you to worrying, but I ... winter can being hard for him, especially if he's beginning with a some cold or virus. He is having the very high temperature for more than a five days, so, I needing to flying there and seeing him to bringing him some medicine—some Canadian or German medicines maybe is better. There's a one normal not so crazy price for flight to Sochi that the traveling agency finds and a stop in a Germany. It's fitting for my work on days I needing to take off. Problem is this: it's on a morning of twenty-first."

"Book it. Are you kidding? Of course—go! I'll have plenty of other birthdays."

"I am afraid to leaving you alone here, but take you with me ... two tickets expensive for such quick trip. And school will not—"

"Mama, come on! Forget about all of that, you need to go be with *Dedushka*. He needs you. I will do everything you say—I won't leave this house—school and back."

She didn't argue or say anything, and after some time, my thoughts grew quiet. I drifted into a dreamless sleep with her arms around me— nothing bad could ever get to me there.

CHAPTER 12

OLIVER

After flipping around in bed, trying to fall asleep for hours, I finally started to doze off around three in the morning, but something woke me up again. The thoughts just kept coming. There was also my severe case of blue balls to consider—more mental than physical. They were restless, obnoxiously loud—the thoughts, not my balls. *Maybe take care of the physical and the mental will take a rest.* I opened the browser on my phone, tapped my fingers against the edge of the device for a while—a nervous tic—but realized that there was no use in pretending with myself. I knew what I needed. I typed "hardcore" and scrolled through endless images of aggression until the rage poured out of me and onto the parquet floor.

Now I can get some sleep. My eyelids got heavier and heavier, until finally I was out. But there was no peace for me in my dream world either— only more restlessness. I was dreaming I was in some kind of tar pit being assaulted by flying demons. The demons bit chunks of my flesh and whipped me with their arrow-shaped tails as I waddled through the rank, sticky tar. Finally, I reached the other side and crawled out, taking off for the woods in the distance. I ran as fast as I could as a fierce wind blew against me. I came to a hard stop when I spotted moonlight reflecting off a body surrounded by redwoods. It was Mina; her wrists and ankles were tied by ropes secured to the surrounding tree trunks. Her skin reflected under the moonlight like the metallic scales of a Koi fish.

"Mina?" I whispered. She was silent. Her expression was calm, weary, like she'd been waiting for me for a long time.

"Touch me," she whispered back. I walked closer and knelt beside her. "Touch me," she repeated, more urgently this time. I reached my hand out and glided my fingers along the length of her body. She arched her spine, revealing something shiny and reflective underneath her. "Take them," she pleaded. I reached for the object, wrapping my fingers around a large pair of metallic scissors and pulling them out from under her.

"The ropes are too thick to cut," I explained to her apologetically, but the look in her eyes was pure seduction. She wasn't listening to a word I was saying. She threw her head back and writhed in snake-like motions. She tried to bend her knees, but the ropes restricted her movement; she moaned with pleasure.

"Touch me," she whispered again. I didn't move. I clutched the scissors, hypnotized by her motions. "Touch me, Oliver." I crawled down to her feet and position myself between her legs, hooking one of the scissor blades under the fabric of her jeans near her ankle and cut up. I didn't stop until I reached her hips. "Yes," she said in a low voice. I did the same to the other side. Then I cut the fabric of her shirt along the center of her chest.

I put the scissors down behind me and ran my hands over her twisting body. I hovered above her, trailing my fingertips gently up her thigh, over her hips, and across her ribs. She gave a muffled cry, and when I looked up, I found someone had wrapped duct tape over her mouth. Tears flooded down her angelic face—my spell shattered. Her body was covered in bruises and deep bite marks. Could I have done this? My eyes darted to her wrists: they were raw and bloody where the ropes restrained them. *No!* I scrambled to untie her. Hate illuminated her eyes. "I'm sorry." The words escaped my mouth as I hit the floor of my bedroom and opened my eyes. The dream receded, replaced by the bleak reality of the dim room. My hip and elbow ached, but I was filled with relief. *It was just a dream.* I pushed myself up to a sitting position, panting.

The neighborhood birds were up too, starting their morning concert like clockwork—not a minute past the butt crack of dawn. At that point, I didn't think I'd be able to get any more sleep. I checked my phone—no messages. *If it weren't Sunday, she'd have no choice but to see me.* I shuffled to the kitchen to put on the coffee, then went into the bathroom to turn on the hot water in the shower. I stood under the scalding cascade until the bathroom walls were covered with a waterdrop lining. I got dressed—lazily poured myself coffee into a dirty cup, and considered sugar, but took it down plain. It was a black coffee kind of day. My phone buzzed with a text and I leapt to check it. *Pathetic.* I was hoping to see Mina's name, but it was CJ. *Get a hold of yourself, Oli. This is getting lame.* I had to break the spell or the hold or whatever the thing was that she'd got over me and get my power back. I read CJ's message, determined to stay super focused on business.

Update: D-Day is the 26th. I'm waiting on 60.

How the hell was I supposed to get sixty units by tomorrow? I'd waited all week on the thirty units from last night. I dialed his number.

"Oliver? You're up? Is there a problem?" he asked, agitation in his voice.

"Sixty? You mean *thirty*, right? I can't do sixty on my own. I've got my bike, but I—"

"Stop—"

"You told me last night that you don't care whether it's twenty or two hundred."

"Oliver, stop. LACMA, main entrance, ten hundred hours."

"Ten hundred hours? Wait, still on the twenty-sixth or—"

"Today." *Click.*

Asswipe. He could've just said, "Let's talk in person" . . . I checked the time: 6:15 a.m. *Ten hundred hours . . . what is that? Like, ten o'clock, right?* Her face returned to the center of my attention. *Why'd she leave like that? I gotta do something. I should call her.* I dialed her number. It rang and rang—no answer. I didn't let it go to voice mail.

Stop messing with your own head. Give her time—it's six in the friggin' morning, I mumbled to myself. *Who calls someone at six in the morning on a Sunday anyway? A friggin' lunatic, that's who.* I could almost hear the nasty voice whispering from some dark corner inside my head: *You don't need this girl messing with your emotions, throwing you off your game just when you landed on your feet.*

"Shut up," I muttered.

I tried to shut the voice off—to silence it—but it got louder. *Asking about my past like it's any of her damn business. I sure as hell don't need to tolerate CJ bulldozing me over the tiniest nonsensical bullshit either.*

My rage swelled like an infected wound and grew more reactive with each new shitty thought until it was as volatile as an operational nuke awaiting detonation. Coherence went out the window, replaced by electric crimson. I looked around the room for a distraction and set my sights on the mermaid in ropes hanging on my wall when it hit me: I was the one who was friggin' trapped. I ground my teeth at the thought of the ropes binding me, choking the breath out of me. I ripped the floating wood frame off the wall and threw the art piece across the room. The sound of breaking glass was like an itch I finally scratched—it was a release—proof that I had turned my anger outward and destroyed something.

I walked over slowly. The mermaid laid on a bed of broken shards—a creature engulfed by night, craving freedom but understanding only captivity. *You're weak, Oliver. Look at what you do—you destroy. Keep going and you won't only be hurting yourself . . . you'll drag her with you.*

I fell to my knees, grabbed a sharp shard of glass off the floor, and manically started cutting the mermaid free from her bonds. Wait—was that blood? Was it bleeding? *Yes*, I realized, it was . . . *I* was. I was a sick boy, kneeling by the result of my most recent tantrum, nursing a canvas mermaid in my bloody hand.

In the bathroom, I held my hand under the cold running water and checked for glass in the wound—the cut bled generously. I should have probably disinfected it, but there was no alcohol there. I reached for my cologne—that would work. I opened the cap with my teeth and gave it a couple of pumps over the open cut. *Shit! It stings.* Rummaging through my drawer with my good hand, I pulled out a clean t-shirt, ripped a long strip of cloth out with my teeth, and tied it tightly around my hand.

Had anyone happened by and seen me in that moment, it would not have been a pretty picture. I was in bad shape. I should've been locked up; I was losing my friggin' mind. I looked down, examining the knuckles on my good hand (which was still messed up from that store wall I'd punched the other day). Los Angeles was a bad idea. It was time for me to leave. *No matter how far you run, even if you hide with the rats in the sewers . . . you'll never outrun those ropes.*

Ignoring the voice, I quickly packed. I threw essentials into my backpack. Head still spinning, I rushed out the door. I started my bike and rode it to its limits out of my neighborhood, not knowing the destination yet. I passed Mina's block, our school, the gym, a freeway, another freeway—I didn't stop until I reached the coast. Now I had to make a choice: north or south. An ocean of possibility laid in both directions. I could leave this place and finally stop worrying about Mina. I could disentangle myself from this net of emotions, cut myself cleanly loose and move on. I didn't have to feel fear or pain or any of that shit. I didn't have to meet with CJ and listen to him try to school me or set up impossible ultimatums for me. I could go somewhere new and start from scratch again. I could head north to Portland or up to Washington. I could head south to San Diego. I could order my passport and go even farther south, all the way down to South America, and then . . . well, anywhere, really. I could have a new life every day. I sat at the fork between thousands of outcomes. Choice was all I'd ever wanted, wasn't it? Now that it was there, I dreaded it. Which way to happiness? Where were the road signs that mattered?

I didn't move. I just sat, torn, unable to make a simple decision between right and left. The sound of the waves crashing onto the shore in the distance distracted me. I got off my bike, plodded through the damp morning sand toward the ocean, and plopped down on the hill near the shore, watching the waves come and go. The monochromatic hues that blended sea with sky were strangely soothing. Even as the noisy families began to roll in by the dozens, I didn't mind the company so much; I found myself smiling at a pair of toddler twins wearing those funny looking bucket beach hats. They helped their mom set up a canopy, and when they were finally finished, they ran into the freezing water, squealing at the top of their lungs. I laughed with them, imagining what it might feel like to be so carefree. The relentless storm in my mind was slowly beginning to clear away.

Things aren't as bad as you think they are. You came here to build a business, and you've already made some pretty big moves. From now on, that's your only focus.

I pulled up to LACMA, parked my bike across the street, and approached the iconic streetlamp exhibit in front of the museum.

"You're late." CJ commented, leaning against one of the streetlamps.

I look down at the time. "It's nine fifty; I'm early," I fired back.

"You're late if I'm standing here, waiting for you," he said through a smile, as if it'd somehow make his words less condescending. His eyes lingered on my bandaged hand.

"If you wanted to be here early, CJ, that's on you. I'm not a mind reader. Listen, I agreed to do business with you because I respect you. You seem like a cultured person. Honorable, even—someone I can learn a thing or two from. But I don't work for you, and I'm not your bitch, so don't talk to me like I am." He stayed silent and downgraded his smile to a slight smirk. I continued, "About the units, I'll find out how many I can promise, and let you know by tonight. You can confirm or dismiss at that point. Later, CJ."

I didn't wait for the smirk to leave his face before turning away and crossing the street to return to my bike. It hurt to squeeze the throttle with my injured hand, but at least my dignity was on the mend.

I was on my way to the gym when I spotted a sign on a billboard that read *Real Deal Martial Arts*. I pulled over and stared at the sign for a while. Something told me martial arts might do more to channel my excess anger than a treadmill and some weights. I typed the name of the business into the search engine on my phone; it said they were open, and the place had over 100 five-star reviews online. Who would've thought? I turned into the empty plaza, where most of the units were up for lease or closed. The exterior building was seriously busted up, covered in old graffiti and the smell of dried piss. It was perfect—this place might actually have been the real deal, not one of those posh rip-offs that went easy on you and didn't teach you shit. When I tried the door, though, it didn't budge. I knocked. The doors and windows were tinted and covered in old martial art competition posters—I couldn't see in. *That sucks.* I figured it was worth a shot, but I guessed it was closed after all. Not sure what I was hoping for, but somehow disappointed, I turned to leave. Just then, the door opened behind me.

"Can I help you?" I stopped and turned to the man speaking to me. He stood in the doorway, analyzing me. I did the same. He was scrawny, ginger-haired, and not a day over thirty, but you could tell he ran things. He had an accent—might have been Irish or Scottish. Despite the broken-down look of the business, this guy seemed sharp. His clothes were tightly fitted over his athletic figure, his beard was well-groomed and clean-cut—and he looked you dead in the eye when he talked to you.

"No, that's okay." I didn't know why I said it, but I also turned to leave. It was like a part of me wanted this and another part of me was fighting against it.

"Well, you knocked, didn't you? The sign says martial arts, so I'm going to take a leap in logic and assume you're interested in learning about the art of defense, correct?"

"I guess," I struggled to find the right words.

"It's not a trick question," he said. "I'm not trying to sucker you into washing my car." He turned and walked back inside, and after a moment I followed him.

There was no one else there, but the place looked a lot better from the inside. This was a legit martial arts studio. Nothing was new, but all the equipment looked clean and the space was huge, sectioned out based on floor surfaces. I looked around for the guy, walking past the carpeted entrance, over the wooden floor section, past a fight cage, and stopped when I reached a black-matted area.

"You in here?" I called out.

"Shoes off."

I jumped, and my eyes darted to the far corner of the space. "Try to be more aware of your surroundings. What's your name?"

"Oliver."

"I'm Master Rig, but call me Rig—only the little ones call me Master. Tell me, Oliver, what do you feel like fighting?"

"My anger, I guess." He said nothing, so I went on. "I can't control it. I think it's starting to control me."

"You've got good instincts, and you listen to them. So you're on the right track already. The body is an intelligent, strategic entity, and it always finds a way to placate its qualms and satisfy its needs. First things first—take your shoes off. High-density mats like these are primarily for karate, tae kwon do, and Muay Thai. That yellow one over there is a grappling mat mostly for wrestling, judo and jujutsu. The blue mat in that corner is a foaming mat for combat training and aerobics."

"Karate, tae kwon do, wrestling, judo, jujutsu, combat training, aerobics—got it."

"And Muay Thai. Good. Anything specific you have your heart set on, or do you want me to suggest one?"

"Can I learn all of them? Do you teach all of them?"

He laughed like it was the funniest thing he'd ever heard, and I clenched my fists.

"What's funny?"

"You sound like me at your age, that's all. Anger is like any other force—it can work for you or against you. By training, you'll develop your strength and focus to inhabit your anger. Once you know it and make it your own, it becomes yours to use. If you choose to. Make sense?"

"Yeah." I did get it. I felt like this guy got a bit of what I was going through as well, which was funny because a few moments ago I'd hated his guts for laughing at me. "Don't worry—I give a shitty first impression too," I told him.

"Very funny. You got any experience at all in martial arts?"

"No," I answered.

"All the better. We'll start from the beginning. How fast you excel is up to you; it all depends on what you want to achieve and how much time you put in. Every Sunday I hold a mandatory boot camp session with a focus on conditioning. In my class, I do something very different from what you will be learning in your practice throughout the week—you'll not likely find this program anywhere else in the city. During the week, you'll practice technique. That is where repetition and focus rule. With me, you'll learn endurance and survival in a series I like to call 'old-school conditioning.'"

"Old-school? Like what?"

"Like hitting truck tires with a sledgehammer in the L.A. heat until you can't raise your arms above your head."

"Sounds fun. Wait, today is Sunday! Are you doing one today?"

"Indeed! You up for it?" He didn't give me a moment to answer. "We meet at noon, and students bring their own sledgehammers. You might want to wear some gloves. Oh, and we meet in a section of the dog park— the gate at the top of Fuller Ave."

"All right, let's do it."

"Last thing: payment. If you're paying by credit card, I gotta charge it here in the office. It's four hundred and eighty for the first month, and two hundred and seventy-five dollars every month after that." He added, "The first month's steep, but it includes one private lesson a week on top of the Sunday boot camp with me, and the two classes a week of whichever discipline you choose—I recommend jujutsu. You can use the space for practice during designated free time throughout the week. We've also got a cardio and weights room through that yellow door in the back. That room's always available during business hours, so you can save on a gym membership."

"Sounds good. I'll see you at twelve." I counted out five hundred dollars and handed him the cash. While I waited for my change, I searched online for the nearest hardware store selling sledgehammers—the last thing I had thought I'd be doing that day.

CHAPTER 13

MINA

It felt like I spent my night in a Goya painting—his late work, judging by my throbbing headache and the owls, bats, and other animals of necromancy had swarmed around me as I slept. Shaking off the chills and wiping sweat away, I propped myself up on my elbows.

What time is it? It couldn't be 1:00 p.m.—my clock must've been on acid. How was it possible to feel like I didn't get any sleep when I slept that long? *Wait, did Oliver call?* I reached for my phone, and it was as though my own personal Hermes had flown in with word that I'd been on Oliver's mind this morning. I was in missed-call heaven.

I shuffled my favorite playlist and jumped out of bed, bubbling with unexpected energy. I had one pant leg on and my toothbrush hanging out the corner of my mouth while humming along to a song I was so annoyed by that I usually just skipped. I hoped Mama and I were on better terms after last night. I wouldn't know for sure unless we had our signature hug sesh that morning, so I pulled my pants on the rest of the way, changed my shirt, and ran downstairs.

"Mom!" I called out.

There was no answer. I ran back up to my room and called her phone.

"*Privet,* Minachka," she answered almost immediately.

"*Dobroye utro,* Mamachka." I told her good morning.

"You just wake up right now?"

"I know, right? I thought my clock was broken when I saw the time."

"Maybe spending the less energy driving me crazy and then maybe you'll needing less sleep."

A joke! She made a joke with me. This was definitely progress. My heart soared. "You're hilarious. Where are you?"

"Costco and then some few errands."

Hmm. That was vague. "What errands? Want me to come?"

"No, I'm just having one more thing to do . . . no point to coming and picking you up then going back to this area."

"Gotcha . . . Mama, would it be okay if I could go see Oliver? Just really quick . . ." There was silence. "Would that please be okay?" Shit, maybe I shouldn't have asked. But it wasn't entirely unheard of for Mama to be apoplectic about something one day, then okay with it the next. "It's just, I left yesterday in . . . a way that might have hurt his feelings, so I just want to make sure everything's all right, if I can."

There was a pause in which I felt like I might slide off the end of the world and hurtle into oblivion. Then she spoke.

"Okay, you go, but if you are not coming back to the house before I do, which will being in approximately one and half hour, then we will having a big problems."

I gave a deep sigh of relief. I couldn't believe she was cool with it. "I promise, love of my eternity, moon of my sun, half and half to my coffee."

"Mm hmm, *davai ztiluyu.*"

"Bye, *lyubimaya.*" *Click.* I called Oliver; the phone rang and rang, and then I got his voicemail. I called him four more times. *Maybe he's in the shower?* I didn't have time to sit around and wait, though. I'd just head over there. If he was there, great. If not, no biggie—I'd pretend I'd never been by at all.

By the time I reached Oliver's, I was beginning to second-guess my impulse. The bus was overcrowded and the traffic heavy; it'd taken me forever to get there. Oli's bike wasn't parked on the street.

As I walked closer to Oliver's apartment at the back of the house, I couldn't shake the feeling that something was off. His door front door was slightly ajar. I tried calling his name and waited around for a few minutes, but there was no answer. Maybe he'd forgotten to lock it? I should have just closed it and left, but I didn't—I went in. After a few steps, I stopped. At first, I didn't realize what the pile of glass, wood, and cloth on the floor was, but I identified the red smeared all over: blood. Not crime-scene-he-could-be-dead amounts, but still. Blood is blood.

What had gone on in here? My heart thudded violently as I scrambled for my phone. My fingertips were numb as I dialed his number. No answer. I redialed. *Come on* . . . No answer. My heart sank. *Don't panic. Use your head.*

Only upon closer observation did I realize the mess was what was left of his mermaid piece, but that she'd been cut out. Why would Oliver do something like that? Maybe the people who lived in the main house knew. *I should go ask them.* I walked back outside where the sweet aroma of blossoming citrus trees filled the air. I turned the corner of a narrow path to the main house when I ran into something small and squishy with a hard thud.

"Oh my God! I'm sorry!" I gasped, realizing it was a little boy. His eyes welled up, but he didn't make a peep; just clenched his fists and sucked in the tears. I knelt. "I'm so sorry! I didn't see you there. Are you hurt? Let me help you up."

He shook his head, but I wasn't sure if it was because he wasn't hurt or because he didn't want me to help him up. I stayed put and waited. After a few more breaths, his eyes were completely tear-free, and he pushed himself up off the ground bravely. He dusted his pants off and then blew on his hands before offering one to me.

"I'm Patrick."

My heart melted, and I shook his hand gently. "I'm Mina," I said, giving him an apologetic smile. "Do you live here?"

"It's my mother's house. Who are you? Are you Oliver's friend?" he asked.

"Yeah, I am. Do you know Oliver? Have you seen him today?"

"I shouldn't talk to you because I don't know you and that means I can't trust you," he explained.

"That's true. You're absolutely right. You shouldn't talk to strangers."

"I know that," he sassed.

"Are your parents home?"

He shrugged, deliberately unhelpful. I walked past him down the path to the front door of the main house and knocked. He followed close behind.

"Patrick?" called a loud, stern voice from the other side of the door.

"Um, no . . . not Patrick, ma'am." The door was opened by a well-dressed woman in an elegant silk blouse and a sophisticated updo—a rare sight in Los Angeles.

"Hello." She studied me, both worried and curious. "Patrick?" she called past me.

"Here, Mother."

"Oh, good, I was wondering where you disappeared to . . . Gloria was looking for you."

"Hello, ma'am." I said, preparing to ask about Oliver when it suddenly occurred to me: *Maybe Oliver doesn't want this woman to know his business.*

"She's a friend of Oliver's," Patrick offered knowingly.

"She is? Well, come on inside, both of you. Let's close this door before all the bugs get in the house." I hesitated for a moment, then walked inside. Patrick followed behind and tried to disappear up the stairs, but his mother caught him by the arm and held him still. "Gloria! I found him, Gloria! Gloria!"

"I'm sorry to bother . . . I should just—"

"I'm Mrs. Goldberg, by the way."

"Mina—"

"There's no need to be sorry, Mina darling. Oliver's friends are always welcome. Patrick, you're bleeding! Oh, no . . . this won't wash out, it's a silk blouse. Honey, did you fall?"

"It doesn't hurt," Patrick said bravely, not mentioning me. What a champ!

"Still, have Gloria disinfect it, sweetie. Go on, I think she's in the kitchen," Patrick ran off. "All right, Mina, how can I help you, dear? Is everything all right?"

"Hmm? Oh, yes, that's right . . . I knocked. Well, that's why I knocked—just to say sorry about Patrick. I was rounding the corner of that pathway and didn't see him running toward me, so we collided, and he fell. It was my fault."

"Don't be silly; it was an accident. He's uncontrollable, that boy. I'm glad you're not hurt." I smiled, unsure of how to respond. This was incredibly awkward. "Is there anything else?"

"No, that's all. I'll see Oliver another time. Well . . . thank you, and sorry about your blouse—"

"Hmm? Oh yes, that. It's just a blouse. Pleasure to meet you, Mina. Hope to see you around."

"You too, Mrs. Goldberg," I exhaled in relief that the exchange was brief and turned to leave.

When I reached the guest house again, Oliver's door was locked. *That's strange.* I didn't lock it behind me. In fact, I was almost certain I left it slightly ajar. I knocked.

The lock clicked and he opened the door, surprised to see me. "Oh, hey. I just saw your missed calls, I was 'bout to get back to you . . . but you're here," he said.

I couldn't read his expression—there were questions in his gaze, but silence on his lips. I searched his body for signs of blood and spotted his bandaged hand. He noticed me looking and hid it behind the door casually. His clothes and hair were drenched in sweat, and he was barely standing on his own two feet as he clutched the door frame to hold himself up.

"Are you okay?" I asked.

He continued staring at me in silence, but his guard started slipping. He was clearly embarrassed. "Did you just get here? Or were you here earlier?" he asked quietly.

"Yeah," I answered vaguely. He hated that answer. The tension in his jaw convinced me of his anger, but suddenly he eased up and started to laugh.

"Yeah?" he asked, like it was a big joke.

"Yeah," I repeated, not budging.

"Okay, well, sorry, but I was just about to hop in the shower." He matched my casual tone.

"It's okay, I should be getting back anyway, but I just wanted to see you and apologize for last night. I had to go, because—"

"It's cool, Mina, no worries. I get it," he said, deadpan.

"You sure?"

"Yeah, you had stuff you needed to take care of . . . so do I. See you tomorrow."

"See you tomorrow." I turned to leave slowly, giving him a chance to change his mind and invite me in, but the door shut behind me. I was crushed.

•••

Tomorrow was a real letdown. He said, "Hey, what's up?" when he saw me, and I answered that not much was up. I waited for him to approach me with more than a casual greeting, but the window of opportunity decreased marginally with every hour, until suddenly, the day was over. The rest of the week was much of the same. I tried to approach him myself a few times at lunch, but I was also trying to avoid rejection like it was the flu, and it was as though he'd become an expert at keeping his distance. Apart from attending our mutual class, he'd been making himself scarce. I brought my focus back to my schoolwork. Playing hard to get with someone who wasn't trying to get you was like running from someone who wasn't chasing you—pathetic.

The infuriating thing was that though we rarely talked in person anymore, we still talked through texts sometimes—mostly commenting on Mr. Gerald's neurotic behavior—like the way he checked his fly fifty times in the course of one lesson. Periodically, we shared these intense moments of eye contact, especially if it was the first time we were seeing each other that day. *Or are they only intense to me?*

I remembered this one time in sixth grade when I accidentally bumped into a girl in the gym locker room. I spent the whole year avoiding her because I thought she was mad-dogging me every time she saw me. It turned out that wasn't a special scowl meant for me—simply the natural expression of her face. Maybe I needed to get used to the fact that not everything was always about me. Maybe I was just one of a whole slew of girls out there who thought they had some deep connection with him.

No. I refuse to believe that. How many of them had been to his place or knew what he did for a living, or knew he'd never had a real family? I'd never seen him talk to anyone at school besides me—not voluntarily, at least. The fact was that I just don't know. That was why today I was finally going to do it. I couldn't keep living like this, in constant limbo, so I wasn't going to. I was going to talk to him. What would I say? I'd improvise.

AWOLNATION's "Sail" blared through my headphones as I was walking through the hall when I spotted Oli by the staircase on the second floor. I didn't know if it was the beat of the music or the prospect of casually running into him in the hallway that propelled me up those stairs at the speed of sound, but three-fourths of the way up, my foot slipped on the edge of the step and I ate it—hard.

If it had just been falling down the stairs, it would not have been that big of a deal. Unfortunately, it happened to be the day that I wore a flared miniskirt and had been carrying an extra-hot vanilla latte. The reality of my ass on display for the entire school was magnified tenfold by the revelation of my day-of-the-week granny panties. Of course, I hadn't paid attention to the day when I put them on that fine Thursday morning, so mine read "Sunday" across the back. It was a sad sight, but I couldn't care less about a bunch of losers laughing at my coffee-stained panties—the photos that they were taking, those would haunt me forever. Humiliation used to be so much more temporary.

"Mina! You hurt?" It was him.

Suddenly, I was mortified. I didn't move, I didn't look up—I just froze, which might not have been the best idea in that particular situation. The best thing to do, probably, was to recover quickly and pretend nothing happened. Yet I was frozen there while the crowd around me multiplied. Finally, I guessed Oliver realized he had to do something, so he covered me with his jacket.

"Can you stand?" he asked in a low voice.

I couldn't answer him and just kept my eyes down, staring at my hands plastered on the steps as he pulled me up, slowly and carefully. Even then, with his arm around me, helping me into the girl's bathroom, I wished I were somewhere else—anywhere else. It was the first physical contact we'd had since that night at his place. I had pictured it happening very differently.

"I'll let you clean up—unless you need me to stay. Can you stand on your own?" He asked once we were in the bathroom. I nodded *yes*. I was more mortified than actually hurt, although I was feeling a slight discomfort in my ankle. Thankfully, no one else had followed us in. I couldn't face him, so I held his jacket out without looking up. "No, it's okay. Keep the jacket," he insisted.

I managed an inaudible thanks, and when he finally turned to leave, I limped to the sink and braced it with both hands for stability, overcome with nausea.

"Mina?" His voice came from the doorway. "I wanna tell you something I wish someone had told me when I needed to hear it." Slowly, I brought my eyes up to meet his in the bathroom mirror. "One day you'll forget about this. This moment isn't forever. One day it won't even be a dot on the canvas of your life," he said before finally shutting the door.

A week had gone by since I first planned to talk to Oliver, and thankfully things had warmed up between us. We were texting more frequently now. We said "Hi" before class starts and "Bye" when it ended. Sometimes we saw each other in the hallway—he nodded at me, and I smiled. Oliver was going through some issues of his own, I thought, and that had me worried. He'd seemed exhausted lately, and earlier that day I saw bruises on his stomach when his shirt rode up mid-stretch before he walked into second period. It was time I tried to talk to him—for real this time.

I waited until lunch and walked to Oliver's usual spot on the ground by the modular classroom buildings behind campus. It used to be my spot, but I'd given it up when I saw him sitting there a couple weeks ago— very uncharacteristic of me. I just didn't want to be clingy or extra, so I gave him his precious space. I noticed he was reading Harding's *Tinkers*. Oliver noticed me approaching and looked up from the book. I didn't sit down next to him; instead, I just looked down at him from where I stood to maintain confidence and strength. He wasn't going to charm his way out of answering.

"How do you like it so far?" I asked about the book nonchalantly, like nothing was up.

"Honestly?"

"Yes, of course." The harder I tried to act natural, the more strained I ended up sounding.

"I'm not sure I do. This is my second attempt at it. I gave it a try earlier this month but couldn't get past the first fifty pages." I tried to maintain a neutral expression. "Obviously Harding's a great writer, but it's more like reading a long-ass poem than a book. But so far, I don't feel anything for the characters," he said with a pained expression, as though I'd be offended.

"Yeah, it isn't for everyone, but to some people, it's everything," I noted vaguely, not specifying where I stood on the matter. He felt me trying to change the subject and shut the book.

"What's up?" he asked.

I decided to just blurt it out. "Earlier, I saw some bruises. Where did you get them?" I asked uncomfortably but firmly.

"Where did you see them?" he asked.

"Before class."

"No. I mean, where? Which ones?"

"Your stomach. Why? Are there more?" It came out panicked.

"Everything's fine."

"But that's the thing, Oli, everything's obviously not fine. Fine doesn't leave marks."

He stood and walked closer to me; we were eye to eye.

My ligaments turned to jelly. It was a tactic, I realized, so I took a step away from him and regained focus.

"Who's hurting you?" I asked firmly.

"It isn't like that."

"Then what's it like?"

"Jesus . . . I'm taking some classes, okay?"

"What classes?"

"It's complicated. Technically, it's jujutsu, but basically, it's MMA."

"MMA did—"

"Mixed martial—"

"I know what it is. You're saying you got those from a class?" I asked in disbelief, but it did make sense. I felt stupid now.

"Yeah, we rough each other up pretty badly," he bragged, exposing his bruised but ripped abdomen. "But it's not as bad as it looks . . . it's all just a roadmap to learning," he explained, reacting to the apparent look of horror on my face.

"You're crazy."

"No pain, no gain. Ever heard of it?"

"How is getting beat up in some violent class going to benefit you?"

"It's the exact opposite of a violent class. The class teaches us how to avoid violence and practice patience. I need that right now, so it is good for me. The bruises are just a side effect—or a bonus, depending on how you look at it."

"How do you have to look at it for it to be a bonus?"

"It got you over here, all bothered and worried, didn't it?"

I did a double take. Was he being a little flirtatious all of a sudden?

"Wow, what an attention whore!"

"You're right. Next time, I should just trip on some stairs."

I reacted on impulse and socked him right in the gut.

"Ah, not there!"

"Oh shit, I'm sorry! Shit, shit, shit. I'm so, so sorry!"

He knelt over, clutching his stomach like it may have flopped open if he let go. I crouched beside him and placed my hand on his back, unsure of what else to do.

"You've got one hell of a right cross," he panted.

I sat beside him and put his head on my lap, wanting to comfort him. At first, he tensed, but then suddenly he let himself relax into me. I stroked his baby-soft hair and looked down to see his eyes were closed as he rested his cheek against my thigh. He looked comfortable—at least the pain had left his face. For the next few minutes, we just sat still and listened to the sounds around us. It was the most content I'd been in a long time. When the shrill sound of the bell finally broke our serenity, it startled me. I could've stayed like that for hours, but let's be real: my butt cheeks had gone numb from sitting on concrete.

"What are you up to this weekend?" he asked, sitting up.

"I'm performing, actually," I said, suddenly remembering that fact.

"For real? Where?"

"Okay, don't laugh. Remember the rave Nyah was talking about? I'm performing at that rave after all. The girl she knew actually came through with audition slots for us, and Nyah dragged me to audition with her this past weekend."

"She still doing all this for that Jake guy?"

"Well, aren't you the modern Lord Peter Wimsey, remembering every detail?" I didn't realize he was paying such close attention to the conversation she and I were having at the *shisha* place.

"So your mom's just letting you go to this rave?"

"She doesn't exactly know about it, as of yet. But, I mean, it is a job—we are getting paid—and there'll be security around the whole time. Plus we get all access. She might be cool with it."

"Yeah! She'll be totally psyched to hear that her little girl's gonna dance for drug peddlers, sex offenders, and creeps."

"Sounds like you're the one who has a problem with it," I pointed out.

"Maybe I do. I don't think it's a good idea for you to be in a place like that. Especially after what happened to you . . . people go missing. People

OD at raves all the time. It's the perfect cover for guys like the ones who came after you before. It's dangerous—"

"You don't know that anyone's still after me."

"I don't know that anyone isn't."

"Can't you just be cool about it?"

He closed his eyes for a moment.

"Yeah, I can be cool. Do what you want, Mina. I'll see you later." He left, and my heart sank into my stomach. The peaceful vibe of just a few moments ago was gone, replaced with disappointment.

I just didn't know which one of us I was disappointed in.

CHAPTER 14

OLIVER

I sipped on a double-shot espresso as I sat on the patio of a new neighborhood café within walking distance from my place. Grapevines covered the outside walls, and the brightly painted French bistro chairs made it feel like this could be a peaceful afternoon somewhere in Europe. School had been out for only half an hour, but it already seemed like the weekend was gonna come and go too quickly. My phone rang and I took the call.

"Hey, CJ. Listen, your wire hasn't come through yet, but I'll keep you posted. Total's one hundred and thirty?"

"That is correct," CJ answered dryly over the phone and hung up.

That's right, one hundred and thirty, as in one hundred and thirty thousand dollars, as in over two hundred units. You're killin' it, Oli. I hyped myself up. Despite my initial doubts, I found a way to acquire the quantity that was necessary to keep CJ happy and elevate my business to a whole other level in the process. Turned out I just needed to make a few changes in my business model. Like everything else, it was about who you knew and, of course, how much money you had. But moving two-hundred-plus units myself wasn't the perfect solution either. My cost per unit had gone up, the risk was higher, and CJ's prices kept dropping, so my margin was taking a hit too. I needed other options—another buyer. CJ needed some competition.

At least I'd gained his trust enough for him to advance my payment a day or two before I delivered the units. That might not seem like a big deal, but it changed the game when it came to cash flow and business growth. Despite everything going on in my life, my profits had tripled in under a month. I was looking at six grand a day, clean. That was just in iPhones alone, not to mention all the side business: TVs, MacBooks, accessories, and appliances. Flipping product for profit was the one thing I knew I could control. It'd become an obsession. That and my jujutsu practice—the only two things that were any good at keeping Mina off my mind and my anger at bay.

I'd decided I wasn't touching that hush money from my court case either, and for good this time. Our goal was never the money—it was to win big and set a precedent, to teach them a lesson. The point was to show them how much it was going to cost them the next time they turned their backs on a complaint filed by a child—by any victim. But the thought of keeping the spoils of that fight made me feel bought; it sickened me. It was as good as blood money to me. I'd only borrow what I needed to build a solid foundation for myself. Then I'd donate everything to the proper cause when the time came. And the time would come when my business evolved into a legitimate corporation with distributor contracts. That was the goal.

It sounded like a longshot, but I could see it so clearly. The business had already evolved so much—no more chump change. I was talking about real money—the kind of cheese that built a white-collar future with a wife draped in Tiffany, kids in private school, and a house on an acre. Okay, fine, I wasn't quite at the pule-for-breakfast level yet, but I was so darn close that I could almost smell that Serbian donkey cheese.

Things really turned for me once I finally rented a van—well, technically, Mrs. Goldberg did. I gave her two grand to cosign the lease with me on top of all the cash for the monthly payments up front. It turned out she really needed the money. She was a beauty (the van, not Mrs. Goldberg)—a spacious Mercedes-Benz Sprinter 2500: affordable and practical, making it possible for me to move quantities I never thought I could when I had only my bike.

All that was left was to bring more hands on deck, but my trust issues were still getting in the way, and I hadn't gotten that far in my jujutsu training yet. I still had to learn how to maintain a level head when I was wedged into a tough situation; that was how I'd been getting all those bruises. The training method worked like this: Your partner put you in a bitch of a bind, and if you could endure the pain while keeping your shit together, you left relatively unscathed. Fight back against your partner with an inappropriate grappling strategy for even a second, though, and you'd end up causing yourself some serious suffering. So, you just didn't move until you had a clear strategy—in practice, not as simple as it sounded.

I rented a vehicle storage space in North Hollywood to store product overnight until I could find a landlord willing to lease a real office to someone with no credit history. I even bought theft insurance. I left the van there overnight, swapped it out for my bike after a meet, and headed home.

Despite all the growth, it'd been a fairly miserable month. I kept telling myself, *Just keep moving, just keep moving, stay busy.* It was hard to stay away from Mina, but I wasn't suited to having a girlfriend or anything like it. Mina didn't seem like the type to be down with casual hookups; I didn't want to lead her on and end up hurting her. So, I tried to avoid her, but that hadn't worked either. I couldn't leave her splattered on the stairs like that with no support while those idiots laughed and took pictures. I was selfish, but I wasn't a monster. We hadn't talked about that stupid rave since the day I lay on her lap at lunch.

Ever since that day, I'd tried avoiding her and staying true to my promise, but there was this indescribably strong pull between us—impossible to resist. I'd write some stupid joke down in class and pass it to her because it gave me so much pleasure just watching her open it and seeing her body shake in silent laughter. I teased her every chance I got about unimportant things—like her messy hair when she overslept and came in late. I'd even been working on a gift for her. It had taken me a couple of weeks to make, but I had finally finished it last night. I'd never made anything for anyone before, so I hoped I'd eventually work up the courage to actually give it to her. Until then, I'd carry it with me in my back pocket. That was where it was right then.

I'd avoided talking about this rave with her because I was afraid it would lead to a real fight between us, and what was the point? She was stubborn and wouldn't listen to me anyway. But the rave was tonight, so there was no avoiding it now. I could've just gone and kept an eye on her, but that might not have been enough. I asked around about the rave and Tee told me this particular rave was something of a front by a group of people who'd be using it to unload drugs, and that the guys behind the rave partnered with some heavy-duty thugs who funded a majority of the project. The word on the street was that they were Russian. What if I failed to protect her, failed to see the danger coming? No—the safest thing would be for her not to go at all. There was only one person I know who would want Mina at that rave less than I did.

That would be really messed up, though. How badly did I not want her to go to this thing? Pretty badly. So, what—I'd just go over there and knock on the door? "Hi, Ms. Arkova. We haven't met, but remember that one time you were worried sick about your daughter and that other time too? Well, I'm the asshole responsible. Nice to meet you. Don't freak out, but your daughter . . . she plans on dancing at this thing called a rave. You're unfamiliar? It's just a place where EDM junkies, druggies of every level, a few sex predators and potentially some Russian thugs get together to

party with the general population. I just thought you'd wanna know."
Yeah, there was no way I was doing that.

I knocked on Mina's front door. No one answered, but I was pretty sure
that was her mom's car parked out front. I knocked again. Still nothing.
Maybe her mom was in the shower? Maybe this was a sign. I was ready
to leave when the door finally opened. A beautiful dark-haired woman
stood in the doorway.

She and Mina had the same eyes: a very particular mix of green and
honey. You could sense she'd lived life on both ends of the spectrum—
seen its beauty and ugliness. There was also a warmth about her. She was
guarded with me, though, and by the looks of her dark circles, hadn't
been sleeping very well. Still, she looked too young to be the mother of
anyone out of diapers.

"Yes? Can I helping you with a something?" That's when it became unde-
niable that they were related, because her voice had the exact same tone
as Mina's. *I should say something before she thinks I'm a weirdo.*

"Ms. Arkova, we haven't met, but I'm—"

"Oliver?"

"Yes," I said with a nervous laugh. "It's nice to finally meet you."

"It can possible be pleasant to finally meeting me, if you stop to
encouraging my daughter to skipping her classes and to disrespect-
ing me."

I took a deep breath.

"I never—Look, Ms. Arkova, I respect you. Even though I don't know
you, my respect for you is automatic. Well, not automatic like innocent
until proven guilty; not like respected until proven unrespect-worthy,
or disrespect-worthy, or— shit. I mean, crap! I mean . . . I'm sorry."
*Take a damn breath, Oliver. You sound like a nutcase. Calm down. She's
just a person.* "Sorry, guess I'm nervous. What I mean is that I have a
lot of respect for you and for your daughter. I would never stand in the

way of her education or her safety. In fact, that's why I'm here. I came here to tell you something Mina will probably never forgive me for, but . . . she's going to a rave tonight. A rave is—" I cut myself off when Ms. Arkova's neutral expression shifted from confusion to an intense glare. "I'm guessing you know what a rave is, then?"

"Yes, Oliver, I knowing what is rave." She shook her head, muttering something in Russian under her breath. Whatever it was, it didn't sound positive. "Deaths reported on news program each year."

"It's not just that." I hesitated but continued. "I heard that the guys behind the rave are some Russian thugs looking to unload drugs in bulk. I think it's important that Mina stays away from there." Mina was going to kill me; her mom looked so pissed right now.

"Thank you for to telling this to me. I cannot believing this. She telling me can she please sleeping over at her friend house . . . just a more lies." She waited for me to say something. "Anything else you wanting to say to me?"

"Huh? Um, no, that's it. It was nice to meet—oh, wait! Actually, ma'am, there is something. Can you please not say that you heard it from me?"

"But Mina home right now. She is upstairs and California construction making a very thin walls, poor insulation; sound travel very easily." Crap. I thought she was supposed to be at rehearsal already. "She could sitting at top of a stairs, listening to each every word we saying, or be in bathroom, getting ready for fake slumber party. No matter which is true, she still a very smart girl and will figuring out anyway, but I promising you I will not telling to her information came from you. Is not my style anyway. Oliver, I must to go talking to my daughter now. Thank you."

"Here's my card, Ms. Arkova," I handed her my business card with my cell number on it. She took it and examined it like she was an elementary school science judge reviewing a project. "Please call me if you need anything."

"Very fancy." She smiled. "Goodbye, Oliver."

I turned to go, and the door closed behind me. As soon as I neared the sidewalk, I looked back to find a pissed-off Mina glaring down at me from her window. She disappeared out of sight. *Bing.* My phone got a text from her.

Are you freakin' kidding me?

Perfect. **just looking out 4 u**, I replied.

She texted back. *I barely fixed my relationship with her!*

so maybe u shouldn't b lying 2 her?

What the hell is your problem? From now on, just stay out of my life.

Shit. I looked back to the window, but she was gone. Well, I guess that was the end of that. My phone *binged* again. What more could she possibly have to say? I was afraid to look, but by the time I risked a glance at my phone, it was just CJ. *Good. Keep working, keep moving. Stay busy.* I opened his message as I walked back to my bike.

130K Wired.

I responded quickly: **meet 4 PM ?**

Westfield Century City, enter central structure via Santa Monica, take ramp down, then an immediate left and all the way until you reach the wall. Look for a white G550. 203 units. Confirmed? The ultra-specific directions were typical, and one of the things I liked about dealing with him.

It was strange, though—we'd never met at that location before. Either way, my account showed the wire went through, so I texted back **confirmed**. It was 3:05. If I could get back to the storage unit and load up the van in the next half-hour, then I'd have more time to get to Century City.

I pulled up into an empty space adjacent to the G-Wagon that CJ described. The windows were tinted, so I couldn't tell who it was in the car. To my surprise, when the door opened it was the sound of stilettos hitting the pavement that echoed through the parking garage. The woman walking toward me had gorgeous golden-brown skin and long dark hair, and was wearing a pair of black shades. Her clothes were sleek, business professional, yet still sexy—probably designer. She walked with purpose, accompanied by two figures: one was an asset from CJ's security team, but the second one I didn't recognize. Who the hell was this? CJ's sister, maybe?

She spoke to me as I get out of my van. "Calvin didn't mention how bloody young you were." She was very attractive, and it wasn't just the distinguished accent. She was probably somewhere in her midthirties, but could easily pull off midtwenties if she wanted to. I looked around. Where was CJ? Why did I get the strange feeling that I was about to get shafted?

"CJ never mentioned you. I'm supposed to be meeting him today. You work for him?"

"Not exactly. My name is Kiran Kaur. I mind the business while he's out of town. Now, I'm assuming—"

"I'll need to verify that with him. So—you'll have to excuse me, Ms. Kaur, but there's no way I'm handing over this much merchandise to someone I don't know—"

She quickly interjected. "It's Mrs., actually—Calvin's my husband. Notice that I am under the protection of Calvin's personal security detail. Surely you recognize that man?"

I opted to ignore her, instead taking out my phone to text CJ.

I'm here but ur not . . . am I handing all units 2 the mrs? confirm?

So, the C in CJ stood for Calvin? I always thought CJ was his whole name. "So what's the J stand for?" I approached her security detail, or, as I liked to refer to him, Titus #2, because he was slightly shorter than the other one. "Hey, man, what's up? Listen, don't trip. Of course I recognize you. How could I forget this face? So, what happened? Did CJ—or CK—go on holiday and leave you behind? That's messed up. I feel for you, bro." I offered a fist bump, but he left me hanging, so I turned back to her. "Who was this guy? Ex-queen's guard?"

"You're hilarious. Good on you—razor-sharp humor, truly. But Kaur is my maiden name. Calvin's last name will remain an unsolved mystery to you, I'm afraid." The look on her face told me she didn't find humor in much of anything.

"Didn't take his last name, huh?" I asked Titus #2, who rolled his eyes. Finally, a reaction. "Interesting. Very interesting. That says a lot about a woman. Emotional ties to her last name, especially her father? Most likely comes from money? Values her independence?"

Her eyes narrowed. "Don't read so far into it. It's simple really—too busy to bother. I despise unnecessary paperwork. Also, it's not quite any of your business, is it?"

"True. I apologize. He should think about taking your last name, though. CK has a ring to it, plus . . . I can think of a major underwear company with those exact initials. I'd be stoked to coincidentally have my initials stamped on all my underwear for free."

"Note that I'm being patient with your utter absence of respect, but my patience is growing thin."

"No, come on, no disrespect intended. Just killing time till he gets around to responding. He's the one who lacks respect, in my opinion, by wasting both our time like this." I dropped my smile, and she didn't have anything to say in response. She knew I was right.

My phone finally buzzed. ***Good. Always confirm with me. Confirmed.*** What the hell did he mean "good"? Was this another friggin' test? I should be past all that. I clenched my jaw.

She walked closer to me, looked down at my phone, read the confirmation, and exclaimed, "Oh, goody, a confirmation! Let's do this shall we?" She lowered her voice so the others didn't hear. "You're carrying quite a load," she said, before raising her voice back to normal and pointing to the van. "The units—let's have a gander." I swallowed audibly. Did she just say what I thought she did? I stayed still and silent. "Something the matter? Two hundred and three units, is that right?" I recovered and gave her my keys. She took them and smiled deviously.

"Would you mind terribly if one of my men drives your van to deliver these units straight to our warehouse? We'll make sure to top off the petrol for you, and Calvin would be very appreciative of the gesture."

I scowled. "Why would we do that? How would I get around? Why don't we just transfer the units to your SUV and you can take it to the warehouse yourself?"

"Jason's having it serviced for me in a few minutes. Something's been setting off the check engine light lately, so I'm afraid I'm carless. How about we grab a bite to eat upstairs while these two do the heavy lifting?"

What else did I have to do today? Other than trying to avoid thinking about Mina, pretty much nothing. So why the hell not?—I nodded.

She handed my keys to Titus #2. "Zavier, please drive his van to warehouse five and unload it at the dock; they're waiting on these units. Afterwards, just drive Oliver's van back to my place. We'll head over there after Justin gets back here with my own car. Send Calvin an update and then you're free the rest of the night. I'll give you a ring if there's anything else."

"Yes, ma'am," Zavier said, not thrilled with the idea. "Parking stub?" He held his hand open to me.

"What happened to 'please,' Zavier?" He looked like he was itching to slug me. I raised both hands in a "don't shoot" gesture, gave him the stub, and ran to catch up with Kiran, who was already at the escalators.

It didn't take long to pick out a place: a patio overlooking the Century City high-rises surrounded by lush greenery and exotic Asian décor. When the waiter came to take our order, Kiran briefly lowered her sunglasses to look at the menu, and I finally caught a glimpse of her almond-shaped, honey colored eyes, warm in color only. Her gaze was stone cold. She struck me as a woman who should never be underestimated.

"So, Oliver, tell me about yourself," she asked casually, but it felt like more of a command than a question.

"I'm from a city in northern California, before I moved to L.A.—mostly 'cause business opportunities grow on trees out here. That's pretty much it. You?" She pressed her lips together tightly—my answer was too short and impersonal. That, and the ball was in her court now.

"Whereabouts in Northern California?"

Nice try, but no. "Have you lived in America very long? You may not be familiar with the cities up north."

"Try me" she smirked.

"Santa Clarita."

Our waiter was back with whiskey. She took hers down as soon as it touched the table and ordered another. "All right, so . . . Santa Clarita, or, as the advertising hoardings call it, Awesometown. Continue." She was relentless, and knowing that nickname off the top of her head was downright bizarre.

"Please never call it that." I cleared my throat. "What, you've been there before?"

"We used to have a warehouse out there."

"No way."

She nodded. "Land's cheap."

"That's crazy . . . what're the odds?"

Once again, she steamrolled right past me. "So, Oliver, how'd you get into all of this?" she asked.

I could give a full answer, a real answer—put in some effort—but I just didn't feel like it. "I grew up under humble circumstances and got into this field by chance," I said.

I studied her, but she offered nothing. She just sat there, unmoved, staring at me for several long moments. Suddenly, she pulled her sunglasses up and set them on the crown of her head.

"I see," was all she said at first. Then she leaned back and looked away. "I grew up in the London borough of Harrow. My father was a cryobiologist at the Royal National Orthopedic Hospital. His expectations for me were always impossibly high, but I was consistent in reaching them. I grew up in a stable home environment, privileged even—"

"Go ahead, rub it in."

"—until the summer of my sixteenth birthday. My entire life changed that summer. I lost my father in a car wreck." Caught off guard, I quickly wiped the stupid smile from earlier off my face. "I didn't just lose my father that day—my mother became a ghost. We soon learned he had debts. His life insurance helped, but in the end, we had to sell the house and were left with close to nothing.

"I met Calvin at Stanford, and it has been a relentless quest, keeping up with that man," she finished. What did you say to all that? She'd overcome some hurdles . . . so she knew how to own a narrative. I respected that.

"From London, huh? Fancy a cup o' tea? Cheers, mate . . . cheerio . . . tea and crumpets—or is it biscuits . . . ?" I made a lame joke to avoid commenting on her life story.

She rolled her eyes. "You about finished?"

"Yeah, I'm done."

She didn't look amused. In fact, she scowled at me. But then a tiny smile slipped through the cracks when she asked, "That's really all you've got? That story usually leaves an impression with people."

"I was like you once."

"In what way?" she asked.

"Very serious. It's okay—I can show you how I got that stick out of my ass. I'm thinking we might need to rent an excavator to get yours out, though . . ." Thankfully she laughed instead of throwing something at me. She'd let her guard down a little, finally.

"I must be feverish; your horrid sense of humor is starting to grow on me."

"Finally." Neither of us said much more after our food arrived. After we'd finished, I asked for the check, but the waitress said it'd been taken care of. Kiran smiled and invited me for a walk around the shopping center while we waited for her replacement vehicle to arrive. We made small talk—she exaggerated the American obsession with social media and commented on how dramatic the shift in corporate marketing strategy had become while I talked shit about hypocritical Europeans who called Americans capitalistic pigs while eating the same supersized combo and scrolling through the same apps.

Jason dropped off Kiran's service loner vehicle in the parking garage for us and disappeared up the escalators after she dismissed him. The drive to her place was silent except for the bougie opera station blasts over the radio. I didn't think opera music was meant to be played that loud, but what the hell did I know? My van was nowhere in sight as we pulled up to her apartment complex.

"Isn't my van supposed to be here?"

"Zavier will call when he's almost here, should be any time now. He probably hit traffic—the port's down in Long Beach." She gave her keys to the valet and the doorman greeted her as I offered a handshake goodbye.

"Nonsense, you'll wait upstairs with me."

"I don't think that's—"

"I could actually use your help with something. Maybe you can take a look . . . it's tech, so I bet it would only take you a second. Would you mind?"

"I mean, I guess," I had a bad feeling that CJ wouldn't be happy about this, but I followed her into the building and up to the penthouse level anyway. The place managed to be decadent and tasteful at the same time, but what was really great as the view. From where I stood on the spacious balcony, the Wilshire Corridor looked like a winding river flowing into the setting sun.

"So . . . what's the tech issue?" I called inside.

She joined me out on the balcony with more whiskey.

"Nah, I'm good, thank you," I said, declining the beverage.

"You sure?" I nodded in response.

"I'll need to drive soon, and I'm technically underage."

She shrugged. "More for me," she downed hers and mine, one after the other. I was about to go back inside when she stopped me by my forearm.

"What?" But as I looked down at her, she pushed me down onto the patio chair and started unbuttoning the top of her blouse as she sat on top of me. I felt Mina's gift in my back pocket; the USB drive pressed into my backside. I almost forgot it was there. *Forget it, you ruined that for good.*

"Kiran, what are you doing?" She maintained eye contact and continued. She peeled off her blouse and threw it on the floor. I lifted her off me and stood. "You're beautiful, don't get me wrong, but CJ would friggin' kill me." I picked up her blouse off the floor and handed it to her. She tossed it. When I say she tossed it, I mean she tossed it over the balcony railing. Where was it going to land? Would it fall all the way down to street level? What if it landed on someone's head? What would the doorman think? *Crap, CJ's going to murder me. Is she crazy?* I was about to look over the railing to find out what the deal with this blouse was when she prowled toward me like a leopard. I imagined her throwing me over the balcony railing next. Instead, she stopped and knelt on the floor with her knees spread apart. Her voluptuous chest could barely be contained by that black lace bra. She held her head high, eyes hungrily fixed on mine. I froze, completely caught off guard. For a moment, temptation flashed across my mind. *What if . . . no, you can't do this.*

"Go inside," I ordered.

She didn't move at first, but suddenly she stood, turned, and went inside. *This is nuts, you need to leave right now,* I told myself. *You need this,* demanded a louder, more dominant voice. *No, you don't. This isn't worth it.* I walked inside, where Kiran was pouring herself another drink. "Will you put a shirt on, please? Did Zavier say when he'll be here?" I sat on the couch, shut my eyes, and rubbed them with the palms of my hands, frustrated. There they were—Mina's eyes, those soulful hazel portals with specks of green that lived in my head, her milky skin, and soft pillow lips. Before I could open my eyes back up, she was on top of me again, her lips on mine. Kiran unbuttoned my shirt, kissing my chest, then my ribs—all the way down to my stomach. I acted like I was lifting her away, but I wasn't trying very hard at all, I was letting her. Why was I letting her? It felt so good. Having lost control, the panic set in.

"Stop." She did. She stood, rolled her eyes, and went to pour herself another drink. My heart hammered against my chest as my mind reeled, igniting a terrible memory dripping in darkness, pushed so far back in my mind that I thought it was out of reach. I rubbed my eyes, trying to get rid of it. Heat spread through my gut and expanded into my limbs until every inch of me was on fire.

Now the nausea gripped me. My hearing went fuzzy. For a moment it was as though I was fading, no longer in my body. Something in my core was dragging me down, below the ground, under the soil, to the dwelling of my demons. I tried to stay present, but it felt like punching in a dream. I knew I couldn't go back there—I clawed to stay in the present, but I was already engrossed in terror. Light—I remembered the light, a blinding light, and I shut my eyes from it. I remembered the rolling sound of a camcorder, the cold—my bare feet on cement—the basement floor, the bite of ropes . . . *You're not there. You're here. Open your eyes, look around. You're not there. It's over.*

Just then, my phone rang, pulling me out of the trance completely. I stood abruptly and reached around to take my phone out of my back pocket, holding onto it like a lifeline. I looked at Kiran, still half-naked and walking around the kitchen.

"Get dressed, please. I'm gonna take this call. Where's your bathroom?"

She pointed at the hallway.

"Hello?" I answered the phone breathlessly as I walk away from Kiran as fast as I could.

"Oliver?" the panicked voice cut through the phone.

"M-Ms. Arkova? What is it? What's wrong?" My head spun from the anxiety of earlier. I found the bathroom, went inside, and locked the door. I scrambled into a corner on the floor like a rat and tried to listen to what she was saying, but my mind was all over the place.

"Oliver, please say to me she's with you."

"M-Mina? No. Mina . . . she isn't. Why? You can't find her?" The fear in her voice took my mind off myself as I imagined the hideous possibilities of what could've happened to Mina, images, varying scenarios. She'd been taken, she was lying on a street somewhere.

"How can I finding her? Do you know how can I finding her? I just calling Nyah parents and her mother saying to me the girls go to perform at concert. I tell to her it's rave, not concert, and she say, 'Oh, okay.' Just like everything normal about this. Oliver, I don't know what to do, just please telling to me that you know how I will locating her at this place. Should I needing ticket to going inside or will a mother of child can to walk inside with no ticket?"

"I . . . I have to see if—"

"Where is address for this place, this rave? Give to me . . . helping me to find an address, please—"

"I'll find her, Ms. Arkova."

"You?"

"I'll find her. Don't worry, I'll get her home safely."

"Please, Oliver, I'm beg to you . . . thank you, thank you, Oliver. She's just . . . she in a danger, she cannot to be alone right now, you understanding what I mean? Like this day in alley of school? I cannot to believe why she is such a reckless. P-please just l-look—"

"I'm sorry, let . . . can I . . . Ms. Arkova, I'm on my way over there right now. I'll let you know when I find her." I hung up, stood, and leaned over the sink. Running my hands under cold water, I covered them in soap and manically scrubbed them clean with my fingernails. I remembered Rig's words. *Clear your thoughts, Oliver. Find the balance between focus and freedom. If your anxiety was a tangible thing, how would you visualize clearing it? Find your way.* My thoughts felt so heavy that a helium balloon wouldn't do shit to them. They needed more of a high-alloy stainless-steel time capsule–type situation in a rocket ship they launch into space. I pictured the rocket ship, time capsule in tow, taking off as I dried my hands, envisioning it leaving our atmosphere into outer space, looping around on a trajectory that propelled it out of our galaxy and into a black hole. *Shit. I'm gonna need a fake ID to get in. Where am I going to get a fake ID so last minute?*

I walked back into the living room. Kiran was in a robe, sipping on yet another glass of whiskey. "You know where I can get a fake ID really fast—like, in an hour or so, by any chance?"

"You can't tell CJ about us," she ignored my question.

"Nothing to tell."

"I'm serious. He'd kill you—or worse."

"Me? What about you? And what do you mean 'or worse'?" Was she kidding me? What could be worse?

"Life in prison."

"For what?"

"Doesn't matter—he'll plant it on you or pin it on you. You're already on the FBI's radar, from what I overheard . . . they might be surveilling your storage unit."

"What? Why? I'm on the straight and narrow, everything legal. How do you know?"

"They asked him for a list of everyone he deals with. He cooperated, of course. The feds here do that from time to time when they're following a lead to the source of stolen merchandise. Maybe you unintentionally bought some hot units off someone?" She must have sensed my total panic. "Relax. If they're tailing you, it's just until you lead them to your source . . . or your source's source. Let them—the faster they find the source, the sooner they'll move on from you. Trust me, they're after bigger fish . . . credit card fraud and all that fun stuff, that's what they're looking for. The important thing is to conduct business as usual. If you don't, they'll think you're hiding something, and that's when they'll get you."

"Why didn't CJ tell me?" I asked.

"Not sure . . . I don't think he likes you very much." She smirked. "MacArthur Park. Northeast of downtown."

"Hmm?"

"You said you need ID? On Alvarado and 6th, there are guys on the street who approach you. It won't be airport quality, but it'll be fast—an hour, maybe less."

I was almost out the door when I turned back. "Thank you, Kiran, I appreciate the heads up. And I'm sorry the, umm . . ."

"That's all right, darling. You made your choice. Don't come crawling back to me unless you're ready to beg for it." She pushed the elevator button for me and disappeared into a room down the hallway. As soon as the elevator doors closed and it started to descend, I called Mina. No answer. I texted her: **call me when u can plz**. Then I added **i'm sri about going to her. I shoulda stayed out of it. let me make it up 2 u?**

I headed straight to downtown in my van. I left it on the northeast corner of MacArthur Park, then walked the rest of the way—Alvarado Street was only a few blocks south. The farther down I went, the more congested the sidewalk became. Soon the smell of portable bacon-dog grills and swap meet aesthetics filled the street with an intense energy. *Is this the place? This has gotta be it—right? How am I supposed to spot the ID guys in all this?* As if he'd heard my thoughts, a small man passed by me and spoke in a hushed voice. "ID? ID, mister? You need it?" I turned to him like the messiah himself had come to answer my prayers.

"Yes."

"Come."

I followed him to a nearby bruja shop. It was equipped with all your average necessities: hex candles, rat legs hanging from the ceiling on strings, and musty smells galore. Toward the back of the shop, a makeshift photobooth sat next to a massive blinged-out skeleton. He asked me to stand in front of a blue backdrop duct-taped to the bathroom door. I pivoted my shoulders toward another man who held a foam cup of instant soup in one hand and a camera in the other. A picture was taken before I could rub away the dust projected into my eyeball.

"Open please your eye, sir, for picture."

"Yeah, sorry . . . I wasn't ready."

He took another one quickly. He then immediately extended his hand and said, "Ten dólares."

"Ten dollars for the ID?" I asked, and the question was followed shortly by a roar of laughter.

"No, my friend, just for picture."

"Can I pay for everything together when it's ready?"

"No posible, my friend. Pay to him for picture eh, separate. Pay to me *para* ID when is ready, no problem," explained the guy who led me there.

It made sense—the photo guy played innocent bystander this way.

I gave ten bucks to the man with the camera and then turned to the presumed ID guy.

"How much ID?" I asked.

"Alaska ID?"

"I feel like Alaska would be too obvious. Maybe Utah?"

"Oh," filled the tiny bruja shop. "Utah ID *es muy caro*, much expensive."

"How much?"

"Three hundred."

"How about eighty?"

"No, no, no, my friend," he laughed at the amount like it was a joke. "Two fifty *dólares*."

I didn't have time to bargain, but . . . "Come on, I can get it online for, like, a hundred bucks. I'll give you a hundred fifty, but it's gotta have all the holograms, pass the blacklight test, and scannable, yes?"

"*Sí, sí*. Eh, blackligh' *y* scan, Utah, *muy bien*, two hundred *dólares* okay, okay."

"Don't forget the holograms—and you mean one fifty."

"*Ay, pinche gringo* . . . Okay . . . okay. Meet me one *hora*. Same place like before."

"Out there on the street?"

"*Sí*, my friend."

"Okay, see you in an hour. Thank you."

I called Mina a few more times—still no answer. How to kill an hour? I went for a walk around the pond or lake or whatever Los Angeles called the dirty pigeon puddle I was looking at. I'd been redirecting my focus away from what happened with Kiran ever since I left her place, but now that I was distraction-free, those events looped over and over in my mind. What was insane is how badly my darkest, oldest memories could still mess me up—all because I let the wrong person get too close to me. Kiran's aggression had flipped a switch and triggered an anxiety attack that brought back memories I locked so far away and long ago that I thought I'd never have to face them again. I mean . . . if I hadn't stopped myself, if that call hadn't come in, who knows how vivid the flashbacks would have gotten, and where that would have left me mentally? *You need to be more friggin' careful who you're letting near you.*

It was fate that Ms. Arkova called me when she did. I'd never believed in fate before, but when certain things happened, you tended to change your mind—like the time I knocked over the bookstand in the library that Remi had just alphabetized; that must have been fate, because it made Remi notice me. After that, she started noticing other things—like how I stole food when people left their stuff on the table to go find a different book. I'd probably be dead if she hadn't taken an interest—dead or locked away. Remi made me better.

Mina made me better too. I saw that now. The more I got to know her, the more I realized how different she was from everyone else. She was the kind of person who was trying to leave a mark in the world, and probably would. I thought subconsciously my recent business growth had stemmed from some competitive need to make something of my own. *No matter how hard you've tried to ignore her, you know she's the one who inspired that need.* I'd have to at least try and fix things between us. I couldn't give up—not now.

I checked my phone again; still no response from Mina. She was ignoring me. How was I gonna find her? Now I knew how helpless her mom must have felt. I texted Ms. Arkova: **Ms. Arkova can u plz send me Nyah's # if u have it?** As soon as she replied, I dial the number.

"Hello?" Nyah picked up after a few rings.

"Hello, Nyah? Listen, is Mina with you?" I asked.

"Who is it?" I could hear Mina's irritated voice in the background. I almost shouted out loud with relief.

"It's Oliver," I responded. "Can you tell her I—"

"Oliver? Hold on . . . she says she doesn't want to talk to you. And . . . she's asking me to hang up."

"Nyah, wait! I want to come by and make sure she's safe."

"I don't think that's—they're not gonna let you back here anyway. She's safe—we're fine. We're working, though. I can't be on my phone right now. I gotta go. We're finishing up hair and makeup." *Click.*

All right, well, that was pointless. I still had no clue how I was going to find her. I'd probably need a backstage pass or something or they wouldn't let me anywhere near her. I face-palmed. Instead of taking an aimless walk around this smelly pigeon pond, I should've been online, scoping out an all-access pass to the rave.

After digging around online for a few minutes, I found an ad a guy posted who was selling passes that looked relatively authentic. Of course, this asshole was asking for $1,500 each, which was crazy. But I didn't really have options at this point, and every other listing looked like bullshit. It was almost dark—I had to make it to the bank before it closed.

First I contacted the guy to see if the tickets were still available. He responded by the time I had gotten back to my van and driven to the downtown branch of my bank.

YA they R bro but I'm selling the pair 2gether.

Bro? Seriously? **I need just the 1 tick. let me know if that's cool w u**

He responded almost immediately, *LMAO can you read? I'm selling the pair 2gether so naw i'm good bro.*

I texted back: **unless u see some pigs flying chances are slim of someone walking around out there w/ 3k cash in their pocket a couple of hours before the headliners come on. hit me up when u change your mind.**

He didn't respond. Shit; maybe pigs *were* flying tonight. Meanwhile, I withdrew $2,000 from my account anyway, just in case, and drove back to pick up my fake ID. A cop car cruised past me as I walked back to the meet spot and my heart raced a bit, but I tried to act like I wasn't doing anything wrong—which I wasn't; I was just walking. Suddenly I remembered what Kiran said about the feds, that they could be watching me. I looked around for a suspicious car or an undercover set of eyes, but nothing stood out. *Consider what you're risking to buy this thing. This isn't smart, Oli.*

I was standing in the exact spot where the ID guy approached me an hour before, wondering if I should just bail. *Maybe you should just go home, text Ms. Arkova the address of the rave, and let her deal with her daughter in her own way. No—there's no version of the universe where that happens. I can't bail on her.* This was what I should've been doing in the first place, not screwing around with CJ's wife in their penthouse. I cared about Mina, and feelings like that didn't just happen every day—not for me. It wasn't just the feelings; a girl like her didn't come around every day, either—and who knew? Maybe never again.

"Not here." The same guy from before spoke in a hushed voice. "More privacy—coming this way."

"I was just thinking the same thing," I said before following him around the corner and in through the emergency exit of the plaza's parking structure.

He led me up the stairwell of the parking garage to the third floor where another guy in a dark hoodie waited for us, hands in his pockets. I gave him the cash as soon as he showed me the ID, which I bent it back and forth to make sure it was solid. It looked right to me—this could actually work. I shook his hand. By the time I got back to my van, more good news arrived.

Exposition Park. Meet me at the fountain. I'm already here.

Plan B was buying a regular ticket off of someone and then bribing as many security guards as it might take to get to the backstage area, and even then, I still might've been kicked out. This was a safer plan. The traffic into the event was bad, as expected. I left my van parked in a lot belonging to the local college, paid the daily rate, and went the rest of the way on foot. It'd be faster that way. Past old campus buildings, modern campus buildings, through a long stinky tunnel, and beyond an impressive rose garden emerged a circular fountain featuring four women carrying the weight of the world on their shoulders. I looked around for a nervous guy with a "bro" vibe.

I didn't need to look for long. A guy sat by the water, buried in his phone, nervously shaking his leg up and down. Weird, though, that he was by himself. Didn't bros normally travel in packs?

"You the one selling all-access?" I asked him as I approached.

He looked up at me, surprised. I waited, but he stared in silence.

"Wrong guy, I guess. Sorry," I turned away and kept looking.

"You've got the cash?" the guy asked me. *Why take so long to speak up?* I turned back to him.

"Let me see it first," I demanded, suspiciously.

"It's right here." I snatched the pass out of the open envelope he was holding and examined it. It looked legit—same colors and symbols as the ones in the photos on social media hash-tagged by all-access pass holders. I secured the wristband and dropped the cash into his envelope. As I turned and walked away toward the entrance gates, he called out, "Wait up. I have to count it!"

I kept walking. "You do that." *Amateur. What an easy target.* He was lucky I was an honorable guy.

It was chaos at the general gate. I'd never seen so many people sardined into a fenced-off area. The VIP entrance may have been bourgeois, but after witnessing all those people huddled like livestock near troughs at feeding time, I was grateful for an alternative. Security barely glanced at my fake ID, but when the guy scanned my wristband against the monitor, it lit up red. He scanned it again . . . and again.

It kept coming up red on the monitor, signifying an error. *That little douche.* Adrenaline surged through me like lightning, but suddenly the monitor lit up green.

"Monitor's been glitchy today. Sorry 'bout that. Have a good time, sir," said the security guy. Sweet relief—it was all good. Everything was going smoothly. Too smoothly, almost.

"Question: Do you know where I can find my friend? She was hired with the event as a dancer. I have all-access—"

"Keep moving sir. You're holding up the line ... you have to keep walking,"

"But I—"

"Keep moving, sir. Ask your questions inside," said a different security guy. I did what they said. He was right; even the VIP entrance was getting congested now.

My eyes beheld the madness before me with a wonder as I walked deeper into the field. I almost forgot what I was there for. This was like nothing I'd ever seen before. The scale of everything was massive—the giant neon mushroom sculptures erected from the dirt-like buildings, electric daisy installations, and, on ground level, bouncing titties covered in emoji stickers surrounded me like something out of a hallucination. I wound through waves of bodies as one face blurred into the next. I was a drop in a massive ocean of people and, strangely enough, at peace in an atmosphere of pure mayhem. Grown men in skull masks ground on glittered fairies, and circus clowns on stilts walked through the masses of ecstatic bodies. Apart from the clowns, it was hard to distinguish between the patrons and the performers. I was wandering through the crowd aimlessly when Mina's name came to me like a whisper. I walked up to a guy with a radio who looked like he might know some information.

"Quick question: Where can I find the dancer area backstage? I have all-access—" I showed him my wristband—"I'm trying to meet up with a friend hired as a dancer tonight."

"Is your friend performing with a DJ for a set on one of the stages, or hired by the event as a crowd dancer?"

Shit. "I don't really know."

"Then I can't really help you. The all-access designated areas are at the front of every stage. The dancers have a changing and break area back there, but even with all-access, that area is restricted to artists and crew only."

"Thanks."

"Yeah, no problem. Good luck man."

Great. How was I gonna find her in all of this? I picked up the pace and kept a lookout for groups of dancers traveling through the crowd, but there were groups like that in every direction I looked. I scanned the faces of the dancing glow-in-the-dark aliens stationed by the electric daisies, then of a group in blue spandex with gold wigs, next a clan of pink-haired fairies with purple eyes and silver wings, and then a threesome covered in gold glitter showcasing their sunflower nipples. No one in sight even resembled Mina or Nyah.

I moved toward the seductive siren call of trance music coming from a nearby stage—a sign designated it the "Solar Meadow Stage." A floating glimmer caught my eye, and I did a double take. A long green tail stretched out beneath a girl who was rigged above the DJ by wires. She was meant to be a mermaid, but hovering in the air like that, she looked more like a dragon. In contrast with her twenty-foot emerald colored mermaid tail, the girl's dark hair cascaded over her naked breasts. *It can't be.* I squinted to make out her face and realized it was Mina. *Of course it is.*

I moved toward her, a moth to a flame. My feet were moving on their own. I'd made it through the grinding crowd to the front corner of the stage, where she was now directly overhead. She was breathtaking. I looked up at her, a mortal kneeling to a goddess at the base of Mount Olympus. Glowing under the lights like a deity, she was perched maybe forty feet in the air on a metal swing by wires. She rocked forward, back, then forward again and then, abruptly, let go and backflipped off the swing. Her body hurtled toward the ground. I gasped, my heart in my mouth. She didn't land on her face and break her neck like I imagined she would, though; the wire system kicked in toward the end and she descended gracefully.

"Back up!"

I peeled my focus off Mina to find the face of an angry security guard that I must have rammed into during my freak-out. "Oh, shit, sorry! I thought she was falling!"

He laughed. I looked back to the stage to find that Mina was gone. *Where'd she go?* I had to get back there quick or I might miss her.

"Back up, Romeo! This area's restricted." The security guard pushed me back aggressively.

I pulled up my sleeve and showed him my wristband. He shone his flashlight on it, and then said reluctantly, "All right, go ahead."

Rushing past him, I kept moving until I reached a large white tent between two rows of honey wagons. I pushed through the glass doors, ignoring the "Talent Only" sign, and found a tent full of performers. Some of them were resting in the corner while others stretched or did their makeup. A few people looked up at me, but no one said anything.

Feeling out of place, I turned to leave when suddenly I heard, "Oliver?"

I stopped just short of the door. "Nyah! Where is she?"

"She's performing. You can't be in here. Is she expecting you?"

"No."

"Shit. Look, Oliver, I'm sorry, but I don't think she wants to see you—especially here, in the talent tent. Just trust me, I've been with her all day—she's really pissed. Personally, I think it's sweet of you to come and apologize in person, though. How'd you even get past security?"

"Long story."

"I bet." She looked around, then drew me aside, tugging gently on my elbow. "Look, I don't know much about the situation, and she'd kill me if she knew I was saying this, but I know Mina's never cared about anyone like this before. For real, I will deny that if you quote me. It's just . . . she can't see that you're in here. She's big on things like privacy and personal space—you know—basic shit." *Yeah, except when it comes to mine.* But Nyah had a point—this didn't feel right. Nyah took pity on me. "Maybe I can come up with something, though. It's not gonna be easy. I mean, ratting on her to her mom? Come on! What were you thinking? Never mess with Mina and her mom, Oliver. Those two are inseparable. You managed to not only come between them, but also to drive a wedge right through their relationship at its most fragile moment."

"I had my reasons, and they were good ones," I fired back, defensive.

"Everyone lies to their parents to go to parties or to do stuff their parents would never let them do. I do it all the time! Thank God no one comes over and randomly tells them what I'm really up to. They would murder me."

"Mina's mom said your parents didn't care about you going to a rave."

"Yeah . . . because there's nothing wrong with going to a rave. I told them it's like a giant carnival with music, plus they're thrilled that I'm working. They've been begging me to get a job. How do you know that, anyway? Are you still talking to Ms. Arkova? I feel so bad, because she keeps calling me and crying. I told her Mina's okay, but it's like she isn't really listening to me. Honestly, I've never seen Ms. Arkova like this before . . . she's usually so chill. I mean, what is the big deal about her performing here, anyway?"

"It isn't safe for her to be here."

Nyah rolled her eyes.

"You sound exactly like her mom. I feel like there's something else going on that you guys aren't telling me."

"No." I quickly changed the subject.

"Anyway, we've gotta get you out of here—she'll be here any second. I think they're just getting her out of the tail. Aw,"—she cupped my face, and I jerked away instinctively—"Don't stress. We'll come up with something."

I followed her toward the doors, but as we approached, they swung open, and it was too late. There she was, right in front of me, and, like an idiot, I grinned, happy to see her. She shook her head and walked right past me like I wasn't there.

As she passed, I heard her mutter, "You've gotta be kidding me. Leave me the hell alone."

Expecting that reaction, I was nonetheless stung by it and my temper surged. "No, I'm not kidding. Actually, I don't think there's anything funny about flashing half of Los Angeles in a strap-on mermaid tail while your mom's having a panic attack at home."

I turned and left the tent.

"Are you out of your mind?" Her voice was cold but steady as she followed me out of the talent tent. She spoke quietly. "Don't you *ever* put me down like that. First you come to my house and stick your nose into something that's completely none of your business. You scare my mother with bullshit stories about how this rave was funded by some Russian thugs when everyone knows that the company running it, the company that's been running it all these years, is Wide Awake Inc., a legit American corporation. Now you come here and berate me in front of my co-workers? You don't have the right. My mom didn't need to know about today; she didn't need to worry. I could've performed here and gone home. She would never have known, and everything would still be good. But you took that from me. Why? I have the right to do whatever I want with my life—with my body. Don't you get that?" She paused, evaluating me and composing herself. "And I wasn't 'flashing' anyone. This isn't Mardi Gras. I'm in a beige body suit. This is expression—it's . . . it's art. If you don't understand that, then—"

I wrapped my hands around her, and my mouth found hers. She shoved me and then slapped my face. It stung, but I knew I deserve it.

"No, Oliver, that's not going to work. You can't just kiss me and make it better. You hurt me, you asshole. My mom doesn't trust me anymore, and part of that is on you."

"I'm sorry, but what I said, it's was true. Tee wouldn't bullshit me. He told me himself that these guys running this event are dangerous. They're pushing their drugs tonight on a massive scale and Wide Awake Inc. is looking the other way and collecting their profits quietly. Still, I'm sorry. I should've found another way to protect you."

"I don't need protection." She shook her head. "They're gone—they left us alone. I have to believe that. I can't keep living in fear. I have to move on." I needed to fix this. I held her, trying to make up for the pain I'd caused. After a while, she stopped resisting.

She's looked up at me, conflicted, with furrowed brows. "You smell different."

"Hmm?" I asked, even though I heard her just fine.

She stayed quiet for a while. "Never mind." She turned to head back inside.

"I love you, Mina."

She whipped back around, a fire in her eyes. "You—" She cut herself off; she was furious. She didn't believe me. I pulled her gift out of my back pocket but hid it behind a clenched fist. *This isn't the right time, you idiot. What are you doing? You're ruining everything.* I put in back in my pocket.

"I love you. I'm sorry. I know I'm an idiot. I don't know why I went to your mom when I should've just talked to you. I should've fully told you how I felt about you coming here—convinced you somehow. And I don't know why I said what I did just now in that tent—I was so stupid, angry. You deserve so much better than me, but I can't not have you in my life.

I tried—I got on my bike and I rode off. I wasn't supposed to come back, but I just couldn't do it. I didn't want to go down a path when I knew you wouldn't be there. I had to come back. I don't know what it's going to take, but I'll do anything for you. Just tell me what to do."

There—all of it was just hanging out there, waiting on her. Still, she said nothing. She just stared at me with her beautiful, sad eyes. She turned around and went into the tent, and my heart sank to the pit of my stomach. I couldn't feel the ground under my feet, so I shifted toward a nearby fence and slumped down against it. I repeated the words I'd just said over and over in my mind.

I closed my eyes, trying to disappear.

Feel it, really feel the pain of this. You deserve it this time . . . you did it to yourself. Nope. No more. Uh-uh, no more for me. No more dating, no more girls, no more love. Love was another thing I'd just never have, like family. *You cling to this world like a leech when it doesn't want you, just like you're clinging to Mina. Leave her alone.* There was a ringing in my ear. It was disorienting.

"Come on." I looked up to find her outstretched hand. The ringing stopped. I stared at her hand, waiting for the punchline. "I called my mom and apologized . . . again. I told her I'm fine and that you're with me—keeping me safe or whatever. She's . . . well . . . you know, fed up with me. Anyway, what's done is done. Might as well go out there and salvage what's left of the night—one last hoorah before she locks me away forever. Come or don't—your choice." She turned and headed for the gated area that I entered through.

A lady ran after her from the side of the stage, calling out her name, "Mina! Where are you going?"

Mina looked over to her, shrugged, and ventured straight into the crowd. *Shit.* Without a second thought, I jumped up and followed her before it was too late.

CHAPTER 15

MINA

The words "I love you" lingered in my ears. It may have been a lie, but it'd colored my night in shades of ultraviolet. I hydroplaned through a sea of bodies, my heart drumming with the beat of the bass. I checked that he was still with me—he was. I smiled at him; he smiled back, following close behind. I held a course, but I didn't have a destination in mind. Finally, I veered from the crowd and toward the food tents. Everything smelled so good, but what I really wanted was a drink just to relax a little. The sticky counter of the makeshift tent-bar reeked of cheap liquor and Margarita mixer.

"Want a drink?" His whisper tickled the back of my neck. He swooped around next to me and offered his signature smoldering stare. "Are we okay?" he asked.

"Sure, I'd love one." I answered his first question because I didn't know the answer to the second one yet. But before I had the chance to tell him what I wanted, my bladder sent me an urgent reminder. I looked around for the restrooms, spotting the porta potties about one hundred yards away—but the line was massive. Even if I could have held it that long, there was no way I was waiting twenty minutes to pee inside a closet of toxic sludge. I couldn't go back to the backstage area either. They'd be looking for me there. "Be right back!"

I ran into a dark clearing hidden behind a cluster of trees by the perimeter of the venue. It could be safe to squat there if I were lightning quick about it. After I was done, instead of heading straight back to Oliver, I snuck over to a restricted area behind the bar booth tent. No one was back there manning the access. I stuck my hand under the tent flap, feeling around for the crate I noticed when I was standing by the counter. Jackpot! My fingers found a wooden crate. I gripped a bottleneck and pulled it up without clanking the sides of the crate—it was vodka. I wasn't sure what'd gotten into me—ditching my performance team without a word of explanation, peeing behind a tree instead of waiting in line like normal—and now I was a booze poacher? An impatient, electric energy buzzed through me, a wild and sudden vitality that seemed to be driving me to commit those acts. I knew it was wrong, but I couldn't help it. I stashed the bottle in a deserted area further along the perimeter and went back to Oliver.

"Miss me?" I asked.

"They said I need some special wristband to get a drink here. The ID-check booth is over there—"

"You don't say. It's like I had a premonition," I laughed to myself.

"What do you mean?"

I took his hand and led him to the place where I stashed the bottle of vodka. "Open it for me?" I waited for him to argue, but he didn't. Instead, he took the bottle out of my hands, twisted it open, and held it out to me, all the while laughing and shaking his head in disbelief.

"Just take it easy, okay? You don't want to face your mom hammered when you get home."

"I told her I'd be working here till 2 am . . . which was true at the time." He looked at me nervously. *What the hell,* I told myself. I never had fun. I always did the responsible thing. I just wanted to relax and be a little reckless. I lifted the bottle and filled my mouth with vodka, fighting back the gag reflex after I swallowed. Despite my better judgement, I took a few more swigs from the bottle. The taste improved with each swig, and it got progressively easier to swallow. My eyes teared up, my throat burned, and my nose ran a little. I wiped my lips with the back of my hand. "Whoo!" I yelled, and shook it off. Finally, I looked at him and offered him the bottle, but he just shook his head.

"Hey!" a voice exclaimed from somewhere nearby. "You can't do that!"

"Run!" I exclaimed. I threw the bottle toward the bushes and pushed back into the crowd. When I looked back, though, Oliver was still there. It looked like he was giving some money to the guy working the booth. When he saw me, he ran in my direction. I smiled to cover my guilt and continued ahead, dancing, spinning, and skipping along the way. I did my best not to step on anyone lying in the grass.

There was a group of about five people huddled in a circle passing around a blunt. Behind them, in the distance, the Ferris wheel came into view. It beckoned me, making me forget about the pot. Strange— normally, I would want nothing to do with that rotating catastrophe waiting to happen, but tonight it looked alluring and luminous against the dark sky. Just as Oliver finally caught up to me, I took his hand and pulled him toward the Ferris wheel. A line three times longer than the one for the porta-potties led up to it. "You've gotta be kidding me," I cried out in frustration. *Screw it.* I made my way forward around the whole line and squeezed through the metal railing surrounding the ride.

"Where you going, sweetie? Line starts back there," said an amused security guard doubling as a ticket taker.

"Hi," I smiled at him, sweetly. I leaned over and spoke softly so others can't hear. "I'm working tonight too—I'm a dancer from main stage, the mermaid on the trapeze. Anyway, the Ferris wheel's my favorite, but they only gave me a ten-minute break—you know how it is. Can you help a girl out and do me a favor?" I pled, maintaining eye contact and not giving him an easy way out.

He gave it real thought, looked around to see who else was watching, then nodded. "All right, come on."

"Seriously? Thank you. How much for two?"

"Naw, it's cool—just get on quick. Come hang out after work," he winked.

"I really appreciate it," I walked back to grab Oli's hand, pulled him in along with me, and hopped up on the rocking seat, beaming. The security guard frowned when he saw Oli get on with me and didn't bother helping us with our seatbelts before securing the bar over our laps. I looked to Oliver for a reaction regarding the miracle front-of-line pass; he was shaking his head in disbelief again. *I hope you're impressed, Oli, 'cause even I didn't think that would work.* My heart thudded louder.

The chair started swinging and up we went. Even through the light pollution of the city and festival thirty feet below us, the stars shone more brilliantly than I'd ever seen them in L.A. Maybe it was all the adrenaline that was making everything look so lovely—not to mention the alcohol. Or maybe it was those simple words he'd said to me earlier, blazing like shooting stars across a clear night sky. *I love you.*

I chuckled. "I'm normally super apprehensive of carnival rides; I don't trust their structural integrity. But strangely, today, I don't really care."

He took that in and didn't respond at first, but then he said softly, "I'm normally apprehensive around you, but strangely, today I'm not." His jaw muscle flexed independently, the way it did from time to time. It probably meant something too, but again, I didn't know what.

"Yeah, not today. Today . . . you love me." I teased, but instantly regretted bringing it up.

He took a heavy breath, and it was as though I could hear him thinking: *What am I going to do with you?* Then he rested his arm behind me, along the back of the seat. "You're wild, unpredictable, stubborn . . . infuriating, really smart . . . and crazy beautiful. I'd be an idiot not to fall for you."

He didn't deny it. My body trembled. *Please don't break my heart, Oliver.* Coping with that possibility was too much. I pulled his arm off of my shoulder but then brought his hand into my lap and laced our fingers. I didn't say anything. I looked away, out toward the far end of the arena. He must have sensed it—my fear, my internal conflict—so he rubbed his thumb against mine softly and looked out in the other direction. The ride was over too quickly.

I hopped off first and swiftly moved toward the exit, itching to get back into the crowd, to tap into all that exuberant energy. We walked to a nearby stage. I moved toward the center of the stadium, avoiding areas with gaps. I wanted to be sandwiched in vibes of comfort and chaos. I wanted to melt into the masses and flow with the music. Our bodies swayed like a thousand buoys drifting in the tranquil Mediterranean. I raised my arms into the air, mouthing words of the song over my shoulder to Oliver, who stood behind me, suddenly very still. As his arms wrapped tightly around my waist, he drifted with the rest of us. My head spun and blood rushed to my stomach as he pressed against me. Drifting morphed into something more intense as our mutual desire for intimacy grew. He kissed my neck, and I ran my hands through his hair. I was transported. Everything blinked away—it was as if nothing was left but the two of us and the music. We were in a meadow of weeping love grass. We swayed in the wind with each blade. We were an orchestra of violence and peace.

"Come back with me," he whispered softly, each word like a dandelion seed tickling my ear. I turned around to face him and nodded without a thought.

"Wait, I have to get my things," I remembered. "They're back at the tent. My supervisor, though—she's gonna . . . well, I don't know exactly what she's gonna do, but we should probably try to avoid her."

"We'll figure something out." He smiled and led me out of the crowd. We walked back to the main stage, fingers laced, letting go of each other opnly when we re-entered the backstage area. Just as we got past security, I spotted my supervisor walking toward the wardrobe tent.

"Come on," I whispered. We ducked behind a table under a portable canopy. "Shit. I think she saw us."

"No, I don't think so. Look, she went in there." He stood back up. "My stuff should be right over there." I pointed toward the dark green tents at the outskirts of the backstage area.

"Let me check if anyone's in there—hold on." Oli ran over to the tents and peeked through the side opening before waving me over.

I ducked inside after him. Squinting through the dim lighting, I searched for my locker number and immediately spotted my giant pink lock—good thing they ran out of grey at the drugstore. I stared at it blankly, trying to remember the combination. I could still feel his lips on my neck. I set the combo to Mama's birth year and the lock clicked open.

I let out a gasp as Oli grabbed my hips and spun me into a corner behind the lockers. Moonlight washed over one side of his face through an opening in the tent corner. His eyes were lit with desire. He kissed my neck, my cheek, my lips.

"Mina?" he whispered.

"Hmm?" I muttered.

"You okay?"

"Mm-hmm."

I wanted to show him I was without words—I wanted to give him goosebumps. I glided my parted lips lightly up the side of his neck until I reached the soft part of his ear. I ran my teeth over it and tugged gently, and he moaned. I started down his chest, undoing a few buttons as I went and leaving kisses on both the bruised and not-so-bruised parts. That's when I noticed it.

"Oli, what's this . . . ? Is this blood?" My stomach sank. I was lying to myself, hoping—praying—he had the perfect explanation as to why it wasn't what I thought it was. I'd accept anything but what it looked like: cherry-red lipstick. Not even close to my shade.

I waited, but he didn't answer me. That was when I knew there was no magical explanation. It was everything I knew it was. *Don't be upset. You have no claim on him . . . you're the one who sent him away*—pushed *him away. He was free to do whatever he wanted.* Still, I needed him to say it.

"Is it lipstick?" He didn't answer me. *I can't do this.* I grabbed my things from my locker and ran away as fast as my legs could carry me.

"Mina, wait!" I heard behind me. "Wait!" He caught up and grabbed my arm to stop me. I couldn't face him as he buttoned his shirt back up, so I stared at my feet. "I didn't want you to . . . I wanted to tell you. I was gonna, but I thought there was no point in hurting you for no reason. Nothing happened with her."

I glared at him. "It's fine. I'm fine." *No, you're not.* "You screwed someone, then tracked me down and told me you loved me. I think you've got stuff of your own to work out." I shrugged.

"It's not what you think. She and I didn't do anything. I got a call from your mom and I was so grateful for it and it helped me see—"

"Maybe you should have . . . maybe you shouldn't have come here." I yanked myself out of his grasp, ran across the path toward the exit, and didn't stop until I finally reached the street.

I walked along the sidewalk, bumping into people as tears streamed down my cheek. I pulled my phone out to shoot a quick message to Nyah. **Csn you plesse send mr Cassie's adsress?**

The sidewalk was filled with drunk people, angry people, crying people, laughing people, scary people—people like me, I guessed. It was overwhelming. *Get your shit together. Don't be pathetic.* I wiped the tears off my face. A rapid-fire series of notification tones lit up my phone. Nyah'd responded, to say the least.

ARE U KIDDING????

U just up & leave middle of the show no warning & leave me all alone? then ignore all my texts!

I was worried about u like crazy!

And when u finally find the decency to text me it's not to let me know ur alright or to apologize but to ask about the DAMN address to the DAMN after party?!

I only then realized how my leaving might've affected Nyah and how she must have felt when I disappeared. I'd been so selfish. It was like I wasn't myself anymore. I'd lost touch with all the important things. I felt like shit. *You should've paid more attention to your best friend—someone who actually cares about you and who's always there for you, never hurts you, never lets you down.* I texted back: **You're right. I should've texted you earlier. I'm really sorry. I kinda lost my head back there for a bit, but I found it now . . . I promise. So is the party still on or . . . ,** I typed. She was going to kill me.

Wow.

I sent her a kissy face.

6911 Queens Way

Yes! Perfect—now I could order a ride. I stepped to the edge of the sidewalk, and just like that, I lost my balance and tipped over into the street. Everything else happened so fast. I heard horns and saw bright headlights, and then fingers closed around my arm and I was hoisted back to the sidewalk. My arm was almost yanked out of its socket. The pain was intense, but it was a small price to pay considering what could have been. I looked up to thank my savior. It was Oliver. Of course it was Oliver.

"Listen to me." He was angry; a vein in his neck bulged. "You're upset. I get it. But you can't do shit like this. You can't be texting on your phone while walking down a busy street completely wasted and alone."

"Screw you! I'm not wasted!" I was overcome with laughter. It was a defense mechanism. My body was still in shock after what had just happened. My hands trembled and my phone slipped from my fingers, but I continued laughing.

He picked my phone up off the ground and handed it to me.

"You think it's funny? You could've been run over—"

I grabbed it. "Shit! It's cracked."

"Let me see." He held his hand out and I gave him the phone reluctantly. He examined it and then tried to unlock it. "Code?"

"Yeah, right." I grabbed it, typed it in, and handed it back. He shook his head and checked out the phone.

"Everything's working fine, I think. The screen . . . I can replace it for you tomorrow if you want—I have some spare parts at home." I didn't answer. I couldn't look him in the eye. "You need a ride home?" he asked.

"No."

"Come on, let me give you a ride."

"I'm not going home yet. I still have some time."

"I don't know if that's—where do you want to go?"

"One of the dancers is doing an after party at her place. I can get my own ride, though."

"I'll take you," he said.

I opened my mouth to refuse, but suddenly the night seemed to catch up with me. My feet ached, and I was burping vodka. I looked at him and nodded. "Okay . . . thanks."

Oliver and I were in his van heading north on the freeway in silence. No music—just radio commercials. I didn't touch the station dial. When city lights merged and separated like accordion bellows, you knew you were either hammered or in desperate need of prescription lenses.

"What happened to your bike?"

"She's still around."

The dashboard was spinning. I leaned back and waited for the sensation to stop, but that almost made it worse. I looked to him to ground

278 • EMILIA ARES

myself; even though there were remnants of sadness in his expression, he was still effortlessly sexy, and I couldn't help but admire the classical lines of his bone structure.

What a shame. Maybe he wouldn't have hooked up with some other chick if we'd just had one honest conversation with each other. Why hadn't we talked about all those weeks of ignoring each other? Why didn't we figure out why that had even happened? Oh, that was right—because we both loved our colossal three-headed dog named Pride and because the taste in my mouth was growing sour.

"Oh, God. Pull . . . pull over . . ."

"Why? You okay? We're on the freeway. I dunno if . . ."

"Please—can you just pull over?" I cupped my mouth with my hand. As soon as the van neared a stop on the highway, I swung the door open, lurched out, and heaved onto a shrub. He got out and brought over a water bottle and some napkins, then placed his hand on my shoulder. Tears filled my eyes. I didn't want his pity. I moved away from him, my heart torn to pieces at the thought of him with someone else.

"Why didn't you do it?" I blurted.

"Do what?"

"Sleep with her."

"Mina—"

"Just answer the question."

"I already told you. I didn't sleep with anyone."

I threw my hands up. "I wasn't listening before. My brain pretty much malfunctioned after I saw the lipstick. Tell me again—I want a visual. She's kissing your chest with her red lips, and then what? Do you expect me to believe you just up and left in the middle of all that? You just walked out that door and came here because—and this is my favorite part—you got a call from my mom?" I laughed hysterically as tears fell down my cheeks.

"Stop." He held his hand out to wipe my tears, but I slapped it away and walked back to the van. He got in, started the engine, and pulled onto the freeway as I rummaged through my bag for my mints. We didn't say another word to each other.

Finally, we reached the house. It was perched on the peak of Laurel Canyon. He pulled into a semicircular driveway, walked around, and opened the door for me. I took the hand he offered, but as soon as I hopped down, we both let go. I started for the entrance, but before I reached the front door, I heard the engine rev. I turned to see Oliver back in the driver's seat, ready to drive off. Was he really just dropping me off? He was just going to leave me, after everything? *Well, isn't that what you wanted?* He was probably leaving to meet her, whoever she was, and finish what they started. My heart sank to the pit of my stomach, but I called out "Thank you for catching me back there." He rolled down the passenger side window. "I . . . um, I said thank you for catching me back there on the street when I lost my balance, and thanks for the ride." I waited for him to say something, anything. He didn't; he nodded. I smiled goodbye and turned away. His car was gone by the time I reached the front door.

I walked robotically into an empty entryway. My heart hurt and my head throbbed. I wanted to go home, curl up in bed, and cry, but I needed to see Nyah more. A crystal chandelier hung above a rich arrangement of peonies in a white porcelain vase at the center of a dark marble table with carved wooden legs. Music was thumping somewhere, but the house was empty. I explored. *Imagine if Nyah was so upset with you that she texted you the wrong address on purpose and now you're just trespassing on private property!* I laughed at the thought. "That would be so messed up, Nyah," I muttered to myself.

Continuing forward, I squinted past the bright lights coming from more crystal chandeliers in the living area. That was when I realized I wasn't alone; the adults of the household were gathered for a nightcap on the couch in the family room. They broke off their conversation abruptly and stared at me. A man and woman, both in their forties or fifties, sat on one side of the couch, and on the opposite side sat an older couple, probably in their eighties, who inspected me like a show dog.

The wide-eyed woman—maybe Cassie's mother—pursed her lips and then said "Who are you, and why did you come into the house?" She looked me up and down like I was a freakshow act traveling with the three-ring circus.

What am I doing here again? That's right . . . "Is this the right address for Cassie's party, by any chance?"

She sighed.

"The party is outside the house. In the yard. Not in our living room. Are you a friend?"

"I'm Mina." This whole answering-without-answering-the-question thing was becoming a habit—thanks, Oliver.

Don't think about him.

"Everyone's out back . . . you're supposed to enter through the side gate. There's a sign outside," she remarked in an unpleasant, condescending tone.

I was about to apologize when the man beside her stood, shook his head sheepishly, and said, "It's all right. Just take this hallway all the way down. There's a door at the end that leads to the backyard." The woman gave him a frightening glare and he shrank before my eyes, taking his seat.

It was terrible, but strangely, I wanted to giggle at the two of them and their cartoonish dynamic—she, a man-eating predator with laser vision, and he, a timid Cinderella man bound to live out the rest of his days in this prison. Maybe she was tired after a long day at work and didn't want to come home to the criticism of her in-laws and the fallout from yet another of her daughter's parties. And maybe he'd been laid off after amassing an overwhelming number of sexual harassment complaints from his female co-workers despite his shy, intellectual, sweater-vested façade. I nodded and smiled politely. "I'm sorry, and thank you." I turned away from them and continued down the hall. On my way out, though, I did peek through one of the open doors in the hallway, trying to find the bathroom.

"Need something, dear?" asked the woman through her teeth. She'd been tailing me—probably to make sure I didn't steal anything. I understood her. "Restroom?" she guessed. I nodded. "There's one outside," she gave a forced smile.

"Would you mind if I just . . . I really need to go," I pointed to the one in the hallway.

"Oh, all right, go ahead," she agreed with irritation. I smiled politely and hurried in to freshen up. She was still waiting for me just outside the bathroom door when I finished. "The backyard is right through there." She pointed to the door with textured glass at the end of the hall through which you could see the silhouettes of people in the backyard. She walked me out and locked the door behind me.

After wandering through the party aimlessly and with no one to talk to for what felt like ages but was probably more like ten minutes, I finally spotted Nyah on the other side of the backyard talking to a group of people that I didn't recognize. Relieved to see a familiar face, I ran over to her. "Nybear!" She turned to look at me with an expression less welcoming than the one I'd received inside the house.

"Don't you Nybear me," she warned, her eyes on fire. Puzzled, I furrowed my brow. "And don't look at me with those innocent eyes, either. You don't even care, do you?"

"What do you mean? I told you, I'm really sorry for leaving without saying anything."

"'Sorry' is just a word. That was super shady, what you did, not to mention completely unprofessional. You were getting paid for that gig! People vouched for you, and you let us down so bad. Becka Silverman is Lydia's supervisor, and you really pissed her off. I heard her say she's sending you a bill for a full-priced entrance ticket as punishment. Someone like her could blacklist you in the dance community—"

"I messed up. I'm sorry."

"That's not gonna cut it in the real world, Mina—"

"There are bigger problems in the real world than a threat from some Peter Pan-bloused, pearl-clutching beauty pageant runner-up. I came here to get away from all the bullshit, to have fun, and unwind before I have to go home and face my mom, who's gonna lock me away for the rest of eternity. You obviously don't want me here, so why did you text me the address? For a chance to berate me? Well, you've had it. Now can we please just get over it?"

"Mina, do you hear yourself? You sound like a total bitch. Get your shit together—call your mom and let her know you're alive. She deserves at least that."

"I already did. I don't need you telling me what to do or talking down to me, okay? Calm down." I rolled my eyes and turned to leave, but she called after me.

"Oh, and by the way, the pearl-clutching beauty pageant runner-up forced me into the harness to replace you. No one else knew the routine; I did. So I did it. How's that for 'just getting over it'?"

I turned back to her. "What? Please tell me you're joking."

"Oh, now you get it, huh?"

I definitely did. Nyah had such a bad fear of heights; it normally made her freeze up completely.

"How did you get through it?"

"Because I had no choice. I'm a professional, and . . . fear is overrated." I wrapped my arms around her tiny body, and she let me.

"You are . . . it is. You're unbelievable." I rocked side to side, hugging her tightly, then took a step back to give her space. "Shit, Nyah. I'm 'bout to bow down—"

"You should. Go ahead."

I got on my knees and bowed my head, then raised both arms to the sky and fanned them up and down in supplication. She didn't expect it and rushed to pull me up. We both laughed as I struggled to my feet. "I'm truly, truly sorry, Nybear. Seriously, not just with the word 'sorry', but remorse—the real stuff—from the bottom of my heart. I wish I could go back. I . . . I wouldn't have left like that, like a . . . I don't even know what. I'm such shit. I'm really sorry, okay? I just can't seem to stop pushing everyone I love away right now: my mom, Oliver, even you. I don't know why."

"Mina, you and I are good. We'll always be good. I'll always be here for you, even when you're being a selfish bitch. So go on, tell me what happened. Just get it out."

I shook my head, disappointed in myself. "What's there to say, Ny? I suck at relationships." I took her hand and steered us further away from the group she was talking to before I'd joined her. "I pushed him away at all the wrong times, ignored him when I thought he was ignoring me, and then, just as things were getting good between us, I told him to stay out of my life when all he wanted was to protect me. So he did. He went away. Apparently, he was hooking up with some chick right before coming to the rave, my mom called him asking for help, and he came to the rave to make sure I was, you know, safe. And then he just put me down in front of all you guys, so I went after him to put him in his place and he blurted out that he loves me—like, what? It was too much."

"Babe, he's right behind you. He just walked in. Don't look," She indicated aggressively with her eyes, so naturally, I had to look. "I said don't! Don't freak out."

He hadn't seen us yet.

I turned away.

"Okay, Mina, listen. Pretend you don't even know he's here for a minute, okay? First things first—text your mom. Yes, even though you already called her. There's a bench under the willow tree by the fence—go over there, sit down, and tell her you're finished performing, you're okay, you're coming home soon, and you love her."

"Okay, Nyah, I think I know to say I love her."

"I know you do. Now, if Oliver is here for you—and why else would he be here?—he'll approach you. You two need to have an honest conversation. You have to tell him what he really means to you. No games. No bullshit."

"When did you get so bossy?"

"When's the last time a guy went that far out of his way to make sure you're safe?"

I couldn't say anything. *Never—not even close.*

"Think about that." She nudged me toward the bench.

A figure stood near the backyard entrance by the side gate. *Is that him?* I avoided looking in that direction and rummaged through my bag for my phone instead. Finally, my fingers found it, but as I pulled it out, it slipped out of my grasp like a bar of soap and landed on the concrete with a loud clatter. Blood rushed to my cheeks. Well, if he hadn't spotted me earlier, he sure had now. Reluctantly, I reached for my phone. I turned it over to find that where it had cracked from dropping it earlier, the entire screen had shattered. I hoped I could still text. Ignoring the dozens of microscopic glass shards stabbing my fingers, I focused on typing a message to Mama.

We've finished the performance Mamachka. I'm okay everything's fine. im sorry for everything Mamachka Ill be home in an hour. I love you. Please dont worry and forgive me pleease.

I looked over to the side gate. Oli and Nyah were talking. What was she doing? *She knows what she's doing. Trust her.*

He looked at me after something she told him. His eyes were smiling at me.

I smiled back even though I had no clue what they were saying to each other.

"Hi," came a deep voice from somewhere to the left.

I disregarded it as I watched Oliver and Nyah. Oliver seemed to be pulling out his wallet.

"Those your friends—that guy and girl over there you've been eyeballing?" asked the deep-voiced guy in a polo shirt with dark, smooth hair and pronounced, expressive eyebrows. He took a seat beside me.

"Hi. Um . . . yeah." I barely glanced at him. Now Oliver was handing Nyah some cash.

"You a matchmaker or something? Hello? Well, okay, sorry to bother you, I guess."

I snapped out of it. "You're not bothering me. I'm sorry. I'm just . . ."

He took that as a signal to sit back down but even closer this time.

Great going, girl. Now how are you gonna get rid of him?

"So, did you play matchmaker for those two? Did he just give her money? Is there, like, a drug deal going down? You ever play that game when you guess what strangers do for a living?"

"Them? No, it's not like that. He's—"

"Hey, do you go to Notre Dame?"

"What? No."

"Yeah, I figured. I would've remembered passing a face like yours in the hallway. But you look so familiar."

"I'm pretty sure we don't know each other." I tried to keep it light.

"Were you at the rave tonight?"

"Yeah." *What are they still talking about all this time?*

"Nice! It was sick, right? I'm still rolling . . . *whoo*," He ran his fingers up and down my arm. *Wonderful, he's handsy and on drugs.*

I moved his hand away. "I'm not rolling."

Polo shirt guy suddenly grabbed my wrist. "All-access? Nice! How much did you score this for? Or was it a favor?" He winked suggestively.

"Work. I performed trapeze and—"

"Oh, shit! See, I knew I recognized you. *Aggh!* You were so hot up there—but you know that. Wanna know something? I've kinda always had a thing for mermaids."

"You're not the only one," I muttered.

"Yeah, yeah . . . listen, I can't believe I'm opening up to you like this. It's so crazy. It's, like, so deep, our connection." He scooted closer, and my entire body tensed. "Yeah, I was high as hell, and I was looking up at you and I could have sworn you were the real thing for a minute there. Plus, you have these perfect tits. *Ahh.*" My eyes widened in shock as he actually tried to reach out and touch my breast, but just as I pushed him away from me, Oliver appeared and dragged him toward the pool.

"What the f—?" the guy whined.

"Mina? You guys were done talking?" Oliver stopped and asked, bending the guy's hand over like a pretzel.

"Yeah," I answered, still shaken.

"All right, buddy, come on, let's go over here. Don't fight it. You're only making it worse—trust me." Oliver dragged him farther away from the bench as the guy yelped out in pain, but gave in and hopped over toward the pool. "I know it hurts—it's just sprained. Don't worry—the pool is probably nice and cold. Here, put your dirty little fingers in there," he shoved the guy's hand into the pool and then patted him on the head. Nyah and I exchanged incredulous looks. For a minute, I thought she was crying, but then I realized she was shaking with laughter at the sight of Oliver schooling the poor lech. "Next time, just keep your hands to yourself, all right, buddy? Sorry about that sprain. It'll be better in a week. Ice it when you get home. But if I see you within twenty feet of her again, I'll break every bone in your body."

He walked back over to me. Tired of all the drama, I buried my face in my hands and slumped over. He sat beside me, releasing a hyperbolic sigh. "Enjoying the party?"

I laughed through my hands. "More now that you're here," I answered sincerely and somewhat defeatedly.

He tilted his head to the side quizzically. "I'm confused. Are you being nice to me, or is that some new, advanced form of sarcasm?"

"I'm just speaking my mind. Nyah recommended I try it—commanded would be more accurate."

"That girl is really something."

"One way to put it, yeah. I'm lucky…" I looked around for her, only to find her talking to the polo shirt guy, who was still nursing his wrist, but was in much better spirits. Suddenly, he grabbed one arm and swung her into the pool, cannonballing in after her. I stood, prepared to go after the guy myself. She came up for air and climbed out on the other end, unamused. I eased up—at least she wasn't hurt—but I started toward her to help track down a towel or something. She made eye contact with me and shook her head *no*. She pointed to the bench where I was sitting with Oliver and gestured for me to sit back down. She then found what looked like a cluster of grapes and chucked them at polo shirt guy, one by one, throwing every other grape in her mouth while yelling profane remarks at him. Oliver stood next to me by the pool, watching Nyah with a look of wry amusement.

"So, Nyah's encouraging you to speak some truth? I didn't realize you weren't already doing that," Oliver hinted as we walked back to the bench. I felt a sudden flare of defensiveness.

"That's rich, coming from you—"

"Then tell me something. What do you really feel for me, Mina?" He shifted his hand over so that his pinky finger rested along mine on the bench. *Who was she? Where did he meet her?* Under all the booze, dizziness, and poor judgement, the fact of their encounter still hurt like a raw wound. "Don't think about it, just tell me," he insisted.

"What do I feel? Like a large winged creature dropped you into my life but forgot to leave the operating manual." My answer was, of course, a defense mechanism—making light of pain to avoid vulnerability. *But you'll have to be vulnerable for this to work, won't you?* "No, I'm sorry. That wasn't real. Or maybe it was on the surface, but it wasn't what I meant. I don't know how to describe it." I looked to the sky as if an answer was waiting there for me. There was nothing out there, though, so I closed my eyes, where there was only the fog of my mind and more darkness. *Don't hide. Own it.* I opened my eyes and faced him. "There is nothing ambivalent about my feelings for you." I struggled through the words, finding them slowly, letting them out quietly, almost in a whisper, as if verbalizing this secret would give away all my power irrevocably. "I want an intimacy with you that I'm not even sure you can give me, but also there's this paralyzing fear that if we ever do reach that depth together—the fear is that when—if—one day, I lose you, I'll be broken in a way that's unfixable."

He didn't say anything. I mean, what could he have said? It was a lot to process. It was also a redundant fear, because anyone who'd ever fallen in love had risked heartbreak.

It was time to flip the switch, so I smile as lightheartedly as I could manage. "And you?"

"Not yet."

"What? What do you mean 'not yet'? I just—"

"It's not the right time," he explained calmly, juxtaposing my frustration.

"How convenient. Maybe it wasn't the right time for me either. You know, whatever." I looked away, searching for patience in the gravel beneath my feet and finding nothing but rocks.

"Come on, don't be—there's a lotta people here. I just want, you know, some privacy to, um, to share my—but I will try, I promise. Just not now. Okay?" He searched my face for understanding. I gave him a little nod, though I felt far from understanding.

"Don't be mad at me." He tickled my side. I couldn't help but smile. He tickled me again, this time closer to my underarm, and as a reflex I jumped back and pushed him away. He reeled back, his arms pinwheeling, and it was only then that I realized how close we'd gotten to the pool.

The look on his face just as he hit the water was absolutely priceless. He surfaced quickly, shook the water out of his hair, and pulled himself out of the pool without a problem. He walked over to me, and before I realize what was happening, he picked me up by the waist and threw me over his shoulder.

"Oh, yeah? You think that was funny? Then you'll love what happens next!" He warned, teasing me.

"No! Oli, no, please! No!" It was too late; I was airborne. I hit the water like a sack of potatoes. *I'll just make him a little nervous. It couldn't hurt, right?* I sank to the bottom of the pool dramatically, making sure to produce plenty of bubbles. I prepared to go back up before he freaked out, but someone was already wrapping an arm around my neck, yanking me toward the surface. *Ouch.* Getting saved was no picnic. I helped carry my weight as we resurfaced and tried to let him know that I was okay quickly, but when I opened my mouth to speak, I choked on some water and started coughing violently. Must've been all the excitement. A crowd had gathered around the pool. *How humiliating!*

"I've got you!" I heard him panting. "I've got you, Mina!" He vigorously swam to the edge with me in tow. *Good going, Mina, you idiot. More drama, coming right up. You just can't help yourself, can you?*

Say something! "Oli—"

"It's okay, I got you. You're okay," he panted, swimming vigorously.

"No Oli, I—" But we'd reached the edge of the pool.

He climbed out and pulled me up to sit on the edge. My skin scraped against the concrete. *"Ah!"*

"Move! I can't see anything! Did someone get hurt?" Nyah pushed through a crowd of voyeurs, and as soon as she made eye contact with me, she started cracking up. "What happened? Was the bathroom line too long?"

"How is that funny? This chick can't swim, and he threw her in." A girl with a pixie cut in a rainbow unicorn heavy metal tank top defended me.

"How's it funny? Let's see . . . maybe 'cause *this chick* happens to hold the record for fastest swim time in the fifty-yard freestyle relay at Wazzy's Masemaggen Summer Camp."

I turned to Oliver, who was still panting and now very confused, and not just by the name of our old summer camp. Slowly, that confusion turned into comprehension, and then slight anger just as my shoulders and the corners of my mouth curled up apologetically.

"You sank like a stone. I saw you."

"I was trying to tell you I'm okay, but you were super focused on saving me, so—"

"You kidding me?" He splashed water at me. I coughed, cracking up with Nyah. She returned to her friends, and, thankfully most of the crowd dissipated, already bored. I jumped in and swam to the other side. He peeled off his jacket and boots and then decided his shirt was slowing him down too. I admired his body from across the pool. He dove and reached me in no time.

"I'm sorry, I'm sorry!" I said, holding my hands out protectively, ready to wrestle.

He stopped before he reached me and read my guarded expression. "Let's call it even." He smirked.

I smiled, relieved, and leapt at him playfully, placing both hands over his shoulders, and pushed him down with all my weight. He pulled me down with him, yanking my calf, and I took a big gulp of air and went under. He let go and I drifted, eyes closed, weightless. The weekend at Rancho Mirage felt like years ago, that easy playfulness Mama and I had shared that day. I hadn't been swimming since then, and I'd missed the water. I needed to come up for air soon, so I opened my eyes and there he was, drifting beside me. He reached out to me, touching his finger to my cheek and then to my bottom lip.

He looked at me like he knew I'd made a decision—that I didn't want to be alone anymore, and that loving him was worth the pain, the risk. We drifted toward each other, drawn together. Our lips met and parted, opening a passage of breath. He gave me his first, and I gave it back, along with mine. It was intimate . . . a strange and beautiful feeling. We were breathing life into each other.

The tips of my fingers buzzed with an electric energy. My lips were still pressed together; my toes found the pool floor. I wrapped my arms and legs around him tightly. He squatted and pushed off the bottom, taking us to the surface. We both gasped for air. Even as I was submerged in the cool water, a fire was burning in me.

I pressed my forehead to his. I kissed him without closing my eyes, not caring who was around us or where we were. I pressed my whole body against his, and he reciprocated, swimming us to the edge and pressing me against the pool wall. He placed one hand on my cheek—a gentle gesture. His other hand was on the edge of the pool, holding us up. He trailed his fingers down to my hips as his tongue parted my lips. I was losing myself in this; it felt so good to kiss him again that I couldn't even think. The pressure of his body against mine was the only thing keeping me from slipping under water.

Suddenly, like someone pulled the power cord, he backed off. He swam away, and then after a lap swam up beside me. "You're lucky these nice people are all here," he whispered in my ear and kissed my cheek.

"Or what?" I whispered back. *No one's paying attention to us anymore.*

"Or I'd show you what I really want to do to you right here in this pool." My heart raced with anticipation, but my stomach flipped.

"Take me home?" I asked him, changing the subject.

He tried to read me, but then said, "Yeah, of course." He climbed out of the deep end like it was nothing—the muscles on his back glistening as they flexed. He ran into the guest house and had returned with a couple of towels by the time I climbed out of the water.

I found my phone by my bag on the bench where I'd left it. Grateful no one took it, I checked my messages. Mama replied **Okay**, and nothing more. It was definitely time to go home. We said goodbye to Nyah and left through the side gate. Oli and I took turns changing into dry clothes in the back of his van. Once inside the van, I reclined my seat all the way back. *I just need to rest my eyes for a bit.*

Oli touched my arm to wake me. I sat up on my elbows. We were parked in front of my house. "Here already?" I asked redundantly, buying time to reorient myself. *My head is killing me.*

"Mm-hmm."

I turned to him. He watched me with a soft smile on his lips. I reached out and traced his hand with my fingertips. "I don't want to leave."

"You think I want you to go? It's hard for me too. If I were selfish, I'd take you home and stay in bed with you until . . . I dunno, the end of time."

"Okay, so let's do it."

"I promised her, Mina. I can't blow it off. Please, just go inside."

"I know. I will. Can't a girl play a little make-believe?"

"You're going in?"

"Yes."

"Good." He hopped out and ran around to open my door.

"If you come in with me," I added.

"I thought you'd sober up by now."

"I am sober—almost."

"Come on, crazy girl. Asking me to come in with you to face your mom like I don't value my life . . ." He carried me out of the van, mumbling to himself. He brought me to the front door, where he put me down, kissed my cheek, and nudged me forward. He tested the handle. The door was unlocked; he pushed it open for me. I walked inside, but just before he closed it, I turned and wrapped my arms around his neck, pulling him in closely.

"Thank you," I whispered.

"Everything's gonna be okay."

CHAPTER 16

OLIVER

I ascended the branches of the fifty foot willow tree as if it were a ladder straight to Mina's bedroom window. At first, the tree was a huge advantage, because I didn't think I could've gotten that far up climbing the flimsy gutter pipe. But the higher I went, the more this tree was becoming a pain in the ass, literally—twigs poked at me from all directions.

You can still turn around, get in your van, and drive home. What if her mom sees you? You'll make things so much worse for Mina. I stopped, considering various scenarios and playing them out. I could fall—*that's unlikely.* The window could be jammed—*it's already cracked open and there's no net.* Her mom could hear me—*just be stealthy.* Mina could get scared and push me back out of the window before realizing who I was—*let her know it's you before going in. Don't be a coward.*

I had to be there for her tonight. She needed to hear the truth. It couldn't wait anymore. I patted my pocket, making sure Mina's gift hadn't fallen out—good thing I left the USB in the glove compartment of the van before I went into that pool or we'd need a cup of rice and twenty-four hours before she could play it, which would have been lame.

I reached my hand out toward her windowsill and used it for balance as I slowly stood up on the branch that I'd been holding onto all that time. But as I leaned forward to grip the window glass, one of my feet slipped off the branch. I grabbed onto the ledge and felt a nail dig into my palm, but I couldn't let go or I'd fall and break my neck. My dangling foot found the branch again. I squatted down, breathing heavily. I gripped the ledge again, but in a different place, stood, and this time I had the stability to grip the glass and push the window open wider. "Mina, it's me. Don't get scared . . . and please don't push me out the window or punch me in the head," I whispered. Then I pull myself through the window.

"Mina?" There was no one there. Where was she? The lights were off in the rest of the house; they should have both been asleep by then. I crouched in the corner by the open window and looked out at the night sky through the sheer curtains.

Minutes passed as I sat in silence, trying to decide what to do, when, suddenly, the doorknob turned and in walked Mina.

"Don't get scared—it's just me." She jumped back reflexively, slamming her shoulder against the doorway.

"Sorry, I tried to warn you," I whispered.

She whispered back pointedly after she shut the bedroom door, "Oli . . . what the hell? You scared the shit out of me. How did you even get in here?"

"Window."

"My mom's asleep, but if she catches us, it'll be really messed up. I spent the past hour begging for her forgiveness. She almost canceled her flight to Russia because she was so worried about me, and that flight is really important. My grandfather's sick and she needs to see him."

"I'm sorry. I hope he's gonna be okay. She'll never know I was here at all. We'll be really quiet. Is she a light sleeper?"

"Not at all, I've seen her sleep through a magnitude 4 earthquake."

"Good. Then can I give you something before you kick me out?"

"A present?"

"It's a . . . yeah, I guess so." I reached into my pocket and pulled out the USB. "Just don't laugh."

"Anything else?"

"That's it." I walked over and placed it in her hand. She hopped onto her bed and reached for her laptop to plug the USB in. "Just in time for my birthday."

"On Sunday, isn't it?" I asked.

"Technically, midnight tomorrow," she said.

Mina opened the only folder on the USB drive. I titled it with her name. Inside were 11 mp3 files. My pulse raced. Nervous, I picked at the loose skin at the edge of my thumb.

"Is this a mixtape?" She asked.

I shrugged. "Just play it; you'll see."

She Airdropped the audio files to her phone and got comfy against her pillows before plugging her headphones in, throwing them on, and pressing play. The muffled sound of my voice came through her headphones—she smiled.

Mina wore a puzzled but giddy expression as she listened. Finally, it dawned on her, and her mouth dropped open. She paused the audio. "Did you—is this—?"

"It's my favorite book, Camus's *The Stranger*. I know you prefer audiobooks, so I read it to you—"

"You recorded the whole book for me?"

"Yeah." I chuckled, remembering how hard it had gotten after the first couple of chapters. "I almost lost my voice and gave up halfway through, but I figured it'd be shitty to leave you hanging just when it's getting good."

"Oli, I . . . this is . . ." She didn't know what to say. She pressed play again, listened some more, and paused it. She fast-forwarded through the audio file. "Oh, yeah, I can hear the suffering in your voice at this point—like you've been chain-smoking." We both chuckled quietly and sort of just stared at one another for several moments until she finally uttered, "Thank you."

All I could muster was, "Happy birthday."

I moved closer to her. She stood still as I traced the delicate skin of her cheek with the back of my fingers. I left a gentle kiss on her lips, on her cheek, and another under her ear by her neck. I whispered, "Good night," and turned to the open window. Her hand held on to mine, pulling me back.

"Stay."

"I can't Mina. You're right. Your mom—"

"It'll be fine."

"But you said—"

"I was being paranoid." She pulled me closer. "Just stay for a little," she insisted. I'd hoped she would.

She walked back to her bed and I followed awkwardly, more nervous than a guy with a toupée in a stiff breeze. It was like a sauna in the room; I was sweating through my shirt. Her fingers were cool against the heat of my skin—it felt good.

She lay down and I sat beside her. The back of my head found her pillow in the darkness, and we both stared at the ceiling, side by side. I closed my eyes to get a handle on my nerves, but it only made me more self-conscious. *You're fine. Be cool.* I rubbed my eyes, trying to physically wipe the anxiety away.

"Tired?" she asked quietly.

"No."

"What's wrong, then?"

"Nothing."

"No, don't do that, Oli. Don't shut me out. You wanted privacy? Well, here it is. At least try, try to explain what you couldn't tell me before."

But that's what I do, Mina. I bottle it in and let it fester. "I don't know how," I said. I couldn't find the words. I couldn't connect. I couldn't let go. I couldn't let anyone peek into the festering nightmare dwelling inside me.

She turned my face toward hers and furrowed her brows in frustration, tears flooding her eyes. "You know what, Oli? I understand loss, all right? You think I don't know what pain feels like? Sometimes it's just easier to . . . to just walk around and pretend that I'm numb when, really, inside I'm . . . I feel broken. And it's my own fault. I told you that I lost my sister before she was even born. But that's not the whole story. Back then, we lived on the second floor of this apartment building, and I used to play on the stairwell landing on the porch outside our apartment door. My mom didn't like me playing there because of the stairs—she always scolded me and said it was too dangerous to play there, that I could . . . could fall—so when I heard her coming that day, I got scared and I ran and hid behind a planter. But I'd left one of my toy cars out and she stepped right on it and went over backwards. Down the stairs." I grabbed her hand.

"You were a child, Mina. It was an accident." I told her. "You're not broken. You're strong."

She continued. "I never forgave myself for losing my sister. Losing that baby changed everything for my parents. It was like the grief was eating away at them inside, turning them against one another. Their worst selves came out; they fought about everything until one day they just started ignoring each other completely. My father's on his own now—alone, no family, no real home—that's on me, too."

She wiped the tears away and looked up at the ceiling. "They would have stayed together. We would've been hap—"

"It wasn't your—"

"My fault? I get that, I do—but ultimately, Oli, who knows? No one. My mom's miscarriage was a dark time, and pretending that dark time didn't change their relationship is delusional—"

"I'm sorry, but I don't see why you'd assume they would have stayed together. What happened to your family was a tragedy, but it was an accident, and marriages have survived worse things, and they've crumbled for smaller reasons. It wasn't up to you: It was up to them." She shook her head, disagreeing. "Your sister was more loved in her few months of existence in a womb than I have ever been in my entire life. There are worse things, Mina, than divorce, than dying before you're born. I promise you that I would have gladly traded places with her."

She looked horrified by my words. "How could you say something like that? You got a chance to live."

"You said you wanted to hear the truth. Well, the truth isn't pretty. I'm just now getting to have the things that many people were born with and take for granted every day—like freedom and choices. Living came at a great cost for me, so yes, there were times when I grew tired of paying that price. Things go well for a couple of days and I start to think, 'Finally, I'm getting better,' and then, out of nowhere, something triggers me and I spiral into my next anxiety attack. It can be anything that does it, too—something simple like looking at my own reflection for too long. 'Cause sometimes when I see my face, I start wondering stupid, pointless shit, like, 'What parts of me look like her? Do I have her eyes'?"

Mina's eyes softened, slowly letting go of some of the judgement. "Your mother's?" she asked cautiously. "She must have been beautiful."

"I never knew her face, but I'm living proof of her choices," I mumbled, afraid to say more. If I did, there was no going back. She'd know everything. The image I'd worked hard to create would crumble, replaced by a lonely reject with mommy issues.

"What choices?" Mina asked gently. She patiently waited for me to go on, her eyes bright with warmth and acceptance, like everything was going to be all right after I confessed or something—like she thought she knew what I was about to say.

Why did it feel like I was on the edge of a cliff? If I jumped, I'd either bring this relationship to a deeper level of trust or scare her away for good and mess up my chance at true happiness. Before I could conjure up some third option, I did it—I leapt.

"My mother tried to abort me," I blurted, still ashamed to say it out loud, even after all that time. Her eyes widened in disbelief. "It didn't work, obviously—I guess I just refused to die . . . stubborn bastard from the start."

"Oh, God . . . Oli," she took my hand and held it between both of hers.

"They say she was a mess—an addict. She came in for a sickeningly late-term abortion. All that crap she smoked and pumped into her veins was reason enough for the clinic to sign off on it. The saline solution they injected was supposed to kill me, but by some miracle, after twenty hours, she gave birth to me. I was premature and drug-addicted, but alive. The nurse at the clinic couldn't go through with it, I guess, leaving me on the table to die—"

"Oh, God—"

"So the nurse called an ambulance, which took me to the hospital, where they put me in the NICU." Mina shook her head at me like I was missing something obvious. She was itching to say something but bit her lip and resisted. "Anyway, she saved me, and my mother disappeared.

"I spent the first few months of life connected to a machine that breathed for me. Eventually they diagnosed me with cerebral palsy, which was shit luck and made getting adopted very difficult. No one wants a sick kid—raising a healthy one's hard enough. I was lucky my CP wasn't as severe as it could have been, though. They kept calling me a medical miracle 'cause I was resilient as a cockroach, considering the oxygen depletion I experienced at birth." I laughed. Mina's eyes were wide with compassion.

"So I grew up in foster homes. I tried hard to make friends with the other kids, but I developed slower than they did. According to my file, I started walking and talking later than normal; the milestones just weren't happening for me. I had this fight inside me, though, like I had something to prove—maybe to show everyone they were wrong about me, or that she was wrong and should have kept me despite everything. I fought hard against my CP, and even though eventually I caught up to everyone and you could barely tell it was ever there, I was never adopted. So I kept being moved from one foster home to another—overcrowding.

"By the time I was ten, I was thrown in juvie for serious behavioral issues or some shit. And in there, you're surrounded by violence on a daily basis. Some of those kids have killed people; some haven't done shit. It's brutal in there—survival mode 24/7."

"Oh, my God, Oli—"

"Yeah, and if you fought or made any kind of trouble, you were pepper-sprayed and sent to solitary as punishment—even the kids with mental health issues—"

"Jesus—"

"There was this one asshole, much older than me, who loved giving me a hard time—the bastard got a kick out of spreading misery. He . . . uh, he cut my wrists one night in my sleep. It was nothing major—just surface wounds made by broken plastic—but they put me on suicide watch, stripped me to my underwear, and locked me in solitary confinement for six days with no windows and no light—just a drain in the floor, cold food, and the smell of dried shit everywhere." There was an electricity in Mina's eyes; they were filled with horror and she was speechless. But our connection was palpable as she held my hand tightly. These were things I'd never said out loud before—not like this. This confession was cathartic, with each word bringing us closer together—not further apart like I was afraid it would.

"No one tried to stop this?"

"No one cared. We were the rejects of society. We got groped by the staff during body checks, taken into a separate room, or pulled out of bed in the middle of the night for some unwanted touching. It's never who you'd expect. I'm talking about female staff—desperate and lonely women enjoying the taste of power. Some would groom you and bring you nice things—even alcohol and drugs, if you were lucky. Others would use punishment and force and manipulation. No one's gonna believe a problem kid locked up in juvie. I mean, after living in a place like that for almost five years, you can imagine my stupid, naïve ass, and how excited I was when they eventually released me into a foster home again. If only I knew what was waiting for me there, I would've begged to live out the remainder of my youth in juvie and promise a smile on my face the whole time." Mina sat up higher and squared off toward me, tense, fearful of what I might say next.

"I ended up in a new foster home, and the guy who ran it—there was something wrong with him. At home, he couldn't keep his hands out of his pants and would just be itching it, touching it all day, so we nicknamed him Jack the Crack." I could still remember the smells of that house, the taste of fear—a metallic taste, acidic. Mina kept eye contact with me, not looking away for a second. I looked away. "He forced us to do messed up, disturbing things . . . wipe for him after he'd used the bathroom, take showers with him, and—other messed up shit you don't need to know." I checked in with her to see if she could still look at me. Nothing had changed— still the same compassionate gaze, with only kindness in her eyes. "Caretaker was his official title."

"What a joke."

"If anyone pissed him off, he brought out his insane homemade bat that he'd driven old nails into—he feasted on fear. And at night, when it was your turn, he'd take you down to the basement for a couple of hours and make a movie. But those he paid for, in the end." Mina covered her mouth with her hands and shook her head incredulously.

"Is that the world we live in? Where tax-paying, law-abiding gay couples have a harder time adopting kids than some heartless piece-of-shit pervert lunatic—"

"Yeah . . . I mean, he was damaged to the core. Irredeemable. Dishonorably discharged from the military. He was a conspiracy theorist, a doomsday fanatic, and on top of everything, he was diagnosed with severe PTSD. Yet somehow, the system looked over all that shit and deemed him proper. He was essentially collecting paychecks from the state, then turning around and violating and abusing and starving us."

"That's so messed up."

"It wasn't until I started sneaking to the library after school that I met the person who changed my life forever. Remi—she's a librarian. She was the first truly decent person I'd ever known. She noticed something was off with me, and despite the fact that I kept pushing her away, she just kept trying to help me. To get me justice. I was terrified that Jack would find out I'd opened my mouth about him. He could've killed me and called it an accident, for all I knew."

"Couldn't you report it?"

"We did. It's a long story. Basically, they'd come investigate and no one would speak up in front of him—and he hid evidence well. After the first couple of complaints filed by us were marked false, they stopped taking the investigations seriously all together."

"But you fought back, didn't you?" she squeezed my hand, eyes wide with excitement. "You got away. You're here." None of this seemed to repel her. I thought she would be disgusted by it and by me. But it was the opposite, it's like she was committing to me with all her body language and her heart. I kept going, suddenly feeling empowered by my own story.

"Once Remi figured out how bad the abuse was, she helped me find the right lawyer for our case. Even with a corrupt, messed-up system, the neglect, the cover-ups, the lies . . . still, we worked our asses off. And we also got lucky. It took, like, four months of research and desperate faith and a shit load of favors and sheer friggin' luck—getting the right judge and a good jury. But we won the case, and now he's serving his life sentence. We got a monster off the street and now he can't ever touch another kid. In my case, the judge granted me two million dollars in the trial against the state."

"Holy shit."

"I still can't touch most of that money, but it gave me my start—enough to move, get settled, and get my business running. So there's my silver lining for getting aborted and raped—"

"You're a survivor. Think of how many kids were spared that violence because you put him away." No one had ever looked at me the way she did—with admiration. It was overwhelming and unexpected. The warmth in her eyes had this healing energy, so hard to describe.

"So, what about your mother?"

"What about her?" I frowned. "She wanted me dead. She's probably dead herself by now. They never told me who my father was—she probably had no clue." One question and now I was fraying at the ends. She pulled my head to her chest. I'd never been held like that before. Realizing how good it felt made my eyes tear up.

I sat up, rubbed my face with my palms, took a heavy breath, and let it go. "I don't want you to feel obligated to do anything now that you've heard all of this. It's a lot for anyone, and I don't want you feeling trapped. This is your life and we only get one. We can't build this from a place of pity, because it won't last. Just think about it before you decide what you want. After everything you've been through, maybe something lighter— someone lighter—would be right for you—"

"Oli, stop."

"No, just listen to me. I don't want to wake up to an empty house one day because you finally realized you've been with me out of kindness and sympathy and can't live that lie anymore. It'll—I won't survive it.

You should know everything about me right now, up front, so you can make your decision based on facts instead of giving me shit about it later because you didn't know how hard it was gonna be."

"What do you mean, 'give you shit'? I wouldn't do that. I know it's not gonna be easy—"

"I have—I, uh, I still battle feelings of shame when it comes to sex...so I've slept with women who prefer...who like when it's intense, basically. I sought out aggressively sexual women and it's always been exclusively physical, not emotional at all. I've never been with anyone like you. You were talking about wanting intimacy earlier. I don't know if I can ever give that to you." For the first time, she was uncomfortable. She wrapped her arms around her knees and rested her chin on her legs, lost in thought. "I have issues controlling my anger. That part I'm working on. But it's gonna take time and trial and error to make progress, and...I'm scared, I'm friggin' terrified to commit to this—to us. If I lose you along the way, it would be brutal. It would set me so far back—"

"Oli—"

"I don't trust people, Mina. Most of the ones I ever met were liars or manipulators. I've never loved anyone before. I don't know how because I've never been loved."

"Oli, I—"

"I'm afraid of myself around you—like, I become overprotective. I really wanted to hurt that guy on the bike the day we got the spare helmet. And then tonight, the joker at the party, it's like I'm blinded by my rage—"

"I love you," she whispered, and kissed me. I forgot everything I was going to say. She let go of my hand and wrapped her arms around my neck. "I love you," she said again. We laid down together, face to face, legs intertwined, my arms wrapped around her waist.

I kissed her forehead and held her soft cheek in my palm. This was the best feeling in the world. I was weightless and invincible. "I love you too,

Mina—I've never cared for anyone the way I care for you. I'm gonna give this everything I've got, no holding back—" I promised her. "I'm all in—you can trust me."

She nestled up to me and rested her cheek against my chest.

"I trust you," she whispered.

CHAPTER 17

MINA

Have you ever woken up and thought, *What a beautiful world this is—full of magic, where sunshine is food for the soul?* Usually I opened my eyes and it was like someone smashed a lead hammer against my skull, but this morning was different. In spite of the cramp in my left shoulder from sleeping in the same position all night, the ringing in my head, the sleep in my eyes, and the dryness in my mouth, this morning I woke up with a smile on my face. I turned over to find Oli asleep beside me. *Oh, shit, he's still here! If Mama comes in here, I'm dead! What time is it?* Somehow, he looked even more gorgeous in his sleep. I sat up, massaging the feeling back into my arm and fixing my hair. His long eyelashes fluttered open.

"I'm sorry, I must have conked out. Crap," he muttered while he stretched his limbs. He inhaled deeply and whispered, "Good morning."

"Good morning," I answered hoarsely. *I feel like a boiled turd.*

"How do you feel?" he asked, curling up across my lap.

"Shh . . . good." *Like death warmed up, but happy.*

"I haven't slept that well in . . . well, probably never," he whispered.

"Same." *Like I've been scraped off a shoe, but in a good way.*

"Get over here." He lifted his head to kiss me, I ducked and hugged him instead.

"Morning cuddle sesh." *I refuse to share my morning breath with you, you perfect creature.*

"You're beautiful."

"You are." *My head is going to explode.*

He kissed me. *Lord, I must smell like a smoothie in the Sahara.* He didn't seem to mind as he slipped his tongue into my mouth. *How great is this? I'm so happy in this moment that I need for nothing, except maybe a gallon of water. And two Tylenols. And a pound of bacon.*

Oli's stomach growled as if on cue. "I'll go downstairs and bring us up some breakfast," I told him. "Do you mind waiting in my closet, just in case? Oh, yeah, and if you need to use the bathroom, just don't flush the toilet."

"No worries—it's better I sneak out before I get you in trouble."

"Shh! Did you hear that?" I whispered.

He listened. "No, what?"

"The clinging of pans—she's up. She's in the kitchen."

"Could she have come in and seen us while we slept?"

"No," I whispered.

"How do you know?"

"Because, trust me, she'd have let us know. And she's definitely gonna notice someone climbing down her tree by the kitchen window. Hold on, let me think. I'll have to distract her somehow before you climb out." I pulled on a pair of jeans and changed my T-shirt. Oli sat up and put on his shoes, but I could feel his eyes on me. I started for the door and he headed to the window.

"Just give me a minute," I said in a hushed voice. "I need to come up with something to get her out of the kitchen without being too obvious."

Oli whispered into an imaginary radio. "*Kshh* . . . we've got a potential code three, and we're definitely gonna need back up if Arkova's distraction fails."

"*Shh!*" I chuckled quietly and ran over for a goodbye hug, "Thank you for my gift—and for getting me home, and for—"

He cupped my face in his hands and gave me the kind of kiss I'd always imagined lovers gave each other when they were saying goodbye. Sweeping me up, Oliver wrapped my legs around his waist as he pressed me against the wall. He kissed my neck, then pulled down the strap of my camisole and kissed my shoulder. He continued to kiss my neck. My fingers wove through his hair. His hands caressed my sides, slithered over my hips, and finally landed on my bottom curves, squeezing. I moaned. I wrapped my hand around the back of his neck and pulled his toward me gently, kissing him, inviting him to open my mouth. His hand slid down my thighs, lifting them up around his hips again after I slid down a bit. I pressed into him as his hips moved forward, rubbing into me.

I whispered, breathless. "Oli—" I climbed down, stopping him.

"Yeah, no . . . I know, another time. You're just so . . . I can't get enough of you." He bit his knuckle, breathed out loudly, and walked it off. He leaned against the windowsill and gave me his signature smirk. "Go on, I'll give you a few minutes. Good luck, Mina."

I gave him a short kiss on the lips, but it turned into five, then five more, then a long one, then a longer one. I broke away and looked over his shoulder down at the tree. "Yikes, keep the luck—looks like you'll need it more than me."

"Don't worry—just a potentially broken arm, rib, leg, and/or ass bone if something goes wrong. Better than my broken heart if you get grounded for life."

"No pressure, right? Give me, like . . . five minutes."

"Five? All right, into the closet I go, then."

After quickly hitting the bathroom to freshen up, I ran downstairs and into the kitchen almost as my five minutes expired.

"Mama!" She turned to me just as Oliver's foot reached for a tree branch. "Good morning!"

"Good morning, *lyubimaya*. You awake so early. Happy birthday, Minachka, I already been in a hospital eighteen years before on this day in a labor—the starting of a long, long labor," she recalled as she walks over to me and too me into her arms for a long hug. "I loving you more than anything, my baby. You are my life. All I wishing is for you to be safe and not to killing my nerves anymore." I felt terrible, as I was basically deceiving her again right then. *This is the last time—no more lies*, I swore to myself.

"Safe and *happy*, right?" I stalled.

"Not so important. Fine . . . yes, yes, and a happy." She rolled her eyes. "Safe and a happy," she repeated, emphasizing the word *safe* again. I embraced her again, holding her tight.

"You smell nice, Mama."

"*Da?*" I was lucky long hugs were a norm for us, especially after a stressful fight. I kissed her cheek and continued hugging her as I led her out of the kitchen. Oli was in plain sight through the kitchen window—he was in the tree. I looked back to her quickly before she got curious and turned to see what was so interesting. I pulled her along with me out of the kitchen.

"Where we going?"

"Can you help me, please? I need help with laundry."

"You laundry? Now? *Zachem?* I making us the breakfast."

"Mamachka, please, it's for the, umm . . . the costumes I have to return. What if I put in the wrong powder or choose the wrong temperature? Plus, I don't know which settings to choose."

"Eighteen years old, AP Calculus, AP Physics, and AP anything with no problem, but still can't figuring out to do a simple laundry. Your *babushka* will be in a shock. Okay, where this costume?"

"Upstairs."

"Well, go to bring it—or do you needing some help for this too?"

"Maybe."

"I don't want eggs to burn."

I hoped Oli was down by then. "Mama," she was about to go back, but turned to me.

"*Chto?*"

"I love you."

"I loving you more," she smiled and shook her head at my strange behavior. She walked back to the stove and muttered, "*Oy, Minachka, chto mne delat s toboy?* One day you running out of this house, next day you can't make one single step upstairs without me."

"I know, Mama, I've been a handful. I'm sorry."

When I got back to my room, I went straight to the window. Oli was all the way down and using the tree trunk for cover. "Took you long enough," I said in a hushed voice.

He beamed up at me. "It's harder than it looks, Mina."

"M-hmm. Bye, Oli," I couldn't believe we were together.

"I love you, Mina," he whispered. "God, you're gorgeous."

I was covered in goosebumps. "I love you," I whispered back, almost too quietly.

"What?" he asked, cracking up.

"*Tsk* . . . you heard me," I blushed, stomach filled with restless butterflies. "I miss you already."

"I'll see you soon, baby," he winked, then peeked out to check the kitchen window and took off in a flash. My knees went weak from the way he called me *baby*, like he'd been saying it to me for years. I watched him move across my backyard like a ninja, fleet-footed and athletic. He flashed me a final sexy smile before disappearing around the corner hedges of our neighbor's property.

Dear God, that boy is too attractive for his own good. I took a deep breath and let it go with a sigh. I did it, finally. I found my happiness, and somehow, I didn't mess it up. I still couldn't believe how much he'd gone through. To be so strong, hold himself together, and rise after being knocked down so many times? I had a lot to learn from him. I was so afraid of saying the wrong thing the night before, but then I realized there was no wrong thing to say. All I had to do was be honest, and the truth was that I loved him, and he deserved to know. I still couldn't believe we were actually together. *This is crazy!* They couldn't scrape the smile off my face with an excavator.

Now to manifest a costume for Mama to help me wash. I rummaged through my closet, trying to come up with an idea. I considered bringing down an old performance costume, but she knew them all too well. I could just say I'd thought I had it, but it turned out that Nyah grabbed both of ours by mistake—yeah, that could work—

Thunk! I jumped, startled by the sound. It came from downstairs, like a door slam. *What the hell was that?* That had to be Mama. I mean, who else would it have been?

I rushed back over to my window. *What was that?* That's when I spotted it—the black SUV in our driveway, blocking Mama's car. *It could be an Uber.* Then I heard the voices of men downstairs—Russian men. *They're in the house.* Fear shocked my system, making my ears ring. I was frozen—petrified. The walls began to rotate around me as my breathing got more and more shallow. My feet had turned to lead. I needed to do something, hide, find a weapon. *Pew. Pew. Thunk.* The sound was closer to the stairs this time.

Mama! I put one foot in front of the other and I ran.

Acknowledgments

To my best friend and sister, Sofia, you are my greatest inspiration—if I could touch the heart of a single reader with this book the way you touched mine with your music, I would be truly fulfilled. I don't know where I would be without your encouragement and unwavering support. Thank you for being my first reader and for pushing me to write the rest of it. Thank you for being my trusty eyes and ears and always pointing me toward the path of honesty. Thank you for being by my side every step of the way, especially for the hardest steps.

My journey, this book, along with everything else, I owe to my mother and father. I am unbelievably grateful to my mother, Mila, for being by my side through every moment in my life without fail. You taught me how to love deeply and with all my heart. Thank you for those sleepless nights, for kissing all the bumps and bruises, and for going above and beyond what was required. The things you did for us were not easy—they were choices. Every day, you woke up and chose to do your best; you chose to do the hard things because you always knew they were the right things. I will try to do the same.

A big thank you to my father, Ares, who I knew I could always turn to. Anyone who's ever met you would call you generous, kind, funny, and humble. Those are the qualities I have learned just by watching you live. You were both so brave to move away from your friends and family to come to America with close to nothing and start over from scratch. You both did it for us, for my little sister and me. You both wanted us to not only dream big but for those dreams to have a chance of coming to fruition. Thank you for bringing us to a country of opportunity and a city of tolerance, where I got to grow up in diversity among people of varying socioeconomic statuses, races, heritages, beliefs, and worldviews.

I am forever grateful to my companion, Slava, who has been my adventure partner and my greatest love. You came into my life during some dark times and in my most vulnerable years; you brought light. Suddenly, the world wasn't such an awful place. You made me feel like I could do anything. I was a dreamer, and somehow, you convinced me it would all come true. You constantly remind me of my inner strength; we all need someone like that, especially when we lose faith in ourselves. I feel so blessed to have found you. We have given each other the greatest gift life can offer, our children. Sebastian and Vivienne, I love you both so much. Sebastian, thank you for always being so kind and understanding, for sharing me with your sister so beautifully and reawakening my inner child. Vivienne, thank you for showing me unconditional love and unabashed emotions every moment of everyday. You reinvigorate me with the essence of what it means to be alive.

To my grandparents, the most selfless, kind, loving, and beautiful souls I've ever known. Your words of encouragement, your belief in me, your love, and everything you both have done to keep our family together have made me who I am. I don't know what I did to deserve such wonderful people in my life, but I have been blessed to have you two angels by my side. Grandma, a favorite memory always comes to mind: the day I learned about your life. I loved interviewing you for my school project and hearing about the experiences of your childhood—the hardships of war and the sacrifices in the name of propriety. It helped me understand the origins of your strength. You took care of all your siblings even though you were the youngest; you still take care of everyone around you before taking care of yourself. You are a living saint and inspire me every day. Grandpa, you are the rock of our family. Your wisdom has influenced my love for history and literature. Your strength, patience, and kindness challenge me to be better than I am.

Thank you to Lina, Yurik, Zhorik, and Sergey for all your love and support. Thank you to the talented David Drummond for the most amazing cover design. I was stumped for weeks trying to choose between the options you created because they were all so excellent. Thank you to my brilliant editor, Elizabeth Cody Kimmel, who always encouraged me to make the hard choices; in hindsight, they were the right choices. Thank you to my amazing team at The Cadence Group: Bethany, Gwyn, and Kim for helping me put it all together in the home stretch. And a big thank you to Kristi, Mallory, and Mike of Smith Publicity for helping me get the word out.

IT'S NOT OVER.

WHAT HAPPENS TO MINA AND OLIVER?
FIND OUT IN THE SECOND INSTALLMENT OF
LOVE AND OTHER SINS BY EMILIA ARES.

LOVE AND OTHER CAGES

EMILIA ARES

COMING SOON

SERA
PRESS

Printed in Great Britain
by Amazon

81884679R00192